RIO HONDO

THREE RIVERS TRILOGY, BOOK 3

RIO HONDO

PRESTON LEWIS

WHEELER PUBLISHING
A part of Gale, a Cengage Company

LIBRARY OF CONGRESS CIP DATA ON FILE.
CATALOGUING IN PUBLICATION FOR THIS BOOK
IS AVAILABLE FROM THE LIBRARY OF CONGRESS.

ISBN-13: 978-1-4328-9141-1 (softcover alk. paper)

Published in 2023 by arrangement with Preston Lewis

Printed in the USA
1 2 3 4 5   26 25 24 23 22

In Memory of My Father
John Bracken Lewis
1926–2020

CHAPTER 1

The land lay as fallow as his dreams. From astride his sorrel stallion, Wes Bracken studied the remains of the Mirror B. Since arriving in Lincoln County in 1873, five years of sweat and toil had been washed away by the crimson bloodshed that stained his piece of New Mexico Territory. Beyond the worthless, overgrown field stood the cross that marked his brother's grave beneath a cottonwood tree, its leaves murmuring in the breeze and shading a stretch of the noisy waters that bestowed upon the stream its Spanish name of Rio Ruidoso. Wes had followed his brother to Lincoln County to breed the finest horses around, but his dream was a hallucination as dead as the shriveled-hide and bleached-bone carcasses of those horses scattered around the demolished corral. All that remained of the barn he believed was once the best in Lincoln County was the charred timbers that angled over a pile of blackened debris.

While the adobe dwelling he had built for his Hispanic wife still stood, its roof had been torched and its insides blackened. The structure reeked of arson as he nudged his stallion by the ruins of what had been his home. Even the modest adobe cabin his brother had first claimed for their partnership was scorched by flames, and its roof collapsed. Though Wes had scrupulously avoided taking sides in the animosities that had cut painfully through Lincoln County like a dull knife, he had drawn the enmity of both sides and been targeted by each. But for all his pain and losses, Wes had fared better than many since he had accepted from a grateful widow the abandoned Robert Casey place after he had helped Ellen and her six children escape to Texas with a wagon full of their belongings and the bulk of her husband's cattle herd to start anew in the Lone Star State. Downstream past the merging of the Rio Ruidoso and the Rio Bonito to form the Rio Hondo, the Casey place, as Wes still called it, was built to withstand the Apache troubles of fifteen years earlier. The house came with outbuildings, including a blacksmith shed, a barn, a bunkhouse, and a gristmill that might have brought in food and money this fall except few people had planted crops because of the chaos that had ripped the county apart. So hot had burned the flames of anarchy that even President Rutherford B. Hayes himself was forced to address the chaos.

Painful though it was, Wes had returned to the Mirror B to escape his wife, herself a victim of the lawlessness. Sarafina was showing now, obviously pregnant, and each time he looked at her, he wondered if she was, through no fault of her own, carrying another man's child. The thought tormented him, for Sarafina had been violated, raped by two desperadoes with grudges against Bracken. Wes and his partner Jace Cousins had tracked and ambushed the pair, killing one perpetrator, but the other — Jesse Evans — had escaped, the auburn-haired outlaw's offenses being overlooked if not ignored by the crooked lawmen and judges of Lincoln County. As a result, Jesse Evans freely roamed the region with virtual impunity for Sarafina's assault, for the murder of several residents, and for all the other crimes he had committed in the territory.

Wes guided his sorrel by the front door, his gaze focusing on the place where he had found Sarafina unconscious on the ground after the assault. Despite her humiliation when she regained her consciousness, all she had worried about was her two boys, Luis from her first marriage and Roberto from Wes's union with her. As he reined up his mount over the spot still stained with such horrible memories, he cursed the injustice and vowed retribution. Revisiting the ground where he had found his wife, he questioned whether his trip to the abandoned ranch had been a good idea because nothing brought him peace of mind.

Gritting his teeth, he drew his shirtsleeve across his lips and bushy brown mustache, which concealed a wickedly chipped and discolored incisor, compliments of a Yankee rifle butt to the face at Murfreesboro. His steely gray eyes studied the rough mountains and limestone outcrops that cradled the Rio Ruidoso and the verdant Hondo Valley. As the mountains sloped up from the watercourse toward the furious sun, the earth turned economical, grass sparse, shade scarce, and plants stunted. Dwarf evergreen piñons and junipers dotted the mountainsides. Further up the valley the elevations increased and the stunted vegetation gave way to tall pines that tickled the low-hanging clouds that spawned afternoon showers, especially in the summer months. With the start of September, the wet season would be ending and fall would be setting in with the October freezes that in other years would mark the beginning of harvesting, but most fields, like his own, remained fallow and unproductive. The winter would be harder on man and animal as a result. Just as scarce as crops was the cash to buy staples to make up for the harvest shortfall. Wes's money was dwindling, less than twenty dollars currency to his name, and he knew he might have to choose between food to nourish his family or ammunition to protect them. While he was cash poor, he was cattle rich, managing over two hundred head that could provide his wife and children sustenance during the thin months ahead, but rustlers might drive them off any day and the law would do nothing about it.

Wes grimaced at the winter and the grim choices in the coming months, turning his mount toward the stream so the stallion might water before he returned to the Casey place. He rode Charlie into the stream, then let him dip his head into the bubbling waters that rushed by, ultimately draining into the Pecos River. Charlie relished the refreshing water, then yanked his head up in the air, his ears flicking forward as he twisted around in the stream and looked up the valley toward the road.

His instincts honed by the violence of the

last five years, Wes yanked his Winchester carbine from his saddle scabbard and studied the throng of horsemen approaching at a walk. From afar Wes failed to identify them, their horses unfamiliar. Sliding his finger over the carbine's trigger, he weighed his options — climbing the mountainside to secure the high ground against possible enemies or angling for the trail so he could dash back to the Casey place to protect his family from potential danger. Wes tugged Charlie's reins and pointed him toward the road that led to his substitute home. Fighting his desire to gallop away, Wes put Charlie in an easy trot, not caring to waste the stallion's energy unnecessarily when it might be needed later.

As he angled for the trail, he studied the approaching band, seeing two point at him. Wes cradled the carbine in the crook of his left elbow as he eyed the men, counting eight riders. When none reached for their weapons or put their mounts into a lope, Wes figured they might not be friends, but at least they weren't enemies. Even so, he kept his carbine at the ready, when he reached the road and turned his sorrel about to await their approach until he could identify them or their mounts, which appeared gaunt and lethargic. Three of the horses lowered and dropped their necks constantly, a sign Wes took for exhaustion. Perhaps that was the reason the riders had not given chase, hoping to come within range before drawing their guns and firing. A man had to think this way if he was to survive in Lincoln County.

As they neared, the men seemed as fagged as their mounts, their shoulders slumped, their heads bent, and their hands resting on their saddle horns. They appeared no more eager for a fight than Wes, but they outnumbered him eight to one. Their ragged and dirty clothes identified them as men who had been on the trail for a good spell, though whether by choice or necessity remained unclear.

One horseman in the middle of the group nudged his dappled gray in the flank, drawing just enough energy from the pony for it to take the lead. As the rider straightened in the saddle and lifted his head, Wes recognized the buck-toothed smile on the dirtied face of William H. Bonney. Wes had last seen the Kid two weeks earlier atop a mountain overlooking the Casey place. In the aftermath of the Big Killing that had claimed the life of his nominal boss, Alexander McSween, Bonney had admitted on that mountaintop that he was tired of running. If he was weary then, he looked exhausted now. Wes had promised to do what he could for the young fugitive, but the law in Lincoln County was as crooked as the Rio Ruidoso's meandering course. How else could you explain the death of McSween and four allies as they were cut down in a nighttime flurry of gunfire while trying to escape from a burning house while a troop of cavalry under Lieutenant Colonel Nathan Dudley surrounded the place? Some said — and Wes believed the rumors — that the county's corruption reached all the way to territorial Governor Samuel B. Axtell.

Wes slid his finger from the trigger of his carbine, touched the brim of his hat, and greeted the rider. "How you doing, Kid?"

"I've been better."

"Same can be said for most of us in Lincoln County. Are we meeting as friends or foes?"

"Saddle pals, for certain," Bonney responded. "I'm insulted you even asked."

"I know you, Kid, but I can't say the same for most of your posse."

"All are dependable men. More firepower in case we run into Sheriff Peppin or Jimmy Dolan's outlaws. They've been tracking us since the five-day battle in Lincoln."

Wes reined Charlie in beside the Kid's fatigued dappled gray. "I figured Frank and George Coe would be with you."

Bonney yanked his hat off his head and swatted it against his shirt and vest, raising a veil of trail dust. "They turned tail and ran to Colorado. Not enough grit in their craw to see the troubles to their bitter end."

"When we met two weeks ago, you said you were tired of running. As long as you stay in the vicinity, all you can do is run."

The Kid slapped his hat back on his head. "We're moving up north to Fort Sumner. That's why we're back, so the boys can tell their families and kin where to join them."

"San Miguel County's not far enough, Kid. You need to leave the territory. I promised you two weeks ago I'd help you out of your predicament, but if you remain in New Mexico, you're just asking for trouble."

Bonney shook his head. "Dolan's men started it, killing the Englishman six months ago and then McSween six weeks ago."

"There's been murders on both sides, Kid."

"And you've killed a few yourself during the troubles," Bonney shot back.

"It's not something I'm proud of, but the killings have got to stop."

The Kid laughed, then stared hard at Bracken. "You know that's a lie, Wes, because you intend to kill Jesse Evans. When I last saw you, you told me to let you know if I ran across Jesse."

"I can't forget what he did to Sarafina, Kid, and she's just one of the women he's violated in Lincoln County."

Bonney grinned. "So the killing ends when you get your revenge, but not the rest of us? Is that it, Wes?"

Knowing the Kid was right, Wes bit his lip. "Like I said, I'm not proud of what I've done or what I intend to do. I tried to avoid the troubles, but they found me."

"Same for me, Wes, same for me."

The two men rode silently for half a mile, each understanding that the other was right and that Lincoln County only offered the devil's choices to honest citizens. Only the plop of their horses' hooves on the dusty trail and the murmuring of the other horsemen trailing twenty yards behind broke the icy silence.

Wes looked back over his shoulder at the riders, recognizing only John Middleton and wondering why Carlos Zamora had abandoned Bonney.

"Where's Carlos? Sarafina's always anxious about her kid brother."

Bonney grimaced, then shrugged. "I don't know anymore. He took out on his own with a couple other Mexicans. There's a lot of venom in that boy, especially after the Big Killing."

"He's always been a hothead and never took to me marrying his sister."

Clearing his throat, Bonney spat at the side of the trail. "Wes, he's vowed to kill you."

Wes jerked his chin around and stared hard at Bonney, gauging his truthfulness and deciding the comment was valid. "What brought that on?"

"Many of his people turned against him after two Mexicans he recruited died in the Big Killing. He holds you accountable for their deaths and has vowed to kill you."

"What?" Wes yanked the reins and stopped his sorrel. "How's that?"

Bonney stopped his gray beside Wes, then waited for the other riders to pass. "He heard you and Jace Cousins sat on the mountainside, just watching the McSween house burn and then doing nothing when we escaped. He thinks you and Jace should've helped with your long guns. If you had, his recruits Francisco and Vincente might not have died with the others."

Bracken lowered his head and stared at

his saddle horn. "It wasn't my battle."

"In Lincoln County, every fight is yours, like it or not, Wes."

Nudging his sorrel forward, Wes nodded. "Maybe so, Kid."

Bonney eased his gray beside Bracken's mount, and they followed the horsemen toward the Casey place, riding silently for a spell until the Kid spoke. "Dolan's men, not you, were our enemy, but once Carlos vowed to kill you, I sent him on his way."

"Why the favor to me, Kid?"

"You're the only hope I've got of untangling myself from these troubles, and I don't want to lose your trust. Besides, Carlos never was the same after the McSween shootout."

"What happened that night?"

"We slipped into Lincoln in the darkness early that Monday morning and took up positions in friendly buildings around town. Come daylight, Sheriff Peppin and Dolan's men realized we'd gotten the jump on them. There was shooting, but nothing serious for the next three days. Then on Friday, Colonel Dudley led forty soldiers from Fort Stanton into Lincoln. The soldiers took up positions and aimed a canon and a Gatling gun at the house."

Wes whistled. "A Gatling gun?"

"Yep," Bonney continued, "Dudley told us he had two thousand rounds of ammunition, and he'd use every bullet, if we dared fire near his soldiers. With the army between us and our allies in other buildings, the colonel told us any shot in the direction of his troopers would be considered gunfire *at* his troopers. So our supporters slipped away, and we were on our own, surrounded by Dolan's men and the soldiers. Susan McSween did everything she could to negotiate with Dudley to save her home, her husband, and the rest of us, but he didn't care."

"Then they fired the house?"

Bonney nodded. "We were lucky it was a slow burn that didn't corner us in the kitchen until dark. When we could no longer stand the heat, we broke for it. I led the first group, Carlos the second. Some of us made it; some of us didn't. There wasn't much you or Jace could've done to change the outcome."

"But Carlos thinks otherwise."

Bonney nodded. "You best be careful, Wes, if he visits you or Sarafina. He totes a lot of anger on his shoulders."

"How about you, Bonney? Are you angry?"

"I worked for wages both for the Englishman, who never fully paid me, and for the lawyer McSween, who only paid in promises, not in cash. I intend to get what I'm owed."

"From who, Kid?"

"John Chisum, that's who," Bonney replied, his words hot like a branding iron. "He was a silent partner in their affairs."

"Maybe so, Kid, but the law won't see it that way, nor will Chisum. He won't pay a cent."

"Probably not, but he runs more beeves than he can count. He won't miss a few."

Bracken wagged his head from side to side. "You'll never work your way out of this bind if you keep stealing cattle and horses. His Long Rail brand and Jinglebob earmark are recognized throughout the southwest. No reputable ranchman would buy them from you."

"We'll see about that," Bonney countered. "He's hated by most in this county for trying to keep all the water and grass for his herds. More despise him than like him. If he pays me what I'm due, I'll leave him be."

"Few of us receive what we're owed in life, Kid, but we generally get what we deserve. More banditry and violence will only worsen things."

"So you're forgetting your vendetta against

Jesse Evans?"

Wes shrugged, and by his silence admitted Billy was right.

"Don't hitch your horse to a wagon he can't pull," Bonney admonished. "You let me handle my business my way, and I'll allow the same for you. I'll even tip you off if I find Jesse."

"I'd be obliged," Wes replied.

As they rode on, the two friends visited about the hardships in the winter ahead until they rounded a curve in the trail and spotted the Casey place. Bracken sent his horse into a trot to get past the other riders as he knew their appearance would frighten Sarafina, who seldom left the dwelling any more without carrying the revolver Wes had taught her to use for defense. Bonney tried to stay with Wes, but his gray was too fatigued from weeks on the run to keep pace.

As he turned from the road onto the trail leading to his home, he saw tied to the hitching post three horses he did not recognize. Fear raced through his veins as he thought some new evil might have befallen his wife and boys. As he was turning to slap his sorrel on the flank, he glimpsed his partner Jace Cousins walking around the side of the dwelling, his Henry rifle in his right hand. His partner's nonchalance calmed him, as Wes knew Cousins would allow no harm to reach Wes's family. Not caring to alarm the family, Wes drew back on the reins, slowing Charlie until the Kid's gray caught up with him. Now that he was in the lead and confident Jace's presence meant he had no reason to fret, Wes saw no point in approaching at an abnormal gait and creating unnecessary worry.

Turning to the Kid, Wes told him to order his men to wait where they were. Bonney issued the command, and his allies held their horses. Drawing near the dwelling, Wes glimpsed Billy slowly lowering his right hand to his holster, gently lifting the weapon from the leather and resting it on his thigh.

Before he could ask the Kid what was going on, the door to his house flung open and Sarafina rushed out, a broad smile on her face.

"Guess who came by to see us?" his wife gushed.

Wes shrugged.

"It's Carlos and two of his friends," she announced as five-year-old Luis and two-year-old Roberto darted outside until Sarafina grabbed their arms to keep them from getting too close to the horses.

Now Wes understood that Bonney, recognizing the mounts, had pulled his pistol to protect him from his brother-in-law.

"Isn't it wonderful," Sarafina cried as she lifted Roberto in her arms. "The boys get to see their uncle, and Carlos says he was eager to visit with you." She smiled at Bonney. "Nice to see you are well, Billy."

Wes looked beyond his wife to the shaded doorway where Carlos stood, his face emotionless as he fingered the carbine in his arms.

Carlos stepped from the house into the sunlight. *"Buenos días,"* he scowled.

Before Wes could respond, Carlos's two confederates joined him outside, their hands resting on the butts of their revolvers.

"Get the boys out of the way, Sarafina, so I can visit with your brother."

She hesitated.

"Now," Wes shouted.

Stunned, Sarafina stepped aside.

Nothing now stood between Wes and the brother-in-law who had threatened to kill him.

CHAPTER 2

Carlos Zamora raised the carbine a hair, then froze when Billy Bonney lifted his revolver and when he heard the metallic clicks of Jace Cousins chambering a cartridge in his Henry. Focusing his gaze behind the Kid, Carlos noted the seven horsemen pulling their weapons from their holsters. Zamora's two confederates released the butts of their revolvers and slowly eased their hands away from their sides, nervous smiles cracking their stern gazes.

Confident that his brother-in-law and two allies feared the unfavorable odds, Wes dismounted, dropping his reins and stepping to his brother-in-law, who mumbled Spanish curses.

Offended by her brother's words, Sarafina lowered Roberto to the ground and ordered Luis to take him inside the house. "Such language," she scolded, "before the *chicos.*"

Wes stepped to his brother-in-law. "What

can I do for you, Carlos?"

"Nothing now," he answered. "You could've saved the lives of my friends at the shootout. You just watched and let others die."

Sarafina strode to her husband's side. "Shame on you, Carlos."

"I warned you," Wes answered, "about stepping in a white man's feud. You brought this on yourself and the deceased."

Carlos lifted his chin and spat on Wes's cheek.

Instantly, Sarafina slapped her brother's jaw with such force that his head jerked to the side. "The father of my boys deserves better."

Rubbing his right cheek, Carlos scowled at his sister. "Father of one of your boys."

Sarafina struck him again as Wes wiped the spittle from his cheek and swiped his hand across Carlos's shirt, removing the discharge.

"If you weren't my wife's brother, I'd beat you within an inch of your life," Wes threatened, pointing his finger at Carlos's nose.

Ignoring Bracken, Carlos looked up at Bonney, whose revolver pointed at that same nose. "Why do you favor him, Kid?"

"I trust him. Wes is the only man in Lincoln County that plays straight."

"You can't trust him," Carlos shot back.

"You should. He's my best chance to make right with the law if we finally get honest lawmen and judges. I'm tired of running."

"I'm not," Carlos answered, "not until I settle a few scores."

Sarafina shook her head. "That's foolish talk, Carlos. If you believe such and carry a vendetta against *mi esposo,* stay away from our home."

Carlos nodded slowly. "So I am no longer welcome in *your* house?"

"In *our* home, mine and my husband's."

As Sarafina argued with her brother, Wes studied Carlos's two Mexican gunmen. One wore a sombrero that shaded his narrow black eyes, a broad nose, tobacco-stained teeth, and a scraggly beard. Tall and lean, he wore two right-handed gun belts around his waist, one scabbard resting beside the other on his right hip. His work pants, shirt, and boots showed the rips, tears, and scuffs of a man who had labored hard or a man who cared little for his appearance. His stockier companion had a full, fleshy face sporting a narrow mustache and thick lips. He wore his pistol butt forward on his left hip and stood in brogans rather than boots.

"Let's get out of here," Carlos said, turning to his confederates. "We're not welcome in *la casa de mi hermana.*"

Sarafina crossed her arms over her bosom. "You are welcome in our home as long as you respect my husband. If you cannot value him and my wishes, never call upon us again."

Carlos turned to his partners and pointed to their horses, which showed the strain of too much exertion and too little rest and fodder. "Let's ride," he told them as they untied their mounts and climbed aboard the geldings. As he settled in the saddle, Carlos nodded at Wes. "This is not settled yet."

"Don't do it," Sarafina commanded, her words somewhere between a plea and a threat. "If you force me to choose between *mi hermano* and *mi esposo,* you will lose, Carlos."

He glared at his sister, then spat at her feet. *"Puta del hombre blanco,"* he cried, then yanked the reins of his bay and trotted away before Wes could respond to the insult of his wife.

Wes grabbed Charlie's saddle horn to chase Carlos and demand an apology for calling his wife a white man's whore, but Sarafina clamped her hand around his wrist.

"Let it go, Wes. Promise me you won't

27

harm him no matter what he says. His words have hurt me, but the pain will fade. If I lose him, the loss will be forever."

Releasing the saddle, Wes stood silently staring at his wife. He knew Carlos's blood ran hot with unpredictable rage. Wes realized he could make no honest guarantee, but neither could he deny Sarafina her request, especially when he looked into her eyes.

Tears rolled down her cheeks.

With a sigh, Wes answered, "I vow I won't kill him, but I'll protect myself, you, our boys, and our place."

"*Gracias,*" she said, turning toward the house. "I must tend Luis and Roberto." As she disappeared inside, Wes caught her sobs as she comforted Roberto and Luis, who both cried when they heard their mother weeping.

Bonney dismounted and tied his gray to the hitching rack, then walked over to Wes as Jace Cousins approached, lowering his Henry rifle. "You shouldn't have made that promise," Billy chided. "Carlos is too hot-headed to trust."

"I know." Wes turned to his partner. "Thanks, Jace, for watching out for Sarafina."

Cousins slapped Wes on the shoulder.

"What are partners for, Wes? Besides, I didn't like the looks of Carlos's companions. They showed trouble."

"Good instincts. Bonney here tells me Carlos has threatened to kill us for not rescuing him during the Big Killing."

"Nothing we could do, Wes. We didn't know who was in McSween's place."

"That don't matter to Carlos," Bonney responded.

Wes turned to the Kid. "Who's the pair riding with Carlos?"

"The taller one with the two gun belts is Geraldo Hablador. He's a killing terror among his own people. The hefty one is Andres Mendoza, another bully with the Mexicans, especially among the *señoritas.*"

"Why are they following Carlos's orders?" Jace asked. "He's younger than them both."

Bonney laughed. "Look behind me, boys. I'm younger than those following me."

"But you're good with a gun," Wes noted.

"So's Carlos, and he's ridden with Anglos. I figure Hablador and Mendoza believe Carlos can open doors for thieving and killing among our kind."

Wes shook his head. "Will anything ever change in Lincoln County?"

"Not until law is enforced evenly and the courts are free of corruption," Jace said.

"We'll be lucky if that happens in our lifetime," Bonney added.

Wes informed the Kid that he and his men were welcome to stay the night, though Sarafina could not provide meals as their larder was slim, especially with the winter months ahead. He requested that Bonney and his allies make their camp away from the road so passersby were less likely to see them and start the rumor that he was providing cover for Bonney's Regulators. Jace volunteered to show the Kid and his men where to camp, leading them downstream from the house as Wes went in.

He found Sarafina lying on their bed, the boys whimpering beside her, as tears streamed down her cheek. "I apologize for my brother's words and deeds," she offered. "I am so embarrassed for how he acted in front of others."

Wes sat on the blanket at her side, patting the bulge of her belly where she carried her next child, though Wes remained uncertain if the baby was his. "It's okay," he said, his response as much to his own doubts about paternity as to her words.

Sarafina seemed to read his mind. "You're worried about the little one I carry."

Clenching his jaw, Wes nodded. "It galls me, knowing what he did to you and not knowing whose baby it is."

"We may never know." Sarafina sighed.

"Maybe it's best that way," he replied. "I fear how I might respond if I knew otherwise."

"You understand I would never be unfaithful to you."

"I do, but knowing those men forced themselves upon you gnaws at me."

"You have killed one of them so you have avenged my humiliation."

"Not yet, Sarafina. There's still Jesse Evans."

"Please let it go, Wes. I could not bear to lose you. I have lost one husband. I cannot lose another." Roberto and Luis wormed their way from their mother to Wes, climbing aboard his lap where he hugged and reassured them that things would be okay.

"I can't provide supper for so many," Sarafina announced.

Wes nodded. "I've already told them we had too little food to share. You rest and let's put this behind us."

She smiled. "I can, but I doubt Carlos ever will."

"That's what worries me, but I promised not to kill him. I'll live by my word." Wes wondered if that pledge might one day result in his own death.

■ ■ ■ ■

Come morning, Wes Bracken and Jace Cousins walked to the cottonwood trees by the Rio Hondo where Bonney and his gang had spent the night. The Kid greeted them with a jaunty, buck-toothed grin. Billy and the others had bathed in the river and even washed their clothes as best they could. While the men looked refreshed, their horses watched with exhausted eyes, their energy sapped by weeks on the run as Billy introduced Wes and Jace to his accomplices or "Regulators" as they still called themselves.

Except for John "Doc" Middleton, the rest were strangers to Wes, who shook hands with Fred Waite, Jim French, Henry Brown, Tom O'Folliard, George Bowers, and Charlie Bowdre as the Kid presented them. Wes wondered how many were thrust into the troubles by accident or were simple opportunists hoping to take advantage of the lawlessness. Bonney informed Wes and Jace that the Regulators were headed to Doc's and Charlie's places to load up their wives and what belongings they could manage for the trip north to Fort Sumner where the violence might be less likely to find them.

"It's a shame folks must abandon places where they've worked so hard," Bonney noted.

"Wes knows about that," Jace said. "You've seen the Mirror B or what's left of it."

"Once we get Doc and Charlie on the way to Sumner," Billy said, "a few of us are heading to Lincoln to see if we can flush Dolan or any of his men."

"It'll just make your situation worse," Wes warned.

"Maybe so," Bonney replied, "but I'll sleep better knowing there's fewer of them around to ambush me and my friends."

"Somebody's gotta end it sometime, Kid," Jace added. "Why not you?"

"Because I didn't start it. Dolan and his men did, killing the Englishman and then others." Bonney looked from Jace to Wes and back. "Are the two of you giving up on putting Jesse Evans in his grave?"

"That's different," Jace replied. "I spent two years in a Texas prison for a crime Jesse committed and pinned on me."

Billy shrugged. "I know the story, stealing horses, wasn't it?" He stared at Wes, awaiting a response.

Ignoring the question because everyone knew the answer, Bracken pointed toward the saddle horses. "Those animals won't carry you far, particularly if you run into trouble."

The Kid laughed. "There are plenty of fresh horses in Lincoln County."

"But you're broke," Wes replied.

Chuckling again, Bonney said, "I'm a better horse trader than you are."

"Like the time you stole my horses?" Wes reminded him.

"You're memory's failing you, Wes. I told you then and I'll repeat it now that I relieved some thieves of your horseflesh and was returning them to your place."

"You were going the wrong way when I caught up with you."

Bonney flashed those buckteeth, "My horse trading skills are better than my directions, Wes. You know that."

"Way better," Bracken answered.

The three men strolled to the animals where the others were saddling their mounts. Billy secured the tack to his gray as Wes and Bracken visited with him. One by one the Regulators led their saddled horses to the Rio Hondo to water them a final time. Bonney was the last of the group to offer his animal a drink and the last to climb in the saddle.

"Take care of yourself, Wes. You, too, Jace. I don't trust Carlos Zamora or the ruffians riding with him. They'll shoot you in the back if they get a chance. If something happens to you, Wes, there's no way I'll get out of this mess, so take care of yourself."

"Don't make things worse on yourself, Kid, by riding into Lincoln. No telling what you'll find."

"You worry too much, Wes."

"And you worry too little. You'll never get out of trouble if you make more of it, but as long as you're going to Lincoln, say hello to Juan Patrón, if you run into him. Tell him to come visit when he feels safe."

"You know he's been housing the widow McSween since the Big Killing. That woman's got more guts than the rest of us, staying in town to wind up her husband's affairs when so many still hate her."

Never fond of Susan McSween, Wes simply nodded. "Just the same, ask Juan to stop by the next time he heads this direction."

"I'll not only tell Juan, but I'll extend an invitation to Jesse Evans if I run into him, seeing as how you boys can't wait to settle matters with him." Bonney yanked his hat off his head and waved it at them. "¡Adiós, adiós! Next time you see me I'll be riding a better mount."

Wes responded with a grin and a sweep of his arm as the Regulators aimed their horses

35

toward the Lincoln County trail that always ended in trouble and violence. The two partners watched their visitors disappear, then started silently back for the house. Though Wes couldn't help but like Bonney, Jace Cousins was the one man he could totally trust in all of New Mexico Territory. Besides their mutual loathing of Jesse Evans, the two men shared a moral compass that knew right from wrong, even in wicked Lincoln County.

Cousins possessed an easy manner, though his brown eyes were void of non-sense, and his lip had a peculiar curl about it at the corners. His wavy brown hair gave him a boyish look and the cleft in his chin matched the gap between his two front teeth when he opened his mouth. Bracken wished he had the gap in his teeth rather than the badly chipped incisor that spawned his thick mustache to hide the damaged tooth, which was gradually darkening and loosening.

"I don't get the Kid," Wes said, breaking the silence. "He wants to extract himself from his past and Lincoln's troubles, yet he keeps tempting fate, like going to Lincoln."

"Or stealing horses?"

"Exactly."

"The way I figure it, Jace, he's got a conscience, but he feels he never gets a fair shake, even though he's killed men on his own. And maybe he's right, what with all the chicanery out of the sheriff's office and the Dolan store, how they tried to corner all the trade in the region."

"Why doesn't he just leave?"

Wes shrugged. "I've begged him to do just that, but he thinks Texas is even worse, there being so many Texans involved in our troubles. He doesn't like the cold in Colorado, and apparently he's got a past in Arizona. That leaves Mexico or Indian Territory."

"The way he likes the *señoritas,* I'd point him to Mexico," Jace suggested.

"It'll end badly for him, if he stays around here."

"How's it gonna wind up for us, if we remain, what with Jesse Evans and now Carlos threatening us?"

"I left Arkansas to escape the lawlessness and start over. I'm not abandoning this place, not with a wife and family to support. We'll face problems making it through the winter, but it beats starting over someplace else. You're not thinking of leaving, are you, Jace?"

"Not on your life, but I don't have a wife and kids with another one on the way. And, I don't have a hotheaded brother-in-law.

What'll we do about Carlos?"

"That's a puzzle I haven't solved, Jace."

"At least I didn't promise not to hurt him," Cousins replied.

Bracken shook his head. "I chose my words carefully, promising not to kill him. Never did I say I wouldn't hurt him."

"You're sounding like one of those corrupt lawyers that the Dolan bunch has argue their cases before a crooked court."

Wes scowled. "Don't compare me to a lawyer. That was the crook McSween's line of work. Some of his legal chicanery magnified the problems with Dolan's faction and led to, how many deaths is it now? Twenty? Thirty?"

"By my count since last year, it was thirteen on the streets of Lincoln alone and that many or more in the rest of the county."

"And there'll be more," Wes predicted.

They walked from there to the house in silence. Upon entering they caught the aroma of coffee, fresh tortillas, and boiled goat meat. Inside the kitchen, they greeted Sarafina and smiled at the good breakfast she had prepared before they started their chores. Sarafina motioned for them to sit at the table, and she served them cups of coffee, then a platter of fresh tortillas, and finally a clay bowl of the goat concoction.

Wes and Jace picked up their spoons and ate as Sarafina paced back and forth between the table and the stove, instead of joining them as was her custom.

"Are you okay?" Wes asked his wife.

She offered a weak smile. "I am scared."

"Of Carlos?" Wes asked.

"Not so much him as the two who ride with him." She clutched her throat. "They are evil men. I saw it in their eyes."

"We'll protect you," Jace offered.

Wes arose from his chair and stepped to comfort his wife, wrapping his arms around her.

"But you both won't always be around as you have chores to do and business to attend elsewhere. How will I protect the boys and the new one?"

"I showed you how to use the revolver I gave you," Wes replied.

"But I have no way to carry it, not that I want a holster, but something to keep it on me."

Wes released his grasp on his wife and scratched his head. "I'll think about that, Sarafina."

Jace waved a folded tortilla at the couple. "I learned some things in prison that might solve the problem, Wes. Fetch her revolver and let me finish my breakfast, then I'll head out to the toolshed and fix her up."

"You sure you know what you're doing, Jace?"

"Does a goose know north from south?"

"Okay," Wes laughed, then headed to their bedroom where he found the revolver. By the time he returned to the table, Jace was finishing his coffee. He stood up, swiping the back of his hand across his lips. "Fine breakfast, Sarafina," Jace said, then grabbed the pistol from Wes and marched out the back door. "I'll be in the toolshed."

Wes sat back down at the table and finished his food. Sarafina refilled his coffee cup and joined her husband. "Everything will work out eventually, Sarafina."

She took his left hand and squeezed it in hers.

When he finished, Wes stood, helped his wife from her chair, and hugged her just as Luis called his mother. Wes moved to the back door as Sarafina went to check on the boy. As he stepped outside, Wes considered how lucky he was to have her despite all the troubles. Yes, the Mirror B had been wrecked as had other places in Lincoln County, but he at least had another parcel of land he could call his own. The Casey place was better than the Mirror B with a larger house that had doubled as a store; a barn; a gristmill that would bring in money once farmers could plant again; a bunkhouse for Jace to stay; a blacksmith shed; and a toolshed where Wes headed.

Stepping inside the toolroom, Wes saw Cousins at a workbench where he had removed the grips from the pistol and was drilling a hole in one of the wooden handles. Wes looked at the naked metal frame and mainspring of the revolver handle.

"You pick up odd things in prison," Jace said over his shoulder, his fingers working the hand drill, "like how to carry or hide weapons. That and how to read the Bible were the two best things I learned in captivity."

"I still don't know what you're doing," Wes replied.

"Making Sarafina a necklace."

Wes scratched his head as Jace finished drilling the hole.

When he completed the task, Cousins picked up the other grip and placed them back to back, holding them up for West to see the perfectly matched holes.

"So you defiled the grips. I still don't get it, Jace."

"I removed them to drill holes that would clear the frame without interfering with the spring mechanism." Jace separated the grips, placed the right side back on the frame and screwed it down tight, then repeated the procedure with the left side. He held the revolver up eye level to stare through the hole at Wes. "Now all we need is a leather thong. We slip it through the hole, tie the ends, and Sarafina can hang the gun over her neck or across her shoulder, however she feels most comfortable. Then she can carry it wherever she goes. It might not be as comfortable as a holster, but it'll be less visible."

"Well I'll be," Wes muttered, impressed with Jace's ingenuity.

"Don't thank me," Jace countered. "Thank that redheaded bastard Jesse Evans."

Wes cursed the name.

"If he hadn't set me up for prison, I'd never have gone to the Texas penitentiary. That's how the criminals inside hid their shivs and knives." Jace handed the altered revolver to Wes. "Find you some leathers in the barn, and Sarafina should be set, if she ever needs to use the pistol."

"I hope she never has to," Wes replied, "but I'm obliged anyway."

CHAPTER 3

Wes Bracken rode warily on the trail toward Lincoln, passing the cemetery on the north where the Rio Bonito curved past the graveyard as if paying respect to the dead. Wes had lost track of the number of men buried there because of the violence. Whatever the count, it was only part of the total that had died on either side of Lincoln's dangerous street. Those affiliated with the Murphy-Dolan gang could claim a plot in the Lincoln Cemetery while those aligned with the Tunstall-McSween faction could not. The murdered Englishman Tunstall, whose killing had detonated the simmering animosities in Lincoln County, and the deceased lawyer McSween, whose legal machinations had fanned those flames of rancor, lay buried beside each other behind the fortress of a store that Tunstall had built to challenge the economic stranglehold of L.G. Murphy, now dead and buried in

Santa Fe where he had escaped when the violence turned hot. Murphy's partner, James J. Dolan, had assumed control over the county and its residents.

Beyond the graveyard, Bracken pulled his Winchester from its scabbard as he approached the gentle curve in the road on the outskirts of town. He rested the barrel of the weapon in the crook of his left arm to protect himself from enemies as yet unseen. Wes knew he should have delayed this trip, but he told himself he should purchase what supplies he could to help his family through the winter. In reality it was not food he craved as much as news. If the Kid had ever passed Bracken's invitation along for Juan Patrón to visit him, the leader of Lincoln's Hispanic community had not availed himself of the opportunity, likely because of the dangers inherent in traveling during such turbulent and uncertain times. Bracken respected Patrón for his caution and admitted to himself he should never have left the Casey place for town.

The morning air carried the cool of approaching winter as the calendar had turned to October, which whispered of wintry days ahead. Wes shivered as the road bent toward Lincoln, and he studied each side of the street ahead. As he approached from the

44

east, the valley widened and the Rio Bonito drifted to the north while the town stood out along the south side of the stream. A smattering of nondescript adobes and pole *jacales* stood haphazardly along the dusty street for three-quarters of a mile. Empty of men and horses, the lane had been abandoned to chickens pecking for insects, dogs prowling for food, a meandering hog, and a dozen goats that had escaped from someone's pen. On the north side of the street Wes rode past the sheriff's office, which was little more than a shack covering a pit in the ground that served as the jail. Wes wondered if Sheriff George Peppin was in his office, on the trail searching for the Regulators, or hiding in his home, Peppin never impressing Bracken as a brave man. On the opposite side of the street from the jail stood Patrón's adobe house that boasted a double-pitched roof instead of the flat ones common on the other sun-dried earth-and-straw structures in town. He would return to Patrón's home, but first he wanted to inspect the community and determine if any enemies might be lurking, especially Jesse Evans as Wes burned to avenge the assault on Sarafina.

On the east end of town, he spotted no one on the street, though he suspected residents were peeking out their windows to identify the lone rider new to town. He passed four simple houses on the north side of the street and the Montaño store on the south edge. Beyond the store he saw Squire Wilson, the onetime justice of the peace and apparently the only man in town brave enough to be outside, picking apples in his orchard. Wes rode by the looted Tunstall store with its thick adobe walls and iron shutters installed in anticipation of the trouble that came. Beyond the ransacked store, he saw the blackened ruins of the hacienda style house that had burned during the Big Killing. The roof had caved in and what stood of the adobe walls was scorched from flame and pockmarked from the hundreds of bullets that had targeted McSween and his men. As he advanced by the ruins, Wes saw a black specter moving among the debris. He yanked the reins on his sorrel, drawing the animal to a stop. The ghostly black apparition stopped and turned his way, staring at him through a black veil. Wes realized the phantom was not a spirit at all, but the widow McSween shrouded in mourning attire and digging through the rubble of her past life.

Bracken nodded, then nudged his stallion toward the far side of town, passing the

Wortley Hotel with a hand-painted sign CLOSED FOR NOW in the front window. From the hostelry, Wes studied the imposing two-story adobe building on the west end of town. The edifice, one of the biggest buildings in the territory, had served as the mercantile, saloon, and headquarters for the late L.G. Murphy and his renegades. The sign that once read L.G. MURPHY & CO. now advertised JAS. J. DOLAN & CO. So dominant was Murphy's control over the county that everyone knew his store as "the House." Wes rode past the building searching each window for James J. Dolan, wondering if the merchant was now so poor he couldn't afford to spell out his whole first name on the new sign. The violence had cost the House plenty.

After passing the Dolan store, Wes angled his horse south and guided him around the back of the building to check out the corral that was empty save for two nags that looked thirsty and famished. Nearing the fence, Wes saw that the trough was empty, so he rode over and unhooked the gate, swinging it open so the two horses could find water and forage on their own. As poor a shape as they were in, the animals would not stray far.

Wes returned to the street and trotted his

stallion back to Patrón's house. Dismounting and tying his sorrel's reins to the hitching post, he called out, "Juan, Juan Patrón, it's Wes Bracken come to visit." He stepped to the door and knocked, then retreated five steps as the dwelling lacked a front window. While that architectural defect was inconvenient for identifying visitors, it excelled at stopping stray bullets.

Slowly, the entry cracked, then Juan Patrón poked his head out like a turtle emerging from an adobe shell. Confirming Wes as his visitor, he beamed. "Come in, Wesley Bracken. I got your invitation from Bonney, but these are uncertain times and a man shouldn't be out on the road when he doesn't have to."

Wes stepped to the door, clasped Patrón's outstretched hand, and shook it warmly as he entered the modest but clean parlor. "Good to see you, Juan. How's Beatriz?"

"She's in the back, resting. She's not feeling well, says it's headaches, but she's just tired of our guest."

"Susan McSween?"

Patrón nodded. "She's a trying woman, though I guess any lady would be if she saw her husband murdered, then watched his executioners dance around his body."

"I passed her digging through the ruins of

her home as I rode through town."

"She goes there daily, rummaging through her past life. Have a seat, won't you?" Patrón pointed to a cane-bottomed chair.

Wes sat, removed his hat, and placed his carbine across his knees as his friend settled in another seat.

"Gossip has it that Jimmy Dolan's put out word he'll pay five hundred dollars for anyone that'll kill her, so I suspect Susan will depart shortly to stay with her sister near Santa Fe. She'll be back, though. She's talking of hiring a lawyer to sue Colonel Dudley for his part in the affair."

"Juan, you and I both know the deck's stacked against her, Lincoln County politics being as crooked as you'll find anywhere."

"That may change, Wes. I guess you heard the good news?"

"Not sure, Juan, that's why I came to see you. We don't get many visitors these days as people seldom stray from the road to come to the Casey place now that there's no store there."

"The President removed the territorial governor from office the first part of September."

Wes nodded. "Word has it he was replaced, but I didn't know whether to believe it, not with the connections of the House into politics in Santa Fe and beyond."

"That could be changing, Wes."

Leaning forward in his chair, Bracken responded, "Tell me more."

Patrón ran his fingers through his coal black hair, then scratched his mustache, enjoying the moment that he had news unfamiliar to Bracken. He explained how President Hayes had ordered Governor Samuel B. Axtell to step down and then appointed Lew Wallace as his successor. An Indiana native, longtime abolitionist and onetime Democrat, Wallace changed party affiliation to Republican during the Civil War when he rose to the rank of major general fighting the Battles of Fort Donelson, Shiloh, Corinth, and Monocacy, Patrón continued. "Last I heard, Wallace was to reach Santa Fe and take the oath as the eleventh governor of New Mexico Territory by mid-October at the latest. Once he's sworn in, maybe things will change for the better."

"Finally," Wes replied.

"It's still iffy, though. Judge Bristol's canceled the October court session in Lincoln, so who knows when locals will get any justice from the courts."

Wes shook his head. "What about Dolan and his gang? I rode by the House. It's either vacant or his men fear showing their faces."

"Likely a little of both," Patrón explained. "When the Kid delivered your message to me last month, he made it known he would remain in Lincoln until he could shoot Dolan. That spooked Jimmy and he escaped. Word is the army's protecting him at Fort Stanton."

"I suppose the Kid's been rustling horses and cattle," Wes offered.

"That's what gossip says. They steal New Mexico livestock and sell them at Tascosa over in Texas. On the return trip, they steal Panhandle animals and sell them here."

"I feared as much. The Kid wants out of the vendetta, but won't stop committing the thefts that keep it going. I've tried to warn him he won't receive any leniency until he stops rustling."

Patrón shrugged. "Best I figure he thinks he's just equaling out the injustices done to him, but the law doesn't look at it that way. And, I tell you, Wes, he thinks you'll straighten things out for him."

"Only because I've avoided taking a side in the feud. I don't have any pull with those that make the decisions."

"Maybe that will change with the new governor."

Wes scoffed. "Politics! It never differentiates between right and wrong. All the politicians care about is money and power, not necessarily in that order. Democrat or Republican, it doesn't matter. It makes my blood boil."

"I don't have an answer, Wes, but politics is a part of life we've got to put up with for better or worse."

Wes released a deep breath. "Have you heard news of Carlos and the two fellows running with him, Geraldo Hablador and Andres Mendoza?"

"Both are mean *hombres,* but I don't know about Carlos running with them."

"From what the Kid says, Carlos is leading the gang."

Patrón whistled. "That's not good. Carlos is known among our people for his flash temper and the trouble it causes."

"Keep an ear out if you hear anything on them as they've threatened to kill me and Jace."

Patrón shook his head. "Your own brother-in-law. He's always been foolhardy, but why this?"

"He says Jace and I should've rescued McSween's men during the Big Killing, but I suspect he resents me marrying Sarafina."

Running his fingers through his hair,

Patrón grinned. "For a man that's not taken sides, you sure have plenty of enemies."

Wes studied Patrón's black eyes, then nodded. "That's what happens in Lincoln County, even when you do what's right."

"I hear Jesse Evans is gunning for you."

"And me for him after what he did to Sarafina."

Patrón grimaced, eager to change the subject. "Is news all you came to town for?"

"Supplies, if any of the stores have any."

"Montaño's shelves are empty, same at the Ellis store. There may be a few goods at Dolan's store, but I don't suspect you'd care to spend any money there."

"It'll have to be on credit, things being tight as they are and winter staring at us."

"Everybody's in the same bind in this part of Lincoln County at least, though folks along the Pecos Valley may be doing better, John Chisum especially since the violence hasn't struck him as much."

Wes arose from his chair with his Winchester in one hand and pulled his hat over his head with the other. "I best be going, but if things get tough for you and Beatriz, I can always spare a beef for you to slaughter, if that'll help you through the winter."

"Glad to know that, Wes. Hold on a moment and let me get you something." Patrón stood up from his chair and walked into the kitchen, returning shortly with a burlap bag lumpy at the bottom. "Here's a sack of apples from Squire Wilson's orchard. He's got more than he can eat, and he's giving them away to decent folks. Take these."

Wes took the bag by the neck and thanked Patrón, *"Gracias."* He stepped to the door and out into the crisp morning air, moving to his sorrel and tying the bag to his saddle with a leather strap over his saddlebags. As he cinched the burlap sack to his rig, he looked up to see the woman in black approaching. Once he finished with the apples, he tipped his hat. "Good morning, Mrs. McSween."

She stared, then lifted a black-gloved hand that carried a blackened teacup and pointed at him. "You're Wesley Bracken, aren't you?"

"Yes, ma'am."

"Is it true you watched the fire and breakout that killed my Alex?"

"I was on the hillside."

"Why didn't you help out? Maybe my husband would still be alive."

"It wasn't my fight, ma'am." Wes removed his hat as he stared over his saddle at the widow McSween.

She wagged the soot-stained teacup at him. "He didn't deserve to die."

"And I didn't kill him, ma'am."

"Nobody stands up for what's decent in Lincoln County," she answered, lowering the cup to her side.

"I agree, ma'am, but your husband didn't do right by the men that worked for him."

"What do you mean?" she scowled behind her black veil.

"He owed Billy Bonney and the others wages for riding with him. Keep that in mind as you conduct his affairs. He owes several men money for doing his bidding. You make certain they are paid when you settle his estate."

"There'll be nothing left to share with them. I'm broke."

"Who isn't ruined in Lincoln County now?" Wes yanked his hat back on his head, untied his sorrel from the hitching post, and pulled himself aboard the stallion, keeping his carbine at the ready. "Good day, ma'am." He aimed his mount east toward home and started the twelve-mile journey back to the Casey place, disappointed that he was returning with no food beyond the bag of apples but encouraged with Patrón's news. He studied the hillsides as he paralleled the Rio Bonito, then passed the Lincoln Cemetery. The stream meandered ten miles through the valley before it joined up with the Rio Ruidoso to form the Rio Hondo. Another five miles beyond the converging streams stood the Casey place.

As he neared the convergence of waters, Wes saw Charlie's ears flick forward. Twisting in his saddle, Wes scanned the vicinity, then caught the whiz of a bullet passing by his head an instant before he heard the retort from the south side of the trail. He cursed himself for riding into an ambush, then pushed himself off his sorrel, holding the reins in one hand and his carbine in the other, but the weapon fell to the ground as he fought his nervous stallion, pawing at the earth, as one, two, three bullets splattered at his feet, spitting up dirt and pebbles. Frantically, Wes yanked the sack of apples free and the fruit spilled on the road as he loosened the strap on his saddlebag, quickly shoving his hand inside and pulling out a carton of Winchester cartridges.

The terrified stallion raised on its hind legs, then jerked the reins from Wes's grasp. Wes swatted Charlie's rump and sent him galloping away, then bent unprotected in front of his assassins as he grabbed his carbine. He darted down the slope to the stream and lunged for cover among the boulders that marked the edge of the water.

Catching his breath, he yanked his hat

from his head and tossed it aside, then peered between two stones, scouring the opposite hillside for his assailants. He fought the urge to fire blindly, for he knew he must use his ammunition judiciously.

Wes wondered who his unseen attacker or attackers might be, hoping it was Jesse Evans so he might kill him but fearing it was Carlos and his gang. Wes doubted he could fend off those bushwhackers without risking the death of his brother-in-law, even if Carlos was trying to kill him. He watched. His foes waited, their patience exasperating as Wes could never defend himself until he could spot his enemies.

"Show yourselves," he mumbled. "Let's end it here and now." He sighted down the barrel of his carbine, ready to train the weapon on any form that moved. Nothing. Wes exhaled slowly, steadying his nerves so his hands remained still and his aim would be true when he spotted his enemies.

Then he noticed a slight movement behind a scrub oak a hundred and fifty yards away. It wasn't a person but the twitching brim of a sombrero. Wes cursed. Carlos was behind this ambush. The hat slid out of sight, and Wes aimed where he expected the hat's occupant to be. He aimed high of his intended target, then squeezed the trigger. Wes saw the bush tremble, then saw an attacker jump up and run for new cover. He fired two more shots, kicking up dirt behind the man he identified as Geraldo Hablador.

Barely had he fired a second time than he heard the ping of three bullets hitting the boulders at his side, spraying shards of rock around him. Glancing between the boulders, he spotted a puff of white smoke over a large hillside boulder a hundred yards away. When the gunman raised himself again, Wes recognized Andres Mendoza and instantly loosed a shot his direction.

Bracken had spotted his two henchmen, but where was Carlos? His brother-in-law could be playing for position, working himself around Wes's back for the kill. Biting his lip, Wes realized he should never have promised Sarafina not to slay her brother. Though she might never know if he did, it would be something he would have to live with if he survived. He took a deep breath, wormed his way deeper into the rocks, and awaited the siege to come, wondering if he would survive or break his promise.

CHAPTER 4

Wes tried to keep Geraldo Hablador and Andres Mendoza pinpointed, but for the moment he worried less about them than Carlos as he figured his brother-in-law was slipping around behind him to make the kill. Alternately, he glanced to the hillside across the road and then studied the slope to his back along the Rio Bonito, which flowed placidly toward the Rio Hondo. He fired an occasional shot at Hablador and Mendoza to let them know he hadn't forgotten them, but focused on searching for the unseen assassin he knew must be approaching, likely trying to get within fifty yards of his den for a fatal shot.

Squeezing off a bullet between Hablador and Mendoza, Wes levered the smoking hull from the chamber and rolled over on his back, looking at the mountainside across the rippling waters. In frustration, he squeezed off a round into that slope, warning Carlos that he knew he was out there. As he searched for his brother-in-law, he lowered his right hand and slapped the ground until his fingers found the carton of ammunition. He worked the end flap open and slid out six cartridges, which he thumbed into the Winchester's magazine, then fired across the road to keep Hablador and Mendoza nervous. Wes examined the slope behind him. Since he hadn't spotted Carlos, he hoped his brother-in-law could not see him, but that was a wishful delusion.

A bullet from across the stream pinged against the boulders, alerting Wes that Carlos had spotted him. Wes looked frantically up the mountainside, detecting a veil of white smoke. He fired his Winchester in that direction, aiming at nothing in particular. Another slug whizzed into his den from behind him, then additional shots hit the rocks from across the road. Wes gritted his teeth. They had him in a cross fire. He cursed his luck, again firing blindly toward Carlos's position.

He alternated blasts both to his front and back, realizing it was but a matter of time. Then he heard a shrill whistle from down the road and more gunshots over galloping hooves. If Carlos had more gang members attacking, Wes knew he was as good as dead. He emptied his Winchester in frustration in Carlos's direction, then as he was reloading, he saw his kin jump up and scamper away like a jackrabbit with a wolf on his tail. Wes watched dirt and stones fly up from bullets striking the ground around Carlos.

Quickly, Wes found the carton of cartridges and reloaded his carbine, rolling over and shooting toward Hablador and Mendoza, who had abandoned their positions and scurried away. He looked east toward the Casey place and spotted Jace Cousins racing his direction on his yellow dun with Wes's sorrel following.

"Wes, Wes," Cousins cried, "where are you?"

"Over here." Bracken stood and waved his hat until Jace angled his way.

Jace slowed his dun, directing him off the trail toward Wes's den. Wes watched Carlos mount his bay and ride south across the road, where he joined Hablador and Mendoza on their horses as they raced up the mountain.

"I was afraid we'd lost you when Charlie trotted up riderless. I started backtracking until I heard shots and knew you were in trouble."

Wes picked up the carton of carbine

ammo and stepped from between the rocks. He strode to Jace and took the reins for his sorrel, then paused a moment to reload his carbine, slide it in the scabbard, and pack the carton of cartridges in his saddlebag. Next he led the sorrel to the road where he stopped and picked up the burlap bag and the apples that had fallen onto the trail. He tossed one to Jace, who wiped it off on his sleeve and took a bite. Wes picked up another apple and offered it to Charlie, the animal gobbling it up. A third fruit he gave to the dun, which chomped on it. Wes tied the sack back on his saddle and mounted, turning the sorrel toward home.

"They must've known I was in Lincoln," Wes said, "and waited for me. Hablador and Mendoza positioned themselves on the south side of the road and Carlos on the river side so he could sneak up on me while I held off those two."

"I've had a feeling we've been watched the last week or so, nothing I could put my finger on," Jace replied. "They must've seen you leave this morning and waited for you. Sarafina's terrified something's happened to you. Let's get home and decide what to do about these boys."

Both men spurred their horses, racing through the river crossing and galloping the final five miles to the Casey place. When they came within sight of the house, Wes smiled when his wife emerged from inside. She held her revolver at her waist until she confirmed who it was and then lowered the weapon to her side where it hung from the leather thong. Sarafina ran out to greet Wes.

He reined in his horse and handed the lines to Jace as he jumped to the ground and wrapped his arms around his wife.

She squealed. "I was so worried when Charlie galloped up without you. What happened?"

"They ambushed me."

Sarafina gasped. "Was Carlos involved?"

"Maybe," Wes lied. "I didn't get a good look at them."

"Them?"

"There were three of them."

Sarafina bit her lip, then frowned. "It was Carlos and those evil men. I know it was, even if you won't admit it."

"I can't say for sure," Wes lied again.

"You know it was him, and you don't want to worry me."

"I promised you I wouldn't kill him."

Sarafina patted the revolver dangling at her waist. "I may have to shoot him if he keeps threatening you."

"It's okay, Sarafina. It's okay."

"I am so angry at Carlos for all the trouble he's caused you."

Wes hugged her again. "Get in the house while I tend Charlie. When I'm done, I have something for you and the boys." Releasing her, he turned to his dismounted partner and took the reins to his sorrel. The two men walked silently to the barn.

When they stepped inside, Jace asked, "What are we going to do about it?"

"We'll settle it, though I can't kill Carlos."

"I could do it. He's threatened me, too."

"It'd be the same as me killing him because she'd never be able to trust our word. If you can't shake the feeling we've been watched, they must be staying close enough to spy on us."

"Any ideas, Wes?"

"A few. Let me drop off these apples, then we'll go for a ride."

"Suits me."

They walked the horses to the stream to water. "We'll leave once darkness settles in," Wes said.

When they finished watering their mounts, they led them back to the barn, and Wes took the sack of apples and offered his partner two. "Hang onto these for supper so I can have some time with Sarafina, maybe calm her down."

"Good enough for me," Jace answered as he took the fruit and put both in his pocket.

"See you in a spell." Wes carried the bag with him to the house, entering the front and moving to the kitchen where his wife awaited with the two boys. He opened the sack and handed Luis an apple.

The boy's eyes and mouth widened. *"Gracias, Padre,"* he mumbled before attacking the apple with his teeth.

"Here's one for you, Sarafina, and one for Roberto," he said, giving each the red fruit.

"Roberto can't eat an apple," Sarafina said as her youngest son dropped the orb on the floor. She bent and picked it up for him.

"I know, Sarafina. I'll peel it and cut it in pieces we can mash up with a fork." Wes removed his pocketknife, opened the blade, and took the apple from his wife. As he sat down to peel the fruit, Sarafina brought him a tin plate and a fork. Roberto watched anxiously, licking his lips as his father removed the red skin. After peeling the apple, he quartered it and carved out the core from each piece. Next he chopped the fruit into small pieces, finally taking the fork and mashing them into a mush.

When he finished, he shoved the plate to Sarafina, who motioned for her son to approach. She grabbed him under the arms and sat him on her lap, then spooned a bite into his mouth. He bit down, grimaced at his first taste of apple, before swallowing it and holding out his hands for more.

Wes smiled that his son enjoyed the apple and reached back into the bag to take one for himself. He rubbed it against his sleeve to polish it, then lifted it to his mouth and bit down. A sharp pain raced through his jaw, and Wes yanked the fruit from his mouth, spotting a trickle of blood on the apple. He reached for his gum and felt a wet gap where his chipped tooth had been. Glancing down at the apple, he saw the bloody incisor imbedded in the fruit.

"Damn," he said.

"Such language in front of the boys," Sarafina chided.

Wes turned to his wife, opened his mouth, and watched her grimace at the gap in his teeth.

"Damn," she exclaimed, giggling at her mistake.

He held up the apple and pointed to the tooth, then placed the orb on the table.

Sarafina slid Roberto to the floor, stood up and dipped a tin of water from the barrel in the corner, and carried the cup to her husband.

Taking the tin, he filled his mouth, swished

the water around, and headed out the back door, spitting the pink liquid onto the ground. He rinsed his mouth out again and spat. Stepping back inside, he walked over to the boys and grinned. They laughed at the gap in his teeth, but Sarafina came over and pecked him on the lips.

"You're even more handsome than before."

Wes laughed. "I know better, but *gracias* anyway."

She pointed to the apple. "Do you want to finish it?"

"Let the boys split it once you discard the tooth." Then he added, "Jace and I need to check on some cattle. We may not be back until after dark."

"You're going after Carlos, aren't you?"

"I'd rather not say," he replied.

Sarafina frowned. "You just did."

"I promised you I wouldn't kill him."

"Nor do I want you to die. I've lost one husband and don't care to lose another."

"It's his *compadre*s, Hablador and Mendoza we're after."

Lowering her gaze, Sarafina raised her palms to her face, covering her eyes and shaking her head. "I don't know what to believe anymore. Carlos has wronged you, not once, but many times, but he is still my brother."

"And he's lawless like Lincoln County, but I'm not scared of him. I fear Hablador and Mendoza, for they might violate you, even if they are your brother's friends."

Sarafina lifted her head and lowered her hands from her cheeks. "I have been violated by two white men, never by my own people."

"And one of those attackers is dead, and I intend to kill the other. I suspect Carlos and his men are staying nearby until they can ambush me and Jace. They tried today, and I'd be dead, if Charlie hadn't alarmed Jace to find me."

Tears rolled down Sarafina's cheeks, and Wes comforted her, wrapping his arm around her and kissing her moist cheek. She wormed her way out of his arms.

"Go do what you must," she said, "but don't tell me the result."

Wes nodded. "We may be gone all night, Sarafina. Keep your revolver handy, and I'll load the shotgun for you before I leave so you'll have another weapon."

"*Gracias,*" she said, "now leave." She paused. "But don't tell me the outcome."

Wes started for the back door, then turned around and strode past his wife into the front room where the counter and shelves that had once served as the Casey store stood empty. He reached beneath the counter and removed the double-barreled shotgun that the Caseys had left behind and carefully loaded it and carried it back into the kitchen. He gave it to Sarafina and reminded her how to cock the twin hammers and pull the twin triggers. Wes warned her of the powerful recoil the gun would create if fired and cautioned her to hold it to her side or at her shoulder so the kick would not hurt her swelling belly and the baby growing there. He kissed her a last time and retreated out the back door toward the barn.

Wes saw Jace squatting by the Rio Hondo and wondered what his partner was up to until he stood up, a canteen in each hand. He had been filling their containers with cool water for the task ahead. Cousins ambled toward Bracken, their paths intersecting outside the barn. Jace pitched Wes his canteen.

"I thought we might need these."

Catching the canteen by the strap, Wes grinned.

Jace bobbed his head and stopped in his tracks. "Damn, Wes, did you sass Sarafina one too many times?"

Confused, Wes cocked his head, then

smiled again. "My tooth?"

Cousins nodded. "Seems like your wife taught you a lesson. Whatever your differences with Sarafina, Wes, I'm on her side."

Wes laughed. "The tooth came loose when I bit into an apple. Besides, Sarafina said it made me even better looking."

"Let's just say it didn't hurt your looks." Jace draped his free arm around his partner's shoulders and accompanied him to the barn. "Now tell me what you've got in mind."

"We're going hunting for Carlos and his gang. If you suspect they've been watching us, I have a suspicion where they might be."

"The Mirror B?" Jace asked, dropping his arm from around Wes's shoulders and opening the barn door.

"Possibly," Wes replied, "but more likely at the Zamora cabin where I first met Sarafina."

"And where you met Carlos?"

"Yep. Hard to believe that it's been five years since I arrived in Lincoln County. I left Arkansas thinking I would finally escape the animosities lingering from the War Between the States. Things have been worse here and the rancor more complicated."

"Sorry you came, Wes?"

"I don't regret it because I've got a fine

wife, two boys, and another child on the way. But I must admit I never expected so much violence. I wanted to raise the best horses in the territory with my brother, and all that's left of that dream is the bleaching bones of my herds and Luther's grave on the Mirror B. At least I've still got Charlie."

Hearing his name, Wes's stallion lifted his head and looked over his stall at the two approaching men.

"Lincoln County's where dreams go to die, Wes."

"I don't want to die with them."

The partners tied their canteens to their saddles, then checked the loads in their long guns, Jace confirming his Henry rifle was full and Wes nodding his Winchester carbine was ready as well. After securing the long weapons in their scabbards, the men untied their horses and led them out of the barn. After closing the door, they mounted and rode past the house to the road and turned west down the Ruidoso Valley, which led twenty miles into the tall, pine-shrouded mountains. As they approached the convergence of the Bonito and Ruidoso, each man pulled his long gun from his saddle boot. Splashing through the Hondo crossing, they followed the Ruidoso, studying the slopes and the trees along the stream, looking for enemies that might surprise them.

The cool October air trumped the afternoon sun and the partners rode silently, the clop-clop of their horses being the only sound as they advanced up the valley. Where the two streams joined to form the Rio Hondo stood the forlorn ruins of the Mirror B. Beyond the abandoned ranch, it was two miles to the Zamora place and another two miles to San Patricio where Wes had married Sarafina in the chapel adjoining the graveyard where her first husband lay buried. Nearing the Mirror B, both men wordlessly guided their mounts off the road and toward the remnants of Wes's dream. What had been the best barn in the western half of Lincoln County was a collapsed mass of blackened timbers. The horses he dreamed of breeding were now hide-splotched bones bleaching in the sunlight. What had been the adobe he and his wife called home had been torched as well, its walls scorched and sooted, its roof crumbled inside. Even the small adobe that had been the original cabin Wes's brother had acquired and Jace later used as a bunkhouse had been torched. The men rode past the ruins toward the stream to let their mounts water. Wes directed Charlie toward the cross beneath the massive cottonwood tree that shaded the watercourse and his brother Luther's grave. Stopping at the stone-covered grave, Wes took off his hat, never saying a thing, as he didn't have to. Any brother would've wished things had turned out better. Then he let his sorrel stride into the creek by Jace's dun so Charlie could water.

When both horses had their fill, the riders turned them back toward the road and the Zamora place. As they neared the trail to the lonely adobe, Wes pointed to the village.

"Let's stop at San Patricio first," he said, "then inspect the cabin on the way back."

Jace nodded.

"If my suspicions are right, I figure Carlos and his boys go there for laughs. And if they do, I don't think the locals much appreciate the type of fun they have. Carlos drinks too much and the other two are plain mean."

"We might even catch them in town, commiserating about failing to kill you this morning," Jace noted.

As they rode past the cabin, both men studied it for signs of activity, but nothing gave the place away save maybe a wisp of smoke from the chimney. Then they focused on San Patricio, a sleepy little Mexican village that had been much abused by the various factions in the Lincoln County feud. Nearing the town of forty adobe structures or wooden *jacales* along a single dusty road with trails branching to the outlying adobes, Wes aimed his horse for the cantina. The road through town was empty except for two burros on the opposite side of the street and a mother cat with six kittens trailing her around a house. Seeing no horses at hitching posts, Wes figured Carlos and his men were not in San Patricio.

At the cantina, Wes dismounted and asked Jace to remain outside to watch the horses. Still carrying his carbine, Wes entered the tavern, which was lit by the afternoon light from a single southern window. Seeing the owner asleep on the bar, Wes slammed the door and the proprietor jerked and sat up, fear washing across his face until he recognized Wes Bracken.

"*Buenos días, Señor* Bracken," he said, rolling off the bar and smiling. "*Es bueno verte. ¿Te gustaría un whiskey?*"

"It's good to see you, too," he replied, "and I'll pass on the whiskey." After five years in New Mexico Territory, Wes had picked up enough Spanish to converse with Hispanics. The moment he told the proprietor he was looking for Carlos, Hablador, and Mendoza, the barkeep's expression turned rancid.

"*Hombres muy malos,*" he scowled.

Wes agreed and probed for more information. The cantina owner told him the trio came in daily in the afternoon and drank, threatening the men and tormenting the women, who had learned not to enter when the bad men's horses were tied outside. Further, Hablador and Mendoza had raped two women.

"What about Carlos? Was he involved?"

The proprietor lifted his arms and shrugged. Wes could not be certain if the fellow was telling him the truth or just avoiding it since Carlos was his brother-in-law. He asked the barkeep if they had been in earlier in the day and learned they had not. That was good news because Wes figured they were hiding out after the failed ambush. It was time to find the trio. *"Gracias,"* Wes said, then apologized for his kin's deed. *"Lo siento por las acciones de Carlos."*

The bartender smiled as Wes turned around to leave. *"Buena suerte,"* he called.

Wes stepped outside and mounted Charlie, explaining to Jace what he had learned.

"You think they're at the Zamora place?"

"I'm not sure, Jace, but if not, they are nearby. I think I know where."

Together the partners turned their horses back toward the Zamora cabin and rode cautiously that direction, their long guns at the ready. Wes looked to the west where the sun had gone down behind the mountains and estimated they had an hour of light left.

"Should we wait until dark to approach the cabin, Wes?"

"We can leave the road and slip through the trees by the stream because I don't think anybody's there, but we should confirm that first."

They rode off the trail and worked their way among the foliage until they were two hundred yards away from the adobe. Jace pointed to the chimney. "Smoke," he whispered.

Wes looked and saw a whiff of smoke and a glowing ember rising in the sky over the house. "We'll wait for dark."

Both men slid off their horses and tied them behind bushes to screen them from the house. Then each man retrieved from his saddlebags a box of cartridges for his long gun. Jace pulled two apples from his saddlebag.

"I saved these for supper, Wes. You want one?"

"Sure."

Jace tossed him a piece of fruit. "But don't blame me if you lose any more teeth."

The men seated themselves beside the trunk of a cottonwood, silently eating their fruit and watching the adobe, which was lifeless other than the thin veil of smoke trailing from the corner fireplace. Wes spotted no horses, so he figured his suspicions were true, but the three could hide their horses indoors to make the place appear abandoned.

When darkness fully enveloped the valley, Wes got up and Jace with him. "Let's split up. I'll go around the near side of the house and you circle the east end. When we meet at the front, I'll bust down the door and you knock in the shuttered window. Whistle if you see trouble."

Jace nodded and the two men stalked the adobe, walking stealthily toward the dwelling. They each reached opposite corners together, then proceeded around their side of the noiseless structure. Only the wheeze of the breeze from the valley broke the silence.

Bracken and Cousins made it to the front undetected. Wes leveled his gun, ready to fire when he saw Jace at the shuttered window. Drawing his foot back, Wes kicked open the door and burst inside, praying he didn't kill Carlos in the raid.

CHAPTER 5

The cabin stood empty. Wes looked around the darkened room, dimly lit by the embers in the fireplace.

Jace burst in behind him. "All that work for nothing. I wanted to end it here so I can focus on killing Jesse Evans."

"I know where they are," Wes said.

"Then why'd we waste our time here?"

"I had to be sure with the smoke coming out of the chimney," he responded, taking a deep breath and wrinkling his nose at the smell of horse dung.

"Enlighten me."

"Back during the Horrell troubles when Sarafina was in danger, Carlos hid her in a cave up the mountainside about three-quarters of a mile from here."

"How do you explain the fire?"

"They fix their meals here, keeping their horses inside and out of view. Then they retreat to the cave to sleep so nobody can slip up on them."

"How are we gonna do it?"

"We'll go afoot, less noise and less chance of them spotting us."

"What'll we do with our mounts?"

"Hide them in here like they do."

Jace rubbed his brow and nodded. "You've got it all figured out, don't you?"

"Nothing's certain for now, but we'll know before dawn."

"Then let's fetch our horses and start the party."

The men left the building and retrieved their mounts, leading them inside the adobe and putting hobbles on their legs. They checked the loads in their revolvers and long guns, each retrieving an extra carton of cartridges from their saddlebags in case the siege took a spell. Nodding to each other, the partners stepped outside the cabin where Wes pointed to the southeast. They moved that direction, crossing the Ruidoso on rocks at shallows and angling up the mountainside, moving slowly and quietly.

As Wes's eyes adjusted to the darkness, he spotted familiar markers that confirmed he was on the right path. The men grimaced as they walked up the rocky slopes, trying to move delicately so not to cause a rockslide that might give them away. Taking quiet precautions, the partners inched up the slope, using twice the time they would've needed in daylight.

Halfway to their destination, Jace nudged Wes with his elbow. "What's your plan?"

"Since the law won't do anything, it's either kill Hablador and Mendoza or let them go with another chance to ambush us."

"And Carlos? Does the same apply for him?"

Wes clenched his jaw and hesitated before replying. "I made a promise to Sarafina, Jace, but you do what you have to do."

Cousins nodded. "I won't let him murder you."

"The cave's big enough for them to hide along with their horses, so I doubt we'll see anything until we are almost upon them. Once I can point it out to you, we'll split up, me on the west side, you circling down to the east. When you find cover, give me a bird whistle."

Jace nodded. "How about the call of a piñon jay, queh queh queh?"

Wes nodded and pointed up the mountainside. "Let's go."

They spread about ten yards apart and continued their climb, gradually angling up the slope toward the point Wes believed to be the mouth of the cave. He wondered if his memory or his eyes were failing him until he saw a faint glow flicker from the darkness a hundred yards ahead. Jace froze as he had seen it too. Their quarry had built a fire, and Wes envied them for the heat it provided. Jace waved as he circled east of the cave. Wes crept forward, hiding twenty yards from the cave's mouth behind an outcrop of rocks.

Wes positioned himself and waited. Five minutes later he detected a low whistle.

"Queh queh queh," Jace called.

Wes answered, "Queh queh queh." He lifted his Winchester to his shoulder and rested the barrel on the rock, trying to decide what to do, but his dilemma resolved itself as a man passed through the yellow glimmer and stepped outside the cavern. He was lean and wore a sombrero, oblivious to the danger in front of him as he slipped away from the cave to take a leak. Wes decided it was Hablador. His finger tightened on the trigger, but before he squeezed, he gave the bad man more of a chance than he had received. "Throw up your hands," Wes shouted.

Instantly, Hablador's right hand grabbed for a pistol at his side. Wes fired the instant he heard a rifle shot from the east. The bandit dropped his gun, clutched his chest, and tumbled forward, rolling down the slope before catching on the stub of a piñon bush.

"Geraldo," came a cry from the cave as the yellow glow faded into darkness.

Wes knew the voice belonged to Mendoza, but neither he nor Jace responded.

Carlos shouted out, *"¿Geraldo, estás bien?"*

"He's dead," Wes answered.

"Eres un bastardo, Wes," Carlos cried.

"He got more of a chance than he gave me this morning, Carlos. You might as well surrender, both of you."

"So you can murder us, too?"

"I vowed to your sister I wouldn't kill you. Toss out your guns and come on out."

"I don't trust you, Wes."

"Carlos," Jace cried, "you best do what Wes says. I'm not a patient man like him. I never promised not to kill you, but give up now, and I'll promise not to shoot you tonight."

Wes caught fragments of Spanish as Carlos and Mendoza argued about what to do. "Come on out, Carlos, while you still can."

Only silence answered.

"We've got food and water to last us all night and all day tomorrow," Wes bluffed. "And, we let Sheriff Peppin know where to find you, Carlos. The lawman accompanied Sheriff Brady and Deputy Hindman back in April when you and the Kid ambushed and murdered them. He's still got a hankering to settle scores with you."

"Yeah," Jace shouted. "Peppin wants to kill you. Come out and you can go your own way, as long as you hand over your weapons."

"What about Andres?" Carlos called.

"Mendoza's on his own," Wes answered, then listened to the two trapped men quarrelling.

Mendoza cursed and screamed at Carlos, *"Eres un cobarde."*

With Mendoza calling Carlos a coward, Wes knew the partnership was breaking up and his brother-in-law was terrified.

"I'm coming out," Carlos cried.

"Cobarde," Mendoza screamed.

A gunshot and a flash of light exploded in the cave, the momentary illumination showing the horses hobbled near the cavern's mouth. Carlos shrieked in agony.

Wes jumped up and bolted for Carlos, firing a shot at the top of the cave, hoping the bullet sent enough stony shrapnel into the chasm to stun both men. As he raced for the cave's entrance, he heard Cousins behind him.

"I'm coming, Wes."

Bolting into the cave, Wes leaped behind the nearest horse and rested his Winchester across the saddle. The sounds of the dangerous duo struggling against each other reached his ears, but he could see nothing in the darkness. He lifted his carbine and fired overhead, the flash of the gun illuminating the two antagonists wrestling over a pistol.

"Drop to the ground, Carlos," Wes ordered and shot another bullet into the stony ceiling, the momentary blaze exposing his brother-in-law tumbling backward against the rock wall. Aiming for Mendoza's chest just as the terrified horse twitched, Wes fired.

A scream echoed through the cavern, followed by the sound of a revolver hitting the rock floor and reverberating through the air. Mendoza cursed and screeched in agony.

"Are you okay, Carlos?" he cried.

"I've been hit in the shoulder," he replied.

"What about Mendoza?"

"He's down and groaning. I can't see."

Wes loosed another shot overhead, briefly spotting Mendoza writhing on the ground, his hands holding his bloodstained britches at his groin.

"I'm behind you," Jace called. "Is it safe

to strike a match?"

"They're both down."

Wes listened to Jace extracting a tin of matches from his pocket and flaring one to life with his thumbnail, a ball of light glowing behind Bracken, who stepped around the horse with his carbine still pointed at Mendoza, thrashing around the cave floor. Wes jumped to the wounded man and kicked his revolver out of reach. The sidearm clanged against a lantern by the rock wall as the match faded away.

"There's a lamp to your left," Wes said, as his partner struck another sulfur stick, then walked past him and bent over the lantern, which gradually took hold of the flame and illuminated the back of the cave.

Spinning around, Jace bounded to Carlos, who was holding his right shoulder, and slipped his pistol from the youth's holster. "You won't be needing this, Carlos."

With the gun pointed at his antagonist's head, Wes stepped to Mendoza, who screamed indecipherable Spanish. "What's he saying, Carlos?"

"To kill him and end his agony."

Stepping over him, Wes used the carbine barrel to pry his hands away from his groin, where his soaked britches dripped blood. Mendoza whimpered as Wes stared into his terrified eyes. Wes forced the gun barrel past the bad man's lips and into his mouth, cocking the hammer on the Winchester. Mendoza's eyes widened until Wes yanked the weapon from his lips and fired it into the ground beside his ear. Mendoza screamed, grabbing his ear with a bloody hand.

"You missed," Jace observed as he helped Carlos sit up.

"I thought about killing him, but he got the wound he deserved for what he did to the women in San Patricio. Maybe he'll bleed to death."

Wes turned to Carlos. "Did you rape any señoritas in San Patricio, Carlos?"

"No, I swear to the Blessed Virgin that I did not. What are you going to do to me?"

Stepping to his side while Jace checked the shoulder wound, Wes pushed his hat back with the carbine barrel. "What should I do, Carlos? Turn you over to Sheriff Peppin?"

His eyes and mouth gaping, Carlos shook his head rapidly, then contorted at the sharp pain at his shoulder. "No, you wouldn't do that to your own kin, would you?"

"Flesh and blood that threatened to kill me and my partner. Why wouldn't I?"

"I'm Sarafina's brother."

"And I'm her husband, the one you vowed to kill."

Jace stood up and nodded. "Looks like the bullet missed bones, the best I can tell. He'll live, though he'll be in some pain for a spell."

"What are you planning for me?"

"I'm letting you ride away tonight with Mendoza."

"He shot me," Carlos said.

"Just like the three of you ambushed Wes earlier today," Jace reminded him.

The youth swallowed hard.

"You're not so cocky now, are you, Carlos? Your quick temper gets you in binds you can't handle yourself. Nobody trusts you anymore."

Scowling at Wes, Carlos wagged his head from side to side. "Everything's turned sour since you arrived in Lincoln County. You've done nothing but take, take, take, from me and my sister."

"I saved you both from the Horrells and gave you a horse and a carbine. Your sister offered you the place down in the valley, a piece of land you could work and get by. Instead, you've taken to drinking, killing, and riding with bad men."

Carlos looked at his feet as Jace helped him up and removed his gun belt from his waist. "So, what are you going to do with me?"

"I'm sending you away. Get out of Lincoln County and never come back. If you return, I'll break my promise to your sister and shoot you on sight."

"Where will I go?"

"Figure it out, Carlos. There's El Paso to the south, though I suspect you wouldn't last long around a bunch of drunk Texans, or there's Fort Sumner up north. That's where the Kid and his gang are hiding these days. They're smart enough to stay away from Lincoln County, especially those under indictment for murder like you and the Kid. Which horse is yours?"

Carlos pointed to a bay.

Wes marched to the animal, removing the carbine from its scabbard and rifling through the saddlebags, extracting a carton of carbine cartridges and two of revolver ammunition, which he shoved in his pants pocket, then leaned the weapon and his own Winchester against the wall.

"You're not sending me away without guns and bullets, are you?"

Nodding, Wes pointed his finger at his brother-in-law. "We can't trust you not to shoot us in the back, Carlos, so you'll make do with sticks and stones. Which is Mendoza's mount?"

Carlos pointed toward the second bay, and Wes stepped to the gelding, removing the carbine and another box of ammunition from the saddlebags, placing both beside the other weapons. He also extracted a length of cord, ten feet long.

"You're not tying me up, too, are you?" Carlos demanded.

"No, but your saddle pal will need a little help to stay mounted."

Wes walked over to Mendoza, bent, and securely knotted one end of the cord around his ankle, just above the top of his brogan. The wounded man groaned, then screamed when Wes grabbed his shoulders and boosted him to his feet, then half pushed, half carried him to the side of his bay. Wes pointed for him to mount, but Mendoza shook his head, his terrified eyes widening.

"No, *señor*, no," he pleaded.

Kicking his left foot for him to insert it in the stirrup, Wes bent down and yanked up his knee and forced the brogan into the foothold. Mendoza screeched even more when Wes tugged his britches, forcing him to climb atop his horse. The wounded man twitched and pushed Wes away, deciding it was less painful to obey than to let Wes help. Gently, he climbed into the saddle, settling easily on the leather like a hen on her nest as he gasped and moaned. As soon as he mounted, Wes tossed the loose end of the cord under the saddle and walked around the horse to grab it. He cinched the thong under the bay's belly and around Mendoza's right ankle, binding it tight so Mendoza would stay mounted despite the pain.

Turning to Carlos, he pointed toward his bay. "Get mounted and get out of Lincoln County. If you're going to El Paso, take the road west, then southwest to Tularosa. Should you be aiming for Fort Sumner, ride east out of the Hondo Valley, then turn north. You'll eventually get there. If you go east, don't stop at our house. I left Sarafina with a loaded shotgun with instructions to use it on anyone who stopped by tonight."

"She wouldn't shoot her own brother."

Wes shrugged. "I wouldn't be so sure of that."

Carlos stumbled toward his bay and mounted.

Wes squatted and removed the hobbles first from his and then Mendoza's horse. "Now get out of here and don't come back to Lincoln County."

"What about him?" Carlos said, pointing to Mendoza.

"He's your partner and your problem,"

Wes said. "Now get going and don't stop by Hablador and try to pick up any of his weapons because I'll be watching." Wes stepped to retrieve his carbine and trailed the two horses out into the darkness, seeing them pass the body of their dead confederate. In a few moments after turning east, they disappeared in the gloom of night.

When he stepped back in the cave, Jace was gathering the two carbines and shoving them under the saddle. Wes took the cartons of ammunition from his pocket and placed them in Hablador's saddlebags. Jace picked up Mendoza's and Carlos's pistols and put them in holsters that he buckled and hung over his shoulder as Wes grabbed the lantern. Jace unhobbled the horse and led him outside where the ball of yellow light revealed Hablador's body, two bullet holes in his chest. They stripped him of his two gun belts and hung them over his saddle horn.

"What'll we do with his body?" Jace asked.

"Take him to San Patricio. Let the people bury him. It'll be good for them to see he won't be intimidating them or raping their women again."

Jace nodded as both grabbed an arm and a leg of the dead man. "Mendoza couldn't have been wounded in a better spot."

"I must admit I enjoyed his pain after

what I learned of his assaults. Considering what Jesse Evans did to Sarafina, I take poorly to men attacking women," Wes said as they hoisted the body over the saddle.

"You're still worried about the baby, Wes?"

Wes let out a long sigh like bellows with a hole. "I doubt we'll ever know for certain."

"I'm confident it'll be yours, Wes. There's gotta be a pinch of good in this world. You know I shot and killed a man tonight, and I don't feel an ounce of regret. I know according to the Good Book that I should, but I don't."

Extracting two lengths of cord from the dead man's saddlebags, the two partners secured the dead man to the mount and started back down the mountainside, Wes carrying the lantern and Jace leading the horse. With light and no necessity for stealth on the downhill slope, the two made good time, reaching the cabin and finding their horses hobbled as they had left them. They quickly transferred the cartons of ammunition, the three carbines, and four holsters and pistols to their own mounts, unhobbled them, and headed for San Patricio.

Reaching the village, they returned to the cantina where Wes found the proprietor and three customers having a quiet drink inside, the only sign of life in town beyond the yellow glows coming from the windows of the adobes. Wes asked the proprietor to join him outside.

As the cantina owner stepped out the door and saw the body draped over the horse, he gasped and signed the cross over his chest.

"*Es bueno,*" Wes reassured the Mexican, then told him they had killed Hablador and maimed Mendoza.

"*¿Qué hay de Carlos?*"

Wes explained that he and Cousins had banished Carlos from Lincoln County upon the threat of shooting him on sight. Though it didn't guarantee he would stay away, Wes thought it would scare him off for many months.

"*Gracias, gracias.*"

Next Wes asked the Mexican to see that Hablador was buried somewhere, if not in the cemetery then elsewhere. In exchange for doing that, Wes told him he could sell the bandit's horse and gear to cover his expenses. Wes instructed that whatever money remained after that was to be split between the two women that the deceased and Mendoza had assaulted. "*¿Comprende?*"

"*Sí y gracias.*"

Wes patted the man on the shoulder. "*Gracias.*" He stepped to his sorrel and mounted up, then he and Jace started the ride back

93

to the Casey place as the full moon rose over the mountains. By the time they reached their home shortly after midnight, the moonlight threw a ghostly glow over the countryside. Though the pale glimmer made them more visible to any lurking enemies, it also would give his wife a chance to identify them as they neared the house.

Turning off the road toward his dwelling, Wes called out, "Sarafina, Sarafina, we have returned."

Jace added a shrill whistle to the air, and Wes continued to call his spouse until he saw the front door cracking open. Sarafina stepped outside, holding the double-barreled shotgun.

Confirming the riders were Wes and Jace, she leaned the scattergun against the house and walked out to meet her husband. "I am thankful you have returned, *mi esposo.* I will not ask about my brother so you will not have to tell a lie."

Nearing her, Wes reined up on his mount and slid out of the saddle, holding his reins as he reached for his wife and hugged her. "Hablador died in the shootout and Mendoza took a serious wound to the lower gut. Carlos got shot in the shoulder in a dispute with Mendoza, not with me or Jace, but it was little more than a flesh wound, and he will survive."

"Then what happened to Carlos?"

"I told him to leave Lincoln County and never return because we could no longer trust him." He unwrapped his arms from his wife and shook the reins in his hand. "Let me tend Charlie. After that I'll tell you anything you want to know."

"Give me your reins, partner," Jace said, "and I'll handle him for you."

After handing Jace the leather straps, Wes accompanied Sarafina to the door, grabbing the shotgun as he escorted her inside, shutting and barring the entry behind him.

"What happened to Carlos?"

"He left the cave behind the Zamora place, headed east. I figure he'll go to Fort Sumner, where the Kid and his men are hiding out. He may have passed by here, but I told him not to stop because you were wary of anyone coming to the house in the dark."

"It's strange," Sarafina said, "but I swear I heard him calling my name and saying *adiós* a couple hours ago."

"Might've been him."

"Do you think he will ever visit again?"

"Maybe," Wes replied. "Do you want to see him again?"

She shrugged. "I don't know anymore."

Wes nodded. "That's Lincoln County for you."

CHAPTER 6

Chopping wood for the approaching winter months, Wes recognized Juan Patrón as he guided his black gelding off the road and down the trail to the Bracken house. He was the first to visit the Casey place since Wes and Jace had confronted Carlos's gang. With a powerful swing of his shoulders, Wes planted his ax in a log and picked up his shirt, shoving his arms in and buttoning it up as he walked to the back door, sticking his head inside. "Company's coming, Sarafina. It's Juan Patrón." He backed out of the kitchen and strode around the side of the dwelling to the front where he greeted his visitor.

"Welcome, Juan. What brings you out from Lincoln?"

"News to share with you and Jace."

"He's out checking on the cattle, so I'll have to do."

Patrón drew up his horse and dismounted,

Wes taking the reins and tying them to the hitching post.

As Wes turned around, Patrón grabbed and hugged him. *"Gracias, mi amigo."*

Surprised by his gesture, Wes broke from his friend's grasp. "What brought that on?"

"Word reached us in Lincoln about what you did for our people at San Patricio. Geraldo Hablador and Andres Mendoza were vicious men who deserved to die."

"We only wounded Mendoza."

Patrón shook his head. "His body was found three days ago on the road to Roswell, just after the valley opens out onto the prairie. Best anyone could tell, he bled to death from a gut wound. No Mexican says it aloud, but we know you and Jace gave them their due for attacking those poor girls in San Patricio. And we thank you. You've been a friend of our people ever since you arrived in Lincoln County."

"I'm just trying to do what's right and watch out for my own hide, Juan."

"Maybe so, Wes, but all of us Mexicans are grateful."

Wes patted Patrón on the shoulder. "You're welcome. Any other news?"

"There is."

"Do you want to step inside? Sarafina'd be glad to pour you a cup of coffee."

Juan waved the offer away. "I can't stay long, but you needed to know that on this past Monday, the seventh, President Hayes issued a proclamation admonishing all good citizens of the Territory of New Mexico and especially those who had committed lawless acts to disperse and return to their homes no later than noon this Sunday, the thirteenth. If the violence continues, the president is prepared to declare martial law and use the army to bring offenders to justice."

"Like the soldiers who watched over the murder of McSween and others at the Big Killing?"

His visitor shrugged. "We must start somewhere, if we're to clean this county up."

"I've become too cynical about lawmen and soldiers in Lincoln County. Both are above the law."

"Rumor has it that the president has told the governor to straighten this mess out and end the violence, even if it includes pardons all around. You and I know everyone's tired of the killing and fearing for their own lives."

"Don't get me wrong, Juan, I'm all for peace, but it'll be a long time coming as the animosities run too deep around here for everyone to let bygones be bygones. Something always rears its head to continue the violence, creating more rancor."

"I received a letter from Susan McSween that she's returning to Lincoln, once the presidential proclamation goes into effect."

"What's your wife think of the widow McSween returning to stay with you?"

Juan smiled. "She won't be boarding with us anymore. Her husband owned a couple houses he rented out in town, and she's evicted the Baca family from their home for hers."

"That'll make her more friends."

"And she says she's bringing a lawyer to file charges against Colonel Dudley for his role in the loss of her husband, her home, and her belongings."

Wes spat on the ground. "Lawyers? There's lawyers mired up to their necks in all Lincoln County's problems. One more won't help a damn thing."

"Maybe not, but perhaps the governor's proclamation will. I'll bring you a copy when it arrives."

"Don't bother, Juan. It won't make any difference."

Patrón shook Wes's hand, then stepped to untie his horse. "You're probably right, Wes, but I figured you needed to hear the news. How's Sarafina getting along with the baby?"

Wes smiled. "She manages, even with the

two boys, but she'll be glad when it arrives."

"When will that be?"

"Sarafina figures December sometime."

"I wish you both well when the time comes." Patrón mounted and stared at Wes a final time. "Thanks again for what you did for the San Patricio folks."

With that, Patrón started back for Lincoln, and Wes stepped inside to let his wife know Juan would not be coming in. He saw disappointment in her eyes, "He just came out to deliver news about affairs in Lincoln. He reported that Mendoza died from his wounds."

Sarafina signed the cross over her bosom. "I'm sorry," she started, "sorry that Carlos ever rode with such a wicked man. Did Mendoza's wickedness taint my brother?"

"I can't answer that, Sarafina, but what I can tell you is I need to keep on chopping wood so you'll have plenty for the winter ahead."

Wes slipped out the back door to the woodpile, removed his shirt, grabbed the ax, and resumed his chore, working for a solid hour until he saw his partner riding down a low ridge to the south. Splashing through the Rio Hondo, Jace aimed his horse at Wes and trotted over, shaking his head.

"I was expecting a bigger woodpile by now." He grinned.

"Then you show me how it's done, and I'll check the cattle next time."

"By my count, we're down about a dozen head. Can't tell if they were rustled, wandered off, or just died on us." Jace dismounted.

"Juan Patrón came out to inform us President Hayes has released a proclamation ordering everyone in Lincoln County to return to home and behave."

Cousins laughed. "Our problems are solved then, aren't they?"

"That was my reaction."

"Did you ask him if he'd heard any news about Jesse Evans?"

Wes shook his head. "It slipped my mind."

"Nothing's resolved in my mind until Jesse Evans is dead and buried in an unmarked grave."

The brisk air of October gave way to the chilly nights of early November, Sarafina preparing for a third child, Wes and Jace preparing for winter. The men provided a couple beeves to the villagers of San Patricio in exchange for cornmeal, dried chilies, apples, and two dozen chickens to double the size of Sarafina's flock. Though the

Mexicans got more in value for the trade, Wes felt good about the trade as he dealt with decent people abused by too many other men, both Anglo and Hispanic, over the years. And they had taken to calling him *"nuestro salvador,"* which Sarafina translated as "our savior," an appellation that left Wes uncomfortable, though it provided Jace grist for teasing his partner, especially after reading his Bible each night.

Wes and Jace spent time at the mill the Caseys had constructed beside the Hondo, repairing some slats in the waterwheel and learning how to operate the millstones so they might bring in more revenue the coming fall if people felt safe planting and harvesting corn. The partners cut wild grass along the river and left it to dry so the horses would have fodder come frigid weather.

As winter approached, their first at the Casey place, Jace moved in from the bunkhouse and set up his bed in the front room behind the counter to save on firewood. No sense heating two abodes when there was plenty of space in the house. As they grew, Luis and Roberto became more curious, exploring that room especially, hiding under the counter, climbing on the shelves and pulling the covers off Jace's straw mattress, always giggling and having fun. Sarafina let them play there all they wanted as she was growing heavy and tired with the baby.

With the threat of martial law hanging over everyone, the men and women of Lincoln County warily tried to return to their old way of life, but they trusted no one but family and sometimes not even their kin. By late October word circulated that Billy Bonney and his gang had returned, still intent on settling scores. Wes never knew whether to believe those stories. While the Kid had proclaimed his desire to end the running and lawbreaking, his sense of righteousness about his own cause complicated his intent to go straight. The rumors seemed true when on the second day of November Sheriff George Peppin and his posse visited the Casey place.

Wes left his ax by the woodpile, grabbed his Winchester, and went out to greet the lawmen. Jace followed him from the barn, holding his Henry.

"Afternoon, Sheriff," Wes said.

"We're looking for Billy Bonney. You seen him lately?" Peppin asked.

"Not since early September or so."

"Rumor is he's back in these parts."

"If he is, he hasn't stopped by here."

Peppin studied Wes. "You know he's got

two indictments against him for murdering Sheriff Brady in Lincoln and Buckshot Roberts over at Blazer's Mill."

"I heard."

"You know your brother-in-law's been indicted for killing Deputy Hindman?"

"I haven't seen Carlos for several weeks now."

"What do you know about the shootings of Geraldo Hablador and Andres Mendoza?"

"Seems I heard they got shot up."

"Was that the last time you saw Carlos?"

"When I last saw Carlos, he was headed for Fort Sumner, Sheriff."

"That's where the Kid's been, rustling cattle and horses and taking them into the Texas Panhandle to Tascosa for sale and then stealing Texan livestock to sell in New Mexico Territory. Has Carlos joined up with the Kid?"

"I can't say, Sheriff. Now let me ask you a question. Are you looking for Jesse Evans, too? He's under indictment. What about Jimmy Dolan? Have you arrested him? He's got charges pending against him."

Peppin shrugged. "I can find them later. I'm searching for Bonney. He's a cold-blooded killer. The other two killed in self-defense."

"Every encounter in Lincoln County is self-defense because of the lawlessness, Sheriff. Now unless you have business with me or my partner, get off my place."

The sheriff spat at Wes's feet. "I intend to find the Kid, even if I have to use the cavalry to do it."

"*Adiós,* Sheriff." Wes turned and walked away.

"You're awfully pious for a murderer, Bracken," Peppin said.

Wes froze, slowly turning around until Jace stepped to his side and grabbed his arm.

"The only reason you won't be indicted for murdering Hablador and Mendoza is because they're Mexicans."

Jace waved the sheriff away. "I think you and your posse better ride on, Peppin, before things turn ugly. No white man in Lincoln County is respected more by the Mexicans than Wesley Bracken."

"He's not the hero he thinks he is," Peppin said, yanking his horse about and heading back for the road, his posse trailing him.

Wes felt the veins in his neck throbbing with anger. He jerked his arm away from Jace and lifted his Winchester until his partner grabbed the gun and pushed the barrel downward.

"Let it go, *nuestro salvador,*" Jace cautioned, "let it go."

"It gnaws at me, Jace. So much wickedness in this county, and the law's trying to hang it all around the Kid's neck."

The two men watched the posse reach the road and turn west toward San Patricio. Wes wondered whether the sheriff's intent was to help or intimidate the villagers. Lincoln County was huge, occupying the southeastern fourth of the entire territory, a region so vast that Wes understood the sheriff and a handful of deputies could never cover it all. But when they did impose the law, at least they could do it fairly for all the residents, not just the few with political connections. Wes spat at the ground.

"I've been thinking about the Kid, Wes. He's always where the fire's the hottest. Think about it. He was there when the Englishman was killed, sparking the feud. Bonney was in Black Canyon when two of Tunstall's killers were gunned down. When Sheriff Brady and his deputies were ambushed in Lincoln, he was one of the killers. The same for the shootout at Blazer's Mill where Buckshot Roberts died. Then he was in McSween's place during the Big Killing. We both know others sparked the carnage, but the Kid's an easy target because he seems to be everywhere there is trouble."

Wes nodded. "That's why he needs to leave the territory and start over somewhere else before other people's violence catches up to him."

"Or us," Jace replied.

Two weeks later as a mid-November norther blew through the Hondo Valley, Wes sat at the kitchen table as he and Jace ate noon bowls of chili while Sarafina, her plump belly showing the impending birth of another child, helped feed Luis and Roberto with their meal. The wind howled and whipped against the house.

"If this is a sign of things to come," Wes observed between bites of chili, "this'll be a harsh winter, when we need it least."

"Aren't you a ray of sunshine?" Jace replied. "Always looking at the downside."

"What's good about a severe winter?"

"You've chopped plenty of wood so we should be warm inside, and the foul weather'll keep folks in their homes where they're less likely to cause trouble."

Barely had Jace finished his sentence when a gust of wind was tailed by a banging in the front room, like the storm had blown open the door, though Wes knew it was barred. Wes jumped up and started for the door, when he heard a muffled cry. "Bracken, Bracken, let me in."

Grabbing his Winchester, he bolted out of the kitchen, Jace following him with his Henry. Stepping into the front room, Wes saw the door still barred, then looked out the window and spotted Sheriff Peppin's horse tied to the hitching rack.

"Bracken, open up. It's Sheriff Peppin."

Wes and Jace looked at each other, surprised Peppin was out in such weather. Wes lifted the bar and opened the plank entry, straining to keep the wind from ripping it from his grip. Peppin stepped inside, then Wes shouldered the door shut.

Peppin shivered and spoke. "Damn, it's cold out there."

"What brings you out in such weather, Sheriff?" Wes asked.

"I had papers to deliver to you both."

"Indictments or arrest warrants?" Jace replied.

"Neither. It's a copy of Governor Wallace's pardon proclamation for participants in the Lincoln County difficulties."

Wes and Jace looked at one another, surprise etched in their faces.

"Normally I wouldn't be out in this kind of weather, but I thought it best to spread the word as soon as I could so folks could sleep easier at night and not have so many worries during the day." Peppin stamped his feet and unbuttoned his coat.

"Guess that makes your job easier, doesn't it?" Jace asked.

"It makes it easier on everyone," Peppin replied as he stuck his hand inside his coat and pulled out a stack of papers folded lengthwise. He peeled off twin sheets and handed one to Cousins and another to Bracken. "These were printed up to distribute to the residents of Lincoln County. This should end the difficulties."

The two partners scanned their page, then Wes looked up at Peppin. "Care to share lunch with us? Maybe we can visit to make sure I understand this proclamation."

"I'd be obliged for a meal and some warmth before I deliver the remainder."

Wes nodded. "Stay here and let me check with Sarafina." He slipped into the kitchen.

"Who is it?" Sarafina asked.

"It's the sheriff. Is there chili enough for him?" Wes asked as he propped his Winchester against the wall.

She nodded. "I made plenty, though we may need to skimp for supper."

"Okay," Wes said. "Dip out another bowl, and I'll fetch a chair." He returned to the front room. "You're welcome to join us, Sheriff. If you're warm enough, you can leave your hat and coat on the counter."

Peppin removed his hat, then unbundled himself as Jace stepped behind the counter and placed his Henry atop his bed.

Wes motioned for Peppin to go ahead, and the lawman stepped into the kitchen as Wes grabbed a chair and followed.

"Thank you, ma'am." He nodded to Sarafina. "A hot meal will hit the spot on a chilly day like this." He looked at the boys, who had emptied their bowls and retreated to the corner, suspicious of the visitor. "Greetings, little ones," he said, and Roberto stepped to Luis, who wrapped his arms around him for protection."

"Es bueno," Sarafina said to her sons. "If you like, go play in the front room."

The two slipped past the sheriff, then scurried into the adjacent room, Jace trailing after them. "I best retrieve my Henry before the boys think it a toy."

Wes slid the extra chair to the table and motioned for Peppin to sit down. As the sheriff took his place, Wes joined him, sliding his own bowl aside so he could put the paper down and study it. As he read, Sarafina gave the lawman a bowl of chili, a spoon, and a cup of coffee.

"In a moment I will have fresh corn tortillas for you," Sarafina informed the sheriff as she reached in a wicker basket and removed two, placing them on the griddle atop the stove and warming them. When they were hot, she picked up the tortillas by the edge and carried them to the table, dropping them by Peppin's bowl.

"Thank you, ma'am," he said, grabbing one and biting off a chunk. "Wonderful meal," he offered between bites of chili and sips of coffee.

As his guest ate, Wes studied the proclamation. Jace returned to the table after propping his Henry next to Wes's Winchester, then examined his own copy of the document.

The edict stated that since the citizens of the county had acquiesced to the president's call to stop the violence and had established peace throughout the region over the last month, the governor was hereby granting, with limited exceptions, pardons to all who had committed crimes between February first and the November thirteenth date of this proclamation. Wes found it interesting and perhaps even hopeful that the pardon excluded officers of the United States Army stationed in Lincoln County. The issuance of the mass pardon, though, was conditional upon the grantees maintaining the tranquility and conducting themselves as good citizens from then on.

As he read the final paragraph, Wes grimaced, uncertain if he understood the legal language or its implications, though he feared for the worst. He looked at Jace, his brow furrowed.

Cousins looked up from the sheet and stared at Peppin. "Sheriff, what's the last paragraph mean?"

Peppin wiped his sleeve across his lips, took a sip of coffee, and responded, "Read it to me."

"Neither shall it be pleased by any person in bar of conviction under indictment now found and returned for any such crimes or misdemeanors, nor operate the release of any party undergoing pains and penalties consequent upon sentence heretofore had for any crime or misdemeanor," Jace read. "It's signed by Lew Wallace, governor of the Territory of New Mexico."

Wes nodded. "That confused me as well."

The sheriff picked up his second tortilla, rolled it, and aimed it at Cousins. "Basically what it means is that any person already under indictment for crimes between February first and November thirteenth is not eligible for a pardon and cannot use the pardon as a defense against any subsequent charges."

Wes looked at Sarafina, whose lips mouthed the word "Carlos." He grimaced and nodded back at his wife, whose hand flew to her mouth.

"So the pardon only absolves those who weren't caught and indicted?" Jace asked.

"That's one way to look at it," Peppin admitted. "Another way to view it is you boys are off the hook for any crimes you committed."

Wes shook his head, knowing as long as the law wanted and pursued the Kid, the trouble would continue.

CHAPTER 7

As Wes gathered a load of firewood in his arms and started for the back door in the chill of the first day of December, a gunshot exploded in front of the house, then a second. Tossing the kindling to the ground, Wes stumbled over a piece of wood, caught his balance, and shoved open the door and burst into the kitchen. Grabbing his Winchester standing against the wall, Wes retreated out the back and around the dwelling to the side where he could see the road. Behind him he heard a shrill whistle and knew that Jace was coming from the barn.

At the corner of the house, he stared in disbelief at what he saw. Three riders sat on their horses at the edge of the trail, their mounts pointed down the path to the dwelling. The leader eased his horse forward, his carbine aimed skyward; a white kerchief tied to the muzzle fluttered in the chilly breath of December. The horseman advanced slowly, cautiously as well he should. Wes Bracken cursed at the sight of Jesse Evans.

"Is that who I think it is?" Jace called from the opposite corner of the house.

"That's the son of a bitch himself."

"Should we plug him, white flag or not?"

Wes shuddered, more from anger and hatred than the cold. "What could he want?"

"Nothing honorable," Jace answered as he aimed his rifle at Evans. "It could be a ruse."

Wes turned about and scanned the surrounding countryside, searching for any of the outlaw's allies who might be circling them. Seeing none, he focused on Jesse as he drew within fifty yards.

"What do you want, Jesse?" Wes called.

"I want to parlay with you and Jace. No tricks, just honest talk."

Wes waved his Winchester at the visitor. "Slip your carbine back in its scabbard."

The bad man complied with the command as his bay gelding advanced.

"That's far enough," cried Jace when the rider came within twenty yards of the dwelling. "You and Wes visit all you want, but I'm keeping a bead on your chest."

Wes lowered his own carbine and stepped in front of the house, noticing the curtain twitch in the window. He glimpsed Sarafina peeping out of the glass and in that instant saw terror in her dark eyes.

"You're not welcome on my property, Jesse. Get to the point and get gone."

Evans removed his hat and ran his fingers through his reddish-brown hair, his wide eyes glancing from Wes to Jace and back. His broad face was stubbled with whiskers, and his demeanor was as cold as the breeze sliding down the valley.

"Have you heard about the governor's proclamation and pardons?"

"Sheriff Peppin informed us."

"I'm here to see if we can put the differences between me and you two in the past."

Jace lifted his rifle barrel skyward and pulled the trigger, the gun exploding and echoing off the mountains. "That's my answer, Jesse. You cost me two years in a Texas prison. I'll never get those years back."

"Maybe not, Jace, but you won't lose what years you've got left when I kill you."

Evans turned to Wes. "What about you, Bracken?"

"Nothing doing, Jesse, not after what you did to my wife. She's with child."

"I wish her well," he responded, "but be thankful I didn't kill her like you murdered Tom Hill at the sheep camp, shooting us in the back from ambush. He died. My left arm's still lame, and it will never be as strong as it once was. I live with that daily."

"Sarafina lives with your humiliation every day. That's a wound that will never heal."

"She'll get over it. By refusing my offer, you're endangering both yourself and her."

"The answer's no, Jesse, so get off my land."

"You best accept a truce, Wes, or it's war on you, on Jace, on your wife and your kids, including whatever bastard comes out of your woman."

Wes yanked his carbine to his shoulder and fired a shot over Jesse's head.

Evans never flinched.

"That's a warning, Jesse. One more threat or insult against my family, and I won't miss the next time I pull the trigger."

The outlaw scowled. "You had your chance, both of you. You'll regret refusing a truce."

"Get going, Jesse, and never set foot on my property again."

Evans flashed Wes a sinister grin, then touched the brim of his hat. "Here's another opportunity to back-shoot me," he scowled as he turned his bay and started toward the road.

No sooner had Evans retreated, than Wes

heard the house door creak open. Sarafina emerged, Wes catching the glint of tears on her cheeks. She sobbed and cried, *"¡Bastardo!"*

As he watched, she lifted the pistol hanging at her side and cocked the hammer as she raised the weapon. Clasping the weapon with both quivering hands, she pulled the trigger. The gun exploded, and the bullet kicked up dust on the ground behind Evans, who never flinched.

Without looking back, Evans shouted, "I knew you were back-shooters."

Sarafina burst into tears, sobbing as she ran to the embrace of her husband.

"Lo odio, lo odio," she screamed.

"I hate him, too," Wes growled.

"Do you want me to shoot him?" Jace asked. "I've still got a bead on him."

"Not today, Jace, not with my family around, but if he ever sets foot on our land again or we even see him on the road, kill him."

"I'll be glad to."

As he comforted Sarafina, Wes watched Evans rejoin his companions. The outlaw turned his horse toward the house and pulled his carbine from its scabbard, quickly untying the white kerchief and flinging it to the ground. The moment he did, he raised the long gun over his head and fired it into the air, the three men slapping their horses and heading toward Lincoln.

"We should've shot him, Wes. Intimidating you and me is one thing, but threatening Sarafina and the boys is another. We should've shot him."

Wes sighed. "I know, Jace, but I didn't care to endanger my family. I suppose our sense of fair play has no place in Lincoln County."

Jace nodded. "It can get a man and his family killed."

As Wes turned to steer his wife back into the house, he saw Luis and Roberto standing in the open door, shivering from the cold, their eyes wide with uncertainty and fear.

"Get Sarafina in the house. I'll watch Evans and his boys until they are out of sight."

"Thanks, partner," Wes answered as he guided his spouse indoors. At the door he picked up Luis while Sarafina grabbed Roberto, hugging him tightly to ease his fears and warm his shivering torso. They stepped inside and closed the door.

"I should've killed him," Wes acknowledged.

"You did what you had to do," Sarafina

answered as she comforted Roberto. "So did I. I'm sorry I missed."

"Now that he's threatened you and the boys, I promise I will kill Jesse Evans when I can, provided it doesn't risk harm to you and the boys. Keep wearing your revolver everywhere, and I'll teach you how to handle a carbine. We have the three I took from Carlos and his men."

"Gracias," she said.

"We will get through this, Sarafina, I promise, though it'll take some time." He lowered Luis to the floor and wrapped his arms around his wife again.

After he released her, Sarafina led the boys into the kitchen. When they disappeared, Wes cursed himself for not killing Jesse Evans. He had only delayed the inevitable.

At first Wes planned to start Sarafina's carbine lessons immediately, but she tired easily the closer she got to the delivery date, so he postponed the instruction until after the new baby came. Thankfully, Sarafina had arranged for a Mexican midwife in San Patricio to help with the impending birth.

As they awaited the baby's arrival, Wes decided they needed what supplies they could get from town and asked Cousins to make a trip to Lincoln the next day and bring back what foodstuff he could barter for, plus ammunition, which might be more precious than food in the coming months. After Wes cautioned Cousins to be wary of Jesse Evans, Jace mounted his dun that next morning and started for Lincoln, promising to return as soon as he could.

A couple hours after Cousins departed, Wes heard Sarafina calling from the kitchen, *"Mi esposo,* come quickly *por favor."* He rushed in from the front room where he had been amusing the boys. Sarafina pointed to her stomach. "My belly has shifted. The time is nearing." His wife grimaced as he helped her to their bedroom, where he tucked her in to rest. He hoped the birth would wait until Jace returned so one of them could ride to San Patricio for help.

Barely had he reassured the boys that everything was okay with their mama than Sarafina cried, *"Mi esposo, mi esposo,* my water has broken."

Wes left his sons bewildered as he raced into the bedroom. "Yes, Sarafina."

His wife lay grimacing on the bed. Seeing him, she smiled weakly. "The time has come. The baby is coming."

Wes cursed himself for sending Jace to Lincoln. That trip could've waited; the birth would not. "It's just me and the boys. Jace is gone. Do you want me to stay or ride for the *señora*?"

"Get help," she said. "I'm fear this baby'll be difficult. Bring the boys to me. I will watch them here. Get water and a cloth so they can bathe my face."

Wes dashed to the kitchen, fetching a pail half full of water, a dipper, and a towel, then toted them to their room. He scurried into the front, grabbing a boy under each arm and carrying them to Sarafina's side. "Play with your mother," he said as he placed them on the mattress beside her. They giggled and laughed and bounced on the bed, ignorant of her situation and the pending arrival of a new sibling.

Returning to the front room, he got the shotgun and loaded both barrels, then picked up one of the spare carbines, checking its load, and carried the weapons into the bedroom, propping them in the corner near the bed. "Keep the boys away from these guns," he shouted. "Where's your pistol?"

"Under my pillow," she answered.

"I'm shutting the door so the boys can't get out, then riding to San Patricio."

"Hurry," she implored him.

Wes trotted to the front door, barred it, then ran out the back, closing it, though he had no way of securing it from the outside. He raced to the barn, flung the door open, startling Charlie. Wes quickly threw his saddle blanket over the sorrel's back, then lifted the saddle over his rump and secured it. He dispensed with his saddlebags and put his bridle around the stallion's head. Quickly, he led the sorrel outside, slamming the barn door and latching it, before jumping aboard. As frisky as the morning December air, Charlie relished the idea of a run, so he reacted instantly to the quiver of the reins and the nudge of Wes's bootheel, bounding down the trail toward the road and turning west toward San Patricio. The animal splashed through the water crossing where the Bonito and Ruidoso converged. Only then did Wes realize he had forgotten his carbine and only carried the revolver in his holster. He let Charlie run a half mile at a full gallop, before easing him into a steady lope so as not to exhaust the stallion before the return trip, especially if the stallion had to carry both him and the midwife.

He reached San Patricio as quickly as he could, slowing his mount to a trot so as not to alarm the village and guiding the animal to the far side of town where the midwife lived in an adobe hut with her elderly husband. Reaching the abode, Wes jumped from his saddle, keeping the reins in his hands as he pounded on the front door.

"Señora, señora, el bebé viene," he cried. "The baby is coming."

The entry opened slowly and the old man stood there, nodding that he understood. His wife appeared behind her husband. *"Un momento,"* she responded before issuing instructions to her spouse. He stepped outside, shutting the house behind him and motioning Wes to follow him around the adobe.

The old man limped with age as he led Wes to a small corral made of pickets enclosing a brown donkey that twitched his ears and brayed at the approach of the stranger and his horse. The elderly husband pointed to a trough for Wes to water Charlie, then opened the flimsy gate and stepped inside, taking a bridle from the fence, forcing the bit in the burro's mouth, then sliding the leathers over his head and ears. The burro balked, brayed, and sat down on his haunches, planting himself in the middle of the pen. Wes grimaced, doubtful the animal would budge from his pen, much less make the trip to the Casey place.

As he questioned whether the donkey would ever relent to travel, Wes heard the soft footsteps of the midwife behind him.

He turned. She smiled at him, handing Wes two burlap sacks tied together at the neck. She pointed to his horse for him to throw the sacks behind his saddle. As he took the bags, she lifted her left hand and showed him two apples. She gave Wes one, and he thanked her, lifting the fruit to his mouth to take a bite.

"¡No!" she exclaimed, shaking her head vigorously. "Ver a mi esposo."

Confused, Wes secured the bags behind the cantle as he watched the old man like she instructed.

Reaching the defiant donkey, the midwife wrapped her arms around his neck and lifted her right leg and raised it over the burro's rump until she straddled the stubborn beast. Her spouse handed her the reins as she hugged the animal's neck. When she nodded, the old man held the apple out a foot from the burro's nose. Slowly, the animal lifted its haunches and stood on all four hooves. The old woman gently released the donkey's neck and straightened astride the animal's backbone. As her husband backed out of the pen, the donkey followed, tossing his head in anticipation. Once he led the donkey beyond the pickets, the feeble husband let him catch up and snatch the apple from his hand.

The midwife motioned for Wes to mount up, then wagged her finger from the apple in his hand to the donkey's nose. In the saddle, Wes pulled the reins and circled in front of the burro, leaning over and holding the apple just beyond his nose. The stubborn beast brayed and lurched forward.

"*Sí, sí,*" said the woman as the donkey followed Wes's stallion toward the street.

"*Adiós y buena suerte,*" called her husband in the midwife's wake.

The donkey jogged about a hundred yards, then slowed to a trot when Wes had to entice him again with the apple. Wes made it to the edge of town and wondered if it wouldn't be faster just for him to pick up the donkey and midwife and carry them both. Alternating between walks and jogs, the burro took an hour to reach the Casey place. Wes led the animal around to the back and jumped off his horse, offering the donkey the apple. As soon as he did, the burro sat on its rump, braying success and chomping on the red fruit as the old lady slid off his back.

Wes flung open the back door and rushed inside, terrified at Sarafina's moans and screams. He burst into the bedroom, his sudden entry startling the bewildered boys, and they wailed. Sarafina flung back the covers, her face pimpled with sweat, her white nightshirt drenched with perspiration.

"The midwife is here." He kissed her forehead.

"The boys have been helpful, but scared," she gasped. "Please take them away."

As Wes shooed the boys out, the midwife entered. Sarafina moaned as a wave of contractions rippled through her body. After examining Sarafina, she motioned for Wes to leave and shut the door.

"Let's go outside, Luis and Roberto," Wes said. He herded them to the front room and found their coats, sliding them on each child and buttoning them. "We can unsaddle Charlie."

He escorted them out the back, finding the donkey still sitting on his rump, while Charlie had moved away from the stubborn four-legged visitor. Wes walked over to his sorrel and untied the two burlap bags and carried them to the bedroom. Rapping on the door, he pushed it open enough to slide the sacks in on the floor. *"Señora,"* he cried. She ignored his call and simply shut the door while Sarafina gasped and moaned.

Wes retreated outside, finding his curious sons poking a stick at the stubborn donkey. "Come on, boys, let's go to the barn."

Luis darted ahead, but the distance was

too long for Roberto, so Wes picked him up and angled over to Charlie, grabbing the reins and leading him to the stable. Luis tried to open the barn door, but needed Wes's help. The boy smiled when it swung open, and Roberto wiggled to extract himself from his father's arms. When Wes lowered him to the ground, he scrambled after his half-brother, both giggling as they ran across the straw-specked earth. Wes led Charlie to his stall and removed the tack, then offered the stallion some hay. Leaving the kids in the barn, he fetched two pails and walked to the Hondo, filling the containers and returning with water, which he poured in Charlie's trough.

"Come on, boys," he said, and led the pair outside again.

"Hungry," Luis said.

Wes wondered when they had last eaten as he directed them to the house. In the kitchen he found the basket of tortillas and gave them one apiece. They sat in chairs beside each other, munching on the corn ovals. As they ate, Wes brought in firewood and shoved some in the kitchen stove and in the central fireplace. He was killing time and drowning out the sound of Sarafina's sporadic cries from the pains of childbirth. As the place warmed up, he retreated to his sons and removed their coats, sending the pair into the front room to play. He joined them and waited. And waited.

The afternoon drained away, slowly, tediously. Two hours before dusk, he heard Jace calling outside. "I've returned with the goods and news."

Wes stood up and unbarred the door. When he opened it, he saw Jace dismounting and pointing to four bags draped over his dun's rump.

"I had better luck than you did last trip, Wes," he announced, gigging his friend.

"Sarafina's gone into labor," Wes said as he stepped outside to unload the haul.

"Shouldn't you be with her? I can unpack things."

"The midwife's with her," he answered as he removed two sacks and started for the door.

"So you left her here to ride to San Patricio?" Jace asked, following him inside.

"Longest two hours of my life. I knew she was getting close, but not that close or I never would've sent you."

The cries of Sarafina's anguish carried into the front room. Jace grimaced. "Maybe I should return to the bunkhouse."

"Absolutely not, Jace. Once you tend your horse, I need someone to talk to and keep my mind off her agony."

"Well, I've got news from Lincoln for you. Juan Patrón filled me in, and I met the widow McSween's new lawyer. Now there's a stick of dynamite."

"No sign of Jesse Evans?"

"Nope, but let me put up my horse. Then we can visit."

"You might do the same for the donkey behind the house. The midwife rode him over. Slowest and dumbest animal I've ever seen."

Cousins moved outside as Wes emptied the burlap bags. He found five pounds of coffee, ten pounds of flour, five pounds of dried beans, four boxes of ammo for the long weapons, and three cartons for their sidearms. He also unpacked a jar with twenty thumb-sized marbles inside. They were either for the boys or Jace had run out of ways to amuse himself. Cousins returned in a half hour, saying both animals were secured in the barn, watered, and fed.

"Tell me your news," Wes said as both men boosted themselves up on the counter.

Jace grabbed the jar with the marbles and removed a red one and a blue orb, calling to the boys and giving one to each. "You can roll them on the floor."

Luis did as suggested, but Roberto flung

his across the room, drawing an admonition from his father, who jumped down, squatted by his son, and showed him how to roll the glass toy on the plank floor. Both the kids and the men tried to ignore the periodic cries coming from the other side of the house. Wes sat in a chair opposite Jace.

"With news of the pardons men are warily returning to Lincoln," Jace said. "Jesse Evans passed through after stopping here, and Jimmy Dolan's back in town. Everyone's nervous and no one wants to admit the pardons have complicated rather than solved the problems. No one's seen the Kid for weeks, but everyone agrees it's only a matter of time. Complicating matters is the widow McSween's new lawyer, a one-armed fellow named Huston Chapman."

"Did he lose it during the war?"

"No. From what I'm told, he accidentally blew it off with a shotgun when he was thirteen. It was amputated two inches below the left shoulder. He won't win any fistfights, that's for certain. And how smart can you be to shoot your own arm off? He was a railroad lawyer until a couple years ago when he started practicing law around Santa Fe, where Susan McSween met him. I fear he's a stick of dynamite with a short fuse, doing the widow McSween's dirty work."

"She's a widow scorned and'll only stir the pot of boiling troubles."

"Yep. Chapman's called a community meeting three nights from today to discuss the Lincoln situation. Juan thinks Chapman plans to sue the army's Colonel Dudley for his role in killing her husband and destroying her home."

"Do you suppose the governor's pardon applies to her?"

Jace laughed. "She's too vindictive."

The men continued their conversation as the time drained away. At dusk they lit lamps in the front room and waited, flinching every time Sarafina cried out from the bedroom. Wes fed the boys more tortillas and put them to bed. Next he and Jace ate cold tortillas and drank water, not bothering to boil coffee. After their meager supper, they returned to the front and talked about the developments in Lincoln and what they meant for their own future.

Sarafina's cries became so frequent they adjusted to them, never realizing when they ceased. Not until they caught the jarring wail of a newborn did they realize that the delivery had finally come. For ten or more hours, Sarafina's cries had worried Wes, but now not hearing them terrified him even more. He stared at Jace, pacing around the front room, afraid to check on his Sarafina for fear she had died. How would he take care of the boys and a newborn without her?

When the midwife appeared in the kitchen door, she smiled. *"Es una chica,"* she announced as she wiped her bloody hands on a rag.

"Congratulations, Papa," Jace said, "I hope she gets her mother's looks instead of yours."

Wes raced past the midwife, running into his bedroom, lit by the sickly pale light of a lamp on the bedside stand. He saw Sarafina propped up on a pillow, her eyes filled with sadness and fatigue, as the swaddled newborn suckled at her breast. He rushed to her side, bent over, and kissed his wife on the cheek.

"Are you okay, Sarafina?"

Her lips quivered and tears flowed down her cheeks to her frown.

"You have a daughter, yes?" he asked.

Slowly Sarafina lifted her free hand and pulled the wrap from the baby's head.

Even in the pale yellow light, Wes could see the red tint of the newborn's hair. The baby wasn't his. He sighed, lowered his head, and patted his wife's fingers as they covered the baby's head again. How could he ever look at the baby and not recall the violation of his wife? How could he ever see the little one as anything but Jesse Evans's daughter?

Sarafina managed a somber smile. "Would you do me a favor, *mi esposo*?"

"Yes, Sarafina, anything."

She pulled the whimpering newborn from her breast and offered it to her husband.

Wes carefully took from his wife's hands the daughter that wasn't his. He cradled the infant in his arms as his wife spoke.

"Take her to the river," Sarafina said, "and drown her."

CHAPTER 8

Stunned by Sarafina's request, Wes stood bewildered, his brain roiling, his stomach churning. The newborn, torn from her mother's breast, whimpered to resume her nourishment, her tiny lips suckling at the air. His wife's command astonished Wes; his mind overflowed with questions and doubts about the daughter that was not his and the wife who had never shown such callousness. At least until now! The baby squirmed in his grasp, then wailed and fretted for sustenance. While he could kill men that had threatened him and his family, Wes knew he could never murder an innocent child. He looked from the red-haired newborn to Sarafina, tears streaming down her cheeks. She seemed as confused as him. Wes hesitated to give the little one to his wife for fear she might suffocate or strangle the infant, but yet he could not keep the baby for long because she needed the mother's milk that would sustain her. Wes never felt more helpless in his life, even during tumult of battle for the Confederacy. He understood what was right, and he knew what was wrong. Killing a blameless baby stood as sinful as any deed a man or woman could commit. And while the child was guiltless, she was also tainted by her paternity, something that gnawed at Wes's mind and beliefs.

Sarafina scoured his face with her watery gaze as she lay before him, her breast uncovered for a newborn that might never suckle there again. Wes expected her to repeat her command, but she stared silently at him.

Turning his head from her questioning stare, Wes studied the wailing baby, brushing his forefinger against her reddened cheeks. Instantly, the baby twisted her head and slipped her lips over his fingertip, sucking so hard Wes could feel her toothless gums tightening against his skin and nail. Wes grimaced. No matter how the little one was conceived, he could not avenge one wrong by committing another sin and drowning the girl. The infant sucked on his finger briefly, then turned her head away and cried, frustrated with the lack of nourishment and the futility of her effort.

Shaking his head, he offered the newborn

to his wife. "I can't do it, Sarafina, and I won't drown her, no matter what you wish. And don't you harm her either. You don't want that on your conscience."

His wife's silent tears exploded in great sobs as she lifted her arms to accept the newborn.

Wes stood even more confused. "Promise me you won't harm her, Sarafina."

She nodded vigorously through her sobbing and arose from her pillow, taking the little one from his arms, pressing the newborn to her breast, and covering the girl's red-tinted head with the blanket.

Between snivels, Sarafina answered with a raspy, emotion-soaked voice. "I prayed you wouldn't kill her."

Releasing a long sigh, Wes confessed his confused feelings. "I'm not sure I can ever love her."

"Maybe not," Sarafina replied, "but at least I know you could never harm her."

Wes bent and kissed Sarafina's forehead. "Your words shocked me because they weren't from the woman I married."

"It hurt to say them, but I had to learn how you felt about the new one. We shall name her *Pureza* for the purity of her birth if not her conception."

Wes hesitated.

"You do not approve?"

"I like *Blanca* better, as white can represent the purity she brings into our family."

"Blanca, it is, *mi esposo,*" she answered with a scratchy voice. "I am tired and sleepy. Once I finish nursing our Blanca, I will lay her beside me and rest, but before I sleep, would you do something for me?"

"Sure, Sarafina."

"Would you bring me cool water from the Hondo?"

"You want me to get out in the cold to get water from the stream?" he asked.

She nodded. "Just go."

Wes picked up the empty pail from the floor and marched out of the bedroom and through the kitchen where the midwife sat at the table, her hands clasped beneath her chin and her eyes closed as she prayed. He slipped by her into the front room, where Jace slid off the counter where he had been reading his Bible.

"How's Sarafina?"

"Fine."

"And the baby?" Jace said, grinning.

"She's got red hair."

His smile evaporating, Jace cursed. "I'm sorry, Wes."

"The baby's half Sarafina, so I'll just have to look for her in little Blanca, not her

139

father, though the red mop may make that difficult."

Jace placed the Bible on the counter and walked to Wes. He threw his arms around him. "You're a fine man, Wes."

The gesture embarrassed Wes as he found no decency in the emotions pulsing through his body. "Sarafina asked for cold water from the stream," Wes said, breaking his partner's grip.

Jace grabbed the pail from his hand. "I'll fetch the water. You relax. It's been a hard day on you as well."

Wes thanked his partner and pointed into the kitchen at the midwife still deep in prayer. "I'll toss some blankets on the floor for her."

"Give her my bed. I'll sleep on the floor and return her to San Patricio in the morning."

"*Gracias,*" Wes replied as Jace marched through the kitchen and out the back into the darkness. As he passed, the old woman roused from her prayer, and Jace gestured for her to go into the front room to sleep on his bed. She smiled and nodded that she understood, then marched behind the counter and lay down. Before Jace returned, she was snoring lightly.

Jace entered the kitchen and shivered. "It's

chilly out there." He handed the pail to Wes, who carried it into the bedroom where Sarafina dozed with Blanca bundled beside her. Remembering the revolver under her pillow, Wes slid his hand beneath the feather cushion and extracted it. His movement woke his wife. Her lips thanked him with a thin smile.

"Water," he offered.

She nodded. He took the dipper from the bedside table, filled it half full with the frigid liquid, and lifted it to her mouth. Sarafina arose enough to use her right hand to guide the tin to her lips, gulping the water. "More," she said.

Wes provided her two more dippers before she slid back down on her pillow to rest.

Rather than try to sleep with her and the new baby, Wes slipped out of their room into the small one where the boys slept. He moved them to one side of the bed, slipped out of his clothes down to his long johns, and joined them. Quickly, he fell asleep, his slumber only disturbed by the occasional cries of Blanca for nighttime feedings.

When morning came, Wes awoke but stayed in bed, relishing the rest and pondering if he could ever see Blanca as anything more than the result of his wife's humiliation. The thoughts tormented him until

Roberto roused and then Luis, both surprised to find their father on the mattress with them. They laughed and climbed over him, dragging the covers away and giggling when he snatched the blankets and buried the boys under them.

As he played, he heard the noise of Sarafina cooking on the stove and knew his wife should be resting, so he jumped up and ran into the kitchen in his long johns, barging inside to see the midwife cooking over the cast-iron stove. He spun around to leave the room, but not before he caught the señora's giggle. Back with the boys, he quickly dressed and returned to the kitchen, his face tinted with embarrassment.

"Buenos días, señora," Wes offered.

She turned around and giggled again, reminding Wes she had seen him in his underwear.

Jace ambled in and greeted his partner. "She got up and went to the chicken coop and gathered eggs, then started breakfast for us."

"Gracias," Wes said, as the boys stumbled into the kitchen, rubbing their eyes and looking for their mother, then staring suspiciously at the old lady at the stove.

Grabbing two pails, Jace announced, "I'll fetch cold water for Sarafina, if she wants it, and then milk the cow."

As his partner slipped outside the door, Wes turned to his sons. "You have a little sister, *una hermanita,*" he said. "Her name is Blanca."

The boys looked at each other, not grasping the concept.

"When your mother awakes, I will take you to meet Blanca." He pointed them to their chairs, and they climbed in them, accepting a warm tortilla from the midwife. "Say, *gracias,*" Wes implored them.

"Gracias, gracias," they said meekly as they nibbled at their breakfast.

Wes grabbed a tin cup from the table, filled it at the stove where the midwife was frying two eggs on the griddle. He took his coffee and sat down to watch the boys eat breakfast. Moments later the old woman brought him a plate with a pair of eggs fried over easy and two tortillas. He grabbed his knife and fork, cut the eggs, and watched the yellow pool on his plate. He sopped the liquid with the tortillas and attacked his meal.

As he finished, he heard Blanca's wail from his bedroom. The two boys looked at one another, uncertain what to make of the unfamiliar noise.

"Es tu hermana, niños pequeños," the

midwife informed them.

"Your new sister," Wes said again, the boys sharing bewildered looks. Wes gobbled down his last bite of breakfast and finished his cup of coffee, then stood up and grabbed a boy under each arm, carrying them to the bedroom.

Knocking on the door, he heard Sarafina's raspy voice. "Come in."

Opening the entry, he announced, "I've brought the boys to meet their little sister."

Seeing their mother, both boys wiggled free, Luis dashing to the bed and Roberto toddling behind him.

As Luis climbed beside Sarafina, Wes gave Roberto a boost to join his mother and brother.

"Sit and be still, *chicos*," Sarafina instructed, then picked up the bundle between her and Wes's pillow. Gingerly, she opened the wrap and exposed little Blanca's ruddy face, beneath a thin veil of red-tinted hair.

The boys looked in awe at the little form before them and then at one another.

"This is your sister, Luis and Roberto. Her name is Blanca."

Both boys stared with silent reverence at the newborn. Sarafina motioned for Luis to come closer to his sister, and he reached out and patted her cheek, drawing a coo.

Luis's eyes and mouth widened with a grin. Little Roberto crawled up toward the baby as Wes moved Luis out of the way. Roberto leaned forward and kissed the newborn on the cheek.

Sarafina smiled at Wes. "They love their little sister." She hesitated a moment. "One day, you will too, *mi esposo.*"

Come midmorning, Jace saddled his dun and put the bridle on the donkey to escort the midwife back to San Patricio. For payment, Wes gave her two sitting hens after Jace caught them and tied their legs and wings. She squeezed both birds in one of the burlap sacks that she had brought from her home. Wes and Sarafina thanked her for her care in birthing Blanca before Jace escorted her outside for the trip to home. The journey took almost four hours, the burro having no apples to encourage his pace beyond his natural lethargic gait. Jace returned in the middle of the afternoon and came in the kitchen door.

"I'm back," he called as he entered. "And guess what I drug up along the way?"

Hearing his partner's call, Wes stepped from his bedroom where the two boys sat in wonder on the bed as Blanca nursed. When he reached the kitchen, Wes saw Jace, who he expected, and Billy Bonney, who he hadn't.

"Howdy, Wes," the Kid said, sticking out his hand. "Congratulations. I hear you're a new papa with the cutest little daughter around."

Wes clasped the Kid's hand and wagged it vigorously. "You alone?"

Releasing Wes's grip, Bonney shook his head. "No. Tom O'Folliard, Jim French, and Doc Scurlock are riding with me, but we won't pester you if you'll let us stay the night in the barn, then ride out in the morning, San Patricio way."

Motioning for the Kid to take a chair, Wes joined him at the table.

"I'm gonna tend my horse, Wes, and see the others to the barn," Jace said, exiting the kitchen and leaving the two men alone.

"I thought you were calling Fort Sumner home these days. Is it true you've been stealing stock between Texas and the territory?"

"Just collecting what I'm owed," he replied, lifting his hat and plopping it on the table.

"All you're collecting is more lawlessness to answer for."

"Not anymore," Bonney grinned. "Haven't you heard about the governor's pardon? I'm done with stealing, gonna find steady work and forget the past once I'm pardoned."

"Have you read the proclamation, Kid?"

He nodded. "Way I read it, the governor's pardoning all crimes between February first and the date of the proclamation, November thirteenth as I recall."

Wes stood up from the table. "Let me fetch mine." He stepped into the front room where he had left his copy on one of the empty store shelves. Returning to the kitchen, he sat down. "Did you read the last paragraph?"

"I read it all, can't say I fully understood the language, but I made a point not to steal another beef or horse once I learned of the offer."

"It's the last paragraph, Kid. Let me explain it to you: 'Neither shall it be pleased by any person in bar of conviction under indictment now found and returned for any such crimes or misdemeanors, nor operate the release of any party undergoing pains and penalties consequent upon sentence heretofore had for any crime or misdemeanor.' " Wes looked up from the sheet of paper.

"So?" Bonney asked.

"What it's saying, Kid, is that everyone's

147

pardoned except for those already under indictment for crimes previously committed. It doesn't apply to you and any others already indicted."

Confidence drained from Bonney's face. "Then what good is it? There's more of Dolan's bunch, like him, Jesse Evans and others, under indictment than on our side. The law will never touch them, mark my words, just us that was trying to do right by Tunstall and McSween."

"I'm sorry, Kid. I wish it were different as it would make it easier on everyone."

Bonney sat in his chair, biting his lip and fuming. He banged his hand on the table. "It's not fair, none of it since they murdered Tunstall. The law's been against us every step of the way, even watching Dolan's men trying to burn us alive in McSween's house."

"You're right, Kid, and I'll still do what I can to help you, but nothing has changed for you, Carlos, and the other Regulators."

The Kid picked up his felt hat from the table, rolling and unrolling the brim in his hand. "I ought to ride into Lincoln tonight and shoot the place up, kill or be killed. That's the only way it's gonna end if us Regulators don't get a fair shake."

"Stay out of town, Kid. You'll only make

things worse. I'll help you all I can, but you gotta quit rustling."

"And let others steal from us or kill us?"

"That's not what I mean," Wes said, smiling to reduce the tension.

Bonney cocked his head, stared at Wes's mustache, and laughed. "What happened to your tooth? Did your wife smack you with a skillet?"

Wes just shook his head. "Damaged by Yankee rifle butt during the War, it finally fell out when I bit an apple."

Bonney laughed. "Maybe you're lucky since you don't have two big ole buckteeth like me for all the teasing they've brought me over the years."

The back door opened, and Jace Cousins slid in, closing it quickly behind him. "It's getting colder."

Wes nodded. "I've been explaining to Bonney the pardon's useless to him and the others under indictment."

"It's unfair," Bonney grumbled. "You two get away with murdering Hablador and Mendoza, and I —"

"Where'd you hear that?"

"Ran into Carlos up in Fort Sumner. He was hotter than a chili pepper about losing his gang. He's still threatening to kill the both of you." Bonney paused, his gaze boring into Bracken. "You shouldn't have vowed not to kill him."

"Not me," Jace interjected.

"He's family," Wes replied.

"He don't feel the same way about you," Bonney noted.

"Let's get back to your predicament, Kid." Wes turned to Cousins. "Didn't you say the lawyer for the widow McSween had called a community meeting this week?"

"Yeah. Saturday afternoon in Lincoln. You thinking of attending?"

We shook his head. "I'm staying with Sarafina until she and the baby are stronger."

"I'll go," Bonney volunteered. "Maybe I'll run into some of my acquaintances."

"That's not a good idea, Kid," Wes answered. "You need to remain around San Patricio a few days and avoid Lincoln until Jace can report on the mood there."

Bonney snarled, "The mood? It's is always against me and the Regulators."

Wes waved the comment away. "Many of the people and most of the Mexicans are on your side."

"But none of those that count, those that control the politics and the sheriff," Bonney answered.

"I won't argue that, Kid, but if you ever

hope to get a pardon, you've gotta lay low and avoid trouble."

"I've been hiding out."

"No, Kid. Don't fool yourself. You've been stealing stock Fort Sumner way and selling them in the Panhandle. That's not laying low." Wes could feel his exasperation rising.

"A man's gotta eat."

"An honest living's what a man needs to put food on the table. All you're doing is creating more troubles for yourself. If you want my help, stay out of Lincoln for the next five days."

Bonney plopped his hat on his head and stood up. "I'll think about it."

Wes nodded. "You can consider it tonight in the barn, but move on tomorrow. Return in five days, and we'll tell you what we've learned."

"Why can't we stay here out of sight?" Bonney asked.

"I've got a wife and three young ones to watch after. I've tried to stay impartial, but folks'll think otherwise if they learn ya'll are camped here. That's my price for helping you out, Kid, and I may be your only hope."

Bonney nodded. "We'll leave before sunrise, and I'll return in five days." He spun about and walked outside, shutting the door gently.

Wes shrugged at Jace. "Hope you don't mind going to the lawyer's meeting."

"Not at all, partner. I'm rather curious myself about what a puny one-armed lawyer can do against two-armed thieves and murderers. Now, I've got a question for you: Did you learn anything else about Carlos?"

"Bonney said he's is still blaming us both for his problems."

Jace nodded. "There's more. O'Folliard, French, and Scurlock said he wanted to ride with the Kid and them, but Bonney said no. So, Carlos has organized a few Mexican misfits to rustle cattle like the Kid and play Texan stock off against New Mexican stock."

Wes shook and lowered his head. "Texans don't take too well to Mexicans, especially when they're stealing cattle."

"Scurlock says the Panhandle cattlemen are organizing to hire range detectives to put an end to the rustling, either at the end of a trial or at the end of a rope. It doesn't matter one way or the other to them as long as the stealing ends."

Wes tugged at his mustache. "If he's caught, he better hope he gets a prison sentence, instead of a rope."

Jace grimaced. "I had two years in a Texas prison. There were dark times when I wished I'd gotten a rope instead. Now all I want to get is Jesse Evans."

"Me, too," Wes said, thinking of the red-haired newborn that wasn't his and how he should've killed Evans when he proposed the truce.

CHAPTER 9

When he returned five days later just as the light calmed the morning darkness, Billy Bonney traveled alone. Approaching the house from the Rio Hondo rather than the road, he set the hens to cackling as Wes gathered a half dozen eggs for breakfast, and Jace emerged from the barn after milking the cow. Both partners carried their long weapons, tensing for a moment until they recognized the rider. Wes waved him in, and Bonney tipped his hat at his host.

As their paths converged, Wes greeted him. "Where's the others?"

"They're in San Patricio, waiting on what I find out."

"Has everyone behaved?" Wes inquired.

"We haven't shot at anything besides supper, if that's what you mean."

"It'll do," Wes answered as Jace stepped up.

"Morning, Bonney," he said, lifting the

milk pail. "Care for a snort."

The Kid laughed. "Lost my taste for cow juice years ago."

"It's just as well," Wes replied. "We've got three kids that would arm wrestle you for it."

"I concede," Bonney replied. "Do you boys have time to talk or do you need to finish your girly work?"

"Work is work when it needs doing," Wes said, "but we always have time for you, Kid, if you'll slide off your throne and come inside."

Bonney dismounted. "You want me to hide him in the barn?"

"Here's fine," Wes answered. "One horse won't draw much attention."

The Kid tied his horse to the hitching post and entered the kitchen ahead of Wes and Jace. The three heard the wailing of Blanca as she announced she was ready for a feeding. Shortly, the newborn's cries evaporated. "Hope she didn't wake up the boys," Wes said as he put the basket of eggs on the table and turned to Billy. "We've got coffee boiling, and I can fry you an egg, Kid, but I can't offer you much more other than a couple tortillas."

"Likely that's the best offer I'll have all day, so get to cooking."

Wes grabbed three tin cups from the wooden shelf, filled them, and placed all in the middle of the table. Bonney and Jace took one, the Kid drinking his black, while Cousins spooned two loads of fresh milk from the pail into the coffee. Wes placed a basket of cold tortillas between them, then turned to the stove, sliding more kindling into the firebox and grabbing a skillet to start breakfast. "While I'm cooking, tell him about the meeting in Lincoln."

Jace finished a sip of coffee, looked over the cup at the Kid, and nodded. "This one-armed lawyer is a cocky little bantam rooster," Jace began, "and he's intent on righting the crimes that have plagued Lincoln for the last several years."

Bonney smiled. "Good to know."

"It's the wrongs as seen by the widow McSween," Wes clarified, "not necessarily as viewed by the rest of us." He cracked an egg and dropped the contents in the cast-iron skillet, which took to popping and fizzing.

"I don't like no runny yolks," Bonney said, then turned to Jace.

Cousins reported the meeting had drawn a hundred folks, most of them Mexicans, as well as some Anglos, including Squire Wilson, who had been appointed justice of the peace again, and Sheriff George Peppin, who Jace considered a spy for the Dolan bunch. The lawyer Huston Chapman explained that he intended to press charges against Colonel Nathan Dudley of the U.S. Army for arson and complicity in the murder of McSween and the others. He asked for support and for witnesses of the Big Killing to step forward and report what they saw. Jace said nobody took him up on his request, at least during the public gathering.

"What about the governor's pardons?" Bonney asked.

Jace shook his head. "Chapman explained the conditions just as we understood. They don't apply to men who were already under indictment for crimes committed between February first and November thirteenth."

"It's not right," Bonney responded.

"Nothing's been right in Lincoln County for years," Wes interrupted as he tipped his skillet over a tin and watched the fried egg slide onto the dish. Putting the pan on the stove, he carried the plate to the Kid and sat the dish in front of him. "Squire Wilson tries to do right, but he's always getting overruled by a higher judge or threatened by a stronger opponent."

Bonney grabbed a tortilla and a fork, attacking his meager breakfast and shaking his head in frustration at the futility of Lincoln County.

"Whatever your other problems are, Kid, I don't think Sheriff Peppin is one of them," Jace continued, then turned to Wes. "You remember when he stopped by our place a while back, saying he was searching for Bonney."

"I do."

"It seems he was only looking for the Kid when he was certain he wouldn't find him. Once news got around that Bonney had returned a week ago, he raced to Fort Stanton for protection."

"I never thought Peppin had much grit in his craw," Wes observed. "I figure he'll run at the first sign of trouble."

Bonney finished a sip of coffee and pointed his cup at Cousins. "So there's no hope of anything changing?"

"I can't say for sure, Kid," Jace continued. "The lawyer Chapman announced he was leaving this week for Santa Fe, intent upon meeting with Governor Lew Wallace. I asked him if he would implore the governor to broaden the pardons to forgive all crimes committed during ten months since February first, or at least consider every indicted man's situation on a case-by-case basis."

Wes brought over the coffee pot and refilled Bonney's and Cousins's cups.

"You take up the story from here, Wes."

After he returned the pot to the stove, Wes stepped to the table and sat down, picking up his cup and swallowing the hot liquid. "I wrote a letter to the governor, explaining the unfortunate and unfair circumstances of the cases against you, asking that you receive special consideration, and sent Jace back to Lincoln to deliver it to the lawyer and ask him to present it to Santa Fe."

Bonney smiled. "Will it help?"

Wes pointed to Jace.

"I don't know, Kid. Chapman would make no promises unless I gave him fifty dollars for handling the letter. We don't have that kind of cash anymore."

"Damnation," Billy said, throwing his fork down on his tin plate with a clatter. "Is money the only thing that talks in Lincoln County?"

Wes shrugged. "It carries more weight than doing the right thing. Even if Chapman doesn't deliver the message, maybe he'll let the governor know you're willing to do whatever it requires to put these difficulties behind you."

Jace nodded. "Chapman's making a lot of your enemies as skittish as an unbroken stallion. In fact, several of our allies at the meeting warned him not to come back from his meeting with Wallace, if he valued his life. He didn't take the warning seriously because he doesn't understand the type of men he's dealing with in Dolan and his cronies."

Bonney pushed himself away from the table. "Lincoln County's like a pit you can never climb out of, no matter how much you try."

"That's why you need to leave, Kid," Wes implored him. "You're young enough to start over somewhere else and make a life under a new name."

"Can't do it, fellows." He stood up and drained the last drops of his drink. "I'm rounding up the boys at San Patricio to visit Lincoln. I want to remind folks I haven't forgotten about the Big Killing. It's time to take on Jimmy Dolan or Jesse Evans or the sheriff."

Wes shook his head. "You already are under indictment for shooting Sheriff Brady. Don't add another lawman to your crimes or the governor will never consider your request."

Bonney lowered his gaze and rubbed his eyes with both hands. "I gotta think things through, fellows, but I'm going to Lincoln today to make sure they haven't forgotten me."

"How long you planning on staying, Kid?" Wes asked.

"Can't say for sure. What's it matter to you."

"When Sarafina's stronger, I intend to take her to town so she can show her new daughter off before Christmas gets here. I figure it'll be simpler without you around."

"I'll be there a week at the most, likely less."

"Okay, Kid, but be careful and don't kill anybody else."

Bonney shook Jace's hand and then Wes's. "I appreciate you boys looking out for me, even against all the odds, the law being what it is around here."

"Do me a favor, Kid," Wes said.

"What's that?"

"Let me know if you learn where Jesse Evans is staying during the cold months."

Taking Sarafina and the boys to Lincoln was more complicated since the arson at the Mirror B had consumed their wagon in the barn fire. Wes had no way to get his family to town without borrowing a conveyance, so eight days after Billy Bonney walked out of their kitchen door, Wes told Jace and

Sarafina that he was riding to town to see Juan Patrón and possibly borrow his buckboard for a return visit by the whole family, including Jace. Wes knew the trip was unnecessary, but he desired for his wife to show off the baby as she had been depressed in the days following the birth. He thought having other people brag on the infant might lift her spirits. Further, he was interested in displaying Blanca and her red hair because he knew gossip would follow, and he wanted to move past it. Wes would make do with the consequences, but he didn't care to delay them any longer.

Astride Charlie, Wes rode an uneventful dozen miles to Lincoln, the weather chilly but manageable with a coat and a hat tugged snug over his head. The entire trip, Wes carried his Winchester, hoping he might encounter Jesse Evans as he wearied of waiting for the inevitable confrontation. Nearing town, he passed the cemetery on the north side of the road and wondered how many more graves the plot would hold before the county's troubles ended.

At Patrón's house he tied his sorrel to the hitching post and knocked, calling Juan and identifying himself. Shortly, the door cracked open and his friend's wife greeted him with a smile. *"Por favor entra,"* Beatriz said. *"Juan volverá pronto."*

By her embarrassed eyes, Wes took it that her husband was visiting the outhouse. He sat down when she motioned him to a chair. She seated herself opposite him and picked up a sewing basket, grabbing some cloth and attacking it with a needle and thread, silently smiling while she sewed. After a few minutes, she detected a noise from the back and called out. *"Juan, Wes Bracken está aquí para visitarte."*

Juan entered the room with a broad smile on his face and grabbed Wes's hand as he stood up and shook it warmly. "It's good to see you, friend. I understand you're a new father. Congratulations. We can't wait to see the baby." He motioned for Wes to reclaim his seat.

"That's what I'm here for, Juan. I wanted to borrow your buckboard so I could bring Sarafina, her daughter, and our boys here tomorrow, if you can spare it. I'm dead broke and can't rent it for you, but I'll pay you back somehow."

"What are friends for? Sure, Wes, I'll hitch it up for you and you can take it when you leave town."

"Gracias, amigo. Now tell me what's been going on in Lincoln."

"I guess you know Billy Bonney returned

over a week ago."

"That's what I understand."

"He shook things up and scared some fellows off. Jimmy Dolan was here, but he escaped to Fort Stanton requesting army protection again. Same with Sheriff Peppin. He was talking big several weeks back about scouring the county and bringing the Kid to justice, but when Bonney shows up, our brave sheriff skedaddles to the fort for safety as well. Rumor has it Peppin's so scared now that the Kid's returned that he plans to resign after Christmas. Some said Jesse Evans was hereabouts, but I never saw him."

"What about that new lawyer, Chapman? Has he gone to see the governor?"

"Latest I heard is he leaves on Monday for Santa Fe. He's sure stirred the pot in town, demanding a hearing on Colonel Dudley's role in the Big Killing, and managing Susan McSween's affairs so that she's administering not only her husband's estate but also Tunstall's."

"Where might I find him?"

Juan stroked his chin and grinned. "It depends. His office is in the Tunstall store for business, but rooms with her in the old Baca house, now that she's evicted the Baca family. Their rooming arrangement's causing a lot of gossip around Lincoln. We've all heard the rumors about Mrs. McSween."

Wes nodded. "I don't care for her myself, but it's hard to know what's true about the widow and what's lies spread by the Dolan faction to sully her reputation."

"Maybe so, but the fact is he's living under her roof when everyone knows Tunstall had a bed in the back room of his store."

Wes stood up and thanked Juan for the information. "I'm gonna drop in on the lawyer and then visit Sam Wortley if the hotel's open. I'll be back in an hour."

"The buckboard'll be ready when you return."

"Gracias, Beatriz, por tu hospitalidad," Wes said to Juan's wife, who worked placidly on her sewing.

She nodded and smiled.

Wes took a step to the door, then hesitated as he realized Christmas was approaching. He turned to Juan. "Do you think your wife would mind sewing something for Sarafina and Blanca, maybe a bonnet for each?"

"Ask her yourself."

"Beatriz, would you mind?"

"Es posible," she replied.

"If you will, I'll exchange you a beef for two bonnets and the loan of your buckboard."

165

Beatriz smiled. "I will see what material I can spare, but it will take a few days. Nothing'll be ready tomorrow. Return in a week."

Bracken nodded. "That'll work and give me time to find a yearling for you."

Juan laughed. "We don't want a sickly one, but one with some meat on his bone. No offense, Wes, but you can't trust anyone in Lincoln County and that includes the lawyer you're about to visit."

Wes grinned as he stepped outside. "I'll see you in an hour."

Unhitching his horse, he mounted and rode down the street, a handful of people, mostly Hispanic, out and about, along with the usual smattering of dogs, chickens, hogs, and goats. Beyond Patrón's house, he passed the Montaño store and the courthouse on the south side of the street opposite the Baca adobe, which stood beside the stone *torreón* that the original settlers of Lincoln had built for defense against the Apaches. Beyond the stone tower on the north edge of the road, he stopped in front of the damaged building that had served as Tunstall's mercantile when the Englishman was alive.

Wes dismounted Charlie and tied him to the hitching rack. He stepped up on the plank walk and studied the building that had taken so much abuse from the Dolan partisans. Bullet holes pockmarked the shutters and walls, and shards of glass from several windowpanes still littered the planks. As he entered, a bell on the entry jangled. Inside Wes found the store still showed the destruction and looting that had followed the Big Killing five months earlier.

As he studied the damage, Wes heard noise from the back room that had once been Tunstall's bedroom. He saw a slender wisp of a man emerge in a dark suit with the left sleeve pinned to the shoulder. The attorney wore wire-rimmed glasses over defiant gray eyes and sported a salt-and-pepper mustache and goatee.

"This store is closed."

"The door was unlocked. Are you the lawyer Chapman?"

Nodding, the man stopped and pointed to the front door with his right hand. "I'm not taking new clients. My hands are full handling Mrs. McSween's business, so please seek legal assistance from someone else."

"I don't need a lawyer. My name is Wes Bracken. Jace Cousins, my partner, delivered a letter to you last week that I requested you present to the governor when you go to Santa Fe."

Chapman harrumphed. "I don't do favors

for a man that doesn't contact me in person."

"My wife had just birthed a daughter, and I feared you might leave before I could deliver it myself. It was a plea for consideration of leniency for Billy Bonney."

"The one they call 'the Kid,' am I right?" Wes nodded.

"I told your friend I'd deliver the letter for fifty dollars. That price hasn't changed."

"Have Susan McSween pay your toll."

"How's that?"

"Her husband died owing Bonney and others money for protecting him and their property."

"They failed on both counts," Chapman spat back. "McSween's dead and Susan's house is charred debris."

"The Englishman Tunstall owed Bonney and the others money as well."

"And he's dead, too."

Wes felt anger welling in his gut. "Isn't Mrs. McSween winding up both estates, and aren't you her lawyer?"

"Bonney and his bunch didn't do their job, so why should they receive a cent from either estate?"

"Because they're owed by the deceased, who didn't settle their own debts before their demises. It's the right thing to do."

Chapman's lips tightened and his eyes narrowed. He stared at Wes and finally replied. "It's not my job to do what's right. It's my job to do what's legal. If this kid and others have a claim, they can file it with the courts and resolve it that way."

Wes clenched his fists, fighting the urge to clobber the one-armed attorney. "They don't have the money to file a claim."

"That's their problem, not mine. Now about your letter, I'll deliver it for fifty dollars like I told your shill."

"I'll pay you when you return, and I've got proof you handed it to him."

"In advance."

"I don't have that kind of cash right now."

"Then our business is concluded, Mr. Bracken. Now I suggest you leave so I can attend to more pressing matters." Chapman waved his arm at him like he would shoo away a fly.

Wes spun around and barged outside, slamming the door behind him, cursing the lawyer. Susan McSween harmed her cause, he thought, by hiring a lawyer as pompous and abrasive as Huston Chapman.

Untying his sorrel, Wes led him down the street, past the blackened debris of the McSween house. Behind the demolished dwelling he could see the crosses over the

169

graves of Tunstall and McSween along with four others who had died in the dispute over the last ten months. They were on the wrong side of the feud to receive a plot in the Lincoln Cemetery.

Passing the charred remains of the McSween place, Wes continued west until he came to the Wortley Hotel, where he spotted proprietor Sam Wortley sitting on a rocking chair on the front porch, which spanned the entire length of the hostelry. Wortley pushed himself up from his chair and greeted Bracken.

"Well, look who's finally come to Lincoln, Wes Bracken himself. If you've come for lunch, you're outta luck. I've closed the kitchen and don't cook for anyone but myself these days. Folks don't have money for frivolities, and my cooking doesn't pass muster anymore."

"It never was that good," Wes laughed, tying his sorrel to the hitching post and stepping up on the porch. He grabbed Wortley's hand and shook it warmly. "Glad to see a friendly face."

Wortley grinned and motioned to another rocker. "Have a seat and let's visit for a spell."

Wes sat down and stared across the street at the two-story adobe structure that was headquarters to the crumbling Dolan empire. He wondered if it was safe sitting so close to a store that could hold so many of his enemies. "How's business over there?"

"Slow, real slow, especially after Bonney showed up and scared most of them away."

"What about your hotel, Sam?"

"Pathetic. Nobody's got cash. That may change if this new lawyer fellow drags everybody to court that Susan McSween holds a grudge against. That may bring visitors and some money to town."

"I'm worried about spring plantings. If we can't get crops in the ground again this year, a lot of folks will go under if not outright starve."

Wortley nodded. "There's always other people's cattle, if you have to eat. Word is that Jimmy Dolan's outlaws are stocking his ranch with rustled beeves. Come spring, he may have the best crop of calves this side of John Chisum's ranch."

"I don't mind losing a beef to a family that's trying to eat and survive, but I'll fight thieves like Dolan. At last count, we'd lost a dozen head, but we couldn't tell if it was from thieves or other causes."

"From what I hear, Dolan's boys are swinging wide of the Mirror B and the Casey place, especially Jesse Evans. They know about you and Cousins tracking down and ambushing Hablador and Mendoza."

Wes cocked his head and played innocent. "That's news to me."

Wortley grinned. "Then I'm glad to be the one to tell you about it. From what I hear, Dolan and his men won't come after your cattle or your place, but if they get a chance to bushwhack you away from your land they'll do it, especially Jesse Evans."

"That's some comfort, Sam, but I don't trust them any more than I do Susan McSween's new lawyer."

"I'd sooner face a plague of locusts than a pack of lawyers as they've damaged Lincoln County as much as all the bad men."

"Well, Sam, I best start back to home. Any chance you could cook up a noon meal tomorrow? I'm bringing the family to town so Sarafina can introduce her daughter around. I can't pay you cash, but I can barter or provide you a calf in the spring, if you can fix something for me, Sarafina, Jace, and the boys."

"You haven't announced your return to anyone, have you? If word gets out, Jesse might be laying for you."

"Just Juan and Beatriz Patrón because I need to borrow their buckboard."

Wortley nodded. "I'll see what I can do

about lunch, but you be careful coming in and out of Lincoln."

CHAPTER 10

Wes helped Sarafina and the baby from the buckboard as Jace tied his dun to the hitching post and lifted the bundled boys from the conveyance and placed them on the ground. Both Luis and Roberto scrambled to their mother, grabbing her legs as she inched toward the Patrón dwelling. She moved awkwardly, the infant in her arms, the lads clinging to her thighs and the revolver dangling from the strap over her shoulder.

"Easy boys," cautioned Wes. "Don't trip your mother and your little sister."

The front door opened and Juan Patrón stood there, welcoming them. "Come in out of the cold. Our house is warm."

Sarafina entered first, then Wes herded his sons inside with Jace bringing up the rear and shutting the door. Cousins helped the two boys remove their coats as they studied their new surroundings. Juan and his wife gathered by Sarafina, their smiles wide with the expectation of welcoming Blanca to their home. Wes focused on their expressions as Sarafina removed the wrap and exposed the baby girl's head. Blanca flinched, her eyes flicking open for a second and her nose wiggling before she returned to her slumber. For a moment, Juan's smile froze, then slowly slid away when he saw the reddish tint of her hair and realized its significance.

Juan looked from the infant to Wes and grimaced in an unspoken apology.

Wes nodded that he understood Juan's unspoken message. These were the looks that Wes wanted to get beyond so the gossip would die down before subsequent trips to town.

"What a head of red hair," Beatriz announced, her smile widening even more until Juan nudged her arm with his elbow. Perplexed, his wife threw him a questioning stare, then realized what the hair meant. "She is a beautiful baby, takes after her mother," Beatriz proclaimed, then motioned to the chairs around the room. Everyone took a seat, though Jace squatted on the floor, keeping Luis and Roberto occupied while the Brackens visited with the Patróns for thirty minutes until Blanca fussed for nourishment.

Beatriz arose from her chair and offered Sarafina the privacy of her bedroom to feed the baby. Closing the door behind Sarafina, Beatriz went into the kitchen, fetched her sewing basket, and showed Wes the blue-and-white-checked fabric she had found to make the matching bonnets for Sarafina and Blanca.

"That's perfect," Wes replied.

The seamstress lowered her head. *"Lo siento por mis palabras."*

"You said nothing but the truth. No need to apologize. You are doing me a great favor with your sewing. That is more than I could ask."

Everyone sat back down and visited until Sarafina returned with a satisfied Blanca. Wes announced they had other families to call on and thanked them for their hospitality. Jace assisted the boys with their coats, then escorted them to the buckboard as Wes helped Sarafina bundle up the baby and climb into her seat. They stopped next at the Montaño store and Sarafina introduced the newborn to the family. Wes knew the meaning of the quick glance Jose Montaño shot his way, but he said nothing. From there Sarafina directed Wes to five other Hispanic dwellings to introduce the baby.

Each time Wes drew the glances of understanding that passed wordlessly between them that his new daughter was not actually his.

After the Patrón visit, Jace occupied the boys outside each home, while Sarafina and Wes stepped inside with Blanca. Wes wished he could've stayed with Jace and his sons to avoid the questioning looks, but he felt he should be at Sarafina's side. He knew she could not help but see the quizzical stares, but she took pride in her little daughter, ignoring the brutal paternity.

Leaving one adobe dwelling, Wes saw across the street Squire Wilson, the off-and-on-again justice of the peace for Lincoln. Wilson had tried to navigate the currents of the feud fairly to both sides, but kept getting removed from his position by the Dolan faction through the previous governor's office only to get reelected by the local citizens. Though Wes didn't care so much to introduce Blanca to Wilson, he wanted to see if he could pump him for information. After helping Sarafina and Blanca into the buckboard, he aimed the horse toward Wilson's house, Jace trailing on his dun while monitoring the boys behind the buckboard seat.

Drawing up beside the justice who was

chopping wood, Wes greeted Wilson. "Wanted you to see Sarafina's new daughter, Squire."

Wilson whacked his ax into a log and grinned as Sarafina leaned over in her seat and removed the wrap covering the baby's face. He gandered at the girl and smiled. "She looks just like you, Wes," he said.

Bracken knew Wilson was either bluffing so as not to acknowledge the child's true father or he needed glasses. Wes didn't care, though, as the justice was the only one they had met who had not given away the story.

"Are any of our troubles getting straightened out, Squire?"

"It's a tangled mess, I tell you, Wes," Wilson responded as he ambled around the team to Bracken's side of the wagon. "This lawyer Huston Chapman's stomping on nails, so anxious is he to bring justice for the widow McSween."

"Does she deserve justice?"

"Do any of us, Wes?"

"Maybe not."

"The fact is," Wilson continued, "I'm waiting for Chapman to leave town to serve papers on Colonel Dudley at Fort Stanton for his role in the murder of Alexander McSween and the destruction of the McSween home."

"Why wait?"

Wilson's expression tightened. "I'm trying to keep the new lawyer from getting killed. He's stepping into a washtub full of rattlesnakes. He thinks what's right will triumph, but he doesn't understand the law in Lincoln County."

"Does anybody?"

The justice grinned. "It's like looking in a mirror; everything's backwards."

"Have you heard anything on the whereabouts of Jesse Evans?" Wes asked.

"I haven't seen him, though they say he's in the area. Rumor has it he's avoiding your place since you turned down his offer to let bygones be bygones."

Wes leaned toward Wilson and whispered, "Would you have forgotten what he did to your wife?"

Wilson scratched his whiskered chin and stared at the bundle that held Blanca. "I reckon not, but he's tired of running, tired of having to face all the trouble he's created. I hear it's the same with Bonney and the Regulators."

"What about James Dolan?" Wes asked.

"Jimmy's like Murphy before him. He's got political pull and regrets nothing because he can hire the likes of Jesse Evans to do his dirty work, like all the cattle rustling that's possible when men are afraid to get out and watch their stock."

"I intend to settle up with Jesse," Wes said.

Wilson grinned. "Do me a favor, Wes, will you? Don't kill him in my jurisdiction."

Wes smiled as he rattled the reins and turned the buckboard around. "I'll do my best, Squire, but I can't make any guarantees."

"There are never any guarantees in Lincoln County," Wilson called out as Wes rode past and tipped his hat.

Directing the cart to the street, Wes turned west for the Wortley Hotel as midday and lunch approached. Guiding the rig behind the building where it would be less visible to enemies, Wes wondered if Sam Wortley had scrounged up anything for their meal. After securing the reins, Wes jumped down and strode around the conveyance to help his wife with Blanca while Jace tied his dun and unloaded the lads. As Sarafina started for the entrance, Wes grabbed his carbine. Jace pulled his rifle from its saddle scabbard, and the two armed men herded the boys after their mother.

Wes offered Sarafina his arm as she stepped on the plank walk, then escorted her to the door, opening it for her and the boys to enter, Jace slipping in behind them as Wes brought up the rear. Barely had he closed up than Sam Wortley emerged from the kitchen into the room filled with tables and chairs for diners and a registration desk for overnight guests.

"Welcome, Wes Bracken and family," the proprietor called. "You, too, Jace Cousins." The proprietor pointed to the largest table surrounded by six chairs. "Have a seat and take off your coats." He studied their long guns. "Place your artillery on another table, and I'll finish up in the kitchen and be back with your meals."

"Hold on, Sam," Wes said as he set his carbine on an adjacent table and lifted the strap with Sarafina's pistol over her shoulder, sliding the weapon beside his Winchester. He helped Sarafina remove her coat as she shifted the bundle with the baby from one arm to the other. "Sam, I'd like you to meet Sarafina's daughter, Blanca."

Wortley stepped to his female guest as she parted the cloth covering the baby's face. Wes watched Sam grimace when he saw the red hair. The proprietor squeezed out a sympathetic grin. Like the others Blanca had met that morning, Sam Wortley understood the significance of those auburn locks. "She's a doll," Sam said, "just like her mother."

Sarafina blushed as Sam turned back to the kitchen. Wes held out a chair for her, and she sat down, her sons clambering onto chairs on either side of her. Wes and Jace seated themselves. Turning to her husband, Sarafina said, "Thank you for introducing Blanca to everyone. I know it was difficult for you."

Looking uncomfortable at the conversation, Jace stood up. "Let me see if Sam has some coffee." He strode into the kitchen.

Wes tapped the table with his forefinger, avoiding his wife's gaze. "The sooner we get it over with, the quicker the gossip will die down. Once that happens, we can go on with our lives."

"My life is better because of you, same for the boys and even Blanca, though she doesn't know it yet," Sarafina replied.

Reaching past Luis, Wes patted Sarafina's hand and looked into her dark eyes. "Thank you, but let's not talk of this anymore."

The couple remained silent, listening to the jabber of Roberto and his older brother, who sat on their knees in the chairs, playing with the eating utensils at their places. When Jace returned, he carried coffee in two porcelain cups on matching saucers, placing one dish in front of Sarafina and the other by Wes, before striding back to the kitchen.

Sarafina stared at the cup and saucer, then smiled at her husband. "Someday I hope to serve you coffee and meals on fine dishes like these."

Pushing the sugar bowl to his wife, he nodded, though he wondered if her dream would ever be possible. "It won't be this year or next, not with money so tight."

She patted his hand. "I can wait however long it takes."

Jace returned with two tins of milk for the boys and his own tin of coffee. As Wes glanced from the porcelain dishes for him and his wife to his mug of coffee, Cousins shrugged. "Sam feared I'd break one of his fancy dishes. Besides, you new parents deserved a treat."

Sarafina put two tablespoons of sugar in her drink and stirred it, then took tiny sips of the steaming brew as Wes and Jace blew on their cups.

Wortley appeared at their table carrying a basket with cornbread muffins and two tin plates. Setting the basket in front of Sarafina, he next placed a tin dish in front of Luis and Roberto. "I thought these boys would like cornbread while I dish out the rabbit stew." The proprietor retreated to the kitchen.

The boys' eyes widened as Sarafina picked

up a golden muffin, split it in half, and placed a piece before each boy. Roberto and Luis attacked the food and smiled at the first taste. When they were thirsty, Wes helped Luis and Jace assisted Roberto with a drink while Sarafina gently rocked Blanca in the crook of her left arm.

Wortley returned with porcelain bowls of stew for Wes, Sarafina, and Jace. Then he came back shortly with two half-filled tin cups for the boys.

"It ain't much for a meal," Wortley admitted, "but it was the best I could do on short notice."

Just as Sarafina lifted her spoon to her mouth, Blanca fretted.

"Hold on for a moment," Sam told Sarafina, "and I'll take care of the baby." He stepped to the kitchen, returning in a minute holding a kerchief of thin white cloth bulging at the bottom and tied at the top with a string. "Pardon the language, but it's a sugar teat. You dump a teaspoon of sugar in the center, tie it, and put it in the baby's mouth."

Sarafina took the cloth and touched it to Blanca's fretting lips. Opening her mouth, she took in the little bulge, sucking it as a gentle smile erased the consternation on her lips.

"It'll calm her down."

"Sam," Jace announced, "you'd make some old boy a good wife, what with all your cooking and baby skills."

Wortley grinned. "And I can even change a bed with clean sheets. Bet you've never done that a day in your life, Jace."

"I've thrown a bedroll lots, but I never had clean sheets that often, if I had sheets at all."

While Sarafina worked on her meal, Wes and Jace alternated between feeding themselves and the boys. Blanca suckled contentedly on the sugar teat.

Wes complimented Sam on the stew and the cook smiled. They made small talk until Blanca whimpered after she had drained the cloth teat. Noting the baby's continued hunger, Sam walked to the hotel desk and picked up a key.

"Grab your coat and follow me, Sarafina," he said, then turned to Wes. "I'll open a room for her to feed the baby. I didn't light a fire in the fireplace, but it'll be more private than in here and not as cold as outside."

Sarafina handed Blanca to Wes, arose, and slipped on her coat. She next draped the strap attached to her revolver over her neck.

Wortley shook his head. "It's a shame a

decent woman has to go armed wherever she goes, but that's Lincoln County for you." The proprietor led Sarafina out the front door and down the plank walk to a room. He returned momentarily and sat down with the men and the boys. He pointed out the window to the Dolan store across the street. "It's sure been quiet over there since Bonney came to town. Some men think the Kid's got nine lives like a cat."

"Is the Kid still around?" Wes asked.

"Word is, he's looking for Jesse Evans, just like you boys."

"We haven't been doing much looking," Wes answered, "what with the baby and all. Do any of the stores have supplies left?"

"Perhaps the Ellis store and certainly Dolan's but nobody cares to do business with Jimmy Dolan anymore."

They talked for another twenty minutes when the front door opened. Wes twisted around expecting Sarafina and instead looking into the beady eyes of the one-armed lawyer Huston Chapman.

"Are you open for lunch?" he asked.

Wortley shook his head.

"What about them?"

"They're friends," Sam replied.

"If you'd gotten here earlier," Wes added,

"you could've had my bowl of stew. All it would've cost you was fifty dollars, same price as it takes to get a message to the governor."

Huston scowled and spun around, barging out the door and bumping into Sarafina with enough of a jolt to extract a squeal from Blanca. "Out of my way, you Mexican wench," he grumbled.

Wes shot up from his chair and bolted for the entrance, Jace following him like his shadow. Wes reached the door just as Sarafina stepped in, delaying her husband long enough for Cousins to grab his arm and stop him. "Let it go, Wes."

Sarafina calmed Blanca and reassured her husband. "The baby's fine, as am I. It's nothing I haven't heard before and won't hear again."

"Not in my presence, you won't," Wes cried, yanking himself from Jace's grasp.

His wife pointed to the pistol hanging from the strap around her neck. "Do not worry, *mi esposo*. I can protect myself." Sarafina nudged her husband back into the room and closed the door so Wes would not give chase. "I am tired," she told him, "and ready to return to our place."

Wes turned about and headed to the table where Sam stood. "That lawyer," he said to the proprietor.

"Yeah," Wortley replied, "and he's on our side against the Dolan faction."

"Lawyers are on nobody's side but their own," Wes answered as he picked up Roberto, slipped on the boy's coat, and buttoned it. Jace helped Luis with his.

Both men thanked the proprietor for his hospitality as they gathered their long arms.

"I hope business picks up for you soon, Sam," Wes offered. "I know providing us a free meal didn't help matters."

"You've always played straight with everyone, Wes, and I value that in a man. As for business, it'll be summer at least, or maybe fall when crops come in that things will improve. I can hold on until then. After that, we'll see whether I stay or leave, and that decision turns on when the violence ends as much as when business picks up."

The men herded the boys and Sarafina to the buckboard, where they loaded the family and weapons. Wes told Sarafina the Ellis store might have supplies on the way out of town, if she wanted to stop, but she preferred to head home. He took Jace aside and informed him he was heading straight to the Casey place, but asked him to stop at Juan Patrón's to advise him Wes would return the buckboard the next morning and one of them would come back in a week to provide the promised yearling for the two bonnets Beatriz was making.

Jace mounted as Wes climbed into the rig. Taking hold of the reins, he started the horse and buckboard toward home. After stopping briefly at the Patrón house, Jace caught up with them just east of the Lincoln Cemetery. They completed the trip without incident.

The next morning, Wes returned the buckboard with Charlie tied to the back. He left the rig behind the house, merely knocking on the door to thank Juan for the loan and to confirm that the Christmas bonnets would be ready in a week. Receiving Beatriz's promise, he mounted and headed back home, the solitary ride giving him time to think about all the work that needed completing between then and the spring so he could reverse his fortunes and maybe work his way out of all the problems caused by the Lincoln County violence. As much as anything, he wondered what kind of gift he could pick up for the boys on his return trip to town. Reaching home, he discussed his dilemma with Cousins, who advised him not to worry. Jace reminded Wes of the jar of marbles he had brought home the day Blanca was born. As he had only given the boys one each, figuring they would lose them in short order, he still had several left to offer as Christmas gifts.

"Thanks, Jace."

"That's what partners are for, right?"

A week later Jace drove a beef to Juan Patrón and returned with the two bonnets in his saddlebags, secretly passing them on to Wes, who could not believe how beautiful the sun hats had turned out from mere pieces of cloth and lace. After Jace provided a scrub cedar for a Christmas tree, Wes thought they would have as good a celebration as possible for such dire circumstances.

Then on Christmas Eve, Billy Bonney showed up.

CHAPTER 11

Wes was toting two pails of water from the Rio Hondo when he spotted the two riders stopped astride their horses at the head of the trail to his home. Though he wore his revolver, he had left his carbine in the kitchen. Wes took wider steps, moving as quickly as he could without spilling his load. He studied both men bundled in coats with their collars turned up and their hats tugged low over their foreheads. One lifted his hat over his head, and Wes identified the buck-toothed grin of Billy Bonney. Wes halted and lowered one pail to the earth, waving Bonney forward, then picking up the bucket and delivering his cargo. He entered the back door and announced arriving visitors to Sarafina and Jace.

"Who is it?" Sarafina asked.

"The Kid and somebody."

"Carlos?" asked Sarafina, who paused and reconsidered. "We can't let him ruin our

191

Christmas or threaten you, *mi esposo.*"

Wes placed the pails on the table and shook his head. "Didn't look like Carlos. This rider sat taller in the saddle than your brother."

"Thank you, God," Sarafina replied.

Jace stood up and retreated to the corner where he picked up his Henry rifle. He followed Wes into the front room and outside as the two horsemen reined up.

Wes recognized Bonney and Tom O'Folliard. "Merry Christmas," Wes offered. "What brings you both our way?"

"Most of our *amigos* are with their families," Bonney replied. "Tom and I had no kin to share Christmas with. We're hoping to spend the night and tomorrow with you."

"As I recall, you spent a previous Christmas with us, Kid."

"Yeah, on the Mirror B before all the trouble began, and before they torched your place."

"It's hard to remember the good times, what with all the troubles that followed. Seems like you brought a turkey you shot for our meal that Christmas. Where's this year's bird?"

Bonney laughed, pointing over his shoulder with his thumb at O'Folliard. "Tom will have to do. I can't afford to waste ammunition on something that's not shooting back at me."

"You're welcome to spend tonight and tomorrow night here," Wes said. "Toss down your bedrolls, then tend your horses in the barn."

"We'll sleep there."

"No," Wes answered. "It's Christmas. You can stay in the front room with Jace. He won't mind."

"Just as long as you birds don't snore," Cousins responded to the guests.

Bonney and O'Folliard twisted around in their saddles and untied their bedrolls as Wes stepped over and grabbed each bundle by the straps.

"We won't be feasting, boys, not with things so tight and Sarafina still weak from the birth and taking care of her daughter, but we'll share what we have tonight and tomorrow. Can't promise you anything after that."

"A roof over our heads for two nights will be a fine gift," O'Folliard replied as he and Bonney nudged their horses toward the barn.

"Enter by the kitchen door when you're done," Wes called after them.

Bonney responded with a wave of his arm.

Jace opened the door for Wes to carry in

the bedrolls. When they stepped inside, Jace shook his head. "The fellows look worn down. I've never seen the Kid so faded."

Wes agreed as he dropped the bedrolls on the floor. "Both seem exhausted. At least their horses aren't fagged, though whether they got them legally or not is another question."

Both men entered the kitchen where Wes's sons played on the floor near the warmth of the stove. Sarafina walked in from the bedroom, carrying Blanca, whose wide, unblinking eyes showed she was alert.

"It's Bonney and Tom O'Folliard," Wes told his wife. "They'll be staying two nights."

"But we don't have that much food, and I've Blanca to care for," she replied.

"We'll figure something out, Sarafina, even if Jace and I have to cook. It's Christmas," Wes answered, picking up the water pails and dumping them in the barrel in the corner.

With Blanca cradled in one arm, Sarafina stepped to the table and gathered the empty cups, straightening the kitchen until Wes stepped behind her, put a hand on each shoulder, and steered her to a chair.

"Don't worry about it, Sarafina," he commanded. "Take a seat and relax. These two haven't slept inside for days, if not weeks. They aren't concerned about your house-keeping. They'll feel blessed with a warm place to spend a couple nights."

Sarafina settled into her chair. "I should do more."

"You've done enough," Jace interrupted. "Wes is right. Relax."

No sooner had she sat down than Roberto and Luis scurried over, Luis boosting Roberto onto his mother's lap so he could amuse their baby sister, who fretted at his actions.

A quick rap on the back door announced Bonney and O'Folliard as they entered, each carrying a carbine in his hand and a set of saddlebags over his shoulder.

"Afternoon, ma'am," Bonney said, removing his hat.

"Thanks for letting us stay a few nights," O'Folliard said.

Sarafina smiled as a fearful Roberto slid from her lap and his protective big brother led him to the corner. "It's Christmas."

Wes pointed to the front room. "Put your things in there, fellows."

The two visitors strode past the table into the adjacent room. When they returned, they stepped to the kitchen table, where Bonney placed a large potato.

"It's not much, ma'am," Bonney said, "but it's a gift for putting us up."

O'Folliard dropped a small burlap bag beside the spud. "A half pound of coffee, ma'am. Merry Christmas."

"Gracias," she answered. "Your gifts bless us in these hard times."

Bonney looked at the corner where the two nervous boys stared at him. *"Chicos,"* he said, "you should be smiling. It's almost Christmas." He held out his arms to the brothers, but neither advanced. Instead, the Kid stepped to them, squatted down, and took a bewildered Roberto in his arms, picked him up, and carried him to a chair. Roberto whimpered until the Kid sat down and placed the worried child on his thigh, bouncing him up and down. "Ride that horsey, little one, ride."

Roberto's confusion evaporated in favor of a smile, then a giggle and a laugh as he rode Bonney's knee.

The Kid glanced at Wes. "He's learning to ride fast in case the law's ever on his tail."

Wes wiggled his chin from side to side. "I hope the law never comes after him."

"Don't we all," Bonney replied, "but you're forgetting this is Lincoln County."

After a simple supper of tortillas and beans,

everyone took chairs into the front room, Sarafina easing into the rocking chair and tending Blanca. As the men settled into their seats, Luis and Roberto scurried to Bonney, imploring him for another horse ride on his knee. Jace picked up his well-worn Bible and read the Christmas story as he had done the previous two celebrations. He spoke from the second chapter of Luke on Joseph's and Mary's trip to Bethlehem, of the birth of Jesus, and of peace on earth and goodwill toward men, a concept that seemed so foreign to Lincoln County, New Mexico Territory.

Everyone listened reverently, lost in their thoughts of Christmases past, their memories only interrupted by the intermittent giggles of Luis and Roberto as they rode on Bonney's knee. Afterwards they visited until Blanca fussed for nourishment, and Sarafina excused herself to nurse her daughter. Wes and Jace each took one boy to their bed and prepared them for the night's rest with promises of Christmas gifts in the morning.

When the two partners rejoined Bonney and O'Folliard, the Kid nodded and announced, "We need to talk."

Jace and Wes drew up chairs opposite the visiting pair and sat down. "What about?"

"Ending things," Bonney replied.

"More violence is not the answer, Kid." Wes gauged Bonney's stolid demeanor.

"That's not what I mean. I'm ready to settle things peacefully because I'm plumb tuckered out from running."

"Getting your message to the governor through the lawyer Chapman may not work because he's demanding fifty dollars. We don't have that kind of money right now."

Bonney grimaced. "I'm less worried about the law than I am Jimmy Dolan, Jesse Evans, and everyone that's working for them; even Carlos has fallen in with their gang."

Wes clenched his jaw and his fists, then spoke slowly. "Are you certain?"

"Yep. He wanted to ride with us, but I turned him down as he's still gunning for you. He claims you promised Sarafina not to kill him, but he's made no such vow about you or Jace."

"And Dolan can manipulate him to get back at me," Wes mused.

"Dolan will use him," Bonney said, "that's for certain, but whether you're the target or someone else is the question. Dolan's so crooked he thinks differently than us."

"With so many things working against you, Kid, what are you proposing?" Wes asked as he leaned forward in his seat.

"Seeing if I can arrange a truce with Jimmy Dolan and Jesse Evans. I plan to write a letter to Jesse and set up a meeting with him, Dolan, and any others that are as tired of the fugitive life as I am. Perhaps we can negotiate a truce."

Jace let out a low whistle from across the room and stroked his chin.

"Before I sent the letter, I owed it to you both to let you know."

Before Wes could speak, Jace responded with venom. "Evans and Dolan be damned. I don't want any part of a truce. You can't trust either of them. Jesse still owes me for two years of my life."

Wes released a slow, measured breath. "Everyone knows what Jesse Evans did to Sarafina." He paused, licked his lips, and continued. "Sarafina has a redheaded daughter as a result. Blanca is a daily reminder of that wrong. I intend to kill Jesse for it."

Bonney arose from his chair, stepped to Wes, and patted his shoulder. "I respect you not taking sides," he said. "You've tried to do what's right all along. I'm trying to do the same now, but I didn't want to offer a treaty without informing you."

"Kid, I'm obliged. If you believe that will

end your troubles, go ahead, but count me out."

"I'm with Wes," Jace added.

"Remember, when you deal with the devil you risk a journey to hell," Wes said.

"I'm exhausted looking over my back everywhere I go, Wes, and hell can't be any worse than this life. If the law won't give me a pardon like the others, then I've got to go about it another way, even if it means dealing with my enemies." Bonney lifted his hand from Bracken's shoulder and stepped to the counter. There he toyed with a tin ornament dangling from the Christmas tree. "I don't have a home or family, and I fear I never will unless I straighten this out. Nothing else has turned out right. That's why I'm considering meeting with them."

"Make whatever deal you must with Jesse, but leave me and Jace out of it. Make sure you tell him we declined to join your negotiations. I intend to see him dead."

"I feel the same way," Cousins confirmed.

Bonney laughed. "Maybe if we agree to a truce, I might tip you off where to find Jesse."

Wes cocked his head and stared at Bonney. "Wouldn't that defeat the purpose of your agreement?"

"Yep, but don't you think Jesse would do

the same for me?"

Scratching his head, Wes chuckled. "Then what's the good of a treaty, Kid?"

"I gotta start somewhere," he answered.

"Kid, after hearing this," Jace said, "I don't know whether to be for you or against you."

The Kid cackled. "Pick whichever one'll help you the most."

All four laughed, then talked until midnight, discussing the misdeeds plaguing Lincoln County and the suspects behind them. Word was even circulating that the great John Chisum was thinking of selling his ranching interests and getting out of the area, rustling and thieving being so bad. Bonney noted that several Texas Panhandle cattlemen had united to hire range detectives to stop the thieving overlap between their state and the adjoining territory. Wes wondered if that was the real reason Bonney planned to make entreaties to his Lincoln County enemies. Perhaps the Kid feared he was being boxed in from too many directions to fend off all his foes.

Just after midnight, the men retired. Wes considered himself lucky that he could slip into a warm bed with a decent woman. Whatever his difficulties, at least he had a fine wife to share them with, unlike Cousins,

Bonney, and O'Folliard. He gave a prayer of thanks as he nestled in beside Sarafina and fell asleep.

Come Christmas morning, Wes awoke before dawn, quickly dressed, grabbed a pail and basket, and headed out to milk the cow and gather what hen fruit he could from the chicken coop. He found nine eggs from the chickens, a true Christmas gift, and filled the milk pail three-quarters full before returning to the kitchen and leaving his harvest on the table. He lit a lamp and added kindling to the stove's firebox and stoked the fire until it warmed the room. Next he started a large pot of coffee and wondered what to do for breakfast and dinner. Shortly he heard Blanca wailing for nourishment. Wes knew Sarafina had arisen when Blanca's displeasure faded, so he slipped to the bedroom where she sat in the candlelight nursing her daughter.

"Good morning," he said as he moved to the far side of the bed.

"Merry Christmas," she replied.

"Look the other direction," he ordered as he slid his hand under the mattress. "I don't want you to see your Christmas present."

"I bet it's blue and white," she replied

Wes froze when his hand touched the two bonnets pressed together beneath the covers. She knew. "What are you talking about?"

"I found them when I washed the bedding. It was sweet of you to think of me and Blanca, especially when there's so little money."

Pulling the two presents free, he hid them by his side as he left for the kitchen. "Be sure and thank Beatriz Patrón. She sewed them."

"I will, but first I must thank you. Come here."

Wes walked over to his wife.

"Now bend down where I can kiss you."

He did as ordered, and she planted her lips on his in a loving gesture. Blanca paused in her nursing and cooed her approval. Straightening, Wes headed out the door, poked his head in the boys' room and saw them still sleeping, then continued to the kitchen where he met Jace and O'Folliard yawning and wiping the sleep from their eyes. Checking the front room, Wes found Bonney snoring in the corner in the lamplight seeping from the kitchen. He slid the bonnets under the modest tree beside the jar of marbles that Jace had retrieved for the boys. O'Folliard peeked inside, disappeared for a moment, then returned with the potato and the half pound of coffee, which he slid under the tree. Both men retreated to the table and joined Jace, who poured coffee for them.

As daylight took hold, Sarafina entered the kitchen with Blanca in her arms, smiling at the eggs on the table. A half hour later, Luis and Roberto wandered in, rubbing their eyes. As Sarafina dipped two cups of milk from the pail for the boys, Wes stepped to the front room and saw Bonney still sacked out on his bedroll.

Looking from Bonney to his sons, he called, "Luis, Roberto, come here." He pointed to the corner lump that was the Kid. "Boys, see if you can rouse your horse."

Luis and Roberto looked at him, awaiting confirmation.

Wes nodded. "Go ahead."

The two scampered into the front room, crying "horsey, horsey," and fell on Bonney, who grumbled, rolled over in his bedroll, and grabbed both lads, tickling them under the arms and drawing giggles. When he released them, the two boys scrambled away until Billy got on his hands and knees, tossing his head and neighing like a wild stallion. Roberto and Luis raced back to Bonney and climbed aboard. As soon as they grabbed his shirt, he crawled into the kitchen, drawing more cackles from them both.

O'Folliard laughed. "If my mount ever goes down, I'll saddle Billy and be on my way."

Jace shook his head. "That's the ugliest horse I've ever seen."

Bonney grinned, looking up at Cousins and shaking his head. "My riders disagree. To them I'm a steed."

"I'll find the Mirror B branding iron so the boys can singe your hide and claim you if you're ever stolen," Wes offered.

Another smile cracked Bonney's face. "Now who would steal a fine Lincoln County horse, Wes?"

"Not you, Kid," Wes answered.

"Like I told you before, Wes, I took your horses from the thieves that stole them. I was returning them to your place."

Wes shook his head. "You were going the wrong direction."

"I was taking the long route," Bonney replied.

Wes grimaced. "Looking back, perhaps it would've been better for the horses had you escaped with them. At least they might have survived rather than being slaughtered by Jesse Evans."

"They were good horseflesh," Bonney acknowledged.

Sarafina handed Blanca to Wes, stepped over to her sons, and lifted them from his back. "Get to the table and drink your milk, *chicos,* while I scramble the eggs." They protested, but their mother scolded them. "Uncle Billy needs his rest." She plopped each boy in a chair and helped Roberto manage a sip of the white liquid. Sarafina turned to the men. "It's Christmas. No more talk of the past, just the future." She slid her arm under the basket handle and carried the container to the stove where she took a skillet and placed it on the hot metal and cracked each egg. Sarafina took a wooden spoon and stirred the concoction. Jace sipped coffee, then fetched tin plates for the adults and clay bowls for the boys.

After Sarafina served the eggs and a flour tortilla apiece, everyone ate and retreated to the front room where they exchanged gifts. Jace opened the jar of marbles for Roberto and Luis, squatted, and poured them on the floor. The two lads squealed and herded the orbs together like they were cattle. The adults relished the innocent joy of the two as they rolled the toys to one another, laughing and clapping their tiny hands.

Wes stepped to the small tree atop the counter and offered the two bonnets to

Sarafina and Blanca. Sarafina's smile and the tears welling in her eyes touched him. "I'm glad you remembered Blanca," she said as she removed the wrap from her daughter's head and fit the blue-and-white covering over her red hair.

Wes nodded. "It was the best I could do for her and her mother."

Sarafina knotted the ties beneath Blanca's little chin, her tiny head and face disappearing beneath the blue-and-white-checked cloth. Sarafina's smile widened. "It's big, but she will grow into it when she really needs it." She offered Blanca to Wes, who took her and rocked her in his arms as Sarafina pulled her matching bonnet over her raven hair and tied the strings beneath her jaw. Standing up from her rocker, she smiled and departed. "I'll fetch my mirror," she called as she left.

With Blanca cradled in his left arm, Wes moved the bonnet flap and looked at the little girl, who offered him a toothless smile and a drooling coo.

Sarafina returned, holding her small mirror in one hand and two bulging envelopes in her other. She offered one to Wes and the other to Jace. "These are for the two men in my life. It's not much, but it was the best I could do."

Wes handed Blanca back to her mother.

"Open your present. It's from your sons, Blanca, and me."

Wes lifted the flap. "I hope it's a wad of greenbacks."

"It's blue, not green," Sarafina said.

As she spoke, Wes pulled out a blue-and-white cloth of the same material as the bonnets. "It's a bandanna that Beatriz Patrón made for each of you. It'll come in handy with all the work ahead this spring."

"Thank you," Jace said.

"Try them on," Sarafina replied. "Beatriz had extra material and sewed them for your gifts." She turned to Bonney and O'Folliard. "I'm sorry that I don't have anything for you, especially after you were so generous with the potato and the coffee."

"Your hospitality is gift enough," Bonney answered.

"Yes, ma'am," O'Folliard agreed. "Your letting us sleep under a roof in a warm house for two nights was most considerate, ma'am."

As soon as Wes tied the bandanna around his neck, his wife offered him the hand mirror. He looked at himself and smiled, but his grin disappeared when he focused on the gap from the missing tooth.

"Is something wrong?" Sarafina asked.

"No," he replied. "I wish we had more to share for Christmas."

"What we have is enough, and we will make do, for surely better times are ahead," she answered.

Jace took the mirror and admired the bandanna he had tied over his nose like a bandit. "*Gracias,* Sarafina."

The adults sat back in their chairs and watched the kids play until Sarafina suggested that one man kill a hen that only laid sporadic eggs so she could make a stew for Christmas dinner. Bonney and O'Folliard volunteered to kill, pluck, and gut the bird if Wes would select the hen.

Jace offered to do that for Wes, so he would have a few moments of privacy with his wife and family. When the three men left, Sarafina walked over and hugged Wes, thanking him for providing a gift for little Blanca.

"I know it is difficult for you, *mi esposo,* but you will come to love the innocent one."

Wes sighed and wrapped his arms around Sarafina, the infant pressed between them. "Let's not talk of this today."

Sarafina nodded, "If that is your wish, *mi esposo.*"

When they heard Jace enter through the kitchen door, they broke, Sarafina handing

Blanca to Wes, who sat in the rocker chair and watched the boys as his wife headed for the stove, picking up the potato and coffee as she passed the tree. He observed the boys while Sarafina started their meal.

They ate their Christmas dinner in the early afternoon, a stew of chicken, diced potatoes, onion, and peppers, and then had smaller leftover portions for supper. Come morning, Bonney and O'Folliard saddled up and offered their thanks and goodbyes.

"I'll get word to you if I can arrange a truce with Jesse Evans, Dolan, and the others," Bonney said.

"You be careful, Kid, because I don't trust any of them," Wes replied.

"Nor do I, but I'm tired of running."

"Good luck, Kid."

Bonney smiled and patted the six-gun on his hip. "Here's all the luck I need." He turned east toward the Pecos River, whistled, and put his horse into a trot down the Hondo Valley, O'Folliard riding at his side.

"I hope he knows what he's doing," Jace observed.

"Me, too," Wes answered.

CHAPTER 12

For two cold, blustery months, Wes Bracken
and Jace Cousins worked around the Casey
place, handling the regular chores and
preparing for the spring planting. They
stayed near home except for a monthly foray
upstream to inspect the Mirror B property
and a weekly ride to check on their cattle,
which grazed on the Casey land south of
the Rio Hondo. Though they had heard
from occasional passersby that Billy Bonney
and his Regulators frequented San Patricio,
none had visited since Christmas. The cat-
and-mouse games continued as men of each
faction hunted one another, combatants
avoiding a major confrontation when both
sides were equal, seeking instead to surprise
their enemies in ones and twos so the
outcome would never be in doubt.

Rumors and rustling abounded. Territorial Governor Lew Wallace intended to visit
Lincoln to investigate matters, so the gossip

went, but the speculation had never been confirmed. The previous governor had come to town, ostensibly for the same purpose, but had merely cloistered himself with the Murphy-Dolan faction and never attempted to contact the other side. Since Christmas, some men's cattle herds had dwindled while others had thrived from the ongoing rustling that culminated in a herd of more than two-thousand stolen beeves being driven right past Fort Stanton where Colonel Nathan Dudley let the herd — and Jesse Evans, despite the federal arrest warrants hanging over his head — pass because the cattle were being moved to Dolan's ranch up north near White Oaks. Many suspected Dolan bribed Dudley to look the other way. Meanwhile, the officer's hatred for Susan McSween had only increased because of her unabated legal harassment over the loss of her husband and her home.

After finishing their chores greasing and repairing the gears on the Casey gristmill on a brisk, blustery February day, Wes accompanied Jace back to the house for supper. "You know what today is?" Wes asked.

"Tuesday," Jace replied.

"Yeah, but Tuesday the eighteenth of February. A year ago today the Englishman was murdered, ripping the scab off of

Lincoln County's problems."

Jace tugged his hat down tighter as they strode home. "It's not an anniversary worth celebrating. How many have died as a result?"

Wes shrugged. "I've lost count."

His partner nodded. "Me, too."

At the back door, the men stopped to wash up at the bucket they had left there for that purpose, then shook their hands and wiped them on their pants. Jace dumped the dirty water, and both men entered the kitchen where Sarafina stood over the stove cooking fresh tortillas.

She smiled as the men removed their coats and hats, hanging them on pegs by the entry. "Supper is ready," she said. "It's not much, tortillas and beans."

Wes walked to the corner where his sons were rolling marbles to each other by the warmth of the stove. He squatted, took a pair of agates, and thumbed one to each. The two boys giggled.

Jace stepped to the stove, picked up the coffee pot with a rag, and poured cups for himself and Wes, then sat at the table, relishing the hot liquid and the warm room.

Sarafina carried a platter of fresh tortillas to the table as Wes took his seat. She returned with a bowl of mashed beans, which the men smeared on their tortillas.

"What about our sons?" Wes asked.

"They've eaten," Sarafina replied.

Wes took a bite, then looked at Jace. "We should check on the cattle tomorrow."

"That's fine by me, provided Sarafina's okay being left alone."

Smiling at his wife, Wes asked, "Will you be okay with us gone much of the day?"

Sarafina pointed to the pistol hanging from the lanyard over her shoulder. "I always carry my gun, even when nursing Blanca. Leave a carbine and load the shotgun. I will be fine."

"You sure?" Wes asked.

She nodded firmly. "Nobody'll harm me or my children ever again."

By midafternoon Wes and Jace had tallied their cattle and found their herd down another twenty head. The total disappointed them, but both men knew it could've been worse had rustlers targeted them. The partners drove the animals closer to the Casey house until the dry grass petered out. There they left the animals and started back home, enjoying the time on horseback until six riders appeared over a ridge a half mile distant and headed their direction. Both partners pulled their long arms from their saddle scabbards and confirmed their loads.

"You recognize their mounts?" Jace asked.

"No," Wes replied. "The way horses are being stolen these days, you never know." As the riders approached at a lope, the leader lifted his hat and waved it aloft with a jaunty flick of his hand that reminded Wes of the Kid. "I think it's Bonney."

Wes and Jace studied the men intently. As the Regulators neared, Wes recognized the Kid, Tom O'Folliard, Doc Scurlock, and George Bowers. With them rode two Mexicans, both unknown to Wes. When the riders drew up opposite the two partners, Bonney shook his head. "You almost got us killed, Wes."

"How's that, Kid?"

"Your wife answered your door with a shotgun and a loaded carbine within reach."

"She don't take kindly to visitors when we aren't around."

"I can't say I blame her, after what —" Bonney started, then hesitated, "— you know?"

Wes nodded as he studied the Kid's tight jaw and his nervous eyes. "I take it you didn't come for a social visit."

Cocking his head, he sighed. "You were right, Wes, about making peace with the devil. Another man's dead as a result."

Wes looked from Bonney to Jace, who whistled under his breath. "Who this time?"

"The widow McSween's one-armed lawyer Chapman," Bonney answered.

"Did you or the Regulators have anything to do with it?"

"We were there, but Dolan and Evans murdered him right on the street in Lincoln."

Wes twisted in his saddle and slid his Winchester back in its scabbard. "Tell us about it, Kid. Jace and I have nothing but time."

Bonney explained how he had written a letter to Jesse Evans, and after weeks awaiting an answer had received a note agreeing to a meeting on the eighteenth to discuss the matter.

"You know yesterday was the anniversary of the Englishman's death, don't you, Kid?"

Bonney shrugged. "Hadn't given it a thought. Too much has happened since then." He untied the canteen from his saddle horn and sipped at the contents before continuing his story. "It started as a tense standoff across the street, neither side trusting the other. Jesse even threatened to shoot the first man that crossed the road. They were armed with Colts and Winchesters, as were we. After a wagonload of harsh words, I decided I could never stop running if I didn't step out in the street, so I did. Then Jesse walked out, followed by Billy Campbell, Billy Mathews, two fellows I didn't recognize, and finally by Jimmy Dolan himself. We were wary of each other, but we walked to a saloon and drank and talked, them doing more of both than us."

Bonney explained they agreed to six points. First, anyone who accepted the truce could not kill anyone from the other side without first withdrawing from the agreement. Second, families and friends on either side were not to be harmed. Third, army troops who aided either faction during the difficulties were not to be threatened or harmed. Fourth, no one from either party should testify against any opponent, whether before a grand jury or a trial jury. Fifth, anyone arrested by the law would be assisted by all in resisting capture or escaping jail. And finally, anyone agreeing to the terms of the treaty and later breaking any provision of the agreement should be killed. After Bonney outlined the conditions, he stared at Bracken.

"Will it work, Kid?" Wes asked.

He shrugged. "I thought so when we shook hands, but then Dolan invited us over to his store for free drinks, though he and his men had already drunk so much that they staggered down the street. That's when we ran into Chapman, just back from Santa Fe."

Wes let out a deep breath. "Running into that bunch is plenty dangerous when they're sober, even more so when they're drunk."

Bonney nodded. "Jesse pulled his pistol, sticking it in the lawyer's chest and ordering him to dance. Chapman refused. Dolan lifted his carbine and repeated the demand. When the lawyer declined again, both fired, their guns so close to Chapman that his coat caught fire."

Wes grimaced, then looked at Jace, who was shaking his head.

"The lawyer," Bonney continued, "cried out, 'I'm dead,' then stumbled backward a few steps before tumbling to the ground. We were stunned, weren't we, boys?"

Bonney's companions nodded.

"But Dolan and his men just laughed, and told us now we really had something to celebrate. I swear Jesse Evans came up to me and said, 'I promised God and Colonel Dudley I would kill Chapman, and now it's done!' I couldn't believe he'd admitted that, even if he was drunk. He threw his arm around me and steered me to Dolan's place."

"Why didn't you escape?" Jace asked.

"We were scared. Drunk as they were, I feared they'd shoot us as coldly as they had the lawyer. At the saloon they pulled two tables together, and we sat and celebrated, them downing more whiskey, and us just watching ours. We had to keep our heads about us. After an hour or more of talking about the trouble they were in, they realized Chapman was likely unarmed so Dolan found a pistol behind the bar and said someone needed to plant it on him."

"Hold on, Kid. Chapman's body had stayed on the street for a couple hours?" asked Wes.

"Likely longer," Bonney answered.

"Why didn't the sheriff do anything about it?"

Bonney held up his arm. "Hold on, and I'll get to that. I volunteered to plant the gun on Chapman, seeing it as a way to escape without getting shot. I took the pistol from Dolan. As my pals arose with me, I thanked them for the drinks and slipped out of the saloon. We got our horses and rode out of town as fast as we could for San Patricio, galloping past the lawyer's body. No one was brave enough to cover him, much less get him out of the street, not even us."

After taking another swig from his canteen, he corked the container and continued. "As for the sheriff, Peppin has resigned, and George Kimbrell has been appointed to the job. The new sheriff had been tipped off — likely by Dolan and Evans — that we would be in town, so he had ridden to Fort Stanton for help arresting us. From what we learned, the sheriff and twenty cavalry arrived a half hour after we departed. If we'd stayed, we'd likely be in the stockade at the fort under the colonel's control. I thought it odd that part of the truce protecting soldiers, but now I see they're still in it with Dolan and his bunch."

Wes tapped his fingers against his saddle horn. "I've given up trying to figure out what to do when the law is crooked. Surely, the law will catch up with Dolan and Evans."

Bonney scoffed. "Everyone knows Dolan's behind most of the rustling, but he's hired some Mexicans, Carlos among them, to do his thieving. Once they stock his herds, Dolan plans to have them arrested, hung or sent to prison, making the Mexicans the scapegoats."

Jace snarled. "That sounds like something Jesse would do. Believe me, I know from experience."

"So I've heard," Bonney responded, "but I figured I owed it to the both of you to tell you about the sorry outcome of the truce."

Wes pointed at the Kid. "Billy, you need to leave the territory. That's the only way you'll ever be able to walk down a street without looking over your shoulder and wondering who's trying to kill you."

With a sweep of his arm toward his companions, he shook his head. "I've got no family except these fellows and nowhere else to go."

"One day the violence will catch up to you, Kid."

"You're not bulletproof either, Wes."

"But I'm not riding around looking for trouble."

Bonney grinned. "If you change your mind, Carlos is branding stolen cattle northwest of Fort Stanton toward White Oaks and Carrizozo. From what I hear, there's a ranch up there Dolan's stocking for a Santa Fe Ring member that's not above claiming other men's stock. As for Carlos, once that politician's ranch is stocked, he'll be sacrificed as the biggest cattle thief ever in these parts. Just a caution, though, that area's where Evans, Dolan, and others hide from the law, which is scared to trespass on the politician's ranch."

Wes touched the brim of his hat. "Obliged for the information, Kid."

"One more thing," Bonney said. "Jesse understands neither of you are party to the truce. I made sure he knew that when he was sober and when he was drunk. Don't let him get the drop on you." Twisting around in his saddle, Bonney called to his men. "I've done what I need to do. Let's head back to San Patricio."

The riders reined their horses about and started for the village. Though the Casey place was the same direction, Wes opted not to ride with the Regulators, watching them silently until they rode out of sight.

Finally, Jace broke the quiet. "Young Billy will remain in the territory forever, buried in an unmarked grave."

Wes nodded. "Likely so."

"And another thing I fear, Wes, is that you've got it in your mind to warn Carlos of the danger he's in."

"The thought's entered my mind."

"You remember he's threatened to kill us."

"He's still my wife's brother, and he don't deserve to hang. I'll discuss it with Sarafina when we return, but I'm getting like the Kid and ready to end it with Carlos as well as Jesse."

Four days after encountering William Bonney and armed with more weapons and ammunition than they normally carried, Wes Bracken and Jace Cousins turned up the road toward Lincoln, barely traveling a half mile before they encountered a column of a dozen cavalry troopers, a lieutenant, and a civilian with a star on his coat, a man Wes took to be George Kimbrell, the new sheriff. Wes and Jace guided their mounts off the road as the lawman peeled away from the soldiers and aimed his black gelding their way.

The cavalrymen's horses trod by as Kimbrell reined up.

"Morning, Sheriff," Wes offered.

Kimbrell nodded, eyeing them suspiciously. "Bracken and Cousins, isn't it? You look like you're expecting trouble, two carbines under each saddle and gun belts without an empty cartridge loop."

"One of mine is a rifle. A good Henry rifle," Jace replied.

"You can't be too safe these days," answered Wes, "what with unarmed lawyers being murdered on the street in Lincoln."

"I'm on the trail of Chapman's killers,"

Kimbrell responded. "Billy Bonney and his gang shot the lawyer. Word has it they're holed up in San Patricio."

Wes shook his head. "I heard it was Jimmy Dolan and Jesse Evans that murdered him."

"Where'd you hear a wild tale like that, Bracken?"

"From the Kid himself."

Kimbrell leaned forward in his saddle. "You don't say. Now where might I find him?"

"Can't say for certain. I saw them four afternoons ago. When I saw him, the Kid and a dozen others were headed southeast toward Seven Rivers, saying they were giving up San Patricio, maybe heading to Texas."

"Are you certain?"

"Nothing's certain in Lincoln County, Sheriff. You ought to know that by now. I'd feel better about this matter if you were searching for Dolan and Evans for Chapman's killing."

"This is for Bonney's past crimes, not just for the lawyer's death."

Wes cocked his head. "Did you see Chapman's shooting?"

"No, but I got it on good authority from Dolan and Evans that Bonney fired the deadly shots, even went back to place a pistol in the lawyer's hand to make it look like self-defense."

"Did you find a gun in Chapman's hand?"

"That don't matter, Bracken."

"It does to Bonney," Wes answered, pausing a moment. "And it matters to me. Bonney's been blamed for too many of Lincoln's problems."

Kimbrell stroked his chin whiskers. "Are you taking sides, Bracken?"

"Just trying to stay on the side of what's right, Sheriff."

"What's right in Lincoln County is what the sheriff says, and now I'm the sheriff. Don't forget that. Good day."

Wes tipped his hat at the lawman, who nudged his mount in the flank and trotted off to join the soldiers.

Jace chuckled. "You have a knack for making new friends, partner."

Replacing his hat, Wes shrugged. "Lincoln County's the damndest place I've ever been."

"And it doesn't look like it'll get much better for a while."

Both men nudged their horses on toward Lincoln, passing the town cemetery, then entering the community, drawing suspicious glances from the few people on the street or outside their homes. As they neared the defaced Tunstall store, Wes pointed north toward the Rio Bonito where a dozen men who were bundled against the February chill lowered a coffin into the earth. At the head of the grave stood the widow McSween still dressed in black. Wes realized the lawyer Chapman was being interred beside her late husband and the Englishman. When Wes recognized Juan Patrón, he reined up. "Hold on, Jace," he said as his partner stopped and watched the burial.

As the coffin settled into the earth, the attendants pulled the ropes from beneath the wooden box and three mourners picked up shovels to dump dirt atop the latest victim of Lincoln violence. The others signed the cross over their chests and turned toward their homes.

As Patrón secured his hat, he ambled toward Bracken and Cousins. His lips parted into a smile, his teeth as white as the newly painted grave marker behind him. He greeted his friends.

"You look mighty happy for a man just coming from a funeral," Wes offered, leaning over in his saddle to shake Patrón's proffered hand.

"It's always good to see trustworthy friends," he replied. "And out of bad will come good." He stepped between the two horses to grab and pump Jace's hand.

"What good?" Jace inquired.

"Governor Wallace has promised to visit Lincoln within the month and straighten out this mess."

"We've had a governor here before. It only made matters worse," Wes answered.

"This time it's different. President Hayes himself has ordered the violence stopped."

Jace laughed. "It's easier to proclaim that in Washington than to enforce it in Lincoln."

"We've got to start somewhere," Patrón replied, then eyed the two partners. "What brings you both to Lincoln? I'm sure it wasn't the lawyer's funeral."

Wes hesitated answering until a couple mourners had passed, then leaned down toward his friend. "We've gotten word Carlos is being set up by Dolan and Evans to take the fall for their rustling. We intend to warn him to unhook from the Dolan wagon."

Patrón shook his head, his smile melting away. "He's vowed to kill you."

Wes nodded. "But he's still my brother-in-law."

Jace shrugged at Patrón. "Wasn't my idea."

"Word is they are moving cattle to a ranch White Oaks and Carrizozo way, some place owned by a Santa Fe politician."

"I suspect that's true as Dolan's trying to buy political favors since his empire's been crumbling and his finances have gone to hell, but there's just one problem, Wes."

"What's that?"

Patrón pointed to the grave still being shoveled over, then looked back at Bracken. "Ever since the lawyer's murder, that's where Jimmy Dolan, Jesse Evans, and their men have been hiding out. You best be careful as I don't know Carlos is worth risking your necks over."

"Obliged for the warning, Juan," Wes replied, then shook his reins and started down the road west to Carrizozo.

Jace grinned again. "Wasn't my idea, Juan." He nudged his yellow dun forward.

"Stop by my place on your way home," Patrón called, "if you don't get your fool heads shot off."

For three days Bracken and Cousins rode to the northwest, avoiding the trails and bedding down in cold camps for the night, fighting off the February chill with their blankets and their will. The ragged country ran brown with a thirst broken only by the meager creeks that snaked between the rolling hills and the peaks that glowered into the sky, some crests sporting a cap of snow that glistened in the morning sunlight. They maneuvered among scrub piñon pine and juniper bushes, which sucked the moisture from the parched earth so that only scattered clumps of grass pimpled the land with the forage necessary to sustain cattle.

Each day Bracken and Cousins arose at sunrise, saddled their horses, gnawed on a strip of jerky or one of Sarafina's tortillas for breakfast, and continued their pursuit. Fruitless for three days, their search on the morning of the fourth came upon a trail churned up by cattle on the run and followed it through rough country toward the mountains to the northeast. They tracked the trail for two hours until they saw a puff of dust in the distance and shortly picked out a dozen riders galloping southwest. Uncertain of their mission, Wes and Jace found a gully deep enough to hide their mounts, sliding from their saddles and quickly hobbling their horses. Grabbing their long guns, they peeked over the rim of the ravine and watched the riders come within a mile, but never wavered in their destination and soon passed to the southeast.

"Dolan and Evans?" Jace asked.

"Probably."

"Think Carlos was with them?"

"I doubt it. I figure they'll keep him doing dirty work alone so they can turn him into Sheriff Kimbrell."

When they were certain the riders were well beyond seeing distance, the two men put up their long guns, unhobbled their horses, and resumed their search, spending the rest of the day in the saddle seeking their quarry. Just before dusk, they noticed a plume of smoke too broad just to be a campfire, wafting skyward beyond a tall ridge that screened the source of the fire.

"What do you think?" Jace asked Wes.

"Can't say for sure."

Yanking their long guns from their scabbards, the pair rode toward the ridge. As they neared it, they detected the bellowing of cattle on the other side. Riding halfway up the slope, they dismounted and hobbled their horses, then climbed up the incline and crouched at the peak, leaning forward until they could see down the slope. There in a makeshift pen milled fifty or more beeves, and three men worked a fire, altering brands on the animals.

When the one with the branding iron stood up, Wes recognized Carlos. Jace identified him at the same moment and nudged Wes with his elbow.

"It's him," Jace whispered.

Motioning for Jace to back away from the ridge crest, Wes retreated.

"What do you think?" Jace asked.

"They're changing brands. Let's watch and make sure there's only three of them. It's too risky to ride up on them in a boxed canyon because they only have to watch one end. I figure we eye them until dark, then hit them before dawn."

"They might hear our horses when we ride in."

Wes shook his head. "Let's go over the ridge on foot and surprise them in the morning."

Jace snickered. "Carlos won't like that."

Wes just smiled.

CHAPTER 13

Shivering from the morning cold, Wes Bracken crept toward the bundle where Carlos slept, his heavy breath rasping in the predawn air. The three men snoozed around the large campfire, which had burned down to glowing embers during the night. When Jace Cousins slipped into the circle with his Henry pointed at the other two rustlers, Wes bent over Carlos and poked him in his ribs with the barrel of his Winchester. In his sleeping stupor, Carlos groaned and twisted beneath his blankets, then snorted at the interruption. Wes slid the muzzle of his carbine to Carlos's head, pushed the edge of the blanket aside, and rested the frigid steel of the muzzle against his brother-in-law's cheek. Carlos flinched and brushed his face with his hand until it touched the metal. His fingers froze and his eyes flickered open. Wes could just make out his eyeballs, wide with fear, in the soft light of a fading moon.

"He's awake," Wes whispered to his partner.

Recognizing Wes's voice, Carlos muttered, *"Bastardo."*

"Good to see you, too, Carlos," Wes replied, lifting the gun barrel from his cheek. "Now pull your hands from the blankets and hold them where I can watch them."

Carlos pushed back the blanket and raised his arms.

"Rouse the other two, Jace."

Cousins edged to the campfire and toed his boot into the fire, kicking glowing embers on the two mounds of men and blankets. For a moment the pair slept on, then suddenly awoke in a flurry of curses and flailing arms and legs, flinging their covers back and jumping up, swatting at the fiery particles that stung them like malevolent lightning bugs. As they danced and filled the air with profanities, Jace kicked some kindling near the fire onto the embers, and gradually the flames grew, casting off enough light for both to watch their quarry.

"Tell them to unbuckle their gun belts and drop them to the ground," Wes ordered Carlos, who hesitated. Wes stuck the carbine barrel in his chest. "Tell them."

Carlos cried out hurried orders, and his pals unfastened their holsters and let them fall to earth. "I should've killed you before now, *bastardo,*" he growled.

"I didn't come to kill you, Carlos, but to warn you. Jimmy Dolan is setting you up for arrest as rustlers."

"We're not rustlers," Carlos shot back, "just hands doing honest work."

Wes scowled. "You're altering brands on other men's cattle. You sleep with your boots and holsters on and your horses saddled in case you need to escape. Everyone knows what you're doing. When Dolan's done with you, he's told folks he's turning you in for rustling."

"What folks?"

"Billy Bonney for one."

"I despise the Kid," Carlos spat.

"Why, Carlos?"

"Because he stopped me from killing you when I had a chance, said you and Cousins were the only ones he could trust, but I don't trust you, never have."

"You must believe me, Carlos, that it's time for you to leave Lincoln County and start an honest life elsewhere. You're in waters over your head, and you damn sure can't swim. Now stand and drop your gun belt."

Carlos arose, glaring at Wes as he stood up and unhitched his rig from his waist and slowly let the weapon slide to the ground.

"Don't turn around," Wes ordered, shoving the Winchester barrel against his shoulder.

Carlos spun about, filling the air with profanity.

Wes stepped behind him, placed the carbine muzzle beneath Carlos's jaw as he eased to his brother-in-law, and slipped his hand in his britches pockets, pulling out a pocketknife from Carlos's right and a few bills from his left.

"So you're robbing us, too, are you?"

"Just you, Carlos. We've no quarrel with your rustling buddies. This'll cover our expenses, maybe buy a play-pretty for your niece and nephews. It's better than you'd treat me, if you got the jump on me."

"I'd kill you, *bastardo.*"

"I vowed to your sister not to kill you, Carlos."

"It's a promise you'll regret, *bastardo.*"

Jace cleared his throat. "You're forgetting one thing, Carlos. I never promised anyone I wouldn't kill you. If I see you skulking around our place, I'll shoot you on sight and leave your carcass for the buzzards to devour."

Carlos stiffened and spat on the ground.

Wes lowered his gun barrel. "I promised Sarafina I'd warn you to leave the county before you're thrown in jail or hung. Now that I've done that, I owe you nothing more. We're leaving and taking your horses and guns with us."

Carlos spun around. "You can't do that, leaving us horseless and defenseless out here."

"We'll hobble your horses several miles away and leave your guns with them. That'll give us time to get escape without worrying about you tailing us."

"Bastardo!"

Wes grinned and stepped toward his brother-in-law. "I may've promised Sarafina I wouldn't kill you, but I never vowed not to hurt you." Cat-quick, he yanked the carbine over his shoulder and hammered the butt of the weapon into Carlos's head right over his ear.

Carlos's eyes rolled back and his knees turned to mush as he collapsed.

Seeing that, his two compatriots lifted their arms higher, one crying, *"No más, no más."*

Jace waved his rifle at them, and they backed up. Wes picked up Carlos's gun belt and grabbed the two of his confederates.

Together Wes and Jace eased to the pen where the three rustlers had tied their saddled horses. Untying one of the geldings, Jace mounted first as Wes buckled the holsters and slung the gun belts over his shoulder. He untied the other two horses, and climbed atop the first one, fastening the reins of the second around the saddle horn. When Wes nodded, he and Jace trotted off.

"That fire sure felt good," Jace said, "so much so I hate to leave. It's a shame you can't get along with your kin better."

Wes shook his head. "I have a hard enough time putting up with my partner."

The pair rode out of the box canyon and around the other side of the mountain where they swapped the borrowed horses for their own. They led the three geldings almost five miles from the rustlers' camp, tied them to juniper bushes, and draped the gun belts over the saddle horns. Jace went through their saddlebags, extracting two boxes of cartridges, one he kept and the other he handed to Wes. Both men planted the pistol ammo in their own saddlebag.

"Which way from here, Wes?"

"I figure we're about ten miles from White Oaks. Let's head that direction, buy a hot meal, then follow the roads back home."

"Anything hot sounds good," Jace answered, and they turned their horse to the northwest, ever wary of any riders that might mean trouble.

By midmorning they had followed trails through the rugged mountains and emerged from the ridges to find a basin where the twenty buildings and dwellings of White Oaks had sprouted along a feeble stream of the same name. As strangers in town, they drew the stares of the occasional citizen on the street as they sought sustenance. They stopped by an orange brick building that claimed to be a saloon and eatery. Before dismounting, Jace pointed to a hand-inked sign in the front window: NO SCUM ALLOWED.

"You reckon we're welcome, Wes?"

"As long as we've got money in our pockets, we're not scum."

"Even if it's stolen money?"

Wes laughed. "I figure Carlos paid us for some sound advice."

The two men dropped from their horses, tied their mounts to a hitching post, and entered the building through its tall doors. The interior was lit by a single kerosene lamp and heated by a potbellied stove in the middle of a room with a bar to the side.

"Anybody home?" Wes called, enjoying the

room's warmth. "You've got two customers looking for a hot meal."

"Hold your horses, fellas," came a voice from batwing doors behind the counter. Momentarily, a short fellow with a dirty apron emerged with a frown.

"It's too late for breakfast and too early for lunch."

"Well," Jace asked, "is there any place in town that serves scum at this time of day?"

"Give me thirty minutes, fellas, and I can fix you something."

"How about a steak?" Jace queried.

The proprietor shook his head. "I can give you venison, but no beefsteaks. You'd think as much rustling as goes on in Lincoln County, I could buy cheap beef, but there are crooks on both ends of that tit. Now do you fellas have cash? I don't feed saddle tramps and the needy because I'd go broke. What is it the Good Book says, the poor will be with you always?"

"I thought the Good Book said the scum will inherit the earth. Is that right?" Jace asked.

"Probably so if he was writing about Lincoln County."

"What about a meal?" Wes inquired.

"Special of the day is venison stew."

"What else is on the menu?" Wes asked.

"Stew of venison. Either way, it comes out the same, though I throw in some cornbread to favored customers."

"Are we favored?" Jace asked.

"I favor anybody with cash, but I gotta see it first."

Wes reached for his pocket, but Jace grabbed his arm. "Save that for Sarafina and the kids. I've got a few dollars to cover lunch." He displayed three greenbacks.

Wiping his hands on his apron, the cook licked his lips. "It's fifty cents a bowl."

Jace whistled. "That's a little steep."

"I can go cheaper if you buy whiskey."

Wes shook his head. "Just stew and a cup of coffee."

"I'll throw in the coffee and cornbread for free, if you pay in advance."

Jace peeled off two bills and handed them to the fellow. "Two bowls of stew apiece."

Shoving the bills in his pants pocket, the cook pointed the men to a table. "Take a seat. Coffee'll be out shortly and the stew and cornbread in half an hour." He retreated behind the batwing doors, whistling all the way.

Bracken and Cousins took off their coats and seated themselves in the darkest corner of the room, farthest away from the front door, and sat down facing the entry. They waited ten minutes for their drink and another half hour for their stew and cornbread, but they never complained, enjoying the warmth before what would be a cold overnight camp on the trail and another full day's ride back through Lincoln to home. Both men were ready for coffee refills when the cook brought them their meal on a tray, which he placed in the middle of the table, then pulled out spoons from his pocket and dropped them between his two customers. Wes and Jace grabbed a bowl each and a spoon, then shoveled stew into their mouths, each taking a cornbread muffin, Wes eating his in alternate bites with his stew while Jace crumbled his up in the concoction.

The cook returned with a coffee pot and refilled their tins, then sat the container before them and grabbed a chair. "You fellows figuring on prospecting around here?"

"Just passing through and wanted a hot meal," Wes replied.

"This poor town's built on hope, men thinking there's gold in the mountains. They're always finding good sign, but never any gold. Ol' John Baxter's been looking for a strike for near on three years, and he ain't rich yet. He'd make more money rustling."

Jace pointed at his bowl with his spoon, "Or selling overpriced stew."

The cook grinned. "Yep, but the coffee and cornbread are free." He picked up the pot and refilled their cups.

"The cornbread's good," Wes noted, "but the coffee's a little weak."

"I cut my coffee pretty thin so men'll buy my liquor, something with more punch to it."

"Tell me something —" Wes started as he began his second bowl of stew.

"Dewey's the name."

"Tell me, Dewey, have you seen or heard anything about Jesse Evans or Jimmy Dolan being in these parts?"

Hesitating a moment, Dewey scratched his chin. "Are you lawmen?"

Jace snickered, and Wes shook his head.

Dewey continued, "They've been around off and on, depending on what trouble they're in elsewhere in the county, but I haven't seen them in several days. You a friend of theirs?"

"We've had run-ins with them in the past and don't care to encounter them again."

"Dolan and Evans are meaner than a mama bear with a sore tit, since their fortunes have turned. I hear Dolan's near broke and likely killed a lawyer in Lincoln, though some say the Kid did it. Evans is running from several federal warrants. You know things are bad for them when they avoid the main roads. It's not like it was when L.G. Murphy was alive and the House controlled the county."

Jace laughed as he started his second bowl of stew. "Are they scum?"

Dewey looked over his shoulder to make sure no one had entered and leaned toward Wes and Jace. "Yeah, but I wouldn't want them to know I said so."

"Jesse thinks the same of us," Wes said, "and I've vowed to kill him on sight."

His eyes narrowing, the proprietor twisted his head toward Wes, studying him cautiously. "You wouldn't happen to be Wes Bracken, would you?"

Wes nodded. "That's me."

Dewey frowned. "He got drunk here one night, bragging about how he had, he had —"

Feeling his gut tighten, Wes grimaced. "Violated my wife?" Instantly his appetite turned rancid.

The proprietor clenched his lips as his shoulders sagged. "Didn't mean no harm, Bracken. Only scum would brag about something like that, even when drunk."

Jace interrupted. "We should be going. It's a good ways back home."

"I've lost my appetite, so let's get on the

road," Wes said, pushing himself from the table and grabbing his coat, yanking it on.

"Sorry my hospitality turned sour," Dewey said, arising with Jace.

"The heat from your stove's more than made up for any lack of hospitality, Dewey," Cousins said as put on his coat.

Dewey pointed to the six remaining corn muffins on the tray. "Take those to eat along the way." As Wes stepped toward the door, the cook gestured at Jace's neck. "Lend me your bandanna, and I'll wrap up some more for your trip home."

Wes exited into the cold, which was no match for the anger burning within him. He untied Charlie and mounted, waiting in the street for Jace to join him. As soon as the door opened and Jace appeared with his bandanna plump with cornbread muffins, Wes reined his horse around and started down the road.

Jace jumped on his dun and quickly caught up with him, holding the kerchief by its knotted top. "There's plenty of corn-bread in here to get us home, Wes. Dewey was apologetic for bringing up Sarafina."

Wes nodded. "Let's head for Carrizozo and stick to the roads."

They rode to the southeast in silence the entire twelve miles to Carrizozo, a small

244

community with a store and barely a dozen houses and huts. Reaching town, they turned east toward Lincoln, camping the night another dozen miles from Carrizozo. As dusk settled over the land, they pitched a camp east of Fort Stanton under the cottonwood trees where the road crossed the Rio Bonito. They unsaddled and hobbled their horses, then gathered wood and built a fire to boil a pot of coffee as they threw their bedrolls. When the coffee was ready, they poured themselves a cup apiece and ate cornbread muffins.

In the dying gloom of the day, they heard, then saw, four men coming their way from the east. Without a word, both men grabbed their long guns, slipped behind the broad trunks of two cottonwoods, and waited in silence. As the riders approached, one man hollered.

"Hello the camp. This is Sheriff George Kimbrell and deputies." The riders turned off the road toward the trees.

Wes glanced at Jace, then answered. "State your business, Sheriff. This is Wes Bracken with Jace Cousins."

"We've no quarrel with either of you and just wanted to share a camp."

"Why not head over to Fort Stanton? They'd put you up."

"Don't want anyone there to know our business."

"And what business is that, Sheriff?"

"We've got word on a rustling camp up White Oaks way. You may not want to know, but one rustler is said to be your brother-in-law."

Wes whispered to Jace. "Seems Dolan's pulled the trigger on Carlos. He better have skedaddled like we told him."

"It's nothing against you, Bracken, or Cousins either."

"Come on in, Sheriff. You're welcome to stay the night."

Bracken and Cousins lowered their long guns and returned them to the scabbards by their bedrolls as Kimbrell led his deputies into the circle of light from the fire. He dismounted, ordering his men to tend their horses.

"Obliged, Bracken. What are you doing this way?"

"Take care of your horse, Sheriff. Then we can talk." Wes sat down on his bedroll, holding out his hands toward the warmth of the blaze.

After the lawmen watered, unsaddled, and hobbled their horses, they approached camp and tossed their bedrolls near Backen's and Cousins's. The quartet gathered around the campfire to warm up, then stepped over to their bedrolls and settled in.

"Last time I saw you, Sheriff," Bracken said, "you were riding with soldiers to arrest Billy Bonney? Did you find him?"

"The Kid's like a ghost. Can't find him one day, and the next he shows up and scares the daylights out of you."

"Where have you been, Bracken?"

"White Oaks."

Kimbrell eyed Wes. "What took you to White Oaks? Did you see Carlos?"

"Carlos and I don't gee-haw too well. He's threatened to kill me, so we keep our distance."

"Why the trip to White Oaks then?"

"Money's tight with all the troubles in Lincoln. Some folks say there's gold in the mountains around White Oaks. We did a little prospecting, but didn't find it to our liking. I can starve just as slow back on my place. Who told you about Carlos, Sheriff?"

"Nobody in particular. I hear the rumors and go where they lead me."

"Last time I saw you, gossip said the Kid was in San Patricio. That didn't pan out for you. I doubt this will either."

"Maybe not, Bracken, but I've got to check it out. That's my job."

"The gossip I heard, Sheriff, is that Jimmy

247

Dolan took on Carlos and a couple other Mexicans to help rustle cattle for him, intending to turn them in to take the fall for all the thieving acts of Dolan's gang. Arresting Carlos takes the blame off Dolan and polishes your reputation for bringing him in, even though everyone knows who's behind the thieving."

Kimbrell grimaced. "Keep your thoughts to yourself, Bracken." The sheriff turned to his deputies. "Sleep well, boys. We've got a long day tomorrow if we're to catch the rustlers." After that, the sheriff pulled off his boots and gun belt, placing it at the head of his bedroll. He slid under his blankets without another word.

Wes watched Jace slip into his bedroll and when everyone seemed to be asleep, he removed his coat and got in his bedding, spending a restless night. Come morning, relations in the camp remained as frigid as the air; Kimbrell and his men ignored Wes and Jace, who lingered around the camp, keeping an eye on the lawmen until they had saddled up and departed.

As Wes readied his sorrel for the last leg of the journey home, Jace patted him on the shoulder. "This is Lincoln County. There's only so much you can do. Remember tonight you'll have a warm bed with Sarafina."

"For her sake, I hope Carlos took our advice and left."

"You and I both know he's too stubborn for that."

The men led their horses to the stream to let them water, then mounted and turned east along the road toward home. They split the four remaining pieces of cornbread for breakfast and rode cautiously to Lincoln. Wes wondered if Dolan and Evans had returned. Between worries over his enemies, Wes thought about Sarafina and the boys plus Blanca, the daughter that was not his. He ached that a bartender in White Oaks knew of his wife's humiliation. And his own! He shook his head to try to rattle the thoughts from his brain, but they remained.

"You've been quiet, Wes."

"Yesterday was a bad day. A lot of things to mull over. I need more time to think." Wes said the words, but he knew better, for the events eleven months earlier still tormented him.

As they approached Lincoln, a brisk February wind whipped through the valley, matching the jumble of thoughts blowing around in his mind. Rounding the bend in the road, they saw Dolan's imposing store, which seemed abandoned, no smoke coming from the chimneys. Other buildings showed life, though the street was vacant for so close to noon. The street seemed so tranquil that it was hard to believe all the violence that had occurred there.

"Are you planning on stopping at Juan's, Wes?"

Wes scratched his chin. "I'm ready to get home, but I suppose I should let him know what happened with Carlos and find out if he knows anything about Kimbrell's posse."

They rode past the abandoned Tunstall store and saw the newly mounded grave of the lawyer Chapman. Beside it stood the widow McSween, her head bowed as she stood at the foot of her husband's and lawyer's eternal resting place.

Jace noted the mourning widow. "I've always heard nothing's worse than a woman scorned, but I think it should be nothing's meaner than a widow scorned."

"We know what happened to her husband wasn't right, but when the law won't do anything about it, what else is she to do?"

They rode past the blackened ruins of the McSween home and angled their horses toward Patrón's house on the opposite side of the street.

"I won't be but a minute," Wes said as he jumped down from his horse and tossed his reins to Jace. He knocked and waited.

"Juan, Juan, it's Wes Bracken."

Shortly, the door opened at the hand of a smiling Juan Patrón. "Come in, come in," he said.

"I can't stay long."

"Even so, enter so you don't let the cold wind in because I've got news for you."

Wes nodded and stepped inside, Patrón waving at Jace as he closed the door.

"Good or bad news, Juan?"

"The governor will be in Lincoln in two weeks," he announced. "He's vowed to end the corruption."

"That is good news," Wes answered, though doubtful it would make a difference.

"And he'll need your help to straighten things out."

CHAPTER 14

The heat was stifling in the cramped court-room where the residents of Lincoln had come to hear what Governor Lew Wallace had to say. They murmured among themselves, questioning whether this governor would succeed in bringing law and order back or fail as his predecessor had. Wes Bracken stood along the wall, holding a fretful Roberto, almost three years old. Jace Cousins leaned against the adobe wall beside Wes, managing five-year-old Luis on his hip, while Sarafina sat on the end of a bench at their feet, her coat draped over her bosom as she nursed Blanca. Wes had brought the entire family to the meeting, hoping a show of wives and children would convey the urgency of calming the lawlessness that pervaded the county.

Wes looked around, searching for Juan Patrón among the white and brown faces, but failing to spot him. That was so unlike

Juan to miss a gathering of such importance to the community. People perspired from the heat of so many bodies cramped together, some fanning their faces with their hats or hands. Men on opposite sides of the room opened windows and the frigid March breeze knocked out the sizzle, but made the space no less comfortable as a chill replaced the warmth. Roberto squirmed in Wes's arm, the sudden cold pimpling the boy's skin until he wormed beneath his father's coat.

As Wes looked around for Patrón, he heard a commotion at the door and a voice he recognized as that of Sheriff George Kimbrell.

"Make way for the governor," the lawman called as he squeezed past the attendees, making a path for Wallace behind him. Juan Patrón trailed them both.

The three men inched through the citizens to the front, the governor saying "pardon me" or "excuse me" or "thank you" with every step. Wallace stood ramrod straight in his dark suit and sported a bushy brown mustache and beard speckled with gray. He had attentive eyes behind wire-rimmed glasses with a shock of his russet hair hanging across his forehead. Wes estimated him to be in his fifties.

Once they reached the front, Wallace placed his leather satchel on the table and took the magistrate's seat. As the governor settled into the chair, Patrón turned to face the crowd, holding up his hands for silence. As the throng quieted, Roberto fretted in Wes's arms, drawing a stern gaze from Patrón, who then smiled and nodded when he recognized Bracken. Patrón introduced Wallace as an Indiana native and former Union general, who had fought at Fort Donelson and Shiloh and later served on the military commission in the trial of the conspirators who had assassinated President Lincoln, for whom this very town and county had been named. Patrón lauded Wallace as a published novelist, a lawyer, and a Republican ally of President Hayes, who was committed to ending the violence throughout New Mexico Territory, not just Lincoln.

"And that is why Governor Wallace is among us tonight, to hear your concerns and to address them. I present to you the governor of New Mexico Territory, Lew Wallace."

As the territorial head stood to a smattering of applause, Patrón stepped to his side and whispered something in his ear, drawing a smile and a nod. As the clapping died,

Wallace grabbed the lapels of his coat with his hands and spoke.

"Juan has asked me to speak slowly so he can translate for our Mexican citizens, and I am pleased to do so." He paused, allowing Patrón to convey his message in their native tongue.

"I have been in Lincoln two days and have talked to a dozen men, and I have several more I want to meet, but what I have learned so far is everyone's tired of the violence. I intend to get to the bottom of it and punish those responsible, so that the law-abiding citizens of Lincoln — like yourselves — no longer must worry about their lives and their livelihoods."

Patrón's translation of his words drew nods and smiles from all the Hispanic faces.

Wallace continued. "When the law plays favorites, it erodes our legal system and from what I have seen, the legal system has favored one faction, the one nominally headed by James J. Dolan. Further, the military commander at Fort Stanton has supported the Dolan faction in matters under dispute. I am hereby calling upon the United States Army to relieve Colonel Nathan Dudley of his command."

His comments drew applause from the Anglos and then the Hispanics after Patrón's translation.

"Further, I am ordering the army to arrest James J. Dolan and Jesse Evans for the murder of the lawyer Huston Chapman, who before his death visited me in Santa Fe and apprised me of the depth of corruption that this county has endured for the past decade."

His remarks garnered two more rounds of applause.

He lifted his right hand from his lapel and slipped it inside his coat, extracting a folded sheet of paper that he waved in the air. "I've listed thirty-seven men that have to answer to the law for their crimes. I intend to see they are prosecuted."

Wallace drew more clapping as he returned the list to his shirt pocket and clamped onto his lapel again.

"I cannot say precisely *when* everything will be resolved, but I promise you it *will* be settled while I am governor of New Mexico Territory so you can go about your lives in peace under laws applied equally to all."

With that, he released the lapels of his coat and sat back down as the spectators clapped and cheered.

Patrón stood up and announced that the governor would spend a few minutes meeting with citizens and then retire to the Jose

Montaño home for rest after a tiring two days in Lincoln. He said people desiring to meet with the governor could call upon him at the Montaño residence. As soon as the meeting ended, Patrón worked his way through the crowd, many pushing against him to meet the governor and others retreating outside like Bracken, who escorted his family to their horses.

"Wes, wait up," Patrón yelled as Bracken headed for their mounts.

"Meet us on the east side of the building, Juan," he called as he maneuvered his family past the wagons and horses tethered outside and around the courthouse. He stopped by the window where a shaft of pale yellow light made it easier to see.

Patrón caught up with him. "I'm glad you came, Wes, as we need to discuss a couple things."

"Shoot," Wes answered.

"The governor would like to meet with you in the morning."

Grimacing, Wes shook his head. "Can't do it. We planned to return home tonight and didn't bring any bedding."

"You can stay at our house. Beatriz would be delighted to visit with Sarafina and entertain the children. It's important you meet with Wallace as it's our chance to right things once and for all."

"There's six of us."

"We'll manage," Patrón replied

"What else did you want to talk about?"

Patrón looked at Sarafina, then grimaced. "We should visit in private."

"Just spit it out, Juan. We're tired."

Patrón shrugged. "Carlos has been arrested for rustling."

Sarafina gasped and grabbed her husband's hand, startling Roberto, who whimpered.

"The sheriff captured him and two other Mexicans a week ago, caught them redhanded altering brands. It doesn't look good for him."

"Where is he?" Wes asked. "In jail?"

"If you can call it that, the pit being what it is."

"Pit?" Sarafina said, astonishment in her word.

Wes explained. "It's a hole beneath the floor, nine or ten feet deep, where they toss prisoners."

As soon as he spoke, Wes felt Sarafina's grip tighten around his fingers.

"He should've listened to you, Wes," Jace said, "and gotten out of New Mexico."

"He's too stubborn," Sarafina noted.

Wes looked into his wife's face. Even in

the pale lamplight seeping from the window, he spotted tears welling in her eyes.

"You did what you could, *mi esposo.* I could ask no more of you, though I am ashamed of my brother."

Standing awkwardly before the couple, Patrón apologized. "I should've waited until I was alone with you, Wes."

"It is better I hear it from a friend than a stranger," Sarafina replied. She patted the bundle beneath her coat. "Blanca is cold. Can we go to Juan's home?"

"I'll get the horses," Jace offered.

"It's not that far," Sarafina said. "The walk might help me warm my daughter."

"Let me escort you," Patrón offered, taking her arm and steering her through the dispersing crowd.

Wes and Jace carried the boys to the horses, boosting each in the saddle, both grabbing the saddle horn to hold on as the men untied their mounts and Sarafina's. Taking the reins, the men circled the horses around and ambled toward Patrón's house, the lads giggling as they rode. When they reached their friend's home, Wes pulled the boys from the saddle and carried them inside while Jace led the animals to the corral in back.

Wes entered the house and lowered the

boys to the floor as Beatriz Patrón rushed into the front room to greet them.

"Bienvenido," Beatriz cried, then bent and flung her arms around the two bewildered boys. "My, how you have grown." She escorted them into the adjacent bedroom to find their mother, as Patrón emerged from the kitchen, holding a cup of coffee.

"This'll warm you up," he announced, offering the tin to Wes, who grabbed it and swallowed the liquid's warmth and nodded his appreciation.

When he finished a second sip of coffee, he looked at Patrón in the jaundiced lamplight. "What about the governor?"

"You're to meet him at nine o'clock in the morning. He's been asking about Bonney and how to get in touch with him. I told him you were the man who could reach Bonney. Besides, everybody knows you arranged the Kid's meeting with the Justice Department investigator last summer."

"I don't remember telling anyone about that."

"Perhaps not, but you met in Squire Wilson's house. Wilson talks."

"That's right; he's a talker, not a good trait in a justice of the peace."

"Maybe not, but he's come closer to playing the law straight than anyone else here."

"Now I've a question, Juan. Have you seen the list of thirty-seven names the governor held up for folks?"

He nodded. "I have."

"Am I on that list?"

"No, sir."

"What about Jace?"

"Same answer."

"Carlos?"

"Yes, for the murder of Sheriff Brady and Deputy Hindman, as well as multiple counts for rustling."

"I can't argue with that because I watched him shoot Hindman and caught him altering brands."

"The Kid's on the list as well for the same shooting and for the killing of Buckshot Roberts as well as assorted other crimes."

"So, the governor's taking sides with the Dolan gang, is he?"

Patrón shrugged. "I don't think so, Wes. Of the thirty-seven names, nine are Regulators like the Kid. The rest, three-quarters of them total, are House men, including Dolan and Evans. I believe the governor means what he says and will fight whatever political clout the House once had with the Santa Fe Ring."

"That's good to know," Wes said as Jace entered through the back door.

Cousins walked into the room. "The horses are tended," he announced, then snickered at Wes. "No governor's ever wanted to have anything to do with me. Fact is, they're not high on my list, not after the Texas governor refused to give me a full pardon for the time I spent in prison for a crime Jesse Evans committed. I don't care for governors."

Wes laughed. "I suspect governors don't care for troublemakers like you, either."

Patrón just shook his head. "I don't know how you two stay partners."

"It's my natural charm," Jace replied.

"And you work cheap, *partner,* but only one of us has a meeting with the territorial governor in the morning."

Ten minutes before nine o'clock, Jose Montaño welcomed Wes Bracken into his adobe home, leading him from the entrance through two rooms to a back room with a closed door. The humble man rapped on the entrance. "Governor, *Señor* Bracken, is here."

"*Gracias,* Jose, send him in."

The Mexican opened the door wide enough for Wes to pass, then shut it. Wes entered a windowless bedroom lit by two kerosene lamps. Wallace sat behind a roughhewn table on a high-backed chair, his head down as he scribbled with pen and ink on a sheet of paper beside a stack two inches thick.

Without looking up from his writing, Wallace commented. "I like a man who's early. It's a sign of respect. Have a seat, will you, Wes? Let me finish a couple paragraphs and we'll start promptly at nine."

Wes took the cane-bottomed chair opposite the governor and slid into the seat, noting the open satchel on the end of the table and the open pocket watch beside the pile of papers. He looked around the room, noting the single bed against the wall, two carpetbags on the floor beneath the bed, and the governor's coat hanging from a nail in the wall. The modest quarters held a washstand with a bowl and pitcher atop it and a slop jar beneath it.

Wallace focused on his writing, glancing occasionally at the pocket watch. Precisely at nine o'clock, he placed his pen beside his inkwell, snapped the cover shut on his timepiece, and stood up, offering his hand to Wes, who arose and shook it. "Sorry to keep you waiting, especially when I tell you I like a man who arrives early, but I have a lot to do to stay on schedule, a regimentation I picked up in the army."

Wes pointed at the papers. "I'm sure you're swamped with official business."

"True, but this is my refuge. It's a manuscript about the Holy Land. Parts of New Mexico look like I imagine the lands where Jesus walked. I'm inspired by the landscape." The governor gestured for Wes to be seated, then sat down himself. "I call the book *Ben-Hur,* and it's about a Jewish nobleman falsely accused and convicted of an attempted assassination on a Roman official before he redeems himself at the foot of the Cross on Calvary."

Wes cocked his head and studied the governor's narrow, bewhiskered face, deciding to put his cards on the table. "It sounds a lot like Billy Bonney."

Wallace pursed his lips, then spoke. "Ah, Juan Patrón told you the purpose of our meeting."

"He did, saying you needed me to get to the Kid."

"That's one way of putting it, but I prefer to think of it as getting to the truth and punishing those who have broken the law, especially in taking the lives of others. Bonney's been involved in seven or more murders by my count and has been present at most of the violence. I want to visit with the Kid about the killings, especially that of the lawyer Chapman. From what folks tell me, Bonney trusts you."

"That's what I'm told."

"Can you convince him to meet with me?"

"Perhaps, if there's a pardon at the end of the meeting."

Wallace stroked his whiskered chin. "That can be arranged if I am satisfied he'll give up his thievery and his killing."

"I'll see what I can do, but I need something else from you."

"Does it relate to Carlos Zamora?"

Wes nodded.

Wallace smiled. "Juan has told me things about you and your family."

"My brother-in-law is on your list of thirty-seven."

"And I know he's in that horrid pit that serves as a jail down the street, the same street where he ambushed a sheriff and deputy with the Kid."

"He's my wife's only living kin, a hard-headed young man that followed some wrong men and made some terrible decisions."

"Choices that could get him hanged, Wes."

Bracken nodded. "Prison time might turn him around, make him a better citizen."

"Therein's the problem," Wallace said, standing up from his desk. "New Mexico has never built a prison; it's a poor territory in many respects. We have to pay to house prisoners in penitentiaries in Arizona, Kansas, Colorado, even as far away as Nebraska. It costs the territory money we don't have." The governor studied Wes for a moment, then nodded. "If you get Bonney to meet with me, I'll do what I can for your brother-in-law."

Wes stood up from his chair. Nodding, he shook the governor's hand. "I'll give it a try."

"Have Bonney come alone to meet me."

"He'll never agree to that."

"Then you can come with him, but nobody else. Do remember this: if you can't get Bonney here, then your brother-in-law will get no help from me."

"I understand, sir. We're all obliged for you trying to straighten things out in Lincoln County, but the hatred runs deep. What's right isn't always what's legal."

A smile parted Wallace's bushy goatee. "That's what Ben-Hur learns in my novel. Good luck to you, Wes, because I need your help to restore tranquility to Lincoln County."

Bracken exited the windowless room, figuring that was the reason the governor had opted to stay with Montaño rather than

Patrón because every room in Patrón's house was lit by a window, a convenient opening for a potential assassin. Wes thanked Montaño for hosting Wallace, then exited the place and stepped onto the street, starting first for Juan's abode, then angling instead across the road to the sheriff's office and jail. He heard a whistle behind him and turned to see Jace Cousins leading two of their saddled horses to the front of Patrón's adobe so they could return to the Casey place once Wes concluded his business. Wes waved, then continued toward his intended visit with Carlos.

Wes spotted the sheriff's horse tethered outside and knew George Kimbrell would be in his office, a small adobe square, sixteen feet each way. The so-called jail was a ten-foot-deep, six-foot-diameter pit beneath the plank floor. A hinged two-foot-square trapdoor provided access to the earthen cell that smelled of dirt and sweaty bodies. Wes had seen men in the pit before and had recoiled at the conditions.

As he approached the door, it opened with Kimbrell emerging, a Winchester in his left hand. Startled by Bracken's proximity, the sheriff flinched, then smiled when he saw Wes. "Come for a family visit, Bracken?"

"If you've got the time."

267

Kimbrell nodded. "I'll make time for you. Carlos sure was mad when we caught him, kept blaming you for turning him in, said you'd threatened him a couple days earlier."

"Carlos blames me for all his mistakes."

"I've done nothing to disabuse him of that notion." Kimbrell laughed as he backed into the office and let Wes inside. The sheriff then closed the door and placed his carbine on his desk. Though the room was lit by two windows, Kimbrell picked up a lantern, struck a match, and touched it to the wick until the flame took hold. Grabbing the handle, he offered the lantern to Wes. "You'll need this to see Carlos. It gets a little dark in our cell." The sheriff snickered again. "Before I unlatch the trapdoor, I need your pistol to be on the safe side."

Wes nodded as he took the lantern with his left hand and lifted his revolver from his holster with his right. He stepped to the desk and laid the weapon on a stack of papers.

"Obliged, Bracken." The sheriff squatted by the trapdoor and unscrewed the bolt latch, removing the iron rod, lifting the door, then flipping it on its hinged back. "Hey, Carlos," the sheriff called. "You've got a visitor, your brother-in-law." As Kimbrell backed away from the opening, he motioned for Wes to take his place.

Bracken dropped to his hands and knees at the edge of the opening and lowered the lantern beneath the planks, the light casting a yellow pall on the dark earthen wall, Carlos and his compatriots shielding their eyes against the sudden illumination.

"Bastardo," Carlos growled. "You told the sheriff where we were hiding. I'll kill you for this."

"I didn't point the law your way. The sheriff will confirm that."

Kimbrell scoffed. "I'm not getting in the middle of a family dispute."

"I'll get even with you, Wes," Carlos threatened.

"You better worry about saving your own hide, rather than skinning mine. You should've cleared the territory like I warned you. Dolan and his men were using you to do their dirty work. They planned to betray you all along, once you'd altered enough brands for them. Branding's a lot harder and dirtier work than simply rustling the cattle."

Carlos pulled his hands from over his eyes and stared at Bracken. "They paid me, unlike Tunstall and McSween when I rode with them."

"You're about to pay with your life, Carlos.

They can hang you as well."

"They won't hang me for rustling cattle."

"You're forgetting about the murder charges in Brady's and Hindman's deaths."

"They can't prove anything," Carlos spat back.

"I watched you run out and shoot Hindman —"

"Will you testify to that?" Kimbrell interrupted.

Ignoring the lawman, Wes continued, "— and I'm sure others saw you as well."

Furious, Carlos spat at Wes, but the spittle only showered back on him and his two allies. Carlos wiped at his cheek. "I'll gladly hang, if it's for killing you."

"Something you better understand is that your sister and I are the only two folks in Lincoln County that give a damn about you or your worthless hide."

"You've caused all my problems, including this arrest. I'll get even one day."

Wes shook his head. "I've nothing more to say, Carlos, other than a question. Do you want Sarafina at your hanging?"

"She's welcome, but not you."

Bracken pulled the lantern from the void and reached with his free hand for the trapdoor, which he lifted on its hinges and slammed shut. He blew out the flame, then stood up and offered the lamp to the sheriff.

"He doesn't care for you," Kimbrell said as he took the lantern and sat it on the desk, then picked up Bracken's revolver and handed it to him. "It sounds, Bracken, like you did try to warn him."

As Wes slipped his Colt back in his holster, he shrugged. "He's had a rough life and doesn't know when people are trying to help him. When will Carlos head to a trial?"

"I can't say, Bracken. My job's to arrest them. After that, it depends on what the governor plans to do. He's running things now." Kimbrell paused, then changed the subject. "By the way, how's that little red-haired daughter of yours. Is she fond of her papa?"

Clenching his fists, Wes spun around and barged outside the office into the midmorning chill, which did nothing to douse his anger. He charged across the street to Patrón's house, where Jace had tethered all three of their horses for the return home.

He strode inside, startling Juan and Jace as they conversed in their chairs.

"Wes, you don't look so good," Jace observed.

Shaking his head, Bracken lied. "Carlos angered me." While that was a fib, it was easier than explaining Kimbrell's cruel remark. "Jace, would you get Sarafina and the children outside so we can leave. I want to visit with Juan for a moment. When I'm done, we're leaving."

Jace shot up from his chair and exited the room to round up Wes's family.

Bracken turned to Patrón. "Put out word among your people that I need to find the Kid, and soon. Carlos's life may depend on me scheduling Bonney to meet with the governor, just don't tell anyone that. I'll see if he's around San Patricio, but I've got to see him quick."

Patrón nodded as Jace herded Sarafina and her children through the room and out the front door, Sarafina offering a bewildered look as she passed. Beatriz Patrón followed them out to help. When the room cleared, Juan responded. "I'll do what I can, Wes. We all want Lincoln County to settle down."

The two men went outside to find Sarafina astride her horse with Blanca in her arms. Jace climbed in his saddle, yanked Luis off the ground, and sat him behind him, instructing the boy to hold his gun belt. Little Roberto raced to his father. Wes untied his reins, picked Roberto up, and mounted Charlie, sitting his son between him and the saddle horn. Without a word he turned toward home, the anger still raging through his veins at the sheriff's comment.

Sarafina soon guided her mount to his side. "What about Carlos? Won't we see him?"

Wes shook his head. "I talked to him after the governor. You shouldn't visit him in the jail, it'll just add to your burdens."

"But I want to help him," she said, "give him a little encouragement."

"Right now, the best thing we can do is find Billy Bonney. Carlos's life may depend on me convincing the Kid to meet with Governor Wallace."

Sarafina gasped.

CHAPTER 15

As first light crawled down the Hondo Valley, Wes picked up the pail from the kitchen table and headed out the back door for the barn to milk the cow. A week had passed since his meeting with the governor, and he had heard nothing from Bonney. Other than San Patricio, where he had alerted the people to send the Kid his way, Wes did not know where to look as Bonney had been known to travel north to Fort Sumner or Tascosa in the Texas Panhandle, east to John Chisum's property, and southeast to the Seven Rivers region. Finding the Kid was like chasing a ghost, and neither the law nor the army had caught him. True to his word, Governor Wallace had seen that Jesse Evans and several of his men were captured and jailed in the stockade at Fort Stanton. Wes had relished that news until he learned that James J. Dolan, while arrested with Evans, had subsequently been let go. Was Lew Wallace just another politician that acquiesced to money or political power?

Pondering that question as he opened the barn door, Wes slipped inside and aimed for the corner stall where the milk cow stood chewing cud. As he shut the door, Wes detected the crunch of steps on the barn floor. Dropping the pail, he reached for his pistol, but a quick hand grabbed his wrist. When he looked to his side, he saw two buckteeth smiling at him.

"Morning, Wes," Bonney said. "I've learned from several folks you needed to see me."

Wes felt the tension evaporate from his muscles. "Why didn't you come to the house?"

"Too many people gunning for me. I could hide my horse in the barn and even sleep the night here on a bed of hay, though I notice your supply is dwindling."

"Everyone missed a crop this year, so everything's running low, whether fodder for animals or food for folks. With spring coming, we've got to get a crop in the ground or it'll be terrible this time next year."

Bonney grinned. "I hope you didn't need me to farm your place. I ain't a sodbuster."

Wes bent and retrieved the pail. He

pointed to the corner stall. "Mind if I milk while we talk? Sarafina's daughter and the boys need milk for breakfast."

"I can listen while you milk, Wes."

The two men marched to the stall, and Wes grabbed his stool, placed it by the cow's flank, and sat down, sliding the bucket beneath the udder. Grabbing two teats, he started tugging and squeezing, drawing white strings of liquid that pinged against the metal. "You've wanted to get out of the bind you're in, Kid, and I may have a way."

"I'm listening."

"The governor hopes to meet with you and talk things over. He's especially interested in the killing of the lawyer Huston Chapman. He wants to discuss it with you."

"That ain't happening. I don't trust anybody but you anymore."

"I told Wallace you were unlikely to meet him alone. We agreed I could accompany you, if you would see him. He's staying with the Montaños in Lincoln."

Shaking his head vigorously, Bonney replied. "I'm not seeing him there. I'll agree to a visit only at night, but it must be at Squire Wilson's with you and Jace there, him standing guard and you sitting in the meeting with me."

As he milked, Wes offered an option. "The

governor seemed most concerned with the Chapman killing, maybe because it's still on everybody's mind. You should write a letter outlining your willingness to cooperate, provided a full pardon is available at the end of the line. I'll deliver the letter to Wallace. If he agrees with your conditions, I'll set up a meeting."

"Only as long as you are there to witness what is said."

"I'll be there."

Bonney nodded and walked toward his saddled horse. "I'll get a paper and pencil in San Patricio. Come morning when you milk, you'll find a letter on your milking stool. Read it and if you think it will work, deliver it. I need to ride before it gets lighter, but know I'm hiding at what's left of the old Zamora place."

"Come back the following morning after I've taken your offer to the governor, and I'll give you the day and time for the meeting."

"Any day is fine, but the time must be after dark." Bonney guided his horse out the barn door. "I'll see you in two days."

After Bonney closed the barn, Wes heard him gallop away. Ten minutes later, when he had finished milking, Wes returned to the house, entering the kitchen as Jace started coffee.

"Was that Bonney riding away?"

"Yes, sir. He'll be back overnight with a message for the governor."

"Do you think this will save the Kid?"

Wes shrugged. "Nothing ever seems to work out for Bonney in Lincoln County."

Come morning, Wes found a letter addressed to the governor atop his milking stool in the barn. He shoved it in his shirt pocket, milked the cow, and returned to the house, setting the bucket on the table and lighting a lamp. He sat down and slipped the letter from his pocket. Opening the envelop flap, he pulled out and unfolded the sheet with Bonney's handwriting.

Dear Sir: I have heard that you are interested in the death of Mr. Chapman. I know it is as a witness against those that murdered him. I could give the desired information, but I have indictments against me for things that happened in the late difficulties and am afraid to give up because my enemies would kill me. The day Mr. Chapman was murdered I was in Lincoln at the request of good citizens to meet Mr. J.J. Dolan, to meet as friends, so as to be able to lay aside our arms and go to work.

I was present when Mr. Chapman was murdered and know who did it and if it were not for those indictments I would have made it clear before now. If it is in your power to annul those indictments, I hope you will do so, so as to give me a chance to explain. Please send me an answer telling me what you can do. You can send answer by bearer. I have no wish to fight any more; indeed I have not raised an arm since your proclamation. As to my character, I refer to any of the citizens, for the majority of them are my friends and have been helping me all they could. Waiting for an answer, I remain your obedient servant,

W.H. Bonney

As Wes finished reading the letter, Jace entered the room, stretching his arms and yawning. "Is that Bonney's letter?"

Wes nodded. "He's got a surprising way with words. This should convince the governor of the Kid's sincerity."

"You forget, Wes. This is Lincoln County."

Wes Bracken knocked on the door of the Montaño house, and Jose soon appeared in the doorway. "I'm here to see the governor."

Jose shook his head. "He is not taking visi-

279

tors today. He is writing."

"Tell the governor Wes Bracken has information he requested."

"Please wait," Jose replied, disappearing inside for a moment, then returning and motioning for Wes to hurry inside. Montaño ushered Wes to the governor's room and knocked.

"Enter," answered Lew Wallace.

As Jose backed away, Wes removed his hat and stepped into the room, where Wallace sat at his makeshift desk, working on his novel. When he came to the end of his sentence, he placed his pen by the inkwell and looked up. "Success, I take it?"

"You'll be pleased." Wes reached in his pocket and extracted Bonney's letter, offering it to the governor. "He's willing to meet as long as it's at night at Squire Wilson's home, and he is granted a pardon."

A smile worked its way through Wallace's bushy goatee as he took the letter, pulled it from the envelope, and read the Kid's offer. When he finished, he glanced up, surprise in his eyes. "Bonney's more literate than I was expecting. This is in his own hand, is it not?"

"He's a smart kid and likable, unless you lie to him or don't live up to your word."

"Good! Perhaps we can deal with him

after all." Wallace lifted the sheet he had been writing on from a thin stack of paper and blew on it to dry the ink. "Sometimes I need to work on my novel just to clear my head of all the mischief in Lincoln County." Placing the page aside, he picked up his pen, dipped it in the inkwell, and attacked a clean page.

Wes watched as he dated the missive March 15, 1879, and addressed it to W.H. Bonney. The governor wrote two paragraphs, signing it with his name, then lifted the sheet and blew on the ink. He read the letter to himself, then glanced at Wes and started reading the text aloud.

"Come to the house of old Squire Wilson at nine o'clock next Monday night with the bearer of this letter. Follow along the foot of the mountain south of town, come in on that side, and knock on the east door. I have authority to exempt you from prosecution, if you will testify to what you say you know about the Chapman killing. The object of the meeting is to arrange the matter in a way to make your life safe. To do that, the utmost secrecy is to be used. Don't tell anybody — not a living soul — where you are coming or the object. If you could trust Jesse Evans, you can trust me. Lew Wallace, governor."

Wes nodded. "The words should win him over, but understand that the night the lawyer died, Bonney and other Regulators met with Jimmy Dolan, Jesse Evans, and others. They vowed not to testify against each other in any legal proceedings. Anyone who broke that pact was to be killed by the others. This will endanger the Kid, so he must be able to trust you."

"He has no other options if he is to ever escape these troubles."

"I understand, sir, but he's been betrayed by so many."

"Nothing's certain in Lincoln County, Wes. You should know that by now. I'm trying to clear up this mess as ordered by President Hayes, and I'm his only chance at redemption. I'll see you both Monday night at Squire Wilson's. Good day, sir." Wallace picked up the manuscript page and his pen, then resumed writing.

Wes turned, pulled his hat over his head, and stepped into the hall where Jose escorted him outside. *"Gracias,"* Wes told Jose as he mounted Charlie and headed east, passing Juan Patrón's house without stopping as he didn't care to explain his town business to his friend. Wes would meet Bonney in the morning as planned and later escort him to Lincoln to meet Governor Lew Wallace.

Rather than traveling by road, the trio had ridden over the mountains south of Lincoln to approach the town. They reached the peak by dusk and inched their way down the slope in the darkness. Wes and Bonney dismounted in Squire Wilson's apple orchard, tying their mounts, as Jace rode to the rendezvous site. One rider would draw less attention than three. After circling the house, Jace motioned everything was clear. Bonney pulled his Winchester from his saddle scabbard and lifted his pistol from his holster, then advanced behind Wes. At Wilson's door, Wes knocked three times, and the door cracked, then swung open. There stood the aging Squire Wilson, and behind him sat the governor in a ball of yellow light from the coal oil lamp on his table. Wes entered, looked around, then motioned Bonney inside. The Kid came in, his lips tight, his face drawn until he looked around the room and found no surprises. He slipped his revolver into his holster.

Bonney and Wallace eyed each other, then the governor motioned for him to take a seat opposite him at the table. Wes shut the door and latched it as he and Wilson stood by the back wall. The governor eyed the Kid sternly, neither standing nor offering to shake the youth's hand.

"So, you're the cause of so much trouble in Lincoln County," Wallace mused.

"Trouble found me. I didn't go looking for it," Bonney responded. "If Dolan and his men hadn't murdered John Tunstall, none of the others would've died. Nothing's been done about the Englishman's killing."

"I'm interested in the killing of Huston Chapman, the lawyer murdered last month on the street outside. Did you witness it?"

"I did. Jimmy Dolan fired first and then Jesse Evans."

"Aren't Dolan and Evans your sworn enemies?"

"They are or were. We're all tired of running and living on the run. We wanted to patch things up and go on with our lives. We met for a truce, but they had been drinking before we made our pact and wanted to celebrate after we agreed to it. As we headed to Dolan's saloon, we encountered Chapman. That's when they shot him. He was unarmed."

Wallace nodded. "Will you testify to that in a court of law?"

"I will, as long as I'm protected and

receive a full pardon."

"My powers as governor allow me to pardon you, but not until you testify as you've stated here tonight. Why are you coming forward now, Bonney?"

"I'm tuckered out from running, and I didn't feel safe talking to the law as long as Jesse Evans was on the loose. He'd kill me for breaking the agreement. I don't think Dolan and most of the rest of them are man enough to try. With Evans in the stockade, I feel safer."

"You know we'll have to arrest you, do you not?"

Bonney nodded. "I don't like it, but if that's what it takes to walk clear of these troubles, that's what I'll do, on one condition. I don't want to be thrown in the pit they use for a jail here."

Wallace studied Bonney. "Here's what I propose: You submit to a fake arrest by Sheriff Kimbrell. I may have to keep you in the pit a day or two, but I'll work something out, maybe at Fort Stanton."

"No, sir, I won't go to Fort Stanton," Bonney replied. "The army's favored Dolan and his gang through all these troubles."

"I'll figure something out," Wallace said.

Wes stepped forward. "Perhaps the Kid could stay with Juan Patrón."

Wallace stroked his beard as he looked at Bracken. "That might work." Turning to Bonney, he continued. "Remain in custody until the grand jury meets so you can provide evidence, then testify in the trial against the murderers. Once that's done, I'll let you go scot-free with a pardon in your pocket for all your misdeeds."

Bonney sighed, then smiled and nodded.

"Then we're agreed, yes?"

"Yes, sir."

"Be on your way before word gets out you're in town. I'll get word to Wes what you need to do next."

The Kid arose, smiling and extending his hand. "Thank you, sir."

The governor ignored his handshake offer. "Get going, Bonney."

The Kid spun around and grabbed Bracken's hand. "Thank you, Wes. Maybe now I can lead a regular life."

"You deserve a break, Bonney. Now get out of here, so I can arrange with the governor what happens next."

Bonney unlatched and opened the door, then darted outside for his horse. Wilson closed the door behind him.

"I'll send instructions to you through Juan Patrón and you can pass them to Bonney," Wallace said.

Wes eyed the governor. "Besides the Kid, there's the matter of my brother-in-law, Carlos Zamora. You agreed to pardon him if I brought Bonney to meet with you."

"I hadn't forgotten, but I can't pardon Carlos Zamora. He's a murderer like the Kid."

"But you just agreed to pardon Bonney. He's been involved in more deaths than Carlos."

The governor hesitated.

Then Wes shook his head. "You don't really intend to pardon Bonney, do you?"

Wallace ignored the question. "What I'll do for you, Wes, is this. I'll have the murder charges dropped against Carlos, provided he pleads guilty to rustling and serves two to three years in prison. Without a pardon, the charges can be refiled against him later if he resumes his bad ways. Maybe that will help keep him straight."

Wes felt betrayed, but he could read Wallace's piercing eyes and knew he must take the offer for Carlos. "I'll have my wife convince him to accept the deal. What about Bonney? Do you intend to pardon him or not?"

Wallace bit his lip, then shrugged. "I don't know. He is a murderer. I will assure you one thing, Wes. If he doesn't turn himself in when I send the sheriff for him, he will never get a pardon. Even if I'm undecided, I'm his only option if he ever hopes to clear himself. I'll send instructions by Juan Patrón tomorrow or the next day. That's all I have to say now."

"You just promised him a pardon, that he would walk scot-free for all his misdeeds."

"I have the prerogative to change my mind. You best drop the matter before I revoke my agreement with you on Carlos."

"Yes, sir." Wes spun around and walked out, slamming the door behind him.

Jace Cousins dismounted and walked with Bracken back to the orchard to get Bracken's stallion.

"Trouble?" Jace asked.

"The Kid believes the governor promised him a pardon."

"Well, did he?"

"He made the Kid think so, but Bonney's no better off than before the meeting."

Jace whistled. "Lincoln County."

When Wes went out the next morning to milk the cow, he found Bonney and his horse inside the barn. "I got the best night's sleep I've had in months," he announced. "I can almost feel that pardon in my pocket now."

"Stay wary, Kid, because things could go wrong."

"But I've got the governor's word."

"You do, Bonney, but remember he's still a politician. After you left, he told me he would send Juan Patrón with instructions on surrendering to the sheriff."

"It'll be good to get even with Dolan and Evans." Bonney grinned as Wes moved to the milk cow, picked up his stool, and started milking, uncertain if he was betraying the Kid by not telling him further details of his subsequent conversation with the governor.

"Leave your horse in the barn for the day, Kid, but take your weapons and ammunition to the gristmill. It's got thicker walls than the barn if you have to make a stand."

Bonney grinned like he'd been caught cheating at cards.

"What's so funny, Kid?"

"One of my pals is hiding there now." Bonney laughed.

"O'Folliard?"

"Yep, Tom intends to surrender with me and see if he can't go on with his life."

"There's no guarantee the governor will offer Tom a deal."

"He's got nothing to lose, not having any family and all, so he'll risk it."

Wes finished the milking and stood up, grabbing the pail and moving the stool aside. "Grab your tin and you can have a cup of warm milk for breakfast."

"I'm hungry enough these days to even drink cow juice." Bonney stepped to his horse and extracted a coffee tin from his saddlebags. He dipped it in the bucket and raised it to his lips, sipping it and nodding his approval.

"Fill your cup again and take it to Tom in case he's missed breakfast. Then both of you stay hidden until nightfall."

Bonney dipped his tin in the pail again and thanked Wes, then grabbed his Winchester from his saddle scabbard and slipped outside in the emerging light of day. Wes returned to the house, entering the back door as Jace poured a cup of coffee.

"Morning, Wes," Jace offered, then sipped on his hot drink.

"We've got company."

Jace reached for his revolver.

Wes sat the milk pail on the table. "It's the Kid and O'Folliard. They're hiding out in the mill until we get word from the governor what he's to do next."

"When will that be?"

"Whenever Juan Patrón shows up."

"Good old Juan. He always seems to be in

the middle of things."

"He's one we can trust."

From the bedroom came the cry of Blanca, and Wes knew Sarafina would soon drag into the kitchen once she nursed the baby and put her back to sleep. Wes and his partner discussed all the chores they needed to accomplish as warm weather approached. The list was staggering with all the farm and ranch tasks necessary to make a crop and to calve cattle, especially since they could not trust their Anglo neighbors not to put their own brand on Mirror B stock.

When Sarafina walked in, she rubbed her eyes. She wore her nightgown and carried her revolver on the leather thong over her shoulder. "How did it go last night with the governor?"

Wes explained to his wife the governor's refusal to pardon Carlos, even though Wes had brought the Kid to meet with him as promised. Instead, he explained, Wallace agreed to see that the murder charge was dropped, though it could be refiled later, if Carlos pled guilty to rustling and served two to three years in prison outside the territory.

Sarafina grimaced.

"It was the best I could do for him, Sarafina."

"I know, and he doesn't deserve that much the way he has treated you, but he's still my brother. How did it go for Billy?"

"You should know he and his friend Tom O'Folliard are hiding out in the mill, so don't shoot if you see one of them."

She patted the revolver at her side, then nodded.

"The governor offered a pardon if Bonney identified and testified against the men that murdered Chapman, but I don't know if he's serious because he wouldn't confirm it to me once the Kid left. Juan Patrón will bring us instructions on what Bonney's to do next."

"Do you believe our troubles are ending?"

Wes shrugged. "I can't say for sure, but I doubt it. With so many of the outlaws in jail like Jesse Evans —"

Sarafina clutched her throat, and Wes immediately realized he should never have mentioned her assailant's name.

Jace jumped up from his chair. "I'll go check the henhouse for eggs."

Wes stepped to his wife and wrapped his arms around her. "I'm sorry," he said.

She nestled into his embrace.

"What I meant to say was our major worry is Carlos now. I got the best deal I could for him, but he'll never accept it if I present it to him."

"I am ashamed he is so ungrateful."

"It's up to you Sarafina to offer the arrangement to him and convince him to accept the deal. Otherwise, he might hang for the deputy's death. He has no defense for that."

"He is so embittered, I am uncertain he will even listen to me, his only sister."

Wes kissed her on the cheek. "Once you see the conditions he's jailed in, you'll realize he might do anything to get out of that hole in the ground. Jace survived prison in Texas, you remember. Carlos can do it. Three years in exchange for his life is a good deal."

"When can I visit him?"

"Let's wait until Juan Patrón brings instructions from the governor. Then we'll decide."

"Do you know when he's coming?"

"Today or tomorrow was what Wallace promised."

Sarafina sighed. "I want this to end so I no longer must carry this gun everywhere."

"All the decent folk in Lincoln County feel that way," Wes answered to reassure his wife.

CHAPTER 16

The next afternoon Juan Patrón arrived on horseback, grim-faced and with his Winchester cradled in his arm. Jace whistled to Wes, who was sharpening his ax blade. Wes put aside his file and wiped his hands on his britches before walking out to greet his Lincoln friend. Looking toward the mill, he saw Bonney peeking out the second-floor window. Turning to Jace, Wes suggested he inform Bonney and O'Folliard that Juan was the governor's messenger. Jace nodded and ambled away while Wes strode out to meet the visitor.

Patrón drew up at the front door and dismounted, tying his gelding to the hitching post as Wes welcomed his friend. "Good to see you, Juan," he called, but his guest never smiled, nor did he slip the Winchester back in the saddle boot. The guest stood there, glancing around. "Do you bring word from the governor?"

Looking over his shoulder, Patrón nodded. "I carry news both from Lincoln and Fort Stanton, but Jace needs to hear it as well."

Wes retreated to the corner of the house, whistled to get Jace's attention, and waved him over. As Jace trotted up, Wes returned to Patrón. "Has the governor gone back on his word?"

Patrón shrugged. "I don't know what he promised."

"About pardoning Bonney?"

"He never mentioned a pardon, merely an agreement for Bonney to turn himself in, but there's bad news as well."

Jace jogged up beside Wes and nodded to Patrón. "Good to see you, Juan."

"The governor wants Bonney to surrender tomorrow to Sheriff Kimbrell."

Wes nodded. "I expected that."

Patrón grimaced. "What nobody anticipated, though, was Jesse Evans and Billy Campbell escaping from Fort Stanton."

"Damn," Wes sighed. "I can't figure how this will settle with the Kid. He was fine with surrendering when Jesse was in custody because he knew Evans couldn't get to him. I'm doubtful now."

Patrón tapped the barrel of his carbine. "That's why I'm carrying my Winchester.

Word is Jesse intends to even some scores." He paused. "Both your names came up, him talking in the stockade about killing both of you on sight when he got out."

"How'd he escape?" Jace asked.

"The army's always favored the Dolan faction, but that changed when Wallace had Colonel Dudley replaced. Evidently, there's a soldier that deserted at the same time Evans and Campbell escaped, and they think he helped them."

Wes's mind roiled with the news and what to do next for the Kid and his own family. "Would you like a cup of coffee, Juan? Jace and I need to visit for a minute."

"Coffee'd be good."

Opening the front door, Wes called Sarafina, announcing the visitor and asking her to offer Juan a cup of coffee. Patrón walked inside. "Give us about ten minutes, Juan."

Wes turned to Jace, but before he could speak, his partner spat out a question.

"Are you thinking what I'm thinking?"

"About going after Jesse and settling this once and for all?" Wes replied.

"That's exactly what I intended to propose."

"I'm ready to end it, Jace, one way or another, but there's more to it than that. We've got Sarafina and the children to think about, plus the Kid and O'Folliard. I don't want Juan to find out the Kid's hiding here as word could get out and draw Jesse Evans to our place. Sarafina could not abide that."

"Perhaps she could stay with Patrón while we tracked down Jesse. There'll be no one to watch after the place or milk the cow, but at least we wouldn't worry while we track Evans."

Nodding he liked the idea, Wes tugged at his ear as he pondered how to handle the Kid's situation. "I don't want to talk to Bonney while Juan is here because I fear people would find out we've been hiding him." The two men discussed their options until Juan returned, holding his Winchester with his left hand and tipping a tin of coffee to his lips with his right.

Emptying the cup, he handed it to Wes. "Tell Sarafina thanks again for her hospitality. Do you have a message for the governor?"

"The Kid's worried Wallace won't live up to his end of the agreement to pardon him. I've got to talk to the Kid and see if he intends to go through with it, since there's some doubt about the pardon. He's running with Tom O'Folliard, who's wants the same deal the Kid got. That complicates matters, but if Wallace agreed, it might help bring Bonney in without a fight."

Patrón shrugged. "I'm his messenger. I can't promise what he'll do with O'Folliard."

"I'll get word to the Kid and if he agrees to surrender, he'll either be at my place mid-afternoon tomorrow or at the abandoned Zamora farm about a mile this side of San Patricio. I can't say which because I don't know or if he'll even be there, but send the sheriff anyway."

"I'll inform the governor." Patrón turned for his gelding, but Wes grabbed his arm.

"One other thing, Juan. Could you ride out with the sheriff in your buckboard tomorrow, then take Sarafina and the kids to stay with you and Beatriz? They may be in danger here now that Jesse's loose again."

Patrón shook his head. "I can't —"

Wes flinched with disappointment as Patrón had always been a friend he could count on.

"The governor's appointed me to lead a posse after Evans and Campbell. Once I get back to Lincoln, we're searching for Evans in the mountains south of Fort Stanton."

Wes frowned.

"What I can do," Patrón continued, "is have Beatriz bring the buckboard over with the sheriff and return with them to Lincoln.

It'll be safer for all."

"Don't forget to take the milk cow," Jace suggested.

Patrón stared from Jace back to Wes. "Sounds like you two aren't planning to stay here."

"We're going hunting," Wes answered.

"For Jesse Evans?" Patrón asked.

The two partners grimaced.

Patrón nodded as he mounted his horse. "Good luck. I hope you find him first."

"Be careful, Juan," Wes replied as the governor's emissary started back to Lincoln.

Bracken and Cousins watched him disappear down the road, then returned to their chores for a half hour in case anyone had been spying on Patrón and them. After thirty minutes, both men ambled to the gristmill and climbed up to the second level where Bonney and O'Folliard stood watch over the surrounding country.

"It looked like Juan Patrón," Bonney noted.

"Yep. He was representing the governor, but something's changed."

"No pardon?" Bonney gasped.

"Jesse Evans has escaped and vowed to kill all of us, so I don't know if you still want to go through with this."

Bonney stroked his chin. "I don't mind

dying in a fight when I'm armed and can protect myself, but I don't intend to be shot down unarmed like a mangy dog."

"I'm confounded what to tell you, Kid, as I question if Wallace will keep his word."

"He said so himself. He told me I could go scot-free with a pardon in my pocket. You were there. You heard him."

Wes nodded. "I did."

"And he didn't have to let us know Jesse Evans escaped," Bonney continued. "He may be the only man of authority I can trust in Lincoln County."

Jace turned to O'Folliard. "You haven't spoken, Tom."

"I'm with Billy, today and tomorrow."

"So both of you are ready to surrender and take your chances?"

Bonney and O'Folliard nodded.

"I told Juan that I had to visit with you about it, but if you planned to turn yourselves in tomorrow, you would either be here midafternoon or at the abandoned Zamora place."

"We'll be at the Zamora place," Bonney answered. "Don't want to draw any more suspicions to you or your family, Wes. We'll get our horses after dark and leave, maybe visit San Patricio and spend the night there before hiding out for the rendezvous with the sheriff."

Jace grinned. "If you run into Jesse Evans, give him our regards."

"A posse is heading out after Evans today," Wes informed the Kid, "and as soon as Jace and I see you safely in custody, we're going after him too."

"Good hunting. Put an extra bullet in him for me," Bonney replied.

When the meeting concluded, Wes and Jace returned to their chores until suppertime when they found Luis and Roberto eating at the table while Blanca rested in Sarafina's left arm as her mother's right hand stirred a pot of stew on the stove.

Sarafina turned "Tell me what's worrying Juan. He was solemn and kept his Winchester at his side."

Wes swallowed hard. "A mean man escaped from the Fort Stanton stockade."

"Es él, el mismo diablo," she gasped, dropping the spoon and clutching her throat.

"Yes, the devil himself is running free. Jace and I have vowed to find and kill him."

"But the spring planting and me and the kids."

"We can't put in crops with the threat of him hanging over our heads. We intend to track him down and end the threats."

"I don't know what's worse, him escap-

301

ing, you endangering yourselves to kill him, or me and the little ones being left here alone."

Wes stepped to his wife and put his arm around her shoulder, careful not to disturb Blanca, who slept peacefully in her mother's tender grasp. "I have thought of that, and Beatriz Patrón will ride out tomorrow and take you to stay at her place until we resolve this."

Sarafina seemed relieved and troubled. "The last time we abandoned our home, they burned it and slaughtered our horses."

"I'd rather lose them than you and the boys," Wes answered.

His wife looked up at him with her dark, anguished eyes.

"You and the children," he corrected, anxious to change the subject. "You should carry your pistol and I will send a carbine and shotgun with you. Besides protecting the children, there's one other thing you must do in Lincoln."

"And what is that?"

"Convince Carlos to accept the deal I arranged with the governor. It can keep him off the gallows. Maybe time in prison will slap some sense in his stubborn head."

"Will he even listen to me, *mi esposo*?"

"He'll listen to you before he'll put stock

302

in anything I say. Don't tell him I arranged the deal, as he'd rather hang than accept something I had a hand in."

"I shall try."

Wes leaned over and kissed his wife on the cheek, then joined Jace and the boys at the table for supper.

Standing by his and Jace's saddled horses, Wes watched Sheriff George Kimbrell and his posse approach on the road, then turn down the trail leading to their house. Beatriz Patrón followed the lawmen in her buckboard. The sheriff was right on time, so Wes saved him a few minutes by mounting Charlie and riding out to meet him. The lawman held up his arm and stopped the eight men accompanying him. As Wes neared, Kimbrell eyed his sorrel and rig, taking in the carbine, the two canteens, the thick bedroll, bulging saddlebags, and two burlap supply bags straddling the horse's rump. Wes reined up in the posse's front as Beatriz directed the buckboard around the parlay and continued on to fetch Sarafina and the children.

"You heading somewhere, Bracken?" Kimbrell asked.

"Hunting."

The sheriff pointed to the house. "Looks

like Cousins is going as well. He's saddled up and heavy with gear."

"We're running low on provisions and need to find game."

"You sure you aren't hunting men?"

Wes grinned. "That's your job."

"Then where is he? Where's Bonney? I was told he would be here."

"The message I sent was he would either be here or at the abandoned Zamora place this side of San Patricio. Last time I talked to the Kid, he said that's where he'd surrender as agreed. I doubt you'll have any trouble."

"Then why are you rigged up like you're anticipating it."

"This is Lincoln County, Sheriff. Even if you don't expect trouble, it's always waiting around the bend."

"If the Kid ain't there, I'm coming back for you, Bracken."

"He said he'd be there along with Tom O'Folliard. You shouldn't have any trouble. I'll be here when you return, and I'm obliged for you letting Beatriz ride out with you and escorting my family to town."

"Women and children shouldn't suffer for men's wrongs." Kimbrell yanked the reins on his horse and turned around, crying,

"Let's head for San Patricio and find Bonney."

Wes rode Charlie to the house, just as Sarafina emerged to welcome and thank Beatriz for her help. The two women marched inside as Wes dismounted.

"What did the sheriff have to say?" Jace asked.

"Nothing of note, other than he suspected you and I were up to no good, especially with our horses loaded." Wes tied Charlie to the hitching post.

"It'll take a spell to find Jesse. The longer it takes, the fewer the supplies, the lighter our load."

"And, the weaker our mounts, Jace."

"If there's a chase, we won't be able to run him down, not if he steals fresh mounts."

Wes nodded. "But first we have to find him."

The men went inside to help carry bedding out to the buckboard.

"So you're searching for Jesse Evans like Juan?" Beatriz asked.

"We are, but don't tell the sheriff," Wes instructed.

She squeezed a load of blankets into the buckboard. "I don't understand why the governor sent Juan and his Mexican friends rather than the sheriff."

"I don't know that Wallace trusts Kimbrell, but he has faith in Juan."

"Honest men wind up dead in Lincoln. Beyond that, this county is hard on women and horses."

"Change will come, and killing Jesse Evans will be a good start."

"If we live to see it, Wes, and as long as my husband isn't killed or you or Jace die either." She turned and walked inside.

"I never considered how hard this was on the women," Jace said. "It's a damn shame." He shrugged. "I'll fetch the milk cow and Sarafina's gelding." He ambled off as Wes went inside.

Wes saw Sarafina in her rocker, nursing Blanca. "I am worried for you," Sarafina said. "I'd be lost without you, *mi esposo*."

"You lost one husband, and you'd attract another."

"Maybe," she answered, "but I could never find another you."

She looked from her husband to her daughter and smiled.

Wes studied the infant, who dozed with a smile on her lips, but the fuzz of red hair reminded him of Jesse Evans. He frowned. Sarafina glanced up, beaming at her spouse. "When a sleeping baby smiles, it means she is talking with the angels."

"Maybe so," Wes said, knowing his answer was unconvincing as he could not escape his belief the devil spawned this baby girl.

"You will come to love her one day, *mi esposo*. I know you will."

Ignoring the comment, Wes stepped to the counter that had served the Casey store. He pulled out a carbine and the double-barreled shotgun, which he loaded for his wife. "You should take these with you, in case you need them. I don't know how long we'll be away."

"I will manage provided you are not gone forever."

Picking up the two weapons, Wes stepped around the counter and planted a kiss on his wife's forehead, then walked outside and put the carbine and shotgun on the wagon floorboard. As he returned inside, he asked Sarafina, "You have your pistol?" Then he saw the leather thong over her right shoulder.

She nodded. "It is under the baby."

What an uncivilized country, Wes thought, that a woman should have to keep her gun beneath her sleeping infant. "You shouldn't have any problems riding to Lincoln with the sheriff, but keep your gun within reach. I suspect we've about an hour before the posse returns, so be ready to leave as soon as we spot them up the road."

Wes strode into the kitchen and patted both of his sons on the head as they snacked on tortillas before the trip. They looked up and grinned with tortilla-filled mouths. "You boys behave while you are with Aunt Beatriz and Uncle Juan and do what your mother says." Both nodded, more interested in their tortillas than their dad's instructions.

"They're good boys, like their father," Beatriz said. "We'll have fun."

"Will there be enough room if the governor keeps Bonney and O'Folliard at your house like he promised?"

Beatriz nodded. "We'll make do, and the governor says we'll earn a dollar a day for keeping the prisoners. We can use the money, times being so hard."

"One day, I'll repay both you and Juan for your courtesies to my family," Wes answered.

"You are dependable friends; that is payment enough for now."

Wes smiled. "If you'd be ready in about forty-five minutes, I want to make sure your wagon is rolling when we see the posse returning from San Patricio."

"*Sí*," Beatriz replied

Wes stepped out the back door and studied the place, then marched to the chicken coop. He opened the cage and let the birds wander out. With no one to feed them, he would have to let them range free and hope they survived the varmints for however long it took him and Jace to find Evans. After walking about and shaking his head at all the chores that still needed completing before planting began, Wes returned to the front of the house where Jace stood.

"They'll be back anytime now," Jace offered. "You think Bonney and O'Folliard will be with them?"

"Can't say for certain, but I suspect so. The Kid's ready to stop running."

Jace pointed westward. "There they come. Looks like more riders than before."

Wes scurried into the house. "They're approaching," he told Sarafina as he picked up two burlap bags with clothes and other needs and toted them outside to the buckboard. After tossing them in the back, he herded Sarafina, Beatriz, and the boys out, holding Blanca as his wife stepped onto a wheel rung and into the seat. Wes looked down at the infant, who was still smiling in her sleep. He handed the baby to Sarafina, who bent and kissed his cheek.

"Be careful," she implored.

Nodding, he picked up Roberto first and

placed him in the back of the buckboard, grabbing Luis next and sitting him beside his brother as Jace helped Beatriz take her seat and the reins. The boys settled on the blankets piled in the buckboard as Jace checked that the milk cow and Sarafina's gelding were securely tethered to the back. The boys jabbered to the animals.

Once Beatriz took the reins, she turned the wagon and headed up the trail to intersect the returning posse. As the buckboard lurched up the trail, Wes and Jace mounted, looked at one another, nodded, nudged their horses in the flank, and trotted past the conveyance to meet the lawmen.

Wes saw the Kid and O'Folliard riding with the lawmen and questioned whether to be optimistic or skeptical for Bonney. As the partners neared the posse, Bonney lifted his hands above his head to show that they were bound. He seemed as proud as a boy with a new puppy.

"They caught me, Wes," he called. "I'm done running as long as the law treats me square."

"Glad to hear it," Wes answered as he fell in beside Kimbrell. "Any problems?"

The sheriff shook his head. "Easiest arrest I've ever made. Thanks for convincing the Kid to give it up."

"It was his idea. He's tired of living on the owl hoot trail. And I'm obliged for you watching after my family on the way to Lincoln. These are dangerous times."

Kimbrell studied Jace, then looked back at Wes. "So you're going hunting, are you?"

"Seems the right thing to do with the family safe."

"What game are you hunting? It wouldn't be Jesse Evans, would it?"

"Gracious no, Sheriff. That's your job."

Wes reined his horse about and pointed him toward San Patricio.

"Come on, Jace," he cried, "we've game to find." The two men galloped westward.

CHAPTER 17

As they advanced along the Rio Ruidoso toward San Patricio, their mounts at a trot, Wes Bracken and Jace Cousins pulled their long guns from their saddle scabbards and rode alert to the dangers that grew the deeper they went into the mountains. With good luck, they would surprise Jesse Evans and kill him. With bad luck, he could ambush them. Had the army and civil authorities kept him in the stockade for his crimes, including murder and theft of government mules and horses, Wes and his partner might have been at the Casey place preparing for the spring planting. The injustice pricked Wes's mind with bitterness, especially the assault on his wife with the resulting red-haired daughter. It galled him that he and Jace had to do what the law would not.

The pair stopped at the cantina in San Patricio, questioning the proprietor and the handful of patrons if they had seen or heard anything about Jesse Evans. *"Muy malo,"* answered the Mexican, crossing himself over his chest and responding no one had spotted the bandit recently. The partners mounted and rode to each house where they knew residents, inquiring if anyone had information about Evans. Each man and woman frowned at the mention of his name, then smiled when Wes said he intended to bring the outlaw to justice.

"Buena suerte" or *"Que Dios ande contigo,"* they replied. Their wishes of good luck and that God ride with them confirmed to Wes and Jace that they were doing the right thing, even if it was unlawful. From San Patricio the two man-hunters continued west along the Rio Ruidoso. Shortly after he had arrived in Lincoln County six years earlier from Arkansas, Wes had first traversed this trail to haul timber from the mountains for fence posts on the Mirror B. In those days he had been naïve to the ways of Lincoln County and had actually ridden with Jesse Evans and his two companions — later killed by Jace — to dispatch a band of Mexican horse thieves. Back then, Evans was riding for John Chisum while stealing the cattle baron's beeves and horses. Word was the great cattleman had put a quiet

bounty on Evans's head, but Chisum was too clever to publicly state such a reward. While the county's honest folks despised the thief, the law had for years looked the other way, likely profiting from his misdeeds

Near dusk Bracken and Cousins reached Dowlin's Mill, some twenty miles upriver from San Patricio. Operated by Paul Dowlin and four hands, the mill sawed timber into lumber and provided a small store with limited staples and hardware. Though the venture did modest business, Dowlin survived on the government contracts meeting the lumber needs of Fort Stanton and the Mescalero Apache Reservation south of his place. The political powers had not tried to hone in on the lumber commerce as it required too much work, compared to rustling cattle that came cheap and could actually walk to the market, unlike Dowlin's finished wood.

Approaching the mill, Wes called out. "Hello, the store. Friends coming in." Drawing up outside the wooden structure, he heard the creak of the waterwheel turning in the babbling waters of the Ruidoso. The peaceful noise reminded Wes of the tranquility he sought for his family and for Lincoln County. As he and Jace drew up in front of the building, put their long guns in

314

their scabbards, and dismounted, the door opened slowly, the barrel of a shotgun emerging first, its two malevolent eyes pointed at them. "State your names and lift your hats," came a voice Wes recognized as Paul Dowlin's.

"This is Wes Bracken with my partner, Jace Cousins." He removed his hat, as did Jace.

The scattergun tilted to the ground, and the door swung open, Dowlin exiting with a sheepish smile on his face. "That's no way to greet friends, I know, but not everybody that's stopped by for the last week has been cordial."

"Sorry to hear that, Paul," Wes said, pulling his headgear back on his head and stepping to the door to shake Dowlin's hand.

The mill owner pumped Bracken's hand, then greeted Jace with a hearty shake.

"Sounds like things haven't been going well for you, Paul," Wes said as the three men stepped inside.

"Yeah, last night, three desperadoes visited us."

Wes shot a quick gaze at Jace, then nodded at Dowlin. "One of them wouldn't have been Jesse Evans, would it?"

Dowlin nodded. "The bastard."

"He escaped the stockade at Fort Stanton," Wes replied.

"The umpteenth time he's slipped through the hands of the law," Jace added.

"Somebody ought to do something about it," Dowlin answered.

Wes and Jace grinned.

A sly smile worked its way across Dowlin's lips. "That's what you two are up to."

Evading a direct answer, Wes answered, "We're doing a little hunting, hoping to find plentiful game in the mountains."

"Well, boys, make yourself comfortable and join us for a bite of supper." Dowlin flung his arm around Wes and guided him through the darkened store to the kitchen where four hands sat eating fried bacon and boiled potatoes by lamplight. "Leave some for our visitors," Dowlin ordered, drawing groans.

"We'll manage, boys, so eat up," Wes said, receiving a displeased glance from his partner. "What we're starving for is information on your three visitors last night."

Picking up a fried slice of bacon and pointing it at Wes, a gray-bearded worker said, "They sure weren't three wise men, more like three worried men."

"I'm listening," Wes answered.

"From what I overheard of their whispering, they were planning on spending a day or so on the reservation so they could steal fresh horses, before splitting up so they'd be harder to track. The redheaded was called Jesse, likely Jesse Evans. The other two were Billy and Tex or Jack."

Wes nodded to Jace that the trio was indeed Jesse Evans, Billy Campbell, and the soldier who helped them escape.

"What worried the trio?" Jace asked.

"Guns and horses," said a mill hand wearing a red-checked bandanna around his neck. "They feared running out of bullets or their horses giving out on them."

Dowlin nodded. "They begged me for ammunition and threatened me when I told them I didn't sell bullets to anyone. I keep all I have locked and hidden to defend what's mine."

The gray-bearded fellow bobbed his head. "Best I could tell from all their whispering, Jack was heading to El Paso and Billy to Seven Rivers. Seemed Jesse was intent on skedaddling to Texas once he assassinated two old boys in the Hondo Valley."

Wes nodded at the diners. "Those two would be us."

The quartet at the table grimaced, then froze at the blast of a gunshot outside.

Bracken and Cousins yanked their pistols from their holsters and bolted to the front room, Dowlin behind them, grabbing his shotgun, unlatching the door, and sliding the barrel out.

Wes whispered to Jace. "Let's slip out the back and around the side so we can fight." Both men retreated through the kitchen, exited, and split up, with Wes heading to the east side of the house, Jace to the west in the growing gloom.

"State your business," Dowlin yelled.

"We mean no harm," came a voice Wes had heard before, but it took a moment to place. "We're the law, duly authorized by the governor."

Then Wes realized it was Juan Patrón speaking, though he could barely make him out.

"If you meant no trouble, why did you fire your guns?" Dowlin shouted.

"There's fifteen of us. We didn't care to arrive unannounced after dark."

"Why didn't you yell?" Dowlin continued.

"We did, but got no answer. Your place looked dark."

Confirming the voice was indeed that of Patrón, Wes stepped around the side of the house. "Is that you, Juan?"

"It is. Is that you, Wes Bracken?"

"You nailed it, Juan." Wes marched to the front door and pushed the barrel of Dowlin's shotgun toward the ground. "I can vouch for Juan and whoever rides with him," he informed the mill owner.

Dowlin stepped outside as Jace joined them from the opposite end of the building. The riders advanced cautiously, like men unaccustomed to tracking desperadoes, with Patrón two horse lengths ahead of his posse.

Drawing up beside Bracken's and Cousins's mounts, Patrón slid out of his saddle and landed stiffly on the ground. "I didn't expect to find you two here."

"Same for us," Wes answered.

"We got a slow start, but we've tracked them from Fort Stanton, though we lost their trail for a spell, and it took half a day to pick it up," Juan said.

"You found it," Jace announced, "because they were here last night."

"With a day's lead on us, we'll never catch them," Juan sighed.

"Don't be so sure," Wes said, pointing to Dowlin. "Paul and his hands say they're low on ammunition and worried about their mounts giving out. If that's the case, they'll spend a day or two on the reservation stealing fresh horses, then split up. We need to parlay on a plan, Juan."

Jace pointed to Patrón's posse, "Let your men dismount and settle in."

Dowlin stepped forward. "I don't have room for this many inside, but you're welcome to set up camp by the river. Sorry I can't accommodate you all."

Patrón shrugged. "That's what we've done the last two nights. It's not so bad now that we've got spring weather, at least as long as we don't get caught in any thunderstorms." He turned and ordered his men to camp and build fires by the river.

Dowlin invited Patrón inside with Bracken and Cousins, pointing them to a table in the store. They took chairs and seated themselves while Dowlin lit a candle and sat the holder in the middle of the table before exiting to check on his hands at supper. In the flickering light, Wes saw Patrón's dust-streaked face and the look of uncertainty in his eyes.

"You're worried, aren't you, Juan?"

He nodded. "Those riding with me aren't man-hunters. They're decent men doing me a favor. As long as we stay together, I think I can keep them with me, but if the Evans gang separates, my posse won't split up to follow. They're scared enough as is."

Wes stroked his chin. "Perhaps we can help, Juan."

"Two more won't make a difference in the way they think. They're worried for themselves and their families if they get in a shootout."

Wes studied Juan. "We're interested in Jesse and Jesse alone," he began. "If what the boys here overheard is correct, he plans to leave the territory *after* he kills us. If you and your men can flush him, separate him from the others, and scare him east, we'll be waiting."

Jace shook his head. "How will we catch him, Wes?"

"The way I figure it, Jesse won't risk riding down the valley to reach the Casey place, not with so many possibly looking for him, but will circle the mountains east of here where our cattle graze and come at us from the south. He's ridden the country enough rustling to know there's a draw south of the Casey place that'll lead directly to our home."

Jace nodded. "That might work."

Wes turned to Patrón. "All your posse has to do is flush and separate them. Let the riders that turn south and southeast alone, follow the one that heads east. Keep behind him so he knows you're there and fire off an occasional round so he understands you're serious. Stay far enough away to remain out of Winchester range, but close enough that he doesn't have time to steal another horse. If he has an exhausted horse by the time he reaches us, there's no way he'll escape. Once he turns north for our place, let him go and return home. Can you do that?"

"It may not be a picnic," Jace added, "but it's not a death sentence either."

A smile creased Patrón's face. "They can do that, but they can't match Jesse's gunplay. Still, I'm worried about you two."

"We'll manage," Wes said. "We always have."

"Besides," Jace noted, "we've both got grudges against Jesse."

"And," Wes interjected, "we *will* settle them this time."

The next morning Bracken and Cousins filled their canteens from the Rio Ruidoso and rode with Patrón's men south through the mountains to the reservation, then separated from their companions and turned east to wind through the ridges toward the Casey place. It would've been quicker and easier on the horses to retrace the route from Dowlin's Mill to San Patricio to their home, but if Patrón's posse flushed Jesse sooner, they would be in position to ambush their enemy. By Wes's estimation, the Indian agency was between thirty and thirty-five miles from the Casey place as the crow flies, though more than forty-five miles by the roads. Once they left Patrón's band, they traveled east, their eyes and ears attuned for trouble.

"You think this'll work, Wes, or did we outfox ourselves? Seems a mite suspicious that Evans would let the men at the mill overhear their plans. Perhaps it was intentional and they meant to throw off any pursuers."

Wes pondered the question. "I don't know that Jesse is that smart, but he is vindictive. He wants to kill us and humiliate my family again. He's a mean man."

"Do you fear dying, Wes?"

"I fear waiting."

"What are you talking about?"

"Back in the war, when you realized fighting was imminent, you never knew for certain when it would start. The waiting jarred your nerves, but once the shooting started you had little time to think, just to react. I just want this over so I can enjoy my wife and sons."

Jace hesitated. "Maybe I shouldn't ask this, but what about your girl?"

Wes sighed and studied Jace, quickly realizing there was no malice in his question. Bracken's pause and gaze made his partner shift in his saddle.

"I didn't mean to insult you or Sarafina," Jace continued, "because I've wondered how I would react. You've handled it better than I could have."

Wes shook his head. "The first time I saw Blanca after she was born, Sarafina handed her to me and told me to drown her in the Hondo, if I couldn't accept her. I refused to kill her, but I admit to having trouble loving her. Perhaps that'll change when I kill Jesse, but for now I don't have an answer. Maybe you do, Jace. You read the Bible more than me."

After a long silence, Jace spoke. "There's a verse in Ecclesiastes that says for everything there is a season and a reason for every purpose under heaven, but I can't explain this, other than you understand how Joseph must have felt when he learned Mary carried Jesus. The Good Book also says God will never burden us with a load greater than we can carry."

Wes pondered his partner's response. "Odd isn't it, that we're talking the Bible when we're intent on killing a man. I can't quote the Good Book, but I know thou shalt not kill is one of the commandments."

Jace nodded, "Despite that admonition, there's a lot of killing in the Old Testament, more than either of us could count. From my reading, the Old Testament is about revenge and retribution. The New Testament is about forgiveness. I figure you have to get past the Old Testament to get to the New. Lincoln must be an Old Testament county, and we must get past that before we can patch things up with forgiveness."

"Maybe so, Jace, maybe so."

The men continued their journey by the back route toward the draw leading through the mountains to the Casey place. When they reached the winding course that meandered among the crags to the Rio Hondo, they sat up a cold camp on a flat-topped hill that overlooked the trail. The knoll was tall enough to observe the foot of the twisting trail, but not so high that it would hinder the horses should Bracken and Cousins give chase. The way Wes figured it as dusk approached, if they didn't kill Evans as he advanced, they would have to pursue him all the way to the Pecos River, forty-five miles to the east, or even to the Texas state line, another eighty miles beyond that.

As darkness crept across the foothills and peaks, Wes and Jace unsaddled and hobbled their horses, threw their bedrolls, took measured sips from their canteens, and waited, fighting the lingering boredom of uncertainty that their schemes might all be for naught. Above the mountains to the northeast towered great thunderheads and as the gloom finally enveloped the countryside, the night flashed pink and purple with lightning, the clouds so distant that the thunder was but a low rumble too soft to interfere with their sleep.

Come morning after they saddled their mounts, the boredom continued as doubts crept into their minds. Had their plan been wrong to begin with? Had Jesse Evans slipped past them during the night? Had he and his gang wiped out Patrón's posse? Beyond their misgivings, the wait tormented them past a breakfast of tortillas, beyond a midmorning drink from their canteens, through lunch with another round of tortillas, and then into early afternoon when storm clouds began building to the southwest, thunder resounding in the distance. Seconds passed like time in a dentist's chair, one excruciating hour after another, the approaching storm increasing their anxiety. Now they faced the likelihood they would not only be bored, but soaking wet as well before this day ended.

And then Wes's sorrel stallion neighed, his ears flicking forward. Bracken grabbed his carbine, Cousins his Henry, and both fell to their stomachs on the rocky soil searching for their quarry. Someone advanced cautiously down the trail, maybe fifteen hundred yards away.

"Well, I'll be damned," Jace whispered. "You had it figured right all along."

"I told you Evans wasn't that smart."

"But wait," Jace said. "There's two of them."

Wes squinted, focusing on the trail, shaking his head. "Two horses, but only one man."

"Damnation," Jace replied. "If we miss him, he'll switch mounts and outrun us."

"Then don't miss. Your rifle will carry farther than my carbine. I'll give you the first shot, but I'll fire as soon as you do."

"I can try at a hundred and fifty yards, but I need him a hundred or closer to have a real chance," Jace answered as they both waited.

Nine hundred yards.

Wes gritted his teeth and followed the rider with the sight of his carbine.

Eight hundred yards.

The towering cloud to the southwest blocked out the sun and rumbled with thunder.

Seven hundred yards.

The rider still advanced. Evans rode a bay

and led a gray.

Six hundred yards.

Jace licked his trigger finger and touched his rifle sight.

Five hundred, then four hundred yards.

"That's the bastard," Wes whispered.

Three hundred yards.

Wes could almost taste Jesse's blood.

But then a blazing white flash of light cracked across the sky, and a clap of thunder like a thousand heavenly cannons blasted the air. Terrified, both Wes's sorrel and Jace's yellow dun reared on their hind legs and whinnied.

Two hundred and fifty yards and no more. Evans stopped. The rearing horses caught his eye, giving Jace and Wes away. Evans yanked his mount around and bolted off.

"Damnation," cried Jace.

Both he and Wes jumped to their feet and scrambled to their horses, grabbing the reins of their fidgety mounts and shoving their long guns into the saddle scabbards. "Shuck the supplies and lighten your load," Wes yelled as he tossed aside two burlap bags with their rations.

Jace grabbed his and Wes's canteens from beside their bedrolls and draped them over the saddle horns. "We'll need these," he shouted.

Both men unhobbled their horses and jumped into their saddles as a second clap of thunder resounded over the land. While the thunderclap terrified the horses, they were eager to run and outdistance the horrible noise. Both horses scrambled down the hillside, hitting the trail to outrun the belligerent clouds that roiled with explosions of light and noise. As they raced after Evans, his two horses turned from the trail toward the east and disappeared momentarily. Wes guessed Evans had a minimum half-mile lead on them, maybe more. Wes estimated they had fourteen miles before they cleared the mountains and foothills and reached the grasslands where John Chisum's hands managed his cattle. Then it was thirty or more miles to the Pecos River. Bracken and Cousins let their panicked mounts try to out-gallop the approaching storm, whose cold breath Wes could feel on his neck. He hoped his horses were more rested than his quarry's because that was their only chance.

After a couple miles at full tilt, Wes and Jace pulled back on their reins, easing their mounts into a canter, knowing they would lose ground when they saw Evans slide from one horse to another. Wes lost track of time as he chased Sarafina's assailant. Before he knew it, he was riding on the prairie land, clear of the rough country with Jace a couple lengths behind him. In the distance, he spotted Evans, and he hoped the outlaw felt the same terror as his wife had endured when Jesse had attacked her.

Wes realized he was falling farther behind Evans and could barely see ahead, especially in the muted light from the towering thunderhead that exploded with lightning flashes and growled with thunder. Then he heard a thudding roar as the storm neared. Behind him, Jace yelled "Hail!"

No sooner had he realized Jace had said "hail" rather than "hell," the marble-sized pellets pummeled him and Charlie, the sorrel breaking into another gallop, trying to outdistance the threat he did not understand. Wes grimaced as the hailstones battered him with hundreds of stings like a swarm of frozen bees. Ahead Jesse Evans disappeared in a hazy white veil. And when the hail subsided, a deluge took its place, splattering Wes until his clothes were drenched. The torrent lasted thirty minutes before rumbling to the northeast. When the blue curtain of the rain moved out of the way, Wes scanned the distance and failed to spot Jesse Evans. He cursed, slowing his horse to a trot, allowing Jace to reach him. His soaked partner looked madder than a waterlogged cat.

"He can't get away again," Jace shouted. "We've got to catch him."

They rode another fifteen minutes, then Wes smiled as up ahead he spotted a man afoot, waving a carbine wildly over his head and nearby the gray and the bay that had carried Evans. Both men pulled their long guns, knowing this would be easy shooting, but as they drew closer, they realized the mud-splattered fellow was not Jesse Evans.

"What the hell?" Jace cursed.

Reining their horses up at the man's feet, the cowboy cried out. "That thief stole my horse. I think it was Jesse Evans."

Gasping for breath, Wes cried, "Was . . . your . . . horse . . . fresh?"

"Yep," the cowboy answered, scraping mud off his shirt, "but the joke's on him."

"How's that?" Jace asked.

"When he yanked me off the saddle, I grabbed his waist and as he shoved me aside, I jerked the pistol out of his holster. It's somewhere around here in the mud. As he mounted, I jumped up and pulled my carbine from the saddle boot. Best I know, he's not got a weapon on him. All he did was take time to untie his saddlebag from one horse and secure it to mine before galloping away."

Wes looked at the two fagged animals and noted the carbine sticking up behind the saddle of the bay, but he could only curse. "With a fresh horse, he'll outrun us for sure."

"Maybe not," Jace interjected, jumping from his dun. "A fellow with two tired horses might stand a chance." He handed Wes the reins and shoved his rifle in the scabbard. "Just kill him with my Henry."

Wes saw the Henry in the scabbard and shouted, "I intend to." He slid his carbine in its scabbard and whistled, sending the two horses chasing after Jesse Evans.

Uncertain how long his horses could maintain a canter, he pressed forward, changing mounts every two miles. Always straining against the horizon to see the fleeing Jesse Evans. He rode for two hours through scattered Chisum cattle and an occasional rider, likely cowboys rounding up beeves. As the storm system passed, the sun at his back angled down, casting a jaundiced light across the landscape. He knew as he neared the Pecos that Evans could find a thousand places to hide in the eroded riverbed, but instead he spotted Jesse, riding back and forth along the bank, glancing frightfully over his shoulder before spotting his pursuer.

Nearing him astride Jace's yellow dun, Wes reached behind the saddle and slid his partner's Henry from its scabbard. He advanced, close enough to see the terror in Jesse's face, but not in his eyes. He wanted to stare his wife's assailant in the eye before dispatching him to hell. Wes rode within a hundred yards of Jesse, uncertain why his quarry didn't escape into the riverbed and hide or make a run for it.

Within fifty yards of his enemy, Wes saw the reason for Jesse's hesitation. The Pecos roiled with the muddy brown waters of a flash flood. Only a fool or a desperate man would challenge that river of death. As he drew within thirty yards of the rapist, Wes raised the rifle and aimed at Jesse's heart.

"I'm unarmed," Jesse cried, dropping his reins and raising his hands over his head.

"How's it feel to be helpless like my wife when you raped her?"

Jesse smirked. "She was good."

The words stung Wes. He reined up his horse within twenty yards of Jesse and stared into his evil eyes, then shifted the rifle sight to Jesse's shoulder. Jesse would suffer for those words.

"Take me back to Fort Stanton."

"Not this time." Wes squeezed the trigger. The Henry exploded.

Jesse's left arm flung up to his right shoulder, a blossom of blood appearing on Jesse's shirt. Jesse's jaw dropped in shock as Wes put another bullet in his other shoulder. Evans slumped forward, grabbing the reins, wrapping them around his wrist, then yanking the horse about, kicking at his flank and flailing at his neck with his arms. The animal bolted toward the surging muddy waters and splashed into the flood tide as Evans showered curses upon Bracken.

Wes trotted the dun over to the bank, watching Jesse scream and struggle against the current with his shoulder wounds. He plugged away at Jesse like a kid would throw rocks at a bobbing cork, relishing Evans's terrified screeches whenever a bullet struck flesh. Soon the screams were supplanted by gasps for breath as he struggled to stay afloat. Wes pulled the trigger until the Henry clicked on empty a half dozen times. He watched Jesse slide off his horse, flailing at the raging waters. His terrified horse disappeared beneath the muddy turmoil of the angry Pecos River, and the reins pulled Evans under. His head bobbed up twice for air before Jesse Evans slid beneath the waters, never to be seen again in New Mexico Territory.

CHAPTER 18

Until darkness ended his search, Wes Bracken scoured the embankments along the river, searching for Jesse Evans's body to confirm his demise. When night finally fell, he unsaddled his and Jace's horses and collapsed on the ground, famished and exhausted, but confident he had exterminated Evans like the vermin he was. Without a bedroll, Wes slept on the wet soil, using his saddle for a pillow and the stars overhead for a blanket. Come daybreak, he pushed himself up with aching muscles and sore joints, then brushed the layer of mud and grass off his pants and shirt. With nothing to eat, he saddled his sorrel and Jace's dun, which he tied behind Charlie, mounted, and continued his search for Jesse's sorry carcass. His stomach growled from emptiness, but he plodded southward along the western edge of the Pecos, which had gouged out steep banks on both sides of its course. He

studied each embankment and the occasional sandbar in the middle of the watercourse, hunting for his dead enemy. The
river that had raged like a liquid lion the
day before now purred like a kitten as it
ambled toward Texas, barely knee-deep on
a man.

Wes estimated he had ridden five miles
without a sign of Jesse, and he verged on
giving up when he saw in the distance an
uprooted cottonwood deposited by the
flood on a sandbar. Deciding to ride to the
misshaped tree draped with debris, Wes
advanced, inspecting the river perimeter for
any sign of Jesse if he had died or tracks up
the opposite bank if he had survived. He
discovered nothing. Nearing the fallen tree
trunk, he noticed a discolored clump
wrapped around the whitened wood. Drawing closer to the sandbar, Wes made out the
color and shape of the roan Jesse had stolen
from the Chisum hand. The carcass had
snagged on the trunk, which had dug into
the sand as the roiling floodwaters receded.
Wes found an incline his horses could
descend and guided them to the water's
muddy edge and into the still brown waters
of the Pecos. His two horses fretted at the
pungent smell of death as they splashed
through the stream to the stump of what

had once been a great cottonwood. Reaching the sandbar, Wes dismounted and led the horses upwind from the carcass so they wouldn't fret so much. Dropping his reins, he marched over to the lifeless roan, figuring he could at least retrieve the tack for the Chisum cowhand. Death's aroma drew swarms of flies and attacked Wes's nostrils as he reached the decaying animal. As he inspected the tree trunk and dead horse, he observed the reins snagged on a branch, likely dragging the horse under and drowning it. He swatted at the flies and removed the saddlebags the cowboy said Jesse had secured to the roan. Next he unbuckled the saddle and struggled to pull it free before yanking it clear and tossing it atop the saddlebags. He moved to the carcass's head and loosened the bridle, slipping the bit from between the dead animal's teeth and yanking it clear of the horse, though the reins remained snagged on the tree.

As Wes untangled the reins wrapped around a branch, he spotted something that made him gag: a severed hand entangled in the leather strands and impaled on the sharp stub of a broken limb. He spat bile, revolted at what he saw, yet satisfied that Jesse Evans was indeed dead. As he unwrapped the severed hand from the entangled reins, Wes relished that Evans must have felt the same terror that Sarafina had when he violated her. For a moment, he considered cutting off a finger to take back to Lincoln to prove he had killed the outlaw, but he didn't care to touch the flesh of such an evil man. As he freed the reins from their tangle, he spat on the hand and left it for the flies and the vultures to find.

He took the bridle over to the saddle, which he grabbed by the horn and carried to Jace's dun. Tossing the extra saddle over the gelding, Wes cinched it down and then tied the spare bridle to the saddle horn. Returning for the saddlebags, Wes lifted a flap and looked inside, hoping to find some food. He found a waterlogged carton of pistol ammunition and a large leather pouch, which he extracted. Inside he discovered a roll of soggy bills tied together with string. He didn't know how much money was there, but he pulled out a thick wad and slipped it in his britches pocket. Wes threw the leather pouch in the river, wondering if Jesse had stolen the money or received it from Dolan for misdeeds completed or planned. Next he opened the other side of the saddlebags and found a disintegrating carton of carbine ammo and a saturated stack of tortillas that had turned to mush.

He tossed them aside, removed the soggy container of bullets, and flung the saddlebags into the river, watching the gentle current carry the tack away before it sank out of sight. Stepping to his horses, he slipped the ammunition into his saddlebags, mounted, and started for home across land claimed by John Chisum.

Near dusk he came to the Rio Hondo trickling its way toward the Pecos and spotted to the west the glow of a campfire where four cowboys sat, fixing grub and boiling coffee. Wes counted three horses and smiled when one man arose and ambled his direction. It was Jace.

"I was getting worried," Jace called out.

"It's good to know you fretted over me."

"Not you, my dun. I feared I'd have to walk home if you didn't bring him back."

Wes grinned. "You might have to yet."

"Any luck?"

"Let's talk about it on the way to the Casey place, especially if your friends can spare a cup of coffee and a little grub. It's been more than a day since I had a bite of anything."

When Wes drew up his sorrel, Jace stepped around behind the animal and untied his own horse, noting the two saddles atop his dun. He let out a low whistle.

As Wes dismounted, he recognized the cowboy whose horse Jesse had stolen. "I brought back your saddle and bridle. Your roan drowned in the Pecos."

The cowboy arose and stepped toward Jace, who was removing the spare saddle. "What about Jesse Evans? It was Jesse, wasn't it?"

Wes nodded. "It was him, but I can't confirm his fate. He may have drowned, may have gotten away afoot. I found your horse dead on a sandbar in the middle of the river after the flooding. Never saw Evans or his body after the flood subsided. Can't say anything for certain."

"I'm obliged for you retrieving my saddle," the cowboy answered. "The horse was Chisum's, but he won't mind losing one if it means being rid of Jesse Evans. You're welcome to bed down with us."

"Maybe a cup of coffee and a bite or two to eat, but I need to be on my way, check on my wife and boys."

"We'll share what we've got, but it ain't much," the fellow said.

"It's better than nothing," Wes noted.

Wes spent fifteen minutes suckling coffee and eating four strips of fried bacon and a hard biscuit. He remained silent, not caring to tell what really happened, as he watched

Jace extract his Henry from its saddle scabbard. He checked the load and looked at Wes, nodding slightly that he understood his partner had emptied his rifle at Evans.

After thanking the three Chisum hands for their hospitality, Wes and Jace mounted and started back toward the mountains, following the Rio Hondo to the Casey place in a night lit by a thumbnail of a moon. They rode silently for a mile or two before Wes told Jace of the chase, the confrontation at the river, the terror on Evans's face as he disappeared beneath the roiling floodwaters of the Pecos, and the discovery of the severed hand the next morning.

"If he didn't drown, he bled to death," Wes concluded. "I would've liked to have found his body, but the hand will have to do."

"Was it the left or the right hand?"

Wes scratched his chin, thinking back to the shock of his discovery. He hesitated while he tried to visualize his find. "Must have been his left."

"That would figure," Jace nodded, "to keep his gun hand free."

"But he never fired at me."

"Then Chisum's cowhand was right, that he stripped Jesse of his guns, and the outlaw never knew it until it was too late."

"I'm not sharing this with anyone but you and Sarafina, so she will never fear him again. I'll tell folks he was so terrified he braved floodwaters just to escape and let them know I don't expect ever to see him again in Lincoln County."

"Fine by me, Wes," Jace said, leaning over and pulling his Henry from its scabbard. He thumbed bullets into the magazine as they rode. "I decided not to reload in front of the cowboys, so as not to give anything away. What's next for us?"

"Home, bath, and a good night's sleep. Tomorrow I'll ride into Lincoln and get Sarafina and the boys." Wes could not bring himself to include Blanca among his children. He wondered if Jace would note the omission.

"If you can spare me, I'll fetch the bedrolls and supplies we left behind to chase Jesse."

"There's one other thing I should tell you."

"What's that?"

"We may not be as bad off as we thought. I found a wad of money in Jesse's saddlebags. That's why he grabbed them from his horse without thinking of his weapons."

"How much?"

"I haven't counted it, but I'd say a couple hundred or more."

Jace whistled. "That'll come in handy for you."

"For us," Wes replied.

Wes dismounted and tied his sorrel to the hitching post outside Juan Patrón's home. He glanced both ways down Lincoln's sleepy street as he knocked on the front door. Hearing the sounds of Luis and Roberto playing inside, Wes removed his hat and ran his fingers through his brown hair. He lowered his headgear to his side as the door cracked open. Despite his missing front tooth, he smiled as he saw Sarafina's face appear through the narrow opening that suddenly widened like her arms as she flung herself into his grasp.

"*¡Mis oraciones han sido contestadas!*" Sarafina exclaimed as she buried herself into his chest, wrapping her arms around him and sobbing. "My prayers have been answered! You're home and safe," she sniffled.

Behind his wife, he heard the boys shout, "Papa! Papa!" Both ran to the door and squeezed past their mother, clasping their arms around Wes's legs.

Sarafina looked up into Wes's gray eyes. "I was so worried. You were gone so long." She kissed him full on the mouth until he pulled his lips from hers, placed his hands on her

343

raven hair, and pressed her head against his chest so he could whisper in her ear.

"You don't have to worry any more, Sarafina. The devil will never bother you again."

Sarafina pried herself from his embrace and stared into his eyes. "He's gone?"

Wes nodded, leaned over, and whispered, "Never share that with anyone."

She sighed. "Must I still carry a pistol everywhere I go?"

Grimacing, Wes dipped his head. "He wasn't the only dangerous man in Lincoln County." Feeling the exuberant tugs at his legs, Wes extracted himself away from his wife's hug and handed her his hat. He bent and picked up a son in each arm. They giggled as he lifted them to his chest. "My, how you boys are getting bigger and heavier."

The pair laughed and threw their arms around his neck, kissing him on his cheeks as his wife retreated inside. After he followed her into the front room, Sarafina closed the door. The giggling boys slid from Wes's arms and scampered away to play as he inhaled the aroma of cornbread coming from the kitchen. Sarafina took their place and nestled into Wes's grasp again as Juan Patrón entered.

"The boys are —" Patrón started until he

spotted Bracken. "You're back, Wes. What about Jace? Is he okay?"

"He's at the Casey place, still as mean as ever," Wes answered as he walked over and shook his friend's hand. "Thanks for watching Sarafina and the boys, Juan."

"What about, you know?" Patrón asked without saying Evans's name in front of Sarafina.

Wes broke his grip and slapped Patrón on the back. "You and your posse did your job, driving him our way. We chased him to the Pecos during the thunderstorm, but lost him in the flash flood that followed. Last I saw him, he was struggling to keep his head above the water. I suspect he drowned and doubt we'll see him again in Lincoln County."

Patrón studied the bearer of the news. "Are you telling me more than you're saying?"

Shrugging, Wes answered, "I'm telling you all you need to know."

Patrón sighed. "One less enemy to worry about, but there are so many others."

"What about Bonney?"

"He's staying here. The sheriff kept him in the pit for two days, before placing him under house arrest with us. Fact is, the Kid's meeting with the governor again this afternoon, still trying to confirm a pardon if he testifies before the grand jury next month."

"I'm not sure I trust Wallace."

"He's our best hope if we are to ever right the wrongs of the Santa Fe Ring that protected Murphy and Dolan. They may have been pawns."

Sarafina returned to the room carrying Blanca. The four-month-old infant rested in her mother's grip, cooing and bubbling as her dark eyes glanced around. "Welcome your papa home, Blanca," Sarafina said. "Tell him how much you missed him." Oblivious to her mother's words, Blanca waved her arms wildly. Sarafina toted the baby to Wes's side and held her to his cheek for a kiss, but Blanca whimpered and her mother pulled her away.

Wes stepped away and toward Patrón. "Could I borrow your buckboard and team to take Sarafina and the boys home before dark. I'll return it in the morning."

"You're welcome to stay the night, Wes."

"Obliged, Juan, but we've got too much work to do if we're gonna harvest a crop this fall. First, I gotta find a plow and team I can borrow or times'll grow even harder for us."

Patrón nodded. "Everybody's in the same

shape, Wes. Fortunately, we're getting a few dollars every week for housing Bonney and O'Folliard or I don't know what we'd do. I'll fetch my rig for you."

As Patrón left the room, Wes turned to his wife. "Gather yours and the boys' things so we can get home soon."

Sarafina smiled. "You will come to love Blanca, *mi esposo.* It will take time, but one day you will adore her."

Before he could answer, Wes heard a gunshot outside, then three more right after each other.

Grabbing his pistol, Wes bolted to the door, cracked it, and checked outside. Seeing nothing, he stepped from the house into the street where the sparse spectators stared north across the street toward the Rio Bonito. At the blast of another gunshot, Wes saw three men by the stream and recognized Bonney with a smoking revolver in his outstretched arm. Beside him stood O'Folliard and, surprisingly, Governor Lew Wallace. Fearing Bonney might threaten the governor, Wes bounded for the hitching post, untied his sorrel, and jumped in the saddle, trotting toward the stream. He clenched his pistol grip tightly in his right hand, ready to lift the weapon if circumstances demanded, and approached the trio.

All three turned to greet him with smiles on their faces. Wes slid his pistol back in the holster and eased his sorrel into a walk.

Bonney turned back north, lifted his revolver, fired a sixth shot, raised the weapon to his lips, and blew the trailing smoke away from the muzzle. Turning to Wes, he broke open the pistol, dumped the hulls from the cylinder, and calmly pulled fresh cartridges from the loops of his gun belt to reload the weapon. The Kid offered Wes a buck-toothed grin. "Good to see you, Wes. How was hunting?"

"I didn't bring home any game, Kid," Wes replied. "What are you doing?"

Governor Wallace approached Wes, a smile cracking his thick beard. "Young Bonney is giving me a shooting demonstration. I must admit he's a superb shot."

Wes eyed the territorial appointee. "When are you issuing him his pardon?"

"In good time, Wes Bracken, in good time. He still must testify before the grand jury about the murder of the lawyer Chapman. Then he'll have fulfilled his civic duty and his promise to me. He's doing okay for a man under arrest. How many men in custody are permitted to carry their own guns? I'm allowing that for his own protection."

"It's not men carrying guns that are his

biggest threat, but men carrying law books."

Bonney laughed. "The governor may trust me with a gun, but he doesn't want me running out on him." The kid lifted his leg, which rattled from the iron shackles over his bare feet. Then he pointed to a clump of shade trees hugging the river.

Wes made out a man with a hat pulled low over his forehead and a badge pinned to his vest. "That's Deputy Longworth. The sheriff assigned him to keep watch over me and Tom."

O'Folliard raised his leg for Wes to see his own shackles.

"At least we're not in the pit like Carlos," the Kid continued. "That boy hates you, Wes."

Bracken looked from Bonney to Wallace. "When's the grand jury convene?"

"Monday, April fourteenth, three weeks from today," the governor replied. "Then we'll sort out Lincoln County's troubles and restore order."

"Who's the presiding judge and the prosecutor?" Wes asked.

"Judge Warren Bristol and District Attorney William Rynerson of the Third Judicial District, which covers Doña Ana, Grant, and Lincoln Counties."

Wes shook his head. "They're tied to the

Santa Fe Ring. Like I said, the Kid's got more to fear from those carrying law books than from enemies carrying guns."

"The law's the law," Wallace answered.

"Not in Lincoln County, it's not." Wes turned his sorrel around and started for Patrón's place, certain the governor would never fulfill his promise to Bonney. Wallace was treating the Kid more like the chief attraction at a freak show than a victim of corruption that extended all the way to the territorial capital and maybe even the governor's office.

"You're coming to my court session, aren't you, Wes?" Bonney shouted after him.

Wes twisted around in the saddle, lifted his hat over his head, and nodded. He would return, though he remained uncertain what good it would do. Settling in his saddle and tugging his headgear back in place, Wes smiled when he saw Patrón jumping from his buckboard in front of the house. Juan had tied Sarafina's gelding and their milk cow to the back. So much had transpired since he had stalked Jesse Evans that Wes had forgotten sending the animals with Sarafina when she left for Lincoln.

Reaching Patrón's, Wes dismounted and secured Charlie's reins to the buckboard's rear with the other two animals, then went inside to fetch bedding and belongings. He made three trips, grabbed the carbine and shotgun he had given Sarafina, glad that she never had to fire them, and carried them to the rig. As he passed her with the weapons, he confirmed that she still wore the revolver from a strap over her shoulder. It bothered him that his wife should remain armed in Lincoln County. When he returned indoors, Sarafina asked him to herd the boys outside while she saw to Blanca and thanked Beatriz in the kitchen.

Roberto and Luis giggled as Wes cornered them, lifted one under each arm, and pushed open the front door, emerging into the afternoon sunshine. He tossed each boy onto a bundle of bedding in the back of the wagon, drawing more laughter. Wes tickled each under his arm.

Patrón held the door open for Sarafina, who emerged with Blanca cradled in her left arm. She lifted a cloth-shrouded bundle in her right hand. "It's skillet cornbread," she said. "Beatriz sends her best, but she's been cooking all day and didn't feel presentable."

Wes took the round cloth from her and placed it on the wagon seat until he could help Sarafina into place. "It was thoughtful of her to send cornbread for our return home."

"It's for Carlos, not us. I want to stop at the jail and give it to him since I don't know if I'll see him again before the hearing." Sarafina picked up the round of cornbread as she settled into the seat.

Wes thanked Juan for keeping his family safe, then walked around the wagon, crawled into place, grabbed the reins, and started the team across the street to the jail, barely thirty yards away. Reining up the wagon, he realized it would have been simpler for Sarafina to have strolled across the road than to load her and the baby up, then help her down and assist her back in the buckboard after she completed her errand. Before Wes sat the brake, Sarafina handed him Blanca.

"Wait here with our daughter," she instructed her husband as she stood up and stepped over the sideboard onto a wheel spoke and then the street with the round of cornbread. She took a deep breath and entered the sheriff's office, closing the door behind her.

Wes felt awkward holding Jesse Evans's daughter and bit his lip as he looked down at her, staring back with wide, dark eyes that reminded him of Sarafina's. Shame overcame him, and he refused to view the infant. Rather than look away, he pulled his hat down over his eyes so he could not see her.

As he did, Blanca giggled.

Uncertain what had triggered her, he lifted the brim, drawing a coo, then yanked the hat down over his forehead again.

Blanca erupted in a full-bodied laugh that started deep in her lungs and exploded out of her quivering lips, her little hands reaching toward him. Her merriment came so loudly that Luis scurried to the wagon seat and climbed beside Wes, then helped Roberto over. The two boys stared in awe at their tiny sister.

"Do it again, Papa" cried Luis.

Wes lifted his hat once more, then tugged it past his eyebrows, drawing the loudest guffaw yet. The boys giggled and climbed over each other to see the joy on Blanca's face.

"Again," Luis shouted as he and Roberto slid from the wagon seat and stood on the floorboard grinning at each other and their sister.

Twice more Wes moved his hat up and down, earning two more hysterical responses from the infant girl, whose face reddened from laughing so hard. Wes even grinned at her delight, fascinated that something so simple could draw such a reaction. So focused was he on the baby that Sarafina startled him when she approached.

"Mama, Mama," cried Luis, "Papa made Blanca laugh. It was funny."

Wes saw tears glistening in his wife's eyes.

"Do it again, Papa," Roberto implored.

Feeling foolish, but not wanting to disappoint his boys, Wes lifted his hat, then yanked it down over his eyes.

Silence!

Two, three, four times more Wes yanked his hat brim up and down, drawing nothing but a wide-eyed gaze from the little girl.

"You boys are playing a trick on your mama," Sarafina said as she walked around the buckboard to her side and returned Luis and Roberto to the back.

"No, Mama, she did laugh," Luis answered

Roberto nodded his agreement.

Sarafina pulled herself into the wagon and sat down, taking Blanca from her husband's arm, nestling closer to Wes as he lifted the reins and started the rig toward home.

"It's true," Wes explained, "your daughter did laugh."

"Our daughter," she chided him.

Wes sighed, fearing the girl's paternity

would grate on him for the rest of his life. He was relieved Sarafina said nothing more and glad that they would ride east and not into the afternoon sun. The couple rode wordlessly, the wagon and trail noises plus the chatter of the boys in the back providing the only sounds as they passed the cemetery.

"What about Carlos?"

"He's as hotheaded as ever and still blames you for everything, *mi esposo.*"

"But will he accept the arrangement I worked out with the governor?"

Sarafina hesitated. "I hope so. He is so angry at being kept in the hole, and I've told him he may be there a long time. Bad as it is, it's better than being hanged."

"Court convenes in three weeks. Maybe by then he'll agree to the deal. Two or three years for rustling is preferable to an unforgiving noose forever."

"True, but his bitterness runs deep, and so much of it is aimed at you that it scares me."

"We will get past this just like every other obstacle Lincoln County puts in our way, Sarafina."

She nestled closer to her husband the rest of the journey to their home, where they found Jace Cousins, returned from his excursion to retrieve their supplies and gear. Jace welcomed Sarafina and her children, pulling the boys from the buckboard and letting them scurry inside while Wes helped his wife and Blanca from the wagon. After Wes unloaded the bedding and belongings from the back, Jace took the rig and animals to the barn.

Come dusk, Sarafina had made fresh tortillas for supper, feeding the boys and Blanca first, then putting them to bed and sharing the modest fare with the men. As day gave way to darkness, they lit candles and sat around the table mulling over the events that had consumed their lives in the seven days since the stalking of Jesse Evans began.

"We're safer now, but just as broke," Jace said.

Wes shook his head. "You're forgetting the windfall I told you about."

"You mean the money you found in the saddlebags?"

Reaching into his pants pocket, Wes nodded.

"What's a handful of dollars to us?"

Wes pulled the roll of currency from his pocket and tossed it on the table.

Sarafina gasped.

"I don't know how much is there, but it's

more than a few dollars."

Jace slapped his forehead. "I guess so."

Wes untied the string that bound the cash and massaged the paper to get the curl out of the money. The bills were still damp to his touch as he counted them out, one by one. When he finished, he looked up at Jace and his wife. "Seven hundred and twenty-nine dollars by my count."

"Somos ricos," Sarafina gasped. "We're rich."

"It doesn't make up for what Lincoln County has cost us in horses, land, and family," Wes said, "but it's a start."

CHAPTER 19

Come morning after a night to sleep on their newfound wealth, Bracken arose early and headed out to milk the cow. Though they now had money, Wes knew they must remain discreet in spending it when everyone else was broke. If they were to make a crop this year, they needed a team, a plow, harnesses, and a wagon to replace those destroyed in the arson at his original Mirror B. Inside the barn, Wes grabbed his stool and sat it on the ground by the cow's udder. Taking his seat and shoving the pail under the animal, Wes worked the teats. White threads of milk pinged against the side of the pail. Wes heard Jace whistle as he entered the barn.

"Morning, Wes," he said as he walked over and patted his partner's shoulder. "Don't know about you, but I rested better last night than I have in weeks, knowing we have a few dollars to grubstake us again."

Wes shrugged. "We can't make too big of a splash with it or it'd look too suspicious."

"I've been pondering that as well. Let me toss an idea at you."

"Shoot," Wes replied, stopping his milking and twisting around on his stool to eye his partner in the barn's gloom.

Jace cleared his throat. "Rather than buying anything in Lincoln, I thought I'd ride to Roswell and see what I could find there, maybe run out to John Chisum's headquarters and bargain with him. He promised me a hundred dollars if I would bring him the hull of the cartridge that killed Jesse Evans. I'll let him know the outlaw won't bother him anymore."

Wes scratched his chin, then dipped his head. "I like the idea, save for telling old Chisum anything about Evans. Fact is, I prefer telling him Jesse's been spotted in El Paso or elsewhere in Texas, just to throw anyone off my trail."

Jace grinned. "I like that, spreading gossip. I'll leave after you return Juan's buckboard."

"Don't wait on me. Saddle up and ride out after breakfast. With Jesse dead, I'm not as worried about abandoning Sarafina and the boys for a few hours. I'll give you half the money and see how far you can stretch it." Wes turned to finish his milking.

"By my figuring, we need a plow, a wagon, a team, and harnesses for sure."

"And seed, plenty of seed for Sarafina's garden, for feed corn," Wes noted.

"I suppose we're low on staples, like flour, sugar, and coffee as well."

Wes nodded. "Check with Sarafina on that and buy something for the boys."

"And what about for your girl?"

Wes scowled over his shoulder at his partner. "She's not my girl."

"Maybe not, Wes, but Luis told me how you made her laugh and cackle yesterday in Lincoln. He and Roberto are proud of their sister."

"They don't know the truth."

"And they never should, Wes. They're family. That's more than I've got."

Wes tugged vigorously at the teats to finish milking, though he stewed at Jace's persistence in reminding him about Blanca and her paternity.

His partner stepped to the stall where his dun stood and saddled the animal. "It'll take me three days there and back, maybe four or five depending on what I find."

Wes heard him, but didn't acknowledge his comment.

When he finished prepping his gelding for

the ride to Roswell, Jace led him out of the barn. "I'll see you at the breakfast table," he called as he stepped outside.

While he nodded to himself, Wes ignored his partner, still mad at him for bringing up Blanca and furious at his own mishandling of the situation, for it was neither Sarafina nor the baby's fault. They stood blameless and innocent. The man responsible was dead from Wes's hand. Conflicted, he finished milking and carried the pail back to the house.

As he walked to the kitchen door, he saw Jace's dun tethered outside and then heard a hen cackling and flapping her wings as his partner chased the bird into the pen. Wes remembered he and Jace had released the chickens to range free when everyone abandoned the place during the manhunt. Now it would be a challenge to get them all back in the coop, but never one to waste time, Jace was trying before breakfast. Wes smiled, glad to have Jace as a partner, even if he tweaked Wes's conscience. Jace was a hard worker and a man of unshakable honesty.

Wes entered the house to find Sarafina standing over a skillet on the stove.

"Buenos días, mi esposo," she called. "Jace gathered eggs for us so I am scrambling them now before you return Juan's wagon."

After sitting the pail on the table, he walked over and kissed Sarafina on the cheek. "Good morning, Sarafina. Did Jace tell you he was heading to Roswell for supplies today?"

"Such a long ride when Lincoln is closer," she answered.

"And more dangerous if people realize he has money and start asking where he got it."

Clasping her throat, Sarafina grimaced. "I never considered that."

"We can't be too careful. This is still Lincoln County, and we've plenty of enemies, known and unknown, around us."

"I will speak no more of this, *mi esposo.*"

"Tell Jace of any supplies you'll need. He knows about coffee, flour, and sugar, but give him a list that he can carry to Roswell."

Wes marched from the kitchen into his darkened bedroom, where he could hear the shallow breathing of Blanca in her corner crib. He eased to his bedside and slipped his hand under the mattress, extracting the stack of bills that would pay for their needs. As he tiptoed to the door, Blanca startled, sneezed, and wailed. Shoving the bills in his pants pocket, he marched to the crib and bent, lifting Blanca and resting her head against his left shoulder, gently patting her on the back. "It's okay, girl; it's okay," he whispered. She screamed even louder and fought against Wes's efforts to comfort her. Feeling helpless, Wes turned to the door just as Sarafina burst in, her face showing a frown that bloomed into a smile when she saw her husband holding her daughter.

"Do not worry, *mi esposo*. She is very fussy when hungry in the morning." Sarafina took Blanca from him and cradled the infant in her arms as she moved to the bed, where she opened her gown and nursed the famished one. "I left you and Jace a plate of eggs apiece and a platter of tortillas."

"What about for the boys?"

"Not enough eggs for them. I'll make do for them later. There's coffee boiling."

Wes marched to the kitchen, poured himself a cup of coffee, and sat at the table, gobbling down breakfast. Just as he finished, Jace came in. He pointed to his partner's plate. "It's a good thing you got here because I was considering your breakfast as mine didn't go that far."

"I only found three eggs. I'll find more once we get better sunlight."

"By then, I want you on the way to Roswell," Wes said, fishing the bills out from his pocket and laying them on the table. "I promised you half, so that comes to three hundred and sixty-five dollars." Wes started counting out the money and paused. "I may need to do some calculating if that will be enough."

The way Wes figured it, a team of horses or mules might cost two hundred or more dollars. A farm wagon with iron axles and a double box could run up to a hundred dollars and a steel, sideboard plow another thirty-five. Wes estimated a plow harness at twenty-five bucks and a wagon double harness with hames and collars at fifty-five more. That was near five hundred dollars right there, not including supplies, and that was only if Wes's estimates were solid. Jace had been a fine horse trader, so Wes expected he would drive a solid bargain, but that was assuming he could find their needs for sale. Discouraged at figuring the costs, Wes frowned and counted out twenty-nine dollars, which he stuffed in his shirt pocket. He shoved the remaining seven hundred across the table at his partner.

"I'm giving you all but twenty-nine bucks. Even that may not stretch as far as I hope."

Jace grinned. "Don't keep so much for yourself." He took the stack of bills and folded them in half as he shoved them in his britches. "I'll make do with what you give me. As tight as things are, folks may accept a cheaper price, just to get cash. Do you prefer horses or mules?"

"Mules may be less likely to be stolen, but take whatever you can buy at a good price."

"You know me, Wes, I'm a horse trader. I can bargain a skunk out of his stripes without getting a whiff of perfume in the negotiation."

Wes chuckled as his partner scraped a final bite of breakfast from his tin plate.

After washing down his last mouthful of eggs and tortillas with his coffee, Jace pushed himself away from the table and patted the wad of money in his pants pocket. "I'll take good care of this and us. You want me to harness up Juan's team before I leave?"

"You've got a long ride, so head on to Roswell, and I'll manage. I also plan to slip him five dollars to cover any costs of keeping Sarafina and the boys."

"Aren't you forgetting something?"

Wes felt his face redden. He gritted his teeth, thinking Jace was gigging him about Blanca, but before he could respond his partner continued.

"He stabled the gelding and milk cow." Jace grinned. "What did you think I meant?"

"I'll leave him seven dollars then."

Jace snickered. "I'll fetch my Henry and

some cartridges, then be on my way."

"Ammunition," Wes said. "Buy what you can. Even with Jesse Evans gone, we'll need it. And if you remember, spread word around Roswell that Jesse's been seen in Texas."

"As good as done," Jace replied from the next room. He returned carrying his rifle and a carton of cartridges. "See you in a few days, partner." He exited, and shortly Wes heard his dun trot away.

Wes counted out seven bills and shoved them in his shirt pocket, then stood and carried the remaining twenty-two dollars into the bedroom where Sarafina had finished nursing Blanca. He slid the bills under the mattress, then turned to his wife. "I'm saddling up Charlie and hitching the team to return Juan's buckboard. Maybe when Jace returns, we won't have to borrow so much from folks, and we can stand on our own."

Sarafina smiled. "As long as we've got each other and our three little ones, we'll make do, no matter what, *mi esposo.*" She stood up, put the contented baby back in the crib, then turned to her husband and flung her arms around him. "*Gracias* for what you've done for me and the little ones. I feel safer with that devil dead."

Wes hugged her. "Even so, keep your

pistol handy and remember the shotgun and carbine are in the front room. Use them if you must." He kissed her again, then slipped from her embrace and out the door. "The sooner I get to town, the quicker I'll return."

After saddling his sorrel and hitching the team, Wes tied Charlie to the back and climbed into the wagon. As he rode away, he frowned at how much work remained if they got any crops in the field. And then there were the cattle that had been grazing freely south of the place. Assuming the herd hadn't been rustled, Wes knew he and Jace must round up the beeves and brand the new calves with the Mirror B irons. There was more work than he and Jace could manage, but they would have to try.

Lost in his worries over the awaiting chores, Wes could not believe how fast the trip had gone as he approached Lincoln. He soon drew up outside Patrón's house. As he set the wagon brake, Wes heard the rattle of chains and saw Billy Bonney ambling around the side of the adobe in leg shackles with a gun belt and revolver at his side. Wes shook his head.

"Kid, you go around well-heeled for a fellow in chains."

Bonney flashed a toothy grin. "The governor and I have an understanding. I'll protect

367

myself if attacked, but won't pull a gun for anything else."

"Where's the deputy and O'Folliard?"

"They're around here somewhere."

"How about fetching Juan?" Wes asked as he jumped from the wagon seat and straightened his holster.

The Kid stepped to the door, opened it, and stuck his head inside. "Juan," he yelled, "you've got a visitor."

Before Bonney could shut the door, it swung the rest of the way open. "You don't have to yell, Kid," Patrón chided. "You know how such a clamor annoys Beatriz." When Juan stepped outside, he smiled at the sight of Bracken beside his buckboard. He strode over and clasped Wes's hand. "I didn't expect you back so early. Will you stay for lunch?"

"Obliged for the invitation, Juan, but I've got a lot of work to do, and it won't get done without me. You want me to unhitch the team?" Wes asked as he untied Charlie from the back.

Juan grinned. "The Kid'll do it. He's getting on Beatriz's nerves so the longer I keep him outside and busy, the better it is for all of us."

Bonney laughed. "Beatriz likes me. That's what's gotten Juan all riled up. I'm more fun than he is." The Kid stepped to the side of the wagon, released the brake, and went to the front of the team, grabbing the harness and leading the animals around the house.

As soon as Bonney and the rig disappeared, Wes slipped his hand in his shirt pocket and pulled out the wrinkled bills. "There's seven dollars here, Juan, for keeping my family."

Patrón shook his head. "You keep it. I'm making money boarding the Kid and Tom."

"I'm not broke, Juan. I've still got twenty-two dollars left. I was comforted knowing my family was safe with you while I conducted business on the Pecos." Wes grabbed Juan's hand and pressed the bills into his palm. "Take it."

Before Juan could answer, Wes heard a whistle from the corner of the house.

"Where's my share?" Bonney asked.

"I thought you were taking care of the team and wagon," Wes said as he folded Juan's fingers around the bills.

"I am," Bonney replied.

"It don't look like it to us," Wes answered, drawing a vigorous nod from Juan.

Bonney laughed. "I assigned Tom and my bodyguard to handle the chore. They'll do it, and they'll do a good job."

Wes shook his head and climbed atop Charlie. As he reined the sorrel around, Bonney stepped up and grabbed a bridle strap. "I need a favor from you, Wes."

"What now?"

"I want you here when I go before the grand jury. You know what the governor promised, and I want a witness in case he doesn't live up to the bargain. Do that and when I'm pardoned, I'll make things right with you."

Wes nodded. "I'll be here, Kid."

Looking back over his shoulder at the Casey place as he left his home for Lincoln, Wes Bracken could not believe all they had accomplished since he had returned Juan Patrón's wagon. Jace Cousins had secured from Roswell and the Chisum spread everything on his list and returned with a hundred and eleven dollars plus a puppy for the boys. Not only that, but Jace had told John Chisum himself that Jesse Evans had departed the territory for good and had been causing mischief around Fort Davis and Fort Stockton, Texas. Once Jace returned, the partners had plowed fields, planted four acres of corn, and started a garden for Sarafina and the boys to tend. The men had cleared and repaired the irrigation ditches that would water their thirsty crops. Wes had even put his sons to work herding stray chickens into the pen, a job they did enthusiastically if not efficiently. The work had lasted from before dawn until after dusk. Chores remained, especially rounding up and branding the cattle, but Wes looked with pleasure over their many achievements in such a short time. His muscles ached from all the labor, but he felt optimistic as he headed to Lincoln.

With a little luck on the place and a little justice in Lincoln County, things might just turn around for everyone. Of course, that depended on the court session scheduled to start that morning with the grand jury proceedings. Intent on fulfilling his promise to Bonney, Wes left the Casey place behind and rode toward Lincoln. A handful of other men and women, some on horseback and a few in wagons, journeyed down the road to town as well, drawn by subpoenas or curiosity about the pending legalities that might put Lincoln on a straighter path to law and order. With so many crimes and criminal complaints to sort through, the court session would run two or more weeks, way too long for Wes to spend in town. So, he would ride to and from the sessions from home each day so he could at least get some work done during that time, rather than leave it all for Jace and Sarafina to handle. Besides Bonney's testimony before the grand jury and likely hearings on the murders he was involved in, Wes planned to attend the hearing for his brother-in-law. Wes questioned whether Carlos would see the advantage in pleading guilty to the rustling charge to escape a murder conviction. While Wes knew Bonney would welcome his presence, he suspected Carlos would resent any visit to the jail or his attendance at the hearing.

With the grand jury scheduled to convene at nine o'clock, Wes timed his arrival at Patrón's adobe for a quarter before the hour. Nearing the dwelling, Wes saw the front door open up and Bonney emerge ahead of his guarding deputy. Bonney remained barefooted and shackled at the ankles, but he was also wearing wrist manacles and missing his holster and revolver.

Seeing Wes, the Kid grinned and raised his hands over his head, displaying the cuffs. As he lowered his arms, he cried out. "Thanks for coming, Wes. They don't trust me now that the judge and district attorney are in town."

"If I were you, I wouldn't trust the judge or the prosecutor."

"Hey, I've got the governor on my side."

"I hope you're right, Kid."

The deputy nudged Bonney with his palm and pointed him toward the courthouse a hundred yards southwest of Patrón's place.

"Good luck, Bonney."

"You don't need luck when the governor backs you."

"Kid, you forget this is Lincoln County."

Bonney flashed his buckteeth. "This afternoon I'll be a free man."

If only it were that simple, Wes thought. "I hope so." As Bonney walked to his court destiny, Wes dismounted and tied his horse to Patrón's hitching post. He removed his hat and stretched, enjoying the cool spring morning as he watched men moving toward the courthouse, several of them greeting the Kid and wishing him good luck. Tugging his headgear back in place, Bracken stepped with the crowd, then stopped at the call of a familiar voice.

"Wait up, Wes," shouted Juan Patrón as he emerged from the house. "I'm surprised you didn't come on in."

"We've been enough of a bother for you, Juan. I thought I'd give you a break, even if I am leaving my horse outside your door."

"You could've penned him out back in the corral."

"This'll be fine. I'm not staying the day. Too much work at home."

Juan shook Wes's hand. "From what I understand, the grand jury will meet in the mornings until early afternoon, then the general court sessions will start after lunch each day. They've got plenty to cover."

"Almost two years of outright lawlessness," Wes replied as the friends strode to the courthouse with dozens of others.

While most gathered in front of the courthouse where benches had been moved outside to accommodate them, Juan pointed to the west side of the squat adobe structure. "Let's wait over there where we can visit without being overheard." Patrón looked around to make sure no one was nearby, then whispered, "And where we might hear something." He directed Wes beside an open window, and the pair leaned against the cool adobe wall. Both men heard the murmuring from inside the room and the scraping of chairs against the floor as the grand jury convened to consider evidence against a multitude for innumerable crimes.

"Once Bonney testifies, I'm returning home to chores. Do we know if hearings have been set for him and Carlos?"

Patrón nodded. "They've posted the schedule for this week on the courthouse door. We'll check it once the Kid's done."

The two men pulled their hats down over their heads as if they were resting against the wall rather than listening.

"Judge Bristol and District Attorney Rynerson are Dolan allies, not Bonney's friends," Wes noted.

"Both are tied to the Santa Fe Ring. That's the source of so many of New Mexico's troubles."

"Is Governor Wallace connected to the ring?"

Patrón shrugged. "That's something we'd all like to find out. What I *do* know is Isaac Ellis is chairing the grand jury, and most of those impaneled on the jury have less sympathy for Dolan than for his opposition."

"I've got a bad feeling about the governor. I fear he'll double-cross Bonney. Does the Kid have a lawyer?"

"Yes, sir. Ira Leonard will represent him. Leonard is the widow McSween's new attorney. He knew Chapman before Dolan killed him. Working in the Kid's favor is the governor has taken a liking to Leonard."

"I still fear Bonney knows too much about all the shenanigans in Lincoln County for the Ring to let the governor pardon him."

Patrón held up his hand instead of answering. He pointed to the window. "Listen."

Wes heard the voice of Judge Warren Bristol, giving the oath to the grand jurors, then explaining the role of District Attorney William Rynerson in guiding them through their responsibilities as agents of the courts.

"You will find the D.A. fair, honest, and impartial in presenting the facts behind the many felonies that have come before this court," Bristol said. "Your duty as male citizens of this territory is to faithfully listen to the evidence as outlined by the prosecutor and reach a fair and just conclusion whether each accused should be indicted to stand trial before a jury of his peers."

Bristol then introduced Rynerson to the jurors and excused himself so the grand jury could begin its massive task in unraveling the crimes that had roiled Lincoln County. Rynerson said the first case examined the shooting of the attorney Huston Chapman on the streets of Lincoln on February eighteenth of this year. He called as his first witness, William H. Bonney, also known as Henry Antrim or the Kid.

By the rattling of the Kid's shackles, Wes knew Bonney was entering the room. He took the oath and then Rynerson's questioning began, the first query drawing Wes's ire.

"Is it true that you are under indictment

for the murder of late Sheriff William Brady on the same street that Chapman left this earth and for the murder of Buckshot Roberts at Blazer's Mill and that you have been at the scene of multiple other killings in Lincoln County?"

Wes heard the angry rattle of Bonney's chains as the Kid answered. "Some of that's true, but mostly it's lies."

For half an hour, Wes listened to Rynerson undermine Bonney by focusing on the Kid's transgressions rather than inquiring about Chapman's death. Finally, grand jury foreman Isaac Ellis spoke up. "We know about Bonney. We're here to learn about those involved in Chapman's death."

Rynerson coughed and offered an excuse. "It's my job to get to the truth. You can't get to the truth if you don't know the credibility of the witness."

"Either ask questions about the Chapman murder or we will," Ellis replied.

Chastened by a citizenry tired of all the violence, Rynerson paused, then asked details of the lawyer's death.

Bonney explained the night of the proposed truce and then the encounter with Chapman on the street when James J. Dolan and Jesse Evans shot him. Bonney then detailed how Dolan invited them to his saloon to celebrate the death of the lawyer.

As soon as Bonney finished his statement, Rynerson attacked. "All you're doing is covering for yourself and Tom O'Folliard. You two killed Huston Chapman and tried to blame it on James J. Dolan and Jesse Evans, two of the finest citizens to call Lincoln County home."

His comments drew knowing chuckles from the grand jurors as Bonney responded. "Had we killed the lawyer, Tom and I would never have agreed to turn ourselves over to the sheriff. We met with Dolan, Jesse, and the others to begin a truce to end the killing so we could live in peace. Those of us on the short end of the stick want to go on with our lives. Those that carry a big stick hope to club us down. It ain't right, and it ain't fair."

After a silent pause in the jury room, Wes heard the clap of a single juror, then another citizen joined in and another until the applause sounded like everyone was clapping, except for the district attorney.

"You must remain impartial," Rynerson scolded.

"And so should you," the foreman shot back.

"I have no more questions," Rynerson replied with acid in his tone. "The witness is remanded back to jail for his crimes."

Wes and Juan pushed themselves away from the wall and abandoned the window, rejoining the other attendees. Juan pointed to the court's handwritten schedule on three sheets of paper tacked to the front door. Both moved that way and studied the timetable; Juan pointed to a line that showed Bonney scheduled for his hearing Thursday afternoon. Wes nodded, then spotted his brother-in-law's name on the Friday afternoon calendar.

As the two men backed away from the door and wove their way through the clump of spectators, Bonney and his escort emerged from the courthouse. Bonney threw a wide grin at the crowd as his manacles jingled with each barefooted step. Wes and Patrón angled toward the Kid and intersected him halfway back to Juan's house.

Bonney threw up his arms and rattled the wrist shackles, then winked at his friends. "The district attorney doesn't think much of me," Bonney said, "but it don't matter anymore because I've lived up to my end of the bargain. I'll be walking free in a day or two."

Wes nodded. "I hope you're right, Kid, but you're scheduled for a hearing Thursday afternoon on the Brady and Roberts kill-ings."

"That's just for show," Bonney responded. "You know what the governor said."

"Assuming he lives up to that promise, Kid. I'll return Thursday for your hearing."

CHAPTER 20

Wes Bracken squeezed into the packed courtroom in time for Billy Bonney's Thursday hearing on the killings of Sheriff William Brady and Buckshot Roberts. Wes wormed his way in, standing alongside the wall just as third district Judge Warren Bristol gaveled the room to order in the matter of the Territory of New Mexico versus William H. Bonney. A short man who sat ironing-board straight to make himself appear more imposing, Bristol sported thin gray hair, neatly trimmed because there was so little of it above his brow, and a close-cropped salt-and-pepper goatee. His face tapered into a narrow chin beneath crooked lips and a fine nose. A pair of thick wire-rimmed glasses rested on his beak, giving him the look if not the wisdom of an owl.

Bristol asked the district attorney if he was ready, and William Rynerson stood from his chair, straightening his frame to its full length well over six and a half feet. A physically imposing man, he confirmed the government was prepared to prove the need for Bonney to stand trial. The judge studied the Kid's lawyer, who bounced up without being asked and introduced himself as Ira Leonard, attorney-at-law representing Mr. Bonney.

Wes strained to see the Kid, but the court was too crowded for him to get a clear view, though he could hear the jangling of his chains every time Bonney shifted his hands or feet. A man approaching fifty years of age, Leonard spoke with a firm voice and moved with the confidence of a man who knew he was in the right, even against long odds.

"Your Honor," Leonard began, "might I ask the court's indulgence in permitting my client to sit through these proceedings without shackles on his ankles and wrists?"

Bonney raised his arms over his head for everyone to see the chained cuffs, then shook his hands to rattle the music of the incarcerated.

"The wrist and ankle irons prejudge the issues at debate in this hearing and —"

Bristol banged the gavel on his desk and shook his head. "Mr. Bonney is a known murderer and is not entitled to any such courtesies for the safety of those attending this hearing."

"But Your Honor," Leonard countered, "those are just charges, mere accusations yet to be considered by a jury of his peers. This proceeding will determine whether he faces such a jury. Until that is decided, Your Honor, I beseech you to allow him to sit through this proceeding with the dignity accorded to the accused under our system of justice."

Three times Bristol slammed his gavel against the desk. "Request denied, Mr. Leonard. Please sit so District Attorney Rynerson can present his case against this miscreant."

Bowing his head and sighing loud enough to be heard throughout the courtroom, Leonard returned to his seat. As he sat down, Bonney shook his arms and legs, his chains clanking and drawing snickers from his many friends among the spectators. Rynerson stood up and outlined reasons supporting Bonney's prosecution. The sympathetic Bristol nodded at the prosecutor's points and overruled all objections raised by Leonard. Bonney countered by rattling his cuffs every time Rynerson's comments annoyed him. Several times the judge chastised the Kid.

"A fly keeps pestering me," Bonney explained to the amusement of the spectators. "I'm just trying to shoo him away like the district attorney."

The crowd laughed, drawing another bang from the gavel and a warning from the judge that he would clear the courtroom unless the crowd respected the seriousness of the legal proceeding that everyone soon recognized as a sham. Wes smiled at the Kid's audacity and at the knowledge that no jury in Lincoln County would convict Bonney for his part in the late difficulties. The hearing lasted an hour when Bristol announced the Kid would be held over for a trial on the murder of both Sheriff Brady on the streets of Lincoln and Buckshot Roberts at Blazer's Mill on the Indian reservation. Wes expected the judge's decision, but not the district attorney's subsequent demand.

"Your Honor," said Rynerson, "might I make a final request regarding the trial of William H. Bonney, also known as Henry Antrim."

"Proceed, Counselor," Bristol responded.

"In light of the serious nature of these charges and the difficulties in drawing an unbiased jury from the citizens of this county so ravaged by the murderous rampages of vicious men like William H. Bonney and his consorts, I propose a change of venue for this trial to be conducted in Doña Ana County, where justice can be better served."

The defense attorney shot up from his chair. "Your Honor, I respectfully ask that you deny this change of venue. Let the people who have suffered the most from the violence and depredations be the ones to determine the guilt or innocence of Mr. Bonney."

As soon as Leonard finished his response, the Kid shook his chains and banged them against the table by his lawyer's side.

Bristol slammed the gavel against his desk. "Quiet," the judge screamed, "fly or no fly." He glared at the accused until the Kid rested his hands calmly on the table, offering a smile in return. With vitriol in his voice, the magistrate spoke. "After due consideration, I am granting the prosecutor's request."

"I intend to appeal this decision," Leonard proclaimed.

Bristol banged the gavel a final time. "This proceeding is concluded. Please clear the room for the next hearing." The judge arose, turned about, and marched out.

Rynerson stood up and smirked at Leonard and his client, then followed the judge into the anteroom. Bonney kept rattling his irons as the crowd moved from their chairs toward the exit. Wes lingered until the throng cleared, then approached the table where Bonney's lawyer shook his head and ran his fingers through his hair.

Bonney smirked at Wes. "The district attorney doesn't like me."

Wes nodded. "Nor the judge."

"But it won't matter when the governor pardons me."

Leonard grimaced at the Kid, then turned to Wes. "You are?"

"Wes Bracken, a friend of the Kid."

The lawyer offered a tepid smile. "He speaks highly of you, says you can be trusted."

"I try."

"Few people in Lincoln County would I trust," the lawyer answered.

"Is the governor one of them? He's promised a pardon for the Kid."

Leonard lowered his head. "It's not that simple. The governor has no authority over federal crimes. While the governor might pardon him for the Brady shooting, he can't for the killing at Blazer's Mill, which sits on the Mescalero Reservation. That makes it a federal crime."

Bonney slammed his fist against the table.

"He promised me a pardon."

"What he indicated and what he can do legally are two different animals, Bonney," replied Leonard.

"I demand to talk to the governor," Bonney insisted. "He gave me his word I'd get a pardon and walk away with it in my pocket."

Leonard shrugged. "I wasn't there to hear the governor."

"I was," Wes interjected, "and the Kid's right."

Leonard raised his gaze toward Bracken. "I'll do what I can, but I've been threatened simply for defending Bonney, and the governor's under a lot of pressure to wipe the slate clean in Lincoln County. Rightfully or wrongfully, the Kid's the biggest name in all the difficulties and has been painted as the cause of all the troubles."

"You and I both know that's wrong."

"Agreed, but back east they are now writing dime novels about Billy the Kid, calling him a noted desperado and publishing outlandish tales about him. We know better, as do most of the good folks in Lincoln County, but we're not up against decent people."

Billy rattled his chains again. "No matter what the governor says, I guarantee you I will not step on the trapdoor of any gallows.

They will never hang me."

Leonard nodded. "We're a long way from that possibility, Kid, but we're trying to put out a fire with a mouthful of spittle rather than a bucket full of water."

"I want to speak to Wallace again," Bonney responded as he stood up from his seat and started for the door ahead of his lawyer and the deputy guarding him.

"Carlos's hearing is tomorrow afternoon," Wes announced. "I'll drop by before that to see you."

The Kid lifted his arms and rattled his chains as he left the room.

Wes shook his head, disgusted with Lincoln County and the politics that had stained its soul all the way to bedrock. He stepped outside and spat on the county's corrupt soil before mounting Charlie and returning home.

At high sun the next day, Wes tugged the wagon to a halt outside Juan Patrón's house. Sarafina had insisted on attending her brother's hearing so Wes had loaded her and the three children into the rig and driven to Lincoln. As he tied the lines to the brake lever, Wes heard the front door open and looked up to see Juan inspecting the wagon and team.

"Didn't think you had a wagon, much less a team, Wes."

"Jace did a little horse trading in Roswell and drove a good bargain. Got this and a plow, plus a few supplies to hold us over until the crops come in."

Patrón cocked his head at Bracken. "That's good trading for a man with just twenty-two dollars."

"Jace is good, I tell you."

Patrón nodded. "I heard an interesting rumor yesterday. Word is that Jesse Evans has been prowling around Fort Davis and Fort Stockton in Texas."

Wes grinned, glad that the gossip Jace birthed had made it back to Lincoln. "Can't say for certain, Juan. As long as Jesse never returns here, the rumors don't matter. Is the Kid around?"

Patrón whistled over his shoulder. "Kid, Wes Bracken is here to see you." Juan stepped to the wagon and greeted Sarafina.

Bonney bounded out of the adobe, still in arm and leg chains, but smiling nonetheless. "I met with the governor last evening, and he's got a final request before he grants my pardon. He wants me to testify next month at the court of inquiry for Colonel Nathan Dudley for his role in McSween's death. Once I've done that, he'll issue me a pardon."

Wes forced a grin, suspecting the governor was stringing the Kid along until he had wrung all he needed out of him all the while planning to ignore his promised pardon and abandon the Kid after that. "I hope it works out for you."

"You'll come to Fort Stanton for the inquiry, won't you, Wes?"

"If I get word of the date in time."

Bonney grinned. "I knew you'd be there for me. When I'm free, I'll work as a hand for you to repay my debt."

Patrón nodded. "I'll let you know, Wes, when the inquiry is scheduled. Guess you heard the grand jury issued its findings this morning?"

"It's news to me."

"The grand jurors handed down over two hundred indictments, all but two against Dolan and his allies."

Wes whistled. "That is good news."

"Not entirely," the Kid announced. "They indicted Tom for rustling."

"It's not that bad for O'Folliard," Patrón elaborated, "as the lawyer Leonard says the charge will be dropped because of the governor's general amnesty. Now all we've got to do is get the Kid pardoned and maybe things'll return to normal, though

I'm uncertain how long Leonard will stay here. Somebody fired two shots at him last night. The assassin missed, but we don't know if he was a bad shot or delivering a message from Dolan. Either way, Leonard's terrified, especially knowing that Dolan killed the last lawyer that worked for Susan McSween."

Wes shook his head. "Lincoln County!" He untied the lines from the brake lever. "I doubt there'll be as much interest in Carlos's hearing as in Bonney's, but we came early to claim decent seats." He turned to the Kid. "Good luck with the governor." Wes shook the reins and started for the courthouse, wondering if Wallace would live up to his agreement about Carlos. Would the territory suspend the murder charges if Carlos pled guilty to rustling? Or would the governor ignore the agreement? Wes remained skeptical of the governor's word, but said nothing of his doubts to Sarafina as she fretted about her brother's future.

Halting outside the courthouse, Wes secured the reins and stepped down, helping the boys out of the back, encouraging them to run around and drain some of their excess energy before going inside where they would have to remain still. After setting the boys free, he took Blanca from his wife and offered Sarafina his hand so she could step from the wagon seat. As soon as she stood on the ground, he handed the baby back to her mother. "If you want to go inside, Sarafina, I'll watch after our sons, let them tire themselves out so they'll be easier to manage when the proceedings start. Everything'll work out."

Sarafina took his hand and squeezed it. "I hope you're right, but I worry Carlos is too hotheaded to understand what you have done for him. Painful as a few years in prison might be for him, it beats hanging for his crimes."

Wes nodded. "Go inside, maybe feed Blanca before the session begins so she won't be fussy." After watching his wife enter the courthouse, Wes followed the boys around, enjoying their laughter and antics as they chased each other, then a cottontail rabbit that they flushed from a bush. Once they had drained their boyish energy, Wes called them to the wagon and fished a pair of tortillas from the basket Sarafina had brought for their lunch. When they finished the tortillas, Wes gave each a drink from his canteen and told them they must be still and quiet during the hearing for their uncle. Wes led them past their wagon and a half dozen saddle horses, far fewer than had been present for the Kid's hearing. Few spectators would see the judge hand down Carlos's punishment.

Moving inside, Wes led the boys to their mother, who patted the bench beside her for the boys to sit down. Wes scooted next to the lads and waited. About twenty minutes later, three Hispanic men came in, tipped their hats at Sarafina, and sat. Just before the one o'clock start, Sheriff Kimbrell entered with Carlos. Sarafina gasped when she saw her brother. Always slender, he was now much skinnier, and his loose clothes and face were dirt-stained from time in the pit. Carlos squinted his eyes, even in the dim courtroom, as he had seen so little sunlight since his arrest. As he marched past the front row where Sarafina rested, he smiled briefly, then scowled when he glimpsed Bracken.

"Bastardo," he mumbled.

Sarafina shot up so fast from her seat that it startled the baby in her arms, and Blanca cried. "You will not use such language in front of my children, Carlos. You know better."

Carlos cast his eyes downward.

"How have you been, Carlos?" Sarafina asked.

He lifted his hands so she could see the chains and how they had chafed his wrists and forearms. "How do you think?" he mumbled as the sheriff guided him to his chair.

Before he could say more, Judge Bristol and the district attorney entered the court from the adjacent room. Bristol called the session to order and announced the charges of murder and rustling by the Territory of New Mexico against Carlos Zamora. He called upon Rynerson to make his case.

The lanky Rynerson arose from his chair, thanked the court, and announced that the territory after careful discussions with the accused was prepared to drop the murder charges for his role in the killing of Sheriff Brady and Deputy Hindman, provided Zamora pled guilty to rustling and accepted a prison term of thirty-six months.

Sarafina sighed and lowered her head at the announcement of the sentence, calming herself by rocking Blanca more vigorously in her arms.

Bristol asked the defendant to rise, which he did with prompting from the sheriff.

"Is this a fair and true representation of your agreement?"

Carlos hesitated and finally nodded.

"You are pleading guilty to rustling?"

The defendant bobbed his head again.

"The court hereby sentences you to a term of up to thirty-six months in prison, reducible for good behavior or for budgetary reasons should the Territory of New Mexico be unable to pay for your further imprisonment in the Yuma Territorial Prison. Arizona Territory."

Sarafina looked at Wes, confused by the punishment. "Why Arizona?" she whispered.

"New Mexico has no prison," he whispered back.

She grimaced. "It is so far away."

Wes nodded, then stared at Carlos, who surprised him by remaining silent through the proceeding.

At that point, the judged instructed Kimbrell to carry out the sentence and banged his gavel, declaring the session over. Bishop and Rynerson retreated to the anteroom and just like that the session was over, Bracken relieved that the governor had lived up to his word. The sheriff ordered the convicted defendant to head back to the jail.

Carlos glared at his sister. "Yuma cannot be as horrible as this hole in the ground where they keep me like an animal."

"Wes did everything he could to save you from the hangman, Carlos."

Her brother stared at her, then pointed at the revolver hanging from the leather thong over her shoulder. "You should use that pistol to shoot your husband. He has brought nothing but bad luck to our family."

Sarafina backed away from her brother as he passed. "He's part of the family now. He supports me and my children so we have food in our bellies. You never did that for me. And you wouldn't be in the trouble you're in if you had listened to him."

Carlos raised his manacled hands and shook them at Bracken. "One day, I will kill you for your treachery."

"Dolan and his gang betrayed you. I warned you they were using you. At least I saved you from a murder charge. Don't forget they can revive the murder indictment if you commit any more crimes in New Mexico Territory."

The sheriff shoved Carlos in the back. "Get moving, boy. Yuma's over six hundred miles from here, so you've got a long trip ahead of you."

Carlos cursed the sheriff as he stumbled forward, then blasphemed Bracken as he went out the door.

Wes turned to his wife, tears streaming down her cheeks, her two boys standing on the bench and comforting her with hugs. Not knowing what to say, he simply patted her shoulder. "It's time to go home, Sarafina." He picked up the boys and followed his wife out of the courthouse to the wagon for the ride back to the Casey place. He prayed that this would be the last visit he ever had to make to court.

The spring months turned warmer as summer approached. Bracken and Cousins worked dawn to dusk, not even taking time off on Sundays, to expand their fields and catch up with all the chores around the Casey place for the rest of April. In May the two men put out word to the families along the three rivers that they would grind their corn at the mill for free come fall just to remove one worry from families that were still trying to recuperate from the failure of the previous year's crops. Wes knew they needed to tend their cattle, but there was so much to do with the crops that they couldn't take time away to round up and brand their livestock. The longer they delayed that task, however, the more likely some of Dolan's renegades might rustle their herd and add his brand to their hides. All the troubles had postponed or, in some cases, destroyed Wes's dreams for the future. He did not know what he would've done without Cousins, who had stayed on the place and managed chores while Wes went to Lincoln so often for court hearings and other business brought on by the county's troubles and his efforts to help Billy Bonney.

Eleven days before the end of May, Wes was hoeing weeds in the field when he heard the boy's new puppy yelping. Looking up, he spotted Patrón astride his gelding, then glanced at Jace, who had been spading out a clogged irrigation ditch. Wes knew Patrón's arrival meant he would be riding to Fort Stanton for the court of inquiry as he had promised Bonney. Both Wes and Jace ambled toward Patrón, tools in hand to greet their friend.

"Get down, Juan," Jace offered. "You can have my shovel or Wes's hoe, and you can work with us."

"Can't stay long, *amigos*," Patrón answered. "I came to tell you that the deputy returned from Yuma after delivering Carlos to the Yuma Territorial Prison and —"

"Maybe Carlos'll come back a reformed man," Wes noted.

"— he'll remain in Yuma for thirty-six months or as long as the county pays his room and board," Patrón continued, "but the main thing I wanted to tell you is that the Kid will testify before the Dudley board of inquiry next Wednesday at Fort Stanton. Bonney's getting nervous that the governor won't come through with his promised pardon because he knows if he stands trial in Mesilla, Bristol will hang him."

"He's got reason to fear," Wes answered. "They've always favored the Dolan men."

"What's the penalty for shooting a prosecutor or a judge?" Jace inquired.

Patrón shook his head. "Ask Rynerson. He would know. A dozen years ago he assassinated the territory's chief justice in Santa Fe's Exchange Hotel."

"Damn," Jace answered. "New Mexico's gotta be the crookedest place I've ever been. Got away with murder, did he?"

"Just like Dolan and his bunch. If you've got connections, you can kill without fear."

"And if you don't," Wes interjected, "you're strung along like the Kid. Will the governor be in Fort Stanton for the inquiry?"

"Rumor has it he'll be there," Patrón replied, "but you know about rumors. I'm still hearing that Jesse Evans is causing trouble in Texas."

Cousins cocked his head. "Where in Texas?"

"Fort Stockton and Fort Davis," Patrón

answered.

With a wide grin on his face, Cousins answered. "You don't say? I wouldn't put much stock in those stories, Juan, because any idiot can start a lie."

Patrón shrugged. "I can't say for certain. Jesse always seemed to land on his feet as you fellows both know."

"Thanks for riding out with the news. Any idea what time his testimony will begin?"

"I've heard first thing that morning."

"Tell Bonney I'll be there. You sure you don't want to stay and help us with the chores?"

"That's nothing compared to living with Bonney, O'Folliard, and a sheriff's deputy in your house all the time. At least I'm getting a dollar a day for the trouble."

Wes nodded. "That's more than we're making."

"But you've got it easier than I do!" Patrón reined his horse about and started back for Lincoln. "See you next time, Wes."

Turning to Jace, Wes nodded. "Looks like I'll be out a few days next week. Sorry to abandon you again, partner."

"It's worth it if you can get the Kid's tail out of a crack."

Wes Bracken camped on a ridge overlooking Fort Stanton the night before Bonney's testimony and rode in early the next morning seeking the site for the court of inquiry. He tied his horse on the perimeter of the parade ground and walked by several soldiers in blue uniforms. He still felt uneasy around men wearing the blue uniform he had fought against a decade and a half earlier. Even odder was the sight of black men in that same uniform. By the insignia on their hats, they were members of the Ninth Cavalry. Soon Wes realized the men he was following were headed to the mess hall, so he hailed a young lieutenant who pointed him to the headquarters building. As he neared the white clapboard building, he saw the attorney Ira Leonard who had pushed the inquiry on behalf of Susan McSween. Wes angled for Leonard, who was carrying a satchel of papers and a heavy burden as reflected in the slump of his shoulders and the frown on his face.

"Mr. Leonard," Wes called. "It's Wes Bracken here."

The lawyer glanced up, a slight smile cracking his stiff demeanor for an instant. "Bonney's friend, right? He'll be glad to see you and know that you're here for his testimony. Things are looking bad for Bonney. The board of inquiry is composed of

Dudley's cronies. They are as partisan and corrupt as Judge Bristol and District Attorney Rynerson. We've had a week of testimony with several more days to go, but the outcome is set. I know it in my bones. Without an affirmative recommendation of the board, Colonel Dudley will avoid the court martial he so richly deserves."

"It's Lincoln County, sir. That's the only explanation for it. Is the governor here?"

Leonard nodded, "But he's leaving this afternoon, once Bonney has testified."

Wes felt a sense of relief that just maybe the governor would live up to his bargain once Bonney submitted to the board's inquiries. "Would it be possible to see him?"

"Unlikely as he's consumed in finishing his book in every spare moment, but you can try." Leonard pointed to one of the officer's quarters, a whitewashed clapboard building. "He's staying there."

"How long before the Kid testifies?"

"An hour."

"Tell Bonney, I'll be there." Wes strode toward the governor's quarters. Stepping up on the porch he knocked firmly on the door.

"Enter, Orderly," came the governor's voice.

Wes opened the door and stepped inside.

"You're early, but I'm ready for breakfast,"

402

the governor called, looking up from his stack of papers and shaking his head. "I thought you were the mess orderly. I'm not seeing visitors."

"The name's Wes Bracken, remember? I met with you and the Kid when you promised him a pardon if he testified in all these proceedings."

"I can't pardon him for a crime on the Indian reservation."

"Then pardon him for the shooting of Sheriff Brady."

Lew Wallace stood up from his desk and shook his head. "I can't see how a fellow like him can expect any clemency from me, as he showed none to his victims."

"But you promised him he would walk free with a pardon in his pocket if he testified in the legal proceedings," Wes pleaded. "He's done just that."

"Let me tell you, Bracken, when you get an appointment like governor to a territory as corrupt as New Mexico, you think you will go in and right all the wrongs. You are mistaken. You don't know all the pressures and all the influences that make it near impossible to even tell right from wrong, much less correct it."

"It's the Santa Fe Ring, isn't it? You and everyone else have sold out to their corruption. You don't care who gets crushed."

"Like I said, Bonney doesn't deserve clemency for what he did."

"He tried to make things right, and put his life at risk several times in doing so, and you don't have the decency to abide by your commitment."

Wallace pointed to the door. "It's called politics. Politicians make a lot of promises they have no intention on keeping. It's for the better good. Now leave before I call for soldiers to throw you out."

"In all of Lincoln's bad moments, there's not been one lower than this, Governor. The Kid deserved better."

"Bonney deserves what I'm giving him. Now get out, Bracken, or I'll have you arrested for threatening me."

Wes spun around and rumbled out the door, slamming it behind him.

CHAPTER 21

Wes Bracken waited on the porch of the Fort Stanton headquarters to see Billy Bonney before the court of inquiry resumed into Colonel Nathan Dudley's actions during the climax of Lincoln County's troubles at the Big Killing. Though he was still in shackles when he approached from the stockade with a uniformed guard at each shoulder, the Kid grinned when he saw Wes, who smiled as best he could, knowing that the governor, like Judas, would betray Bonney in the end.

"Morning, Kid. You're plenty chipper for a fellow in chains."

"Each day brings me one day closer to a pardon. It shouldn't be long after I finish testifying before the board of inquiry."

Wes's grin melted away. "I hope you're right, Kid, but I don't trust anyone in New Mexico Territory anymore, save for you and Jace Cousins."

Bonney lifted his manacled hand and grabbed Bracken's, shaking it vigorously, his chains clanging. "I'm obliged for everything you've done for me."

"I fear it hasn't been enough."

"But it was more than anyone else. Your word's always been good." Bonney released his grip as one of his guards motioned toward the entry. The Kid moved on.

"Maybe we can visit during lunch. There's things I need to tell you."

"Talk to you then," Bonney said as a soldier opened the door into the building. The Kid and his guards marched inside and closed the door behind them.

Wes lingered a moment on the porch, enjoying the early morning cool before following two officers into the headquarters building and the modest hearing room where Colonel Dudley and his counsel sat at a table across the aisle from another table for Leonard and Bonney. Behind the Kid stood his two guards. Six officers sat in chairs behind the accused colonel. Wes moved to a seat near a window where he could enjoy the cool of the morning breeze. He took off his hat and placed it on the chair beside him as he studied the military men arrayed before him. By the jovial demeanor of Dudley and the other officers,

Wes decided this hearing was nothing more than a formality to find the colonel blameless for all his actions.

At precisely nine o'clock, a side door opened and four officers entered wearing the formal uniforms of a colonel, a major, and two captains. The other soldiers in the room snapped to attention as the board members stepped to the front table facing the accused and his accuser. As Leonard and Bonney rose from their seats, so did Bracken until the panel members took their chairs and nodded at the others to do likewise. As Wes bent to settle back into his seat, the colonel in charge pointed at him.

"Sir," he said, "I am Colonel Pennypacker of the Sixteenth Infantry. Please state your name and business."

Wes straightened, galled to be challenged by a man in a Union uniform. "I'm Wesley Bracken, a citizen of Lincoln County. I am here at the request of William Bonney with the full knowledge of his attorney Ira Leonard."

"Mr. Bracken, this is an army matter open only to military personnel, witnesses, and appropriate legal counsel. As you fit into none of those categories, I must ask you to leave. Failure to do so on your own volition will result in you being escorted from this hearing room to the stockade until this inquiry is concluded next week. Is that understood?"

"Yes, General."

"It's colonel," Pennypacker corrected.

Wes picked up his hat and looked at the Kid. "Sorry, Bonney. I'll visit with you at lunch as long as your meal's not considered an army matter."

The Kid grinned and rattled his chains as Wes exited the room and strode through the anteroom and outside. For a moment, he wondered how he would kill the time, then remembered the open windows in the hearing room. Deciding to use one of Juan Patrón's tricks, Wes casually stepped off the porch and to the back of the building, where he leaned against the wall beside the opening. There he listened to Pennypacker call the proceedings to order and instruct Leonard to make any opening statement and to introduce his witness.

Wes heard Leonard's chair scrape against the floor as he stood up. The lawyer began by reminding the board that Dudley was charged with directing a detachment of sixty soldiers with one cannon and one Gatling gun into town to support an unlawful attack upon the home and person of Alexander A. McSween. Further, Leonard accused the colonel of forcing Justice of the Peace Squire Wilson to issue an unlawful warrant for the arrest of McSween and his allies and of acquiescing to the plunder and looting of the adjacent Tunstall store in the aftermath of the killing of five innocent citizens, including McSween. The lawyer next charged that Dudley himself threatened and slandered the widow Susan McSween before, during, and even after the attack on the McSween residence. Leonard introduced the Kid as William H. Bonney, sometimes known as Henry Antrim or Billy the Kid, and explained that the witness was present at or affected by all the travesties previously mentioned.

By the rattling of the chains, Wes realized Bonney had stood from his seat and moved to the witness chair where he was sworn in. After the Kid took his seat, Leonard led him through the events of that tragic day. The Kid testified the troops had undermined the McSween advantage in the showdown by taking positions that made it impossible for his allies in other buildings around town to support those in the McSween house without endangering the lives of the soldiers. He further stated that Dudley had made it known he would use the cannon and Gatling gun to demolish any building from which such shots were fired. Bonney further stated that he saw soldiers actually firing into the McSween house and at him when he escaped out the back.

After Leonard finished, Colonel Dudley himself questioned his accuser, trying to get the Kid to confirm he was subject to arrest by the sheriff that day for past crimes. Bonney said that was something he would have to ask the sheriff because he had no way of knowing what was on the lawman's mind.

As the testimony continued, Wes noticed a civilian standing by a nearby barrack and staring at him. At first Wes failed to recognize him, but as the man watched, Bracken realized it was James J. Dolan himself, the kingpin of Lincoln County mischief after the death of his partner, L.G. Murphy. Wes studied the man behind so many of the hardships and bad feelings circulating in Lincoln County. Dolan moved from the building and strode toward Bracken. Fearful Dolan would give away his eavesdropping, Wes stepped from the window and toward Dolan, letting his right hand drop to his side, his fingers wrapping around the butt of his pistol.

Once Dolan saw Bracken's hand on his revolver, he stopped, scowled, and spun around, scurrying off behind the barrack like a cockroach exposed to light. Wes retreated to the window and listened to the testimony for another hour, Dudley trying to rattle the Kid into contradictions and Bonney holding firm to his beliefs and, Wes thought, to the truth of the matter.

When Pennypacker finally called a break for lunch, Wes ambled to the front of the headquarters and awaited Leonard, Bonney, and his two guards.

When they emerged, Leonard pointed to Wes and angled that direction with Bonney and the guards in tow. "Sorry you couldn't stay for the testimony," Leonard said.

"I have a good idea what was said," Wes replied.

"You were listening outside the window, just like at the grand jury, weren't you?" the Kid inquired.

Bracken nodded. "Is there a place where we can talk alone with Bonney?"

Leonard shook his head. "I don't trust anybody around here, Wes."

"Me neither. I saw Jimmy Dolan skulking around during the Kid's testimony."

"Doesn't surprise me," the lawyer replied. "I've heard rumors he was hiding out here, what with all the indictments against him. The army's covering for him just like for Dudley." Leonard pointed to the parade

411

ground. "Let's talk out there under the flagpole. At least we'll know who's around."

"Fine by me," Wes answered.

"I'm with you guys," Bonney said, glancing over his shoulder, "and my twin shadows."

The trio ambled that way, the two uniformed guards trailing in their wake. As they reached the flagpole, a breeze caught the flag, and it snapped in the wind.

Leonard glanced up at the standard waving in the breeze. "Almost makes me ashamed to stand beneath the Stars and Stripes, what with all the corruption being covered up under its auspices." He turned around and pointed at the guards. "Give us some room, fellows, so we can discuss some legalities."

The nearest soldier, a corporal, shook his head. "Not until the new fellow gives us his sidearm."

Wes slid his hand to his holster and pulled the gun out with his thumb and forefinger, giving it to the trooper. Revolver in hand, the corporal and the other guard backed beyond hearing distance.

Eyeing the guards, Wes spoke softly. "I'll be blunt with you both. I visited the governor this morning, and he's more interested in his book than in keeping his promise to

Bonney."

The Kid cocked his head and spat on the ground. "But he gave me his word," he answered, his voice rising.

"Keep it quiet, Billy, so they don't overhear," Leonard said, looking at the guards.

"The governor looked me right in the eye and vowed to put a pardon in my pocket so I could walk away a free man once I testified against Dolan at the grand jury. I did that. Next he said he'd grant my freedom once I appeared before Dudley's board of inquiry. I'm doing that."

"There are forces behind this bigger than us," Wes answered. "If Dolan is walking freely around here under the army's protection while you're in chains, it should tell you something about the power of those we're fighting."

"But he told me to my face I'd get a pardon if I did what he said."

Wes turned to the lawyer. "I hear you are on good terms with Wallace. Am I wrong?"

Leonard pursed his lips, glanced down, and sighed before looking at Bonney. "I'm afraid Wes is right. I suspect he'll never pardon you. Someone or something's gotten to him, whether it's the Santa Fe Ring or his book, I don't know, but I fear he's tired of fighting the corruption and wants out of New Mexico Territory."

Bonney wagged his head from side to side. "I can't believe it. He gave me his word. Is not a governor's word good for anything?"

"He is a politician, Kid. Don't forget that," Wes replied.

"I can't believe he would betray me after I've done everything he's asked. I just can't."

Wes patted Bonney on the shoulder. "I felt you should know, Kid. I tried."

Bonney looked up and bit his lower lip, then shook his head again. "I'll finish my testimony here and give the governor a week to live up to his word. If I haven't received a pardon after this inquiry concludes, I'm escaping because I don't stand a chance in a Mesilla trial. I promise you this, I won't be hanged by them or anyone else, ever!"

"I don't blame you, Kid," Wes said, removing his hand from Bonney's shoulder. "Just don't hurt the Patróns or anyone else when you escape. Don't add to your troubles."

"Juan and Beatriz have treated me squarely. I hold no grudge against them."

"Since I can't attend the hearings, Kid, I'm heading back home. Jace and I still have more days of farm work to do before we can even start rounding up and branding our herd. I fear there's nothing more I can do for you with Wallace."

Bonney nodded. "I'll give him another week before I ride free."

"When you do, Kid, leave New Mexico. Start anew elsewhere, under a different name."

"We'll see what the governor does," the Kid replied.

Wes turned to Leonard. "Thanks for what you're doing for Bonney."

"It's not just for him. I'm working for all the decent folks in the whole territory."

Wes spun around and headed for the guards, retrieving his pistol from the corporal and striding for his sorrel to begin the journey back to the Casey place. There was work to do, and he had done all he could to help the Kid without taking the law into his own hands.

Eight days of hard work followed Wes Bracken's return to the Casey place. Figuring Jace Cousins had pulled more than his fair share of chores during Wes's absences, he suggested on the ninth day that his partner take a couple dollars and go to Lincoln to buy a few drinks for relaxation. Ever practical, Jace accepted the offer but countered that he needed a new work shirt and some socks without holes in them more than he needed some jiggers of whiskey.

Come dusk, Cousins returned with a new shirt, two pairs of socks, and some surprises bundled in brown butcher paper and tied with twine. He dropped off the package at the kitchen door and headed to the barn to unsaddle his dun. When he returned, Jace teased Wes for quitting before dark without him around to keep an eye on things.

"Sarafina called me to supper," Wes replied as he dipped his spoon into a bowl of stew.

As Cousins retrieved his package, Sarafina put a steaming bowl at his place. Jace settled into his seat, placing his bundle in the empty chair by his side and grabbing his spoon. Sarafina put a cornbread muffin on the table by his bowl, and Jace thanked her after taking his first bite.

"Your stew's getting better with each meal," he complimented.

She smiled. "I've learned how to cook on this stove without scorching the stew."

"A little char never hurt anybody," Jace countered. "Where are the boys?"

"They've eaten," Sarafina responded.

"Call them," Jace instructed, "I've got something for them and you two girls."

"Luis, Roberto," Sarafina cried, "come here." Moments later the two boys ambled into the room, looks of uncertainty on their faces. "Uncle Jace has something for you."

Their doubts turned to smiles as Jace unwrapped the bundle in the chair, pulling out a paper sack and offering it to Sarafina. "It's lemon drops. I thought the boys might like them."

Sarafina opened the bag and lifted it to her nose, inhaling the tart sweetness. She took two out, placing one in each little outstretched palm. Uncertain what to do with it, Roberto tried to bounce it on the floor.

"No," Jace instructed. "It's candy. You put it in your mouth and suck on it."

Luis did just that, frowning for a moment at the sour shock before smiling at the sweet aftermath. Roberto picked up his from the floor and slipped it between his lips. Soon, he grinned as well. Moments later both boys scooted away to resume their play.

Sarafina looked in the sack, then at Jace. "There are many. I have never had a lemon drop. May I?"

"Sure," Jace said, "but I've got something else for you and Blanca." He pulled out a yellow ribbon as Sarafina slipped a lemon drop in her mouth. He offered the strand to Sarafina. "There's two yards there. I thought it might look good in your hair or around Blanca's head."

"*Gracias, gracias,*" Sarafina replied, taking the gift from him and bolting to her bedroom.

"What did you bring me?" Wes asked.

"A newspaper from Mesilla and news from Lincoln." Jace tossed the newspaper across the table. "The Kid and Tom O'Folliard escaped from Patrón's place yesterday."

Wes grimaced. "I reckon the governor never pardoned him. Anyone hurt?"

"Not a soul."

"Did the law give chase?"

"Nope. Word is Bonney took enough guns and ammunition to fight off an army. Whether that's true or merely a rumor to scare folks off his tail, I can't say. Neither could Juan."

"The Kid should leave New Mexico forever. That's the best thing he could do now."

Sarafina burst back in the room, carrying in her arms a yawning Blanca with a yellow bow tied around her forehead, accentuating the baby's fuzzy red hair.

"She's a doll, just like her mother," Jace offered.

"Any other news from Lincoln?" Wes asked between bites.

"Seems like Carlos is the only one of the indicted who's been convicted and jailed."

Sarafina stamped her foot until Wes looked up at her. "Aren't you going to say anything about your daughter?"

Wes felt his face redden with embarrassment from being called down in front of his partner. "The ribbon looks nice. Thank you, Jace, for thinking of the girls."

"Your girls," Sarafina snapped, then spun around and exited the kitchen.

"I didn't mean to cause you any trouble, Wes."

"It's nothing," he replied as he tried to change the subject. "We should ride out tomorrow and start rounding up what cattle we can and determining how many we've got left."

"Last count, it was under two hundred," Jace replied, "but I've got work I want to do on the gristmill first."

"But that'll take a couple days."

"A few more days won't matter, especially if we don't have any cattle left, anyway."

Wes shrugged and grabbed his paper. "I'll be up front, reading the news."

"I'll be in after I finish my stew."

Wes stepped from the kitchen to the front room and lit a lamp. He settled in a rocking chair and opened the *Mesilla Valley Independent.* As he read, he heard Sarafina return to the kitchen and start on the dishes. He thought he detected sniffling, like she had been crying.

"It'll be okay," Jace reassured Sarafina. "He'll get over it one day."

"He's a good man," she answered, "better than I deserve, but why should Blanca and I have to suffer for something that wasn't our fault?"

"Time will ease the pain, Sarafina. Be patient."

Wes rattled the paper to let them know he could hear their conversation. He perused the first page, then turned to the next as Jace came in with his Bible and sat down near enough to the lamp to read the scriptures. As Wes examined the second page, he whistled.

"Says here the Dudley investigation has cost the government over twenty-five thousand dollars to date."

Jace released a long, slow breath. "That's some serious money."

Wes nodded. "It's a story reprinted from the *New Mexico Herald.* Here's what it says: 'As long as the people's money is to be squandered, we are glad a little of it comes west. It seems to us the case should have gone to the courts. The opinion prevails at Stanton and Lincoln that no case will be made against Colonel Dudley, resulting in a court martial. We are satisfied, though, that if he is restored to command of Fort Stanton, peace will depart from that section of New Mexico.' "

"That's right," Jace interrupted.

Wes continued. " 'A large portion of the people of Lincoln assert and believe him partisan and claim that they would have no protection under his direction of affairs. Whether this is so or not we are not prepared to say, but of one thing, we are certain: so long as that feeling exists, it will be folly to attempt to restore peace with Dudley in command, and the wiser plan would be to place a good executive officer there, one wholly a stranger to the troubles and let him bring quiet out of the present confusion, even to the proclaiming of martial law.' "

Now Jace whistled. "That was reprinted in the Mesilla paper? Wonder how Bristol and Rynerson feel about that, their local rag publishing an opinion counter to their interests?"

"They'll likely indict the editor for something or have him killed," Wes replied.

The two men resumed their reading until bedtime, Jace excusing himself and slipping behind the counter to his bed while Bracken kept on reading, not because he was interested in news, but because when he retired Sarafina would be cold to him, upset that he had not accepted Blanca. When he slipped into bed, he could not tell if his wife was asleep or playing possum just to ignore him.

Wes slept fretfully and woke up early, glad to get out of the room before Sarafina awoke. He dressed quickly and headed to the kitchen, grabbing the milk pail and starting for the barn when it was barely light enough to see. It was even darker in the barn, but he maneuvered to the cow's stall by rote, reached for the stool, and sat it down beside the cow.

"Well, well," came a voice that startled Wes. He grabbed for his revolver and had it halfway out of his holster poster until he realized Bonney spoke those words.

"Well, well," the Kid repeated, "if it isn't the milkmaid out to tend to her dairy cows."

"Kid, you scared the devil out of me and almost got yourself shot. What in tarnation are you doing here? You should be in Texas or Mexico or Colorado by now."

"I owe you one last favor before I leave Lincoln County."

"Go now, Kid. I'm owed nothing. I just tried to do what was right and decent by you."

"And you did. You mentioned at the court of inquiry that you had to round up and brand your cattle. Has that work been finished?"

"Jace and I plan to get to it in a few days."

"Give me a few days, and Tom and I'll handle that for you."

"I'd rather lose all my cattle than see you shot because you stayed here to do me a favor. Where's Tom and your horses?"

"They're in the gristmill. Didn't figure anyone would look there. Give us your branding irons plus some time, and we'll round up your herd."

"I don't know if it'll do us much good if there's no market for cattle in Lincoln County, times being what they are and the Ring being what it is."

"You worry too much, Wes. Something'll come up. It always does."

Wes nodded. "You wore me down, Bonney. After I finish the milking, I'll fetch our branding irons. Just one thing, though, Kid."

"What's that?"

"Don't be changing any brands on other men's stock."

Bonney laughed. "Wes, I can't believe you think that way, much less believe I would ever do something like that."

"Promise?"

"I give you my word."

"I'll see you at the gristmill in twenty minutes with the branding irons."

Six days later at dusk, Bonney and O'Folliard returned the irons to Bracken and Cousins along with a herd that surpassed three hundred head.

"We didn't get them all branded, but the mamas are marked so the calves will stick with them," Bonney explained.

"I wasn't expecting more than a hundred," Wes replied. "You didn't change any brands, did you?"

The Kid shook his head. "Absolutely not! I promised you we wouldn't, and we didn't, but we sure scorched the hide of every unbranded animal that moved. I even think there's a black bear out there that's got a Mirror B burned into his fur."

Jace shook his head. "What are we gonna do with them all, Wes?"

"At least we'll have beef for our table, even if we can't sell them." Wes turned to Bonney. "We're obliged, Kid, to you and Tom."

"No, sir. My debt to you and my conscience are clear for all you've done for me."

"What next, Bonney?" Wes asked.

"We're returning to Fort Sumner where we know folks."

"That's not far enough, Bonney."

"Maybe not, but it's as far as I'm going," the Kid answered.

With that, Bonney and O'Folliard turned their horses to the north and rode away in the darkness.

CHAPTER 22

By the middle of August, eight weeks after Wes Bracken last implored Billy Bonney to leave the territory, all the hard days of work had produced results on the Casey place. The corn crop was lush and yellowing, and Sarafina's garden produced beans, peppers, squash, and potatoes. Wes and Jace had repaired the gristmill to grind their own corn and that of their neighbors. Jace had even cleaned the smithing shack and put the anvil, forge, and tools to use on horse-shoes for their mounts. At six years old Luis could help his mother in the vegetable patch while three-year-old Roberto tried to emu-late his brother, but often chased bugs, birds, and butterflies, usually followed by the yelping puppy Jace had brought back from Roswell. The boys had named the mutt "Concho" for reasons only they knew, and together they went on daily adventures by the Rio Hondo.

As their crops and luck improved, their greatest asset and liability remained the cattle herd, which grazed farther and farther away from the Casey place as fall approached and the local grass dwindled. Thanks to Bonney and O'Folliard their tally came to just over three hundred head of cows, calves, yearlings, and beeves. Like most cattle raisers around Lincoln except for Dolan, who maintained beef contracts with the Mescalero Reservation and Fort Stanton, Wes and Jace were cattle rich but cash poor, most having to beg or barter to provide anything but beef for their families.

In some ways Wes believed Lincoln County over the past two months had improved and in others was just as crooked as ever. Once the Kid rode north toward Fort Sumner, much of the tension drained from the area and people resumed their lives, hoping that the violence had ended for good. James J. Dolan and his gang seemed more subdued, less confident about continuing their crimes. Even Sarafina noticed, asking Wes if she should still carry her revolver everywhere she went since Jesse Evans was dead and his surviving allies knew to avoid the Casey place. Fearing some still held grudges against him, Wes told her to always keep her pistol nearby until the calendar changed to 1880. But while some things improved, much remained the same, like the army's rigged court of inquiry into Colonel Dudley's handling of the troops at the Big Killing. The officer's cronies vindicated Dudley, finding that he should not stand for a court martial over his actions or inactions during the conflagration and the shootout. Dolan and the others indicted by the grand jury still ran free and Sheriff Kimbrell looked the other way instead of tracking them down for trial, just as he had made only a half-hearted search for Bonney after he walked away from custody. Even the federal marshal had delayed tracking Bonney, so much so that the court's term ended before he might stand trial, meaning it would be 1880 or even 1881 before Bonney would face a jury for his killings.

For Wes and his partner, they worked their crops and waited for the first freeze so they could put a successful end to the 1879 crop. Their larder would be much fuller this year than in 1878 when so much violence consumed Lincoln County. As the corn yellowed, the two partners pulled and shucked the ears, tossing them in the crib. They cut hay by the riverside and left it to dry before gathering it for storage in the barn so the horses and milk cow would have forage during the cold months. They chopped wood to heat the house through winter. Though they still wore their pistols at their side and kept their long arms nearby, Wes and Jace worried less about their enemies and more about completing their chores before winter.

In mid-August, Jace Cousins headed off in the morning for Lincoln to buy coffee and sugar and to start another rumor about Jesse Evans, this time that the outlaw had died in a shootout in Fort Stockton, Texas. Jace relished telling a fib and seeing how long it took the rumor to return to his ears.

Midafternoon of that day, Wes was chopping wood when he heard a galloping horse and a shrill whistle. Tossing his ax aside, he grabbed his carbine and raced around to the front of the house as Jace charged toward him on his dun.

"Trouble?" Wes called as he scanned the trail behind his partner, seeing nothing.

"Good news," Jace cried, reining up hard and jumping from his mount. "There's been a gold strike at White Oaks."

"Don't tell me the gold bug's bitten you."

"No," Jace answered, shaking his head. "Don't you see? It could be easy money."

"Mining's harder work than farming or cowboying. Count me out."

"No, Wes. It'll be a cattle market. There'll be an influx of miners and men with cash."

Wes tugged on his mustache. "I never thought of that."

"If we get there before anyone else thinks of it, we might bring home enough cash to improve our situation for the next year or two."

"It'll take a couple days to round up stock and two or three more to drive them there."

"Then we need to get moving," Jace said, "before someone beats us."

Wes nodded. "We've still got five hours before sunset. I'll let Sarafina know to fix us some grub, and we'll ride out this evening and spend the night on the trail. As soon as I tell her, I'll saddle up and be ready within thirty minutes."

Jace twisted in his saddle and untied a burlap sack. "Here's the coffee and sugar as well as a sack of candy for the boys and a red ribbon for the girls."

Wes took the goods and handed his carbine to Jace to take out to the barn. Then both men rushed away. Wes found Sarafina in their bedroom, nursing Blanca. He quickly explained the plan and instructed his wife to throw together enough tortillas and jerky for two days.

Sarafina nodded and pulled Blanca away

from her breast. The baby wailed with displeasure, even more so when her mother laid her down in the crib. Wes rushed through the house, dropping the burlap bag on the table, and scurrying out the back to the barn where Jace had already started preparing his sorrel. Wes took over while Jace gathered a lariat for each of them, then toted two canteens to the stream to fill. After saddling his horse, Wes led him out of the barn toward the dwelling where he tied the animal. Seeing the ax he had thrown on the ground at Jace's return, Wes picked it up, lifted it over his head, and slammed it into the log he had been cutting. Then he marched inside, where Sarafina had put together two bundles of food and wrapped the provisions in white cloth. Wes told her the burlap sack held the supplies from Lincoln and some surprises for her and the children. He kissed her, reminding her to milk the cow in his absence, then ran out the door, stuffed one sack of food in his saddlebags, then exchanged the other for his canteen when Jace rode up. He mounted, and both men turned their horses to the south to look for their cattle.

They returned home two afternoons later, driving eighty beeves to the Casey place. Sarafina and the boys welcomed the men back, both lads deciding they wanted to accompany the cattle, but Sarafina convinced them to stay at the house and protect her and their sister. Sarafina fixed a supper of fried salt pork, boiled potatoes, roasting ears, and fresh tortillas. Then the two partners slept in their beds, getting up early to start for White Oaks. Sarafina, though, arose first, preparing them a breakfast of scrambled eggs and more salt pork. As they headed out the door, she gave them replenished bundles of food for the drive. Wes asked Jace to carry his grub while he retreated to the front room and got four cartons of ammunition apiece for the trip.

They rounded up the herd for the drive to White Oaks. By their count four had strayed overnight, so they started for White Oaks with seventy-six beeves. They drove the cattle toward Lincoln until they passed the cemetery, then directed them north around the village so they could water the animals in the Rio Bonito and avoid any commotion in town. They pushed the cattle to make thirty miles by sundown. That was a faster pace than the cattle wanted, but Wes knew an exhausted herd was less likely to stampede during the night. They bedded down near the turnoff to Fort Stanton and spent an uneventful night.

Waking early, Wes and Jace resumed the drive, letting the animals take their fill of water in the Rio Bonito before continuing their journey. They drove the cattle another twenty miles to the outskirts of the mining town and bedded them down. Come the next morning, Wes started for White Oaks, confident that he could get a good price because he had beaten other cattle raisers.

He headed to the No Scum Allowed saloon, but the place was closed. The town, though, buzzed with activity as men scurried down its street, and carpenters hammered away on a half dozen new buildings to meet the expected boom that the gold would bring.

Wes asked several men he passed if they knew of anyone needing beef cattle to supply the miners with food, but earned only rejections. As the stores opened, he sought potential buyers, offering good beef at a fair price. After an hour of fruitless inquiries, Wes stopped in an eatery that smelled of fresh coffee, fried bacon, and new lumber. After paying for a cup of coffee, he asked the proprietor, a short fellow in a clean apron, if he would be interested in buying a few beeves to expand his menu. The owner replied he had just opened the place and hadn't paid off the building costs. Wes offered to sell him a beef for twelve dollars. The proprietor whistled.

"That's a fair price," Wes answered.

The fellow nodded. "Plenty fair, but I'm broke. You should know other fellows are going around town trying to sell beef at sixteen dollars a head and threatening folks not to buy beef from anyone but them."

Wes sipped his scalding drink, then pushed the brim of his hat higher on his head. "Did these men say who they were?"

"Nothing other than identifying their boss as Jimmy Dolan. They said Dolan ran things in Lincoln County and got a cut of every dollar made in these parts. They threatened to burn down my place if I bought any beef but theirs."

"I'd go down to eight dollars a head, half what Dolan's beef would cost you."

Wiping his hands on his apron, the proprietor grimaced. "I can't take the chance of them burning me out. I got a wife and young'un to support."

Wes saw fear in the man's eyes.

"What if I gave you a beef? You could butcher it this morning and serve it for lunch and supper. It'd help business."

The fellow hesitated, weighing the threats against the opportunity to increase his profits.

"It's a good beef, not one of those scrawny, diseased cattle that Dolan peddles."

Biting his lip, the owner finally nodded. "Okay, as long as no one sees you deliver it."

"Can't promise you that."

"Then I better pass. I don't want any trouble with those Dolan boys."

Wes gulped down the rest of his coffee. "I understand," he said as he headed out the door, furious that the reach and intimidation of Dolan had beaten him to White Oaks, even if Dolan's cattle hadn't.

As he stepped toward his sorrel, he noticed two men eyeing him from across the street. One of them motioned him over with a wave of his hand. Wes let a freight wagon pass, then crossed over. The clean-shaven one who invited him over wore wire-rimmed spectacles hooked over his ears and two gun belts hanging from his waist. His partner stood taller with a shaggy beard and a double-barreled shotgun in his right hand. Both men smiled as Wes walked up.

"You the fella selling beef around town?" asked the bespectacled one.

Wes nodded. "Ten dollars a head."

The bearded fellow grinned broadly, exposing his tobacco-stained teeth. "We'd like to make a deal."

"How many head do you want? I've got seventy-six."

Spectacles replied, "We want them all —"

"That'll be seven hundred and sixty dollars cash." Wes grinned at his good luck.

"— to get out of town and you with them."

Wes's smile evaporated. "You're Dolan's men, aren't you?"

The bearded fellow grinned, lifting his shotgun at Wes's gut to affirm his affiliation. "Let's just say we know Jimmy. This is his territory. You have no business here."

"It's a free country," Wes replied.

"Maybe so, but this ain't a free town," the beardless fellow answered. "Jimmy Dolan's got the beef contract for White Oaks."

Wes studied the two men, gauging the threat before him and wondering if he could yank his pistol on the bearded fellow before his tormentor pulled the shotgun trigger. Wes responded slowly. "He may hold the beef contract for the reservation and the fort, but there's no contract for a town."

"There is if Jimmy Dolan says so, and Jimmy Dolan sets the price for beef in Lincoln County." The fellow waved the shotgun at Wes's chest, then froze at the sound of another voice.

"Perhaps you should lower that shotgun, friend."

Wes recognized the sound of Billy Bonney, who slipped up behind the shotgun-wielding crook, and poked a gun barrel in his back. Wes pulled his pistol and waved it at the man in glasses.

"How you doing, Wes?" Bonney asked, stepping from behind his adversary and yanking the shotgun from his grasp.

"Much better since you arrived, Kid." Wes stepped to the man in spectacles and lifted the revolvers from his holsters, tucking them in his gun belt. "What are you doing here, Kid?"

"Trying to make an honest living at the gambling table. There's a lot of loose money around White Oaks now that men are finding gold. Gambling's easier than mining."

"Probably more dangerous, too," Wes answered, then studied the two bullies. "Dolan don't control me or my affairs. You two tell him that."

Bonney pulled the pistol from the bearded fellow's holster. "Now scat, both of you!"

"What about our guns?"

"I'm keeping them so you don't hurt yourselves," Bonney replied. "Now get."

The pair looked at each other, then backed down the street, cursing Bonney and Wes.

When they turned the corner, Wes grinned. "Good to see you, Bonney, though it'd be safer for you to stay out of Lincoln County."

Bonney shrugged. "It's where my friends are. What are you doing here?"

"Jace and I drove beeves to market here. He's with the herd outside town."

The Kid shook his head. "Dolan's been trying to sink his teeth into White Oaks now that it's booming. His men are demanding store owners buy his beef at outrageous prices and threatening them if they don't. Dolan's making enemies here like everywhere he goes. A lot of folks are scared, but he's stayed clear of me and the place I work."

"Where would that be?"

"The No Scum Allowed saloon."

"Jace and I ate there on our previous trip to White Oaks. Venison stew we had."

"That's where I was headed when I saw you and your Dolan acquaintances. I had to help, seeing as how you have trouble making new friends."

Wes laughed as they strode to the place, updating each other on events since their last visit. They reached the watering hole just as the owner unlocked the door. He grinned at Bonney, then Wes.

"I remember you from awhile back. Two bowls of venison stew, you and your partner."

"Meet Dewey," Bonney said. "He lets me gamble at his table."

The proprietor shook Wes's hand. "It's true. I've learned that having Billy around keeps the Dolan bunch away so my place can live up to my sign." He shoved open the door for Bonney and Bracken. "If I'm forced to do business with Dolan's bunch, I'll change the name to 'Now Scum Allowed.' "

Bonney pointed to Wes. "He and his partner have driven some beeves to White Oaks, looking for buyers."

"I'm selling at a fair price, ten dollars a head, but I'll go down to eight dollars apiece for a friend of the Kid."

Dewey scratched his chin as he ciphered. "That's half what Dolan's demanding."

"And these are better cattle, not the scrawny scrubs Dolan sells."

"Beef could bring in more customers, Dewey," Bonney noted.

"I'd like eight, but I can only afford four," he responded.

Wes nodded. "I'll sell you eight. Give me thirty-two bucks now and pay the balance to Bonney when you get it. He knows where to find me." Wes turned to the Kid. "Don't lose my money at your gambling table."

"I don't lose at cards," Bonney replied.

They marched to a table and stacked atop it the weapons they had taken from Dolan's men. Dewey stepped behind the bar and into the back room to start a pot of coffee and prepare for the day's business. As Bonney and Bracken took a seat, the front door swung in and Tom O'Folliard ambled in, grinning when he saw the Kid with Wes.

"Morning, Wes," he said, tipping his hat. "Didn't expect to see you here."

"Likewise, Tom. How are you doing?"

"Okay," he answered, then pointed his thumb over his shoulder. "There's two men outside that want to come in and parlay. They said you got their guns."

Wes looked at Bonney. "Dolan's thugs?"

The Kid nodded. As a grin worked its way across his face, he picked up the shotgun and cocked both hammers. "Tell them to come in, Tom, but stay wide of the door." He aimed the twin barrels at the entry.

O'Folliard turned around and stuck his head outside. "Come on in, but no funny business. Bonney's covering the door with his shotgun."

"*My* shotgun," answered the bearded fellow.

As Tom backed away from the entrance, the two gunmen entered cautiously, their hands open and wide of their waists.

"That's far enough," Bonney told them. "Now close the door."

The duo stopped.

"What do you want?" Wes demanded.

"Our guns and a chance to do business with you," the bespectacled fellow replied.

"I'm hanging onto your weapons until I sell my cattle and leave White Oaks," Wes responded.

"We can help," the man in glasses answered. "We talked to our boss, and he's willing to buy your herd at six dollars a head."

"Dolan's in town?" Wes asked.

Both men nodded. "He'll give six dollars a head for up to two hundred beeves."

"So he can turn around and sell them for sixteen dollars a head?"

The bespectacled fellow shrugged. "He's offering cash."

"I'd be careful, Wes," Bonney said softly. "There's been a lot of counterfeit bills circulating in these parts."

Wes bobbed his head, acknowledging Bonney's warning. "Why didn't Dolan come himself?"

"Dolan feared you'd shoot him. He said

he wanted to bury the hatchet with you when he spotted you at Fort Stanton, but you went for your gun and made it clear you weren't interested."

"He wants to bury the hatchet in my back," Bonney said.

Wes nodded. "I won't deal with him, even if I can't sell my cattle. I'll drive them home, before I'll sell to him. He's behind all the county's troubles."

"You need to let bygones be bygones," the bearded man noted.

"The bygones ain't bygone in my mind."

"What about our guns?" the man in glasses asked.

Bonney laughed. "How about I give you a couple loads of buckshot from my shotgun right now? Then we'll see if you still want your weapons back."

"Tell Jimmy Dolan I'll shoot my cattle before I sell them to him," Wes added.

The two men scowled as they backed out the door. "You're making a mistake," the bespectacled man answered. "Dolan will remember this."

"Aw shut up," Bonney cried, "before my trigger finger twitches."

The two spun around and ran outside, slamming the door.

Bonney gently released the hammers on

the shotgun, laughed, then turned to Bracken. "If you'd sold to Dolan, he'd have gotten his money back, either paying you in counterfeit paper or having his men rob you on the way home."

"I couldn't stomach selling my cattle to Dolan for all the evil he's involved in."

"Tell you what, Wes, as soon as Dewey brings us a cup of coffee and we down it, Tom and I'll ride with you to see Jace, and I'll help you sell the cattle around town."

Wes accepted the offer, doubting Bonney could do much good, but willing to give him a chance. Dewey returned shortly with three tins of coffee and the men savored the hot liquid, then headed outside, carrying the shotgun and pistols belonging to Dolan's hands. Wes put the three pistols in his saddlebags and Bonney made a show of toting the shotgun. They mounted their horses and rode south where Jace sat astride his dun keeping watch over the cattle.

Bonney ordered O'Folliard to stay with the herd so Jace could return to town to bargain. "No offense, Wes, but Jace is a better horse trader than you. We'll cut out Dewey's eight head and two more to drive back to town."

After Bonney and Jace had separated ten from the herd, Wes accompanied them to

White Oaks. They penned Dewey's animals in the small corral behind his saloon and drove the other two down the street, Bonney hawking the beeves. "Beef for sale," he cried, "at a fair price for all. Eight dollars a head. Best buy in Lincoln County. Receipts provided."

In ones and twos, men and even two women approached Bonney, attracted by the price but concerned about intimidation from Dolan's cronies. The Kid promised he would stand with them against anybody that threatened them over the purchase of a beef. As the day lengthened, Bonney and Jace sold cattle individually and in pairs, purchasers paying what they could and agreeing to pay the rest to Bonney by the end of the year. Wes accepted those purchasing on credit since Bonney volunteered to collect the money for him and to deliver it to the Casey place by the end of the year. One new mining superintendent planning to build a stamping mill on the edge of town purchased twenty head, paying straight cash. By nightfall, Bonney and Jace had sold and delivered all the cattle. They collected full price on fifty head and half price on the remaining twenty-six. The Mirror B partners would return home with five hundred and four dollars, with another hundred and four dollars due by the new year.

Though Wes and Jace wanted to start for the Casey place that night, Bonney and O'Folliard convinced them to wait until morning when good sunlight would make it harder for robbers to ambush them and steal their profits. At sunrise Wes and Jace began the journey home, accompanied by Bonney and O'Folliard, who rode with them until noon. After a quick bite of jerky for lunch in the saddle, the men separated.

"We're obliged for your help in White Oaks and for your company this far," Wes said. "We should be able to make it home just fine now."

"It's always good to see you, Wes and Jace," Bonney said.

Wes twisted around in his saddle to unbuckle his saddlebags. "You can deliver these pistols back to Dolan's men."

Bonney shook his head. "Keep 'em. I'm giving the shotgun to Dewey, figuring he can use it in the saloon."

"You be careful, Bonney. I still think you ought to leave the territory."

The Kid laughed. "No place else to go. Besides, I'm spending Christmas with you again this year. I'll bring the rest of your money then. *¡Adiós, amigos!* See you Christmas."

With that, Bonney and O'Folliard returned to White Oaks while Bracken and Cousins continued without incident to the Casey place.

CHAPTER 23

As the year neared its end, Wes Bracken atop his sorrel looked with satisfaction across the Casey place, content that they had made a crop in 1879 and had harvested it, unlike the previous year when Lincoln County violence had disrupted everything. With hard work, the windfall from Jesse Evans's saddlebags, and the sale of the cattle in White Oaks, Wes knew the partnership had surpassed their expectations and that 1880, with a little luck, would be even better. For all the advantages of the Casey place with the house, gristmill, blacksmith shop, barns, and pens, Wes still missed the original site he and his brother Luther had managed, despite their differences, where the Rio Ruidoso and the Rio Bonito converged into the Rio Hondo. Six years ago that was where he had hoped to raise the finest horses in all of New Mexico Territory and where he had begun his marriage with

Sarafina. But it was also where Luther had died, his wife was raped, his equine breeding stock slaughtered, and his home and barn torched during all the county's difficulties. Like the territory, the Mirror B had never met his expectations because of the bloodshed and the corruption.

Wes turned his mount to the west, deciding to visit the old place and pay respects to his brother, despite the December cold, which chafed his face and slipped through his coat with icy fingers. He rode slowly, deliberately dreading the return to home because he knew what awaited. A year ago on this day, Blanca had been born with the sheen of fuzzy red hair that confirmed she was the child of another man, an evil man who had violated Sarafina. Wes relished riding alone so he could muddle through the thoughts that plagued him about the daughter that wasn't his on her first birthday. She was walking now and speaking gibberish, much to the delight of Luis and Roberto, who watched over her with a special dedication. She had a cackle of a laugh that started deep in her tummy and erupted from between her rosy cheeks. The laughter of the boys with Blanca brought joy to the entire house, if not to Wes's conscience. As he neared the Mirror B, memories good and bad flooded his mind and reminded him how Lincoln County had devoured his dreams of a new start after leaving Arkansas forever. He studied the burnt remnants of what had once been his home and the best barn in all of southeastern New Mexico. Grimacing at the bleached bones of his breeding herd, Wes turned toward the cottonwood tree beside the Rio Ruidoso where a tiny cross and a mound of stones marked the grave of his brother, whose flirtation with whiskey and an alliance with a family of mean men had resulted in his death on the very property where Wes rode.

Pulling up on the reins of his sorrel, Wes dismounted and stepped to the grave of Luther Bracken. He removed his hat in spite of the biting temperatures and the frigid breeze. Bowing as he studied the crooked cross, Wes spoke. "It could've been different, Luther, if you'd played your hand better." He bit his lip. Could the same thing be said about himself and Blanca? Wes sighed. He was the sole survivor of six brothers, the others lost to the War Between the States and its aftermath. Wes stood at the grave for five minutes, knowing that he was only delaying the inevitable of Blanca's celebration.

Snugging his hat tight over his forehead,

Wes nodded at the grave. "At least you have no more worries, Luther." Wes snickered. "Of course you never worried about much when you were alive, either." He turned and mounted the sorrel for the return ride to the Casey place. While Wes knew the trip had not resolved his doubts, at least now he could face the to-do that Sarafina would make over Blanca's birthday. Riding back home, Wes scanned the slopes of the mountains bordering the valley. Though he rode with care, he suspected men like Dolan and his cronies now focused on White Oaks, draining all the money they could from the honest folks of the mining town. Wes smiled, remembering how the sale of his seventy-six beeves in White Oaks had dented Dolan's larceny, even if only temporarily. The memory stoked Wes, and he nudged Charlie into a full gallop to the Casey place, slowing the sorrel to a walk as he neared home so as not to alarm anyone.

Wes rode out to the barn and put the stallion in his stall, removing his saddle and tack, then watering and feeding him before retreating to the house. As he entered the kitchen door, Sarafina looked up from a pan of churros she was pulling out of the woodstove, then smiled when she saw her husband.

"You're back," she said, placing the hot utensil on the table, then nodding toward Blanca who waddled toward Wes. "There's your papa!"

Blanca shuffled across the room, lifting her arms to Wes as he hung his coat on a peg by the door. Though he ignored her, she flung her arms around his leg and hugged him.

"She missed you," Sarafina said. "And this is her big day. She's a year old."

"I know," Wes sighed. "Let's be done with it."

Sarafina answered with a crooked smile. "You are so sentimental, *mi esposo.*"

"There's been too much work to do," Wes replied. "I didn't get her anything."

"Yes, you did," his wife answered.

Wes scratched his head as he removed his hat. Blanca mumbled. Then Wes looked down at her, placing the hat atop her red locks and jostling it up and down, drawing more laughs from the toddler. "In spite of what you say, Sarafina, I didn't get her anything."

Sarafina walked over, picked up her snickering daughter, and with her spare arm hugged her husband. "Jace did it for you the last time he went to Lincoln. He brought back some cinnamon and sugar for the churros to celebrate her birthday and a surprise from you."

Wes shrugged. "We'll both be surprised, then. I've got a lot on my mind. Let's get this done, Sarafina."

"You are so impatient. Boys," cried Sarafina, "bring your Uncle Jace into the kitchen to celebrate Blanca's birthday."

Roberto and Luis burst into the room, smiles plastered across their faces. Jace strolled in behind them. He carried a rag doll the size of his hand in his grip.

Sarafina motioned for the boys and Jace to take a seat on one side of the table. She sat down on the opposite with Blanca and patted the chair at her side for her husband. Wes slipped next to her.

Their sons sat staring and licking their lips at the pastries. Luis reached for one, but Sarafina chided him. "Wait until I say so, young man."

Chastened, both boys straightened in their seats, eyeing the desserts.

Sarafina stood Blanca in her lap and turned to Cousins. "Do you have something for our little girl?"

He nodded and handed the rag doll across the table toward Blanca. When she saw it, her eyes widened and she smiled, then cackled as she took it from Jace. She cradled the doll against her shoulder, then turned to Wes and offered it to him.

"I'm not good with babies," Wes answered.

"Nor daughters," Jace chided. "That's why I got your gift for her."

Blanca smiled and pulled the doll back to her breast.

"Now, boys," Sarafina asked, "pick out a churro to give to your sister."

Both boys pointed to the smallest pastry, drawing a laugh from her mom, who picked it up, blew on it to cool it, then tore off a small piece to offer her daughter. Blanca grabbed it and shoved it in her mouth, smiling at the sweet taste. Sarafina grinned at her sons. "Now you can each pick one."

They grabbed for the same churro, then Roberto abandoned it for another one.

"Boys, what do you say?" Wes asked.

"Gracias," they said in unison.

Sarafina smiled. "Now, men, you can pick one."

Jace took his, then Wes. After taking a bite and complimenting Sarafina's baking, Jace turned to his partner. "You disappeared for a spell."

"I rode over to the Mirror B."

"How are things there?"

"Nothing's changed."

"If things keep settling down, are you

thinking of rebuilding or staying here?"

"Things won't ease until Bonney leaves the territory or gets hung. He knows too much, and Dolan and his men'll never rest easy until he's dead or gone."

"You think Billy'll return at Christmas with the rest of our cattle proceeds?"

Chewing on a bite, Wes nodded. "Bonney's always lived up to his word with me. I don't expect this to be any different."

"Even with money at stake?"

"The Kid's loyal to those that treat him square. He'll be here. As he's told us once, we're the only family he's got."

Christmas Day came and went with no sign of Billy Bonney. Wes Bracken decided Jace Cousins had been right, and the Kid would keep what was owed them. On the first day of 1880, while the overcast sky began to pinken with the approaching dawn, Wes buttoned up his coat, tugged down his hat, and grabbed the milk pail from the kitchen, then started out for the barn. Nearing the shelter, he noticed the barn door ajar. He knew he had latched it the evening before. Slowly he shifted the pail to his left hand and reached with his right beneath his coat to pull his revolver. Sliding his gun hand in the opening, he slowly pulled the door ajar, the cold hinges creaking in the chill.

"I wondered if you were ever going to show up," called a familiar voice.

At the sound of Bonney, Wes slid his gun back in its holster. "I'd given up on you, Kid, since you didn't make it at Christmas." He spotted Bonney leaning against the stall by the milk cow, strode over, and shook his hand.

"It's no longer safe in White Oaks. Men are looking for me. I have to stay on the run. I slipped in after midnight, less chance somebody might see me and trouble you."

"Did you come alone?"

"Tom's sleeping in the mill, but I owed you the cattle money." Bonney fished a leather pouch from his pocket and tossed it to Wes, who snapped it out of the air. "It's all there."

Wes nodded. "Thank you. Now I hope you're leaving the territory."

Bonney spat at the ground. "I've nowhere else to go. Besides, I've got some scores to settle. The governor went back on his word for a pardon. Dolan and his men are still running free even after murdering so many of my friends. The law's trying to arrest me for murder. If I'm caught, I'll stand trial before Bristol and Rynerson, who hate my guts. John Chisum owes me money for work

I did, but his hands have orders to shoot me on sight. There's so many of them after me now, I can't even stay in White Oaks and make my way gambling. Nobody's played fair with me, save you and Jace."

"Sometimes in life, just like in poker, you're dealt a bad hand. At those times, it's just best to throw in your cards and walk away from the table before you lose everything."

The Kid stared into the gloom, his face ravaged by anger or anguish, Wes could not say which. "They won't leave me alone, even if I walk away."

"If you went far enough away, they'd give up the chase. You're a threat to them and their ring here, but not in Colorado or Texas or Kansas, even Mexico where you speak the language."

"I don't know much," Bonney countered, "but I do know New Mexico Territory."

"You can learn elsewhere."

"But I've got friends here."

"You can make new friends."

Bonney scowled. "Not until I right the wrong that's been done to me and my *amigos.*"

"Kid, I've been on your side up to now, but I can't condone anything you do after this. I won't defend you for any crimes from this day on. It'll only bring more trouble for all."

Lowering his head, Bonney sighed. "I'm no longer welcome here, is that it, Wes?"

"I've got a family and property to consider, Kid. I was burnt out once. I can't let it happen again because I doubt I have the stamina to rebuild or bury more kin."

"So now it's me against everyone, including you?"

"I'm not against you, Kid. I just can't throw in with you anymore."

"Then tell me one thing, Wes, and I'll not bother you or your family again."

"What do you want to know?"

"I've heard a lot of rumors about Jesse Evans, him robbing banks in Texas, him being killed in Fort Stockton, you killing him on the Pecos. Any truth to those stories?"

Wes pursed his lips, debating what to tell Bonney, then nodded. "Let me just say you won't have to look over your shoulder for Jesse."

The Kid's face cracked with a toothy grin. "I hope he died a miserable death for all he did, including to your wife, and I hope he knew who killed him."

"Jesse did. He drowned or bled to death in the flooding Pecos. I didn't find the body, but I discovered his severed hand."

Bonney nodded. "One down, dozens to go."

"Don't do it, Kid. Throw in your cards and get out of the territory or you'll wind up like Jesse Evans."

Releasing Wes's hand, the Kid shrugged. "I can't leave, not until I even the score."

"That'll only lead to more trouble. Folks are tired of it. We want to get on with our lives."

"I understand you've got a family to worry about, so I won't bother you or Jace again." He turned and approached two stalls where his and O'Folliard's horses stood. Grabbing the reins of both, Bonney, his shoulders slumped, led them out the door, leaving it ajar.

Wes tucked the pouch in his pocket, took his stool, placed it and the pail beside the milk cow, and began his chore, tugging on the animal's teats and wondering if he had done the right thing with Bonney. If only the Kid would leave New Mexico Territory, it would be better for him and everyone else, even if he was the one mostly wronged in the dispute. After finishing his milking, Wes walked outside, latched the barn, and started for the house. He heard a whistle from the gristmill and turned to see Bonney and O'Folliard sitting on their horses, staring at him. Bonney lifted his hat and waved, then headed east toward the road and away from Lincoln.

Standing midway between the barn and the house, Wes watched the two men disappear in the morning gloom. Bonney had risked his life to deliver what Wes and Jace were due from the cattle sale. Wes wondered if he'd done right by Bonney. As he continued to the house, he saw the back door open up.

Jace Cousins emerged, holding his Henry rifle. "Did you whistle?"

"It was the Kid. He delivered the rest of our White Oaks cattle proceeds."

Now Jace whistled. "You were right, after all. I feared he'd keep the money."

"Treat him right and he'll be as faithful as a dog. Treat him wrong and he'll bare his teeth. Only problem is, there's a lot in Lincoln County that have treated him poorly, and he's vowed to get even. I told him to stay away, as we didn't need him drawing trouble our way."

Jace nodded as he held the door open for his partner. "He's a likable kid, but I'd hate to have him for an enemy. I wish there was something we could do."

"All I can think of is to write a letter to the governor, pleading with him to pardon

Bonney as he had promised." Wes stepped into the kitchen and put the pail on the table as Jace closed the door and propped his Henry in the corner. Both men took off their coats and hats, hanging them on wall pegs.

"You've got more faith than I do in a politician to live up to his word."

"It may be our only hope for Bonney."

Sitting in the front room in the yellow glow of the lamp on the counter, Wes finished composing the letter and put the pencil down. He held the sheet up to the light and read it silently, then handed the missive to Jace. "What do you think?"

Placing his Bible down beside the lamp, Cousins took the letter, held it to the light, and read aloud, " 'To his Excellency, Lew Wallace, governor of the Territory of New Mexico.' " Looking up from the dispatch, Jace whistled. "Aren't you lathering it on a little thick?"

"I thought about 'Hey, you lying son of a bitch!' but doubted that would help Bonney."

"You're probably right," Jace answered, then continued reading Wes's message aloud. " 'I am writing this letter to implore you to pardon Billy Bonney, as you promised in the meeting you held with him in Squire Wilson's house last spring in Lincoln. As a witness to the meeting, I believe as does Bonney that you promised him a pardon if he provided evidence in the murder of the lawyer Chapman. He did that and testified as well at Colonel Dudley's inquiry, just as you requested back in the spring. Though I heard you promise to pardon him, you have expressed reservations in my subsequent meetings with you of fulfilling that pledge. Your pardon would restore Bonney's faith in justice and help a young man straighten out his life not only from the wrongs he has done, but also from the many wrongs committed against him. Respectfully submitted, Wesley Bracken.' "

Jace handed the letter back to Wes. "I couldn't have said it any better myself. You want me to take it to Lincoln for mailing."

Wes shook his head. "I don't trust the post office in Lincoln or even White Oaks. I want it mailed in Roswell."

Jace nodded. "I'll deliver it as a favor to the Kid, though I doubt it will do any good."

"You're probably right." Wes shrugged. "While you're in Roswell, see if you can find us a couple good horses. With winter ahead, you might buy decent horseflesh from those that can't afford to feed them during the hungry months."

Jace grinned. "You know how I like horse trading."

Wes dug Bonney's pouch out of his pocket and tossed it to his partner. "There's a hundred and four dollars inside."

Snatching the packet from the air, Jace asked, "Did you count it?"

"Nope. I trust the kid."

Jace loosened the leather thong on the neck and pulled out a roll of bills, quickly counting them. He shook his head. "There's not a hundred and four dollars here."

For a moment, Wes felt Bonney had abused his trust.

Then Jace continued, "There's a hundred and ten plus a note."

"The Kid can count better than that."

Jace unfolded the paper, then read it. " 'There's an extra six dollars for you. It's thanks for being a friend. Buy something for Sarafina and the kids. Billy.' "

Wes lowered his head and sighed. "I wish there was more I could do for the Kid."

"Your letter is a start. I'll post it in Roswell tomorrow."

January gave way to February with no response from Santa Fe and the governor. If the letter had been mailed from Lincoln,

Wes knew it could've been intercepted and destroyed by Dolan's men, but with it posted in Roswell, he had faith it had reached the capital. Jace's choices in horses pleased Wes as he returned from Roswell with a chestnut stallion with white stockings and a bay and piebald mares, all purchased for ninety-five dollars. The news, however, was less pleasing as Billy Bonney and his men had been reported stealing cattle from John Chisum and beeves and horses from Texas Panhandle ranchers. March and April came, but no response from the governor as Wes and Jace prepared for planting the 1880 crop and branding new calves for their herd. More accounts of Bonney's cattle thievery filtered to Wes from his occasional visits to Lincoln or sporadic visitors who stopped at his place. By one account, Bonney had stolen a hundred head of Dolan cattle and driven them to the Panhandle. Wes smiled at that news as Dolan deserved anything bad that touched him.

With May and June came warm weather and more chores as the two partners juggled their farm and ranch work. Still, Wes awaited a letter from the governor, but Santa Fe remained silent. News of Bonney's thievery continued unabated, so much so that Wes came to believe every crime in the territory was now being pinned on the Kid and his accomplices. July and August arrived with fall and optimism on the horizon, the crops looking good and a trickle of cash beginning to flow in Lincoln County. The only word coming out of Santa Fe, though, was the governor's pending publication of a book the publisher called *Ben-Hur: A Tale of the Christ.* The governor, though, was anything but Christ-like in his betrayal of William H. Bonney, so much so that Jace had taken to calling his excellency "Judas." By September and October, nothing had changed with the governor, but the crops were ready for harvesting, which consumed Wes, Jace, Sarafina, and the boys, who contributed in their own ways, however small.

Wes managed a trip to Lincoln to buy some supplies in early September and visited with Juan Patrón at his house, expressing his disappointment with Lew Wallace.

"The governor drove the Kid to this lawlessness by denying him the promised pardon," Wes complained. "He hasn't answered my January letter."

"And he won't," Patrón replied. "He's surrendered to the Santa Fe Ring, more interested in his new book and getting another political appointment outside of the territory than he is in fighting the corruption. I've heard the Ring and John Chisum both want the Kid dead, and November's sheriff election may determine his fate."

"Isn't George Kimbrell running again? He's looked the other way on the Kid."

"Rumors are flying around that there's money out to get Bonney and that the Ring or the governor himself are backing a newcomer for sheriff. Others say Chisum's funding this election, or even some Panhandle cattlemen tired of losing their stock. I don't know the answer, but this new candidate out of Roswell is drawing a lot of speculation."

Wes shrugged. "Jace and I've been working too much to follow politics."

"The fellow's name is Pat Garrett."

"Never heard of him."

"If he gets elected, you'll hear plenty about him because word is he's been ordered to bring the Kid to trial or kill him."

Wes shook his head. "The Kid never gets a break."

Patrón nodded. "Unless he leaves the territory, his time is running out."

"I fear you're right, Juan." Wes thanked him for the information and left Lincoln with his supplies. As he rode home, he wondered how much time Bonney had to live.

As November approached, Wes gave up on ever hearing from governor Judas, as he had taken to calling him by Jace's label. Instead, he and Jace focused on gathering the harvest before the first freeze and preparing for the cold winter ahead. Through almost ten months, 1880 had been the second good year in a row, both for crops and for cattle. And, it was inspiring to see the three new horses in the corral, bringing back hope that he might one day resume breeding horses.

As Wes and Jace washed up behind the house near dusk on a cool October evening, they saw a solitary rider angle off the road toward them. A tall, lean fellow astride a coal-black horse, the visitor removed his hat with his gun hand and held it over his heart as he approached the house, a subtle way of saying he meant no harm to anyone. Wes dried his hands and pitched the towel to Jace, who wiped his and followed his partner out to meet the man. The visitor sat straight in the saddle, Wes estimating he was at least six-foot-three, though his lanky frame made his saddle height deceiving. His thick black hair matched the color of his substantial mustache. The nearer he approached, the more dominant became his dark piercing eyes, serious and steady without a glint of foolishness in them. Though his black-and-gray striped pants, black coat, and gray vest showed a film of trail dust, his attire was otherwise fastidious. Wes noticed the bulge of a revolver at his hip and the butt of a Winchester rising above the croup of his mount.

The rider halted as he neared the front of the house and smiled as Wes approached. "Is this the Bracken place?"

Wes nodded. "I'm Wesley Bracken and this is my partner, Jace Cousins."

The fellow nodded as he placed his hat back atop his head. "I'm wondering if we might visit for a moment. I'm running for sheriff of Lincoln County, and I'd like to ask for your vote. My name is Pat Garrett."

Chapter 24

Wes stared at the candidate, focusing on his dark, humorless eyes and wondering who was behind him. Was it the Santa Fe Ring? Or Chisum? Or Panhandle cattlemen? Or somebody else? "Who's backing you, Mr. Garrett?"

"Everybody that wants an end to the bloodletting and stealing in Lincoln County," Garrett responded. "Folks are tired of Billy Bonney running wild. They want him brought to justice for his murders and for his rustling."

"The Kid never harmed me and my family, but his enemies did, the Murphys and the Dolans and their renegades," Wes replied.

"That's a fact," Jace added.

Garrett nodded. "Folks said you were a Bonney sympathizer."

"I'm for what's right in Lincoln County, and Bonney's been wronged more than any man on either side," Wes answered.

"That's for the courts to decide."

"A rigged court in Mesilla won't give Bonney a fair trial, not with Judge Bristol presiding and Rynerson prosecuting. They're crooked Ring men with ties to Dolan and Santa Fe."

"My job is to get him in the jail."

"Or kill him," Jace interjected.

Garrett clenched his jaw and nodded slowly. "That's a possibility," he answered, then removed his hat. "Good day, ma'am."

Wes turned around to see Sarafina standing at the corner of the house, her right hand on the butt of the pistol hanging from her shoulder. "Sarafina, this is Mr. Pat Garrett. He's running for sheriff."

Releasing the gun so that it hung at her side, she acknowledged the visitor. "Sheriffs come and go, but the troubles remain."

Garrett's thin lips turned up at the corners in a slight smile as he replaced his hat on his head. "You're the sister of Carlos Zamora, are you not?"

Sarafina's mouth opened in surprise. "I'm not proud of everything my brother has done. He is serving his time for his wrongs."

"Yuma Territorial Prison is a tough place, ma'am. I hope he learns his lesson when he gets out."

Sarafina lowered her gaze and turned around. "Supper is ready when you are, *mi esposo,*" she announced over her shoulder as she disappeared around the corner of the house.

"My wife is Mexican, too," Garrett said. "They're a fine people."

Wes cocked his head at the candidate. "You seem to know a lot about us."

"I ask around. It's something anyone running for sheriff should do, especially a newcomer to the county like me."

"Who sent you here, Garrett?" Jace asked. "Was it Dolan, Chisum, Judas?"

"Judas?" Garrett responded.

"That's what Jace calls the governor, who's reneged on a promised pardon for Bonney."

"Are you gossiping?" Garrett responded. "It doesn't sound like something the governor would do."

"I heard him promise a pardon in front of the justice of the peace in Lincoln, if Bonney would testify against the murderers of the lawyer Chapman, which the Kid did."

"That's news to me," Garrett answered.

Wes crossed his arms over his chest. "You'll learn, Garrett, there's more double-dealing in Lincoln County and New Mexico

Territory than any place you've ever called home."

"All I ask, Bracken, is that you vote for me. If I'm elected, I'll play straight with you."

"I've always tried to do what's right," Wes answered.

Garrett nodded. "One other question, Bracken, what happened to Jesse Evans?"

Wes swallowed hard, but Jace spoke before he could respond.

"I understand he left the territory for Texas. Last I heard he was robbing banks there and died in a Fort Stockton shoot-out."

Garrett studied Jace, then grinned. "I didn't know that. Word I had was he drowned in the Pecos River, south of Roswell. At least that's what Chisum's cowhands say."

Wes looked at Jace, wondering how much Garrett really knew and how much was bluffing based on rumors.

"Gentlemen, it's getting dark and I've got to get to Lincoln, but I wanted to stop by and introduce myself. I'd appreciate your vote in the election next month."

"Good luck to you," Wes replied, "and thanks for stopping by."

Garrett turned and rode toward Lincoln.

"What do you think of the candidate?" Jace asked.

Wes lowered his arms from his chest and answered softly. "I fear he'll kill the Kid before he's through."

The November election came and went. Though Jace traveled to Lincoln to vote, Wes claimed he had too much work to do and stayed home, managing chores before the cold weather sat in. Wes could not vote for Garrett, fearing he would not give Bonney a fair chance in any encounter. Rumors of Bonney's ongoing rustling and thievery became so common that Wes doubted their veracity, suspecting the crimes were too many to have all been committed by him and his accomplices. After voting Jace returned from Lincoln and apprised Wes of his conversation with Juan Patrón that Sheriff Kimbrell lacked the heart or courage to track down Bonney and had agreed before the election to deputize Garrett so he could begin the hunt for the Kid before he was formally sworn in as sheriff on the first day of 1881.

Sure enough, when the results were tallied and Garrett declared the victor by 141 votes, Kimbrell deputized him and the sheriff-elect put together a posse of hard men, including stock detectives from the Texas Panhandle, to scour the territory for Bonney and his desperadoes. Rumors flew that the range detectives brought money to bribe Bonney's acquaintances for information on his whereabouts. From the scattered news Wes received from passersby and occasional visits to Lincoln, the noose was tightening around Bonney's neck from Garrett's indefatigable efforts to capture or kill him. Further, Governor Lew Wallace had placed a five-hundred-dollar reward on the Kid's head.

As Christmas and the New Year neared, Wes realized this would be the first in years that Bonney had not shared with his family. On Christmas Eve Jace returned from Lincoln with modest presents for everyone and word that Tom O'Folliard had died in a Fort Sumner encounter with Garrett's posse. On Christmas Day Wes watched the boys and Blanca open their simple gifts, but while the boys played with their tops, Blanca, who had just turned two, took her second new doll and climbed in Wes's lap as he sat in the rocking chair. She leaned back against him, and he put his arm around her as she cooed to her baby.

Sarafina smiled at her husband and daughter. "This is the best Christmas ever, seeing you two together and contented."

Wes sighed. He still didn't see Blanca as his daughter, but he merely nodded as he wearied of fighting the idea. Wes still could not bring himself to share his wife's maternal bliss.

Sarafina walked to his chair, leaned down, and kiss her daughter atop her head. Then she grinned at her husband. "Have you noticed anything?" She twirled around in her dress and flashed a shy smile at him.

Shrugging, Wes surrendered. "No, ma'am."

"I'm not wearing my pistol. I didn't think it right on Christmas Day. Do you think I should wear it any longer? It is annoying."

"Maybe not. With the new sheriff, things'll come to a head in the coming year, but keep it in our bedroom where you can find it but the kids won't."

Sarafina smiled. "Thank you, *mi esposo.* You have made me so happy!"

"Over the pistol?"

"No, over Blanca and how you have taken to our daughter."

Wes grimaced. Her daughter, he thought, then grinned when Sarafina leaned over and kissed him on the cheek.

Two days after Christmas, Juan Patrón visited the Casey place, riding across snow-covered roads on a clear but frigid day. Wes welcomed him into the house, but he knew by Juan's somber demeanor that the news was bad.

As Patrón moved to the fireplace for warmth, he grimaced. "Garrett captured Bonney at Stinking Springs outside Fort Sumner. His posse surrounded a cabin where the Kid and his men had gone to get out of the cold. In the shootout, Garrett's men killed Charlie Bowdre and captured the Kid."

Wes whistled, then turned to Jace. "I knew Garrett would stick to it until he caught Bonney, and he isn't officially sheriff for another five days."

"Garrett jailed the Kid in Las Vegas and will transfer him to Santa Fe," Patrón advised.

"Maybe while he's in the capital, he can convince the governor to live up to his promise."

Patrón shrugged. "The newspapers have reported Wallace left Santa Fe for a trip east on book business. His book *Ben-Hur* was published last month, and that's all he cares about now."

Jace shook his head. "Judas was always more interested in his thirty pieces of silver than in pardoning the Kid."

"Wallace let down a lot of us," Patrón responded. "You want to hear another disappointment? You won't believe this, but the county is planning to buy the Murphy-Dolan building as the new courthouse and jail."

"So the building that spawned so much corruption in Lincoln County will now be the center of justice for the county?" Wes asked.

"That's about it," Patrón replied, "and it'll be where Bonney is jailed, if he's convicted."

"Damn if everything isn't askew in this county." Jace whistled.

"Any idea when the Kid'll go to Mesilla for the trial?" Wes asked.

"Best I can tell from what I've read in the papers, it'll be in the spring when the weather clears. Do you plan to attend?"

Wes sighed. "There's nothing we can do for Bonney now."

"Besides," Jace added, "that's planting and branding time."

The kids had already eaten by the time Wes and Jace sat down at the kitchen table for supper, tired from a day of working in the field. Even before Sarafina could serve them bowls of menudo, Blanca climbed into Wes's lap, straddling his right leg until he picked her up and sat her on his left so he could feed himself. She cackled as he jiggled his tired leg. Sarafina sat his bowl and a tin plate of tortillas before him. As Wes spooned a bite into his mouth, Blanca leaned forward and grabbed a tortilla, folding it in half, then taking a bite and twisting around to shove the rest in Wes's mouth. He took a nibble, drawing a chuckle from her. Sarafina smiled at her husband and her daughter as she placed Jace's supper in front of him.

As both men attacked their supper, Sarafina put a large brown envelope on the table by her husband. "A rider delivered this from Juan Patrón. He said it was news from Mesilla."

Wes looked from the envelope to Jace. "Did you hear anyone ride up this afternoon?"

Jace shrugged. "Not a thing."

"Even if we're working hard, we can't let strangers approach our place unnoticed. Somebody could get hurt that way," Wes said as Blanca shoved another bit of tortilla at his mouth. He dodged the bite, and Blanca laughed.

"Maybe so, Wes, but it could be the bad times are behind us. Have you ever thought of that?" Jace asked.

"We think differently."

"My outlook's changed ever since Jesse Evans disappeared."

Wes froze with a spoon of menudo half way to his mouth, then glanced down at Blanca. "In some ways he's still here and will be as long as I live."

"Come on, Blanca, come to Mama so your papa can finish eating." Sarafina took her daughter from her husband's lap. The red-haired girl fussed and grabbed for Wes, but her mother pulled her away. "Why don't you go play with your brothers?"

Wes resumed eating, finishing his supper and opening the envelope and perusing a handwritten note from Patrón, who reported good news in Bonney's trial for the death of Buckshot Roberts. Attorney Ira Leonard had gotten the charges dropped on a technicality, but his accusers were reviving the charge for killing Sheriff Brady, so the Kid would face a second trial. Patrón then wrote that Leonard had stepped down as Bonney's lawyer, the accounts differing on the reason. Supposedly, Leonard had been threatened and had quit for his own safety, while newspapers reported Judge Bristol had replaced him. Either way, a Las Cruces lawyer said to be friendly to the Santa Fe Ring had been appointed instead.

"Damn," Wes said. "The Kid can't get one

break without suffering a bigger setback."

"We know justice is rigged against him in Lincoln County," Jace observed.

"And in all of New Mexico Territory, for that matter," Wes added.

Patrón concluded his letter saying he had enclosed three newspapers with accounts of Bonney's trial and further noted that he intended to ride to Mesilla for the second trial, which was the reason he sent the letter and newspapers by courier.

Jace studied Wes as he glanced up from the letter. "We both know Bonney's as good as dead, don't we?"

Wes let out a long breath. "I'm afraid so."

Both men saw Juan Patrón turn off the road for the house, Wes lowering an irrigation gate as he finished watering the newly planted corn and Jace sharpening their ax. The two men wiped their hands on their britches and strode out to get the latest from their Lincoln confidant. As they approached him, they knew the news was bad from the frown on Patrón's face.

"Climb down and rest a spell, Juan," Wes implored.

"I can't linger. Beatriz is probably worried sick over me as I told her I would be back two days ago, but the judge delayed sentencing for two days."

"So Bonney was convicted?" Jace asked.

Patrón nodded. "And sentenced to hang Friday, May thirteenth!

"It was a sham trial, the Kid's attorney uncertain of the evidence, and Judge Bristol instructing the jury — all Mexicans and none fluent in English — to convict Bonney, threatening their families if they voted him not guilty. It was a travesty of justice."

"What did you expect with Bristol presiding?" Wes asked.

"There's no news other than that. The Kid should be in Lincoln tomorrow."

"With the new courthouse, at least he won't have to spend his last days in that pit of a jail," Wes noted and paused. "It still seems wrong that Dolan's store will be where law's dispensed for Lincoln County. Any idea how Bonney's doing, Juan?"

"I visited with him before I left Mesilla. You know the Kid, he was grinning even with a death sentence hanging over him. He told me he wanted to see you once more before the execution date, but he insisted he wouldn't hang on the thirteenth or ever. He was confident for a condemned man."

"Is there any chance for an appeal to a higher court?" Wes asked.

Patrón smirked. "You know the answer to

that as well as I do, Wes. Those in power want him dead, the sooner the better."

"Maybe the governor will finally pardon him."

"Haven't you heard? Wallace has resigned and headed east to peddle his book."

Wes sighed so deeply he whistled. "The Kid's never gotten corn, just cob."

"You planning on attending the hanging?" Patrón asked.

"I'm not," Jace answered.

"Me neither," Wes added. "I still consider Bonney a friend, perhaps misguided, but even so a friend. I couldn't bear to see him die like a criminal. He deserves better."

"So does Lincoln County," Jace added.

Patrón nodded. "I need to move along to reach home before dark. If you need a place to stay when you visit Bonney, you're always welcome at our place."

"It'll be a couple weeks," Wes said. "We've got too much work to break right now."

"That don't matter as long as you get there before the thirteenth."

"I'll make it, I promise. If you see Bonney, tell him that for me."

Patrón nodded, then turned his horse for Lincoln.

Wes and Jace stood there, disappointed in the outcome, though they expected it.

"Why is it the corrupt politicians not only run but also *ruin* everything in New Mexico Territory?" Wes asked.

Jace had no answer, and both men returned to their chores.

By Wes Bracken's count, Billy Bonney had twenty-two days to live once he was imprisoned in the new Lincoln County Courthouse. Wes vowed to visit Bonney for sure, but he dreaded the day, deciding to put it off as long as he could and go to Lincoln the Friday before the Kid's execution. Bonney was being punished for all Lincoln County's wrongs for the entire eight years since Wes had arrived in the territory. Most frustrating was that Wes was powerless to help the Kid anymore after his conviction in a court of law, even a crooked one that imposed a death sentence. How do you fight a corrupt legal system?

Like a bride counting down to her wedding, Wes tracked the days until Bonney would hang. Late in the afternoon of the fifteenth day out, Wes was hoeing weeds in his cornfield while Jace worked in the blacksmith shack shoeing the piebald. Mired in his thoughts of the injustice done to Bonney by the governor, the courts, and the territory, Wes fumed until he heard a horse galloping down the road from the west and saw him turn toward the Casey place. He did not recognize the horse nor the hatless rider charging toward the house. Throwing his hoe down, Wes pulled his pistol from his holster and jogged to confront the rider, who saw him and waved his free hand, then whistled. Wes stopped in his tracks, stunned.

Billy Bonney had escaped!

Approaching Wes, the Kid reined up his pony and jumped off, stumbling as he hit earth because of the broken shackles on his bare feet. Catching his balance, Bonney flashed a toothy smile. "I decided I'd drop by, rather than waiting for you to visit me."

Wes saw a holstered pistol and another tucked in his pants, plus a Winchester in the pony's scabbard. "What happened, Kid?"

"It don't matter. I need help shedding these shackles and could use a pair of socks and boots if you got them." He handed the pony's reins to Wes. "And I want your stallion. I need a horse with strong lungs to escape."

"Not until you explain things, Bonney," Wes demanded as Jace ran up to join them.

"Kid," Jace cried, "what's going on?"

"They won't hang me after all."

"And you led the posse that's tailing you to my place."

"No. I headed west out of town and circled over the mountains to get here. Besides, nobody's following me."

"How can you be sure?" Wes demanded.

"The two lawmen that were guarding me are dead."

Wes bit his lip, glanced at Jace, then back at the Kid. "Did you kill Garrett?"

"He was in White Oaks buying lumber for my gallows." Bonney laughed. "He'll have to return the lumber for a refund."

"Garrett won't let up now until he kills you."

Bonney glared at Wes and Jace. "At least he won't hang me. Now are you going to help or have you turned against me like everyone else from the governor on down?"

Wes hesitated. The Kid had been wronged, yes, but now he had killed two deputies, compounding his problems.

"What's it gonna be, Wes?"

"I can't let you take my horse."

"Your sorrel is the fastest horseflesh around. I'll get him back to you somehow."

Jace interrupted. "While you're deciding about your horse, Wes, I'll work on the Kid's shackles." Cousins looked at the chain attached to only one of the iron bands around his ankles.

"I had to shoot the chain loose so I could ride."

Bonney handed the pony's reins to Wes, who watched them jog to the blacksmith shed.

As they departed, Jace looked over his shoulder. "Wes, I've got a spare pair of socks in my saddlebags. If you wouldn't mind getting them, I'll let the Kid have them."

Wes nodded, then started for the barn, leading the pony inside. He pondered the Kid's request and looked at his sorrel. Charlie was aging and had lost a step or two, but was still as fast as any mount in the territory. The sorrel stallion was all that remained of Wes's dream of breeding fine horses in New Mexico. Sighing, Wes decided to let go of that dream like so many others. He removed the saddle and bridle from Bonney's stolen horse and placed them on Charlie. Then he put a halter on the pony, planning to leave it hitched outside his house should the law or the owner come looking for it. Along with the pony, he led Charlie toward the barn door for the last time, then remembered Jace's request. He stopped by the stall where his partner's saddlebags hung and quickly fished out his spare socks. Exiting the barn, he headed for the back of the house. As he walked, he heard the clang of a hammer and chisel as Jace worked to free the Kid from his shackles. He tied both animals at the back door, then stepped inside, where the three children rushed over to greet him. As he brushed them aside, he saw his wife with the leather strap on her shoulder, dangling her pistol at her side.

"What's the commotion?" Sarafina asked. "Should I be worried?"

"The Kid's escaped from jail. Killed two deputies."

Sarafina gasped. "The law will look for him here. I'm scared."

"He won't be here long. Gather something he can eat on the trail."

She turned and scurried to the stove as Wes walked into the front room, where he retrieved a carton of cartridges. He returned to the kitchen, the children still following in his wake, and took a stack of tortillas from Sarafina. He exited the house and shoved the grub and ammunition in Bonney's empty saddlebag as the clanging continued from the blacksmith shed.

Wes led the pony around to the front of the house and tied it to the hitching post, then returned to Charlie. He hugged the stallion's neck, knowing the horse was about to begin a desperate ride unlike any before. When the clanging stopped, Wes looked to the shed and saw Bonney and Jace striding toward him. He untied the reins and waited.

The Kid grinned when Wes handed him the straps to the saddled sorrel. "I knew I could count on you, Wes. You've always been there for me. If anyone asks, tell them I stole the stallion at gunpoint."

"There's tortillas and a carton of cartridges in the saddlebags, plus Jace's socks."

"*Gracias* to you both," Bonney said, jumping into the saddle. "You'll get your horse back, Wes, I promise." He rattled the reins and turned the sorrel east, galloping toward his destiny.

"We'll never see the Kid alive again," Wes said.

CHAPTER 25

Two days later, while Jace Cousins was away checking on the cattle, Sheriff Pat Garrett arrived at the Casey place. Wes greeted the lawman, as he dismounted beside Bonney's stolen mount, nodded at the animal, and stretched his lanky arms.

"I see by the pony you know Bonney escaped a couple days ago," the lawman noted.

"That's true, Sheriff."

"Did he tell you he killed two of my deputies in the process?"

"We wormed that out of him, me and Jace."

Garrett looked around. "Where's your partner?"

"Working cattle. He'll be back about sundown."

"I suppose you gave Bonney a fresh horse, am I right?"

"He took my stallion when he was terrified and in a hurry. I figured you'd have a big posse on his tail by now."

Garrett smiled. "Finding Bonney's like chasing the wind. You know it's there, but you can't always see it, unless it kicks up dust. I'll find him. Folks are fed up with his mischief and willing to pass along information on his whereabouts. I doubt you're one to talk, but I thought I'd give you a chance, so you'd be sitting right with the law."

"I last saw him galloping down the road to the east. He didn't say where he was heading, and I didn't ask. Now let me ask you something."

"I'm all ears."

"There are many indictments out there, including ones on Jimmy Dolan. Why hasn't he been arrested, him and others in his gang?"

"I'll level with you, Bracken. It's politics. Dolan's got powerful friends in high places. I can't fight them all. I'm doing what I can to right some wrongs, but I can't fix every one of them."

"So you go after the scapegoats and the powerless?"

"That's one way to put it, but I don't know that I would agree. I look at it as working my way up the ladder. You have to stop on the lower rungs before you can get to the higher ones."

"But you can climb a ladder from either end."

Garrett snickered. "It doesn't matter which end you place on the ground, there's always bottom rungs leading to top ones. That's a fact of life and a fact of politics."

Bracken spat. "Everyone's tired of Lincoln County politics."

"Me, too, but it's just the way things are. As for Dolan, I'll rein him in as best I can, but there's one thing you should know about him."

"What's that?"

"You're the only man in Lincoln County he fears. He says you can't be bought, and you don't back down. I say it's because you try to do the right thing, no matter where the chips fall, at least that's your reputation among the Mexicans, whose opinions I respect more than those of the Anglos."

"It's not easy knowing right from wrong in Lincoln County."

Garrett grinned. "Believe me, as sheriff I know." He pointed to the stolen pony. "I'll return him to his owner in Lincoln."

"That's why I left him there. Now, tell me something else, Sheriff. Do you plan to kill Bonney?"

The sheriff hesitated, then tugged at the

end of his black mustache. "I don't know, Bracken. I knew him in Fort Sumner months back, a friendly, likable kid, but dangerous when riled. Like I've told you, people are tired of the violence, and some of his friends don't know how to keep their mouths shut. Word'll get to me one day, and I'll find him. It'll probably be around Fort Sumner as he favors a *señorita* there, though her brother despises him. The Kid's day will come, just like for the rest of us." Garrett untied the pony. "Mind if I water the animals in your creek?"

"Take all you want, Sheriff."

Garrett led the horses to the stream and let them drink while he filled his canteen. When the animals had their fill, the sheriff pulled his lanky frame into the saddle and rode away.

Four days later Wes awoke and headed to the barn to milk the cow. When he found the barn door unlatched, he slipped his gun from his holster, then slowly eased the door open and slipped in, suspecting something amiss until he heard a familiar whinny. It was Charlie. The horse stood in his stall. Wes did not know who had returned the sorrel or how, only that Charlie was back home. Once again, the Kid had lived up to his word.

■ ■ ■ ■

As May progressed, the Casey place tinted green with the growth of corn and the vegetables in Sarafina's garden, and more cattle carried the Mirror B brand as Wes and Jace worked their herd, now exceeding four hundred. The date of Bonney's scheduled execution came and passed without word of the outlaw or his whereabouts. Rumors still spread about Bonney's activities, but the Kid remained more feared than seen. June arrived, and Wes studied the land with pride as the results of all their work bloomed. He laughed at how Luis and Roberto doted on Blanca and how all three of the children enjoyed playing with Concho.

When July came, Wes and Jace took the family to Lincoln to buy supplies and to celebrate Independence Day, which everyone enjoyed except Blanca, who cried and fretted over the firecrackers and gunshots fired by celebrants during the festivities. Blanca ambled to Wes's arms and quieted only when he held her against his shoulder. Sarafina's smile pleased him, though it suggested he had accepted Blanca as his own.

Before leaving town that evening, Wes

stopped by Juan Patrón's to catch up on the latest news. While Patrón offered little firm information on Bonney, he reported that Governor Wallace's successor, Lionel Sheldon, on the job for a mere seven weeks, was promising to start construction of a penitentiary for the territory to reduce the cost of paying other states or territories for incarcerating New Mexico's criminals, like Carlos Zamora, who had now served more than half of his sentence in the Yuma Territorial Prison. A former Union brigadier general like Wallace, Sheldon was organizing a territorial militia as well to combat the lawlessness in southeastern New Mexico and the Apaches in the southwest corner of the territory. As for Bonney, the governor had said only that he wanted all responsible for the lawlessness brought to justice.

As he drove the wagon back home after the Lincoln celebration, Wes knew Bonney's time was growing short, the outcome inevitable. With Wallace's resignation, any hope of a pardon had vanished. With the killing of the two deputies during his escape, Bonney had forever ruined his own chances for clemency by Governor Sheldon.

Twelve days after the Fourth, Juan Patrón rode out in his wagon with his wife. By the stern look on Patrón's face, Wes feared the news. As soon as Beatriz stepped inside to visit Sarafina and dote on the children, Patrón asked Jace's whereabouts. When Wes informed him his partner was out working the cattle, Patrón grimaced.

"It's done," Patrón said somberly.

"Bonney?"

Patrón nodded. "Two days ago in Fort Sumner. Pat Garrett shot and killed the Kid."

Though he expected the news one day, its finality kicked Wes in the gut.

"I don't have the details, but they don't matter now that he's gone."

"Do you think it will end the county's troubles, Juan?"

"The Kid was the symptom of the problems, not the cause. The cause remains, like Dolan and his men."

"Will the new governor make a difference?"

"Probably not. Folks are weary from the violence, so I suspect it will die down from its own weight."

Wes stared beyond Patrón down the Hondo Valley in the same direction that he had last seen Bonney riding away on Charlie.

"Did I tell you Bonney stopped by here after his escape?"

"I heard it elsewhere."

"He escaped on my stallion, promising to return him. Sure enough, I found him in the barn six days later."

"So the Kid returned him?"

Wes shrugged. "I have no idea. There was no note, no sign who brought him back. It might've been Bonney or it could've been someone else, but who besides him would have known Charlie's proper stall in the barn?"

Patrón nodded. "Bonney kept his word if he trusted you. He was more dependable than most in Lincoln County. Perhaps now things will return to normal."

"I don't know what normal is anymore," Wes replied. "It's been so long since I've seen it. The Kid's gone as well as most of his friends, either dead or fled elsewhere. The only one still standing on their side is John Chisum, but he's far from Lincoln. And the other side? Most are under indictment, including Jimmy Dolan, yet they're still running free and probably always will. It's shameful."

Patrón shrugged. "And there's nothing we can do to change it. That's what I fear."

"Damn Lincoln County," Wes said, shaking his head. "I appreciate you delivering the news, Juan. You're welcome to come in and visit a spell, have a cup of coffee."

"Let me greet Sarafina, but we need to return home. I don't feel like talking much. It's times like these when we need a priest in Lincoln to unburden our souls."

Wes pointed to the house, and they marched inside. As soon as he closed the door and faced his wife, Sarafina gasped, her hand flying to her mouth. "It's the Kid, isn't it?"

Grimacing, Wes nodded.

Sarafina's hand fell to her bosom, and she signed a cross. *"Dios descanse su alma,"* she said. "God rest his soul."

"We're all sorry," Beatriz said, as she held Blanca in her lap while Luis and Roberto played with Concho in the corner. "He was a decent kid."

Juan stepped to Sarafina and patted her shoulder. "We wanted to bring you the news so you wouldn't hear it from his vile enemies."

Wes saw a tear trail down his wife's cheek. He moved to her, and with his forefinger wiped the mournful bead away. Blanca saw her mother's face and squirmed free of Beatriz's lap. The little girl extended her arms and rushed to her mother, climbing into Sarafina's lap to comfort her.

Patrón turned to his wife and offered his

hand. "It's time to go home, Beatriz."

Sarafina handed Blanca to Wes, then stood up and hugged Beatriz. *"Gracias,"* she whispered in her visitor's ear, then started for the entry, taking her daughter from her husband.

As soon as Wes opened the door, the boys scooted out ahead of everyone, their dog chasing after them.

"The sun's shining," Patrón said as he stepped outside. "Maybe it will cheer us up on the way home."

Wes helped Beatriz into the conveyance as Patrón settled into his seat, untying the reins and taking the whip. As Wes backed away, Patrón snapped the cord over the team's flank and the animals lifted their heads and started the buckboard on the trip back to Lincoln. Wes and his family waved as the Patróns reached the road.

"It is so sad about Billy," Sarafina sighed. "I fear the same fate for Carlos, *mi esposo.* He clings to a hatred I never saw in young Billy. It scares me how that hatred burns for you."

"He has more than a year remaining in prison, Sarafina. We will worry about that when he is released."

Wes shooed the boys back in the house along with their mother and sister. Though work remained in the field, he lacked focus and told his wife he was saddling up Charlie to deliver the news to Jace. She lowered Blanca to the floor and hugged her husband. "I am sorry for Billy and for us to lose such a friend. Will the killing ever end?"

"Maybe Bonney's death will stop it, but who knows?"

"Not me," Sarafina replied. "I'm scared for my brother and for you if he returns."

"Let's not worry today, Sarafina, over something that may not happen tomorrow."

Sarafina nodded against his chest. "I hope you're right and that prison has changed Carlos, but I fear otherwise."

Wes ran his hand through Sarafina's long black hair. "I'll not kill him."

She caught her breath. "I am not worried about that, but about him harming you." Sarafina untwined herself from his arms and picked up her whimpering daughter. "Be careful, *mi esposo.*"

Wes marched through the house, grabbing his carbine, and out the kitchen door to the barn where he quickly saddled Charlie and led him outside. After he latched the door, he mounted the sorrel and turned south over the uneven terrain that would lead to his partner. As he rode, he saw scattered cattle with the Mirror B brand and smiled that the animals had fattened on the spring and summer grass, but fall and then winter were approaching. He and Jace were better off than many in the Hondo Valley, but the future always seemed precarious in Lincoln County, especially with Jimmy Dolan still walking free. As he rode, Wes realized Charlie lacked the vigor of his younger years. He suspected that Bonney had fagged the stallion during his desperate escape, and Charlie would never be the same as a mount, though he likely had some good years ahead as a sire. He hated that Charlie's endurance had been drained by Bonney's frantic ride, but Wes considered the sorrel's loan as his final gift to Bonney, one that gave the Kid a few more months of life.

An hour into his ride, Wes spotted Jace coming his way at a trot. Wes took off his hat and waved it at his partner, who lifted his own briefly. Tugging the reins and halting Charlie, Wes held his headgear over his heart as Jace approached.

"Bad news?" Jace inquired.

Wes nodded.

"Bonney?"

"Pat Garrett shot and killed him two days ago in Fort Sumner."

Jace removed his hat again and pursed his lips.

"Juan came out to tell me this afternoon."

Sighing, then clenching his jaw, Jace finally relaxed enough to speak. "I suppose the Ring has finally gotten what they wanted, but I'm not surprised because Garrett had fire in those dark eyes. Will it make any difference in Lincoln County affairs?"

Wes shrugged. "Who knows?" He replaced his hat.

"Bonney remained as loyal as a puppy to the end, Wes. Maybe that was his weakness. He was more devoted to others than to himself."

"Perhaps, Jace, because he ignored all my advice to leave the territory."

"Now he'll remain in New Mexico forever, dead, buried, and forgotten."

Wes nodded. "He deserved better."

Both men turned for home and rode silently as darkness crept across the landscape.

A month later, as August eased toward September, Wes and Jace had just sat for lunch and taken their first sip of hot coffee after working all morning, when Concho started barking, running from the kitchen to the front door. Between growls, Wes heard the call of a distant voice.

"Hello, the house," came the cry.

500

Both partners stood up from the table and grabbed their long guns, Wes heading up front and Jace out back. As Wes slowly opened the door, he knew Jace was providing cover from the side of the house. Peeking through the crack, Wes opened the door fully when he spotted a man fifty yards standing beside his horse, his hands raised to his shoulders. Wes squinted, then stared in disbelief. It was James J. Dolan himself.

"I came to parlay," Dolan shouted. "I'm unarmed." He slowly lowered his hands and opened his riding coat to prove that he wasn't wearing a gun belt. "I want to clear up our differences, Bracken. Everyone's tired of the troubles."

"Talk," cried Wes.

"Let's visit face to face as long as you are unarmed, like me. I'm ready to set aside our differences. I'm coming without a weapon in a show of faith. Let's end the difficulties now." He paused, then pointed to the corner of the house. "And tell Cousins to lower his rifle."

"Do it, Jace," Wes ordered.

"Can you trust him, Wes?"

"I'm willing to risk it, if my family can quit living in fear," he answered. "Let's meet in the kitchen." Turning to Dolan, Wes shouted. "I'll put my guns away and return in a moment."

"Alone," Dolan demanded.

Wes responded, "Alone."

He retreated inside where Jace and his worried wife awaited.

"I don't trust that hotheaded Irishman, Wes."

"Nor do I, Jace, but somebody's gotta take a first step if we're going to end this." Wes propped his carbine in the corner and unhooked his holster, placing it on the table beside his uneaten lunch. He grabbed his coffee cup and took a sip, then asked Sarafina to refill it. As soon as she obliged, he tasted the hot liquid, nodded, and started for Dolan, carrying his drink.

"I'd feel better if you carried a gun, rather than coffee," Jace noted.

"Maybe this'll put him at ease," Wes said.

"Look around to make sure he doesn't have an assassin hiding to ambush you."

"I'd already thought of that," Wes said as he marched out the still open door, the dog following him. "Get back," Wes ordered as he surveyed the surroundings and headed toward the instigator of so many of Lincoln County's troubles.

Dolan again opened his riding coat to show he was unarmed. Then he removed the coat, gently laying it on the saddle of his gelding, careful not to turn his back to Bracken.

Wes studied Dolan, taking in his shield-like face with a narrow chin, thin lips, and broad nose giving way to a high and wide forehead topped by a mop of curly brown hair. Focusing on Dolan's beady serpent eyes, Wes took a small sip of coffee as he stepped within reach of his foe. He swallowed the hot liquid, then spoke. "What have you got to say, Dolan?"

"With the troublemaking Kid dead, I wanted to clear the air, see if we can get along," Dolan started, clasping his hands in front of his waist as if to reassure Wes he carried no weapon or, perhaps, to put Wes at ease in case he did.

"Bonney never created as much mischief as Murphy and you. That's a fact."

"There was wrong on both sides, but the time for pointing fingers is past. We've got to start fresh. What'll it take to do that?"

Wes cleared his throat. "I never want to see you or your men on my property again. If you threaten my wife or my family in any way from this point forward, any agreement is off. It doesn't matter if it was you or one of your cronies, I'll find and hold *you* responsible."

"That sounds like a death threat," Dolan

answered, breaking his hands free and putting them on his hips.

"Then we understand each other. Those demands are my starting point."

"What's the rest?"

"I came here eight years ago to start a place and raise horses. My place was torched and my breeding stock killed. I want to be paid for losses caused by your men."

Dolan shrugged, his beady eyes widening. "My men weren't responsible for that. It was Jesse Evans that did it."

"He was working for you." Wes took a small sip of the scalding coffee.

"Jesse only worked for himself. Now that you brought up, Jesse, I've got a question for you: Did you kill him?"

"Last I saw him, he was swimming his horse across the flooded Pecos. I can't say what happened to him for certain. What difference does it make?"

"I paid him over seven hundred dollars to do a job he never completed. Find Jesse, and you can have that money as compensation."

Wes shrugged. "That money's between you and him. I want what I'm owed from you for destroying my place."

Dolan bowed his back. "Seems odd to me

that after Jesse disappeared, your partner visited Roswell with a wad of money thick enough to buy a wagon, team, and implements." Dolan knotted his fingers on his hips and pressed his fists into his side, widening his stance as he glared at Bracken.

"Take it up with Jesse. Last I heard he was in Texas."

Dolan shook his head, his lips tightening, his serpentine eyes narrowing. "I think you killed Jesse Evans and stole my money."

"You're heading down the wrong trail, Dolan. You better change directions or there's no point in putting our differences aside."

Dolan spewed venom with his response. "I know you killed Jesse just like I know he sired that bastard redheaded daughter of yours."

Wes stepped toward Bracken. "Take it back."

The Irishman backed away, his right fist disappearing behind him, then reappearing in a flash.

Wes eyed a pistol in Dolan's moving hand.

"This is something Jesse should've finished like I paid him to," Dolan shouted, lifting the revolver at Bracken.

The moment he did, Wes flung the scalding coffee into Dolan's eyes.

Dolan screamed, dropping the gun, stumbling backward, and reaching for his face with both hands, shrieking and rubbing his eyes furiously to stop the scorching burn.

Tossing the tin cup aside and knotting his fingers, Wes took two steps toward his foe and powered his right fist into Dolan's nose. As his foe screamed, Wes plastered Dolan's chin with a teeth-rattling uppercut.

As blood flowed from his nose and seeped from his mouth, Dolan stumbled to his horse, which shied away. "Don't," he screeched, "please don't."

Wes jumped to his foe and plunged two powerful punches into his gut, knocking the breath out of him. Dolan folded and gasped for air. As Dolan struggled to fill his lungs, Wes grabbed his ears and jerked his head down as he pistoned his knee into the man's bloodied face. The air and fight leaked from Dolan as he fell to the ground, rolling over on his back, too dazed to do anything but wheeze for his breath.

As Wes stood over him glaring, Jace ran up with his Henry, aiming it at Dolan's head.

Wes waved him away. "This is my fight." Looking at his dazed opponent spread-eagled on the ground, Wes stepped between his opponent's legs, drew back his right foot, and plowed his boot into Dolan's groin.

The injured man squealed, then passed out.

"If you ever insult my wife or her daughter again, I'll make a gelding out of you for sure, you son of a bitch."

Jace grabbed Wes's shoulders, pulling him away. "Don't kill him or the law'll be down on you."

Wes yanked his arm from his partner's grasp and strode to Dolan's gun, which he grabbed and cocked. He marched to Dolan's prone figure and straddled his chest with his feet and fired a bullet into the earth by his left ear and another by his right. Dolan barely flinched.

Without moving from his stance, he called to Jace. "Fetch his canteen from his horse."

"Okay, Wes, just don't kill him." Jace scurried to the nervous animal, grabbing the reins and quickly untying the container. He tossed it to Wes who caught it with his left hand, lifted it to his mouth, and used his teeth to pull out the cork, which he spit aside.

Wes squatted and dribbled water on Dolan's face until he regained a painful consciousness. He moaned and squirmed, his eyes widening in terror when they focused on Wes hovering over him. Wes lowered the revolver over Dolan's pulpy mug and spun the cylinder.

"I fired two bullets while you were asleep, Dolan," Wes snarled. "There are at least two empties in the cylinder." He cocked the gun and shoved the barrel into Dolan's mouth. "Let's see how lucky you are if I pull the trigger."

Dolan's head trembled from side to side as he tried to speak. "N . . . n . . . no . . . nooo," he managed.

Wes spat on his cheek. "Then here's the deal. From this point on, bygones are bygones. If you come anywhere near threatening me, my family, or my partner again, I *will* find you and I *will* kill you, but I'll make a *gelding* out of you first. Do you understand?"

Dolan's entire body trembled, though Wes was uncertain if it was from fear or pain.

"Do you understand?"

"Y . . . y . . . yes . . . yesss," he managed around the gun barrel.

Wes pulled the gun barrel from his mouth and tucked the weapon in his waistband as he stood up. Towering over the prone and bloodied man, he shook his fist in his face. "What's past is past, right Dolan? No more vendetta?"

Dolan nodded, rolling over on his side, grabbing between his legs and moaning. "It's over," he managed.

"Or you're dead, Dolan," Wes reaffirmed, then looked at Jace. "Help him on his horse and send him on his way."

"I . . . ca . . . can't ride," the prone man pleaded.

"You will ride or I'll kick you again."

Jace grabbed him by the shoulders and yanked him to his feet, then walked him to his horse and boosted him into his saddle. Dolan screamed as his bottom hit saddle leather, even though his riding coat provided additional padding. When Jace handed him the reins, Wes slapped the animal's flank and the gelding bounced away, Dolan screaming with the fall of each hoof, then leaning over his horse's neck and vomiting on the trail.

CHAPTER 26

"I've been expecting you, Sheriff," Wes said as he opened the front door and invited Pat Garrett inside.

"Afternoon, Bracken." Garrett removed his hat and dipped his head so he could pass his lanky frame through the doorway.

Wes pointed to a chair in the front room. "Fact is, I expected you here sooner. What's it been, seven or eight days since Jimmy Dolan's visit. I assume that's why you're here."

Garrett tugged at the end of his mustache and grinned. "Yes, sir. Jimmy Dolan was a little sore after he called on you, extending the olive branch as he described it, trying to make things square with the past so everyone could get on with their lives."

Wes pulled up a chair opposite Garrett and plopped himself in the seat. "That's not how I recall it."

"Then tell me, Bracken, your side of the

story. As Dolan relates it, he came here to put past differences aside, and without provocation you beat him up. I will say he's been walking gingerly around town the last several days, and his face is still black and blue."

"I'm glad he remembers me," Wes began, then offered his account of Dolan approaching the Casey place, asking to visit and showing himself to be unarmed. Though the discussion started off about past differences and putting them aside, Wes said it veered toward Jesse Evans and money he had paid the outlaw to handle a job for him. "Dolan accused me of stealing the money and laughed at Evans siring that 'bastard red-headed daughter' of mine as he called Blanca."

Garrett's face drew tight, his eyes narrowing. "I'd be furious, too, if he insulted my Mexican wife."

"As I exploded, he pulled a hidden gun from his back waistband. I threw hot coffee in his face and pummeled him to the ground, then kicked him in the riding britches before shoving the pistol barrel in his mouth and telling him I would kill him if he ever threatened or insulted my family again." Wes paused. "He seemed to understand what I was trying to get across."

Garrett snickered. "I've never seen a man so scared as when he came to my office to have you arrested."

"Are you jailing me?"

"I haven't ruled it out, though I doubt it, because I wanted your side of the story. This money that he accused you of stealing, how much was it?"

"Some seven hundred dollars."

Garrett whistled. "Now it's making sense."

"What?"

"The money, Bracken. You just told me Dolan said he paid Evans seven hundred to handle a matter. You know what that job was?"

Wes shrugged. "No telling as crooked as Dolan is."

The sheriff glanced at the floor, then back at Wes. "Dolan paid to have you and your partner killed."

Wes swallowed hard as Garrett continued.

"Dolan helped Evans escape from Fort Stanton to track you down. He paid Evans five hundred dollars for you and two hundred for Jace Cousins. They didn't expect a posse to give chase to Evans, which ruined Dolan's plan."

The lawman's words confirmed that Evans had indeed been headed to the Casey place to murder them when they turned that scheme inside out and chased him to his death in the Pecos.

"So let's just say you killed Jesse Evans like Dolan is accusing you, to my way of thinking it would've been self-defense. Since his body hasn't been found, there's no crime."

"I'm not concerned about Evans and what became of him, Sheriff. I am worried about my family and their safety. Dolan's as crooked as a washtub full of rattlesnakes and twice as mean."

Garrett grimaced. "I know, but Dolan's got political pull."

Wes wadded his right fist and punched his left palm. "First it was Murphy, and now it's Dolan. They've made Lincoln County a hell of a place to call home."

Garrett leaned forward in his chair. "Listen to me, Bracken, I'm working to make it right. What I've learned about you is you are as respected among the Mexicans as much as Billy Bonney was. You've been straight with my wife's people, and I respect that. Men like Dolan are always trying to cheat them because they may not understand English or our system of laws. Give me a week and then come to my office in the courthouse. Arrive at two o'clock. I'll have Dolan there, and I'll lay down how it'll be. You've got to trust me on this. I've gotten around and listened to people. I know where the problem lies. Give me seven days."

"If it'll protect my family."

"I'll do the best I can, I promise you."

We studied Garrett's face, detecting no guile. "Let me ask you something? How did the Kid die?"

"I was visiting a friend in his darkened bedroom that night when Bonney entered. I couldn't see him but I recognized his voice, calling *'¿Quién es? ¿Quién es?'* I fired twice. He died quickly. Didn't suffer, the best I could tell."

"That's good to know. I liked and trusted him more than anyone on Dolan's side."

Garrett nodded. "I'd known him before at Fort Sumner and found him likable, but folks say he turned mean after he testified against Dolan and his men in the Chapman killing. You know why?"

Wes nodded. "Governor Wallace promised him a pardon."

"You told me that when we first met, but I didn't believe it until the Kid kept talking about a pardon once we arrested him at Stinking Springs. That's all he talked about when we jailed him in Santa Fe, even writing a letter to Wallace. Are you sure about the promise?"

"As sure as I'm sitting here. I was there the night he first met with Governor Wallace at Squire Wilson's house and heard that Judas of a governor say that Bonney would walk away scot-free with a pardon in his pocket once he testified against Dolan and lived up to their agreement. It seems like Dolan always lands on his feet and the rest of us don't."

Garrett stood up and offered Bracken his hand. Wes arose and grasped the sheriff's hand, pumping it vigorously.

"I know Dolan's behind a lot of the problems, and I can't change what's been done, but going forward I intend to make sure decent people in this county can live without fear as long as I'm sheriff."

"Don't let us down, Sheriff," Wes said with a final pump of the hand that had held the gun that had killed Billy the Kid. "Lincoln County justice has disappointed everyone for years."

"I intend to change that." Garrett moved to the door and bent down to exit. He tugged his hat on as Wes followed in his wake.

"Should I bring Jace Cousins with me to meet with Dolan?"

"No, come alone. I'm the only other friend you'll need there."

Wes passed the cemetery and neared the eastern edge of Lincoln. He felt strange atop the white-stockinged chestnut after riding his sorrel stallion for so many years. His new mount had good lungs and an easy gait, but Wes had never ridden him full out to check his speed or stamina. Wes hoped the days when a fast and strong horse meant the difference between life and death were over in Lincoln Country. Perhaps his two o'clock meeting with Sheriff Pat Garrett and Jimmy Dolan would bring peace.

As he reached the first dwelling beside the road, he noticed more people than usual outside their humble abodes, often entire Hispanic families, staring at him. Some spectators removed their hats as he passed and others clapped. Wes looked behind him, to see who had earned such adulation. Even some Anglo men and women acknowledged him as he rode by. Ahead he saw Juan and Beatriz Patrón standing in the road like the others. Ill at ease from the attention, Wes touched his hat brim to acknowledge their recognition, even if he didn't understand the fuss.

He guided the chestnut toward the

Patróns and drew up in front of the couple. "Are folks expecting a circus parade, Juan? What's this all about?"

Patrón stepped to Wes and shook his hand. "You're the parade. It's all for you."

"But why? What did I do?"

"You gave Jimmy Dolan the beating he's long deserved. Folks have been snickering at him behind his back and even to his battered face. They're showing you their appreciation. The sheriff put out word among our people that he was meeting with you and Dolan this afternoon to end the feud. Garrett's made clear the violence will end or else." Juan laughed. "Dolan's bruised and swollen face has lifted people's spirits, especially after the Kid's death. This is their way of thanking you for whipping Dolan."

Wes straightened in his saddle and looked up and down the street at the many hopeful eyes and smiles directed at him. He pursed his lips and nodded, then lifted his hat to acknowledge their thanks. Men, women, and even children cheered and applauded. As he placed his hat back atop his head, Wes looked down at Juan. "I can't say I was righting a wrong. Dolan insulted Sarafina and Blanca, enraging me. If Jace hadn't been there, I might've killed him."

Patrón laughed. "Killing him would not

have hurt him near as much as the whipping you gave him and the humiliation that followed. Word spread quickly in Lincoln and nearby communities that Dolan's iron grip on Lincoln County was at an end, thanks to you. He can't intimidate people like before."

Wes looked down the street where others awaited his passing. He nodded at Patrón. "I best move along so I'm not late for my meeting."

"Enjoy everyone's gratitude, Wes. You have their respect as well. They don't care why you whipped Dolan up, just that you did."

Shaking the reins, Wes started the chestnut moving westward down the street to the imposing building Dolan and his late partner, L.G. Murphy, had built. *"Gracias, gracias,"* he called to those who displayed their gratitude. He rode past the blackened ruins of the McSween house, then the boarded-up store of John Henry Tunstall, whose murder three years earlier at the hands of Dolan's men had precipitated so much of the violence. Riding by the Wortley Hotel, he noted proprietor Sam Wortley on the plank porch giving him a thumbs-up sign. Wes answered Wortley with a nod. Ahead on the south side of the street, he studied the imposing two-story building that now housed the county courthouse and jail. Out front he saw a dozen men and women waiting, including the tall lanky sheriff, who stood a head above those around him.

Reaching the courthouse, Wes dismounted and tied his chestnut to the hitching post as those on the walk clapped softly, save for Garrett who offered a narrow grin as Wes stepped on the planks. The sheriff slapped Wes on the back, then pointed to the door where a spectator opened it for them. As they entered, the lawman spoke.

"Dolan's upstairs waiting, but I wanted folks to see me greeting you. You're a popular man, Bracken. Folks appreciate what you did to Dolan. The friendlier I am with you, the better chance I have of getting reelected when this term ends."

"I'll be honest with you, Sheriff, I didn't vote for you or Kimbrell last fall."

Garrett shut the door, then escorted Wes down a hallway to a narrow staircase leading upstairs. As they turned to start up the stairway, Garrett pointed to a bullet hole in the adobe wall. "That's from Bonney's escape. The bullet that did that killed the first deputy."

At the top of the steps Garrett led Wes into his office, where Dolan sat in a chair by the window, his face still discolored and slightly swollen from Wes's beating. Garrett pointed Wes to a chair on the opposite side of the room as he removed his hat, then hung it on a peg on the gun rack behind his desk. He settled in his chair behind the desk, separating the two foes. Wes placed his hat in his lap, returning the hateful glare that Dolan offered with his beady eyes.

Garrett leaned forward and put his balled fists on the desk. "Gentlemen, it ends today."

"Then arrest him for trying to kill me," Dolan shouted.

The sheriff lifted his finger and pointed at Dolan's misshaped nose. "Shut up, Dolan."

"You don't tell me to shut up, Pat. It's my influence and the Ring's that got you elected to kill Bonney and end the lawlessness."

Garrett sucked in a deep breath and answered in a low and menacing tone. "I got support from more than you and the Ring. The people elected me to straighten out this mess, largely created by you and your band. I intend to do just that."

Dolan flinched, glancing from the sheriff to Bracken and biting his lower lip.

"The folks in this county despise you for how you've swindled and cheated them when this place was a store. They hate you for the killings you spawned, and the cattle you rustled."

"I never stole a single head," Dolan shot back.

"No, but your men did at your direction. And then you filled the government contracts with stolen beef, never costing you anything but the respect of these fine folks, both Mexican and Anglo, who are trying to scrape out a living in an unforgiving land."

Dolan exhaled a frustrated breath, then pointed his trigger finger at the lawman. "I'll see that you never get elected sheriff again, Pat."

Garrett snickered. "No, you won't. Right now, the only man more popular in these parts is Wes Bracken. He might beat me in an election if he runs, but you couldn't. Your days are over running this county by whim and intimidation."

"I've got powerful friends, Pat."

The lawman nodded. "Yes, you do, Dolan, and they are keeping me from arresting you on the outstanding indictments for the murder of the lawyer Chapman and for other offenses, but they can't keep me from killing you."

Dolan flinched and sat back in his chair, his eyes widening.

"That's why I brought Bracken here to meet with you, Dolan, as I want an understanding as we move forward, and I want both of you to hear it."

Wes nodded. "As long as my family is safe and free from intimidation, I'll go along with anything, Sheriff."

Garrett studied Dolan. "It ends here, and it ends today, Dolan. Everything that is past is past, including the whipping he gave you."

"He should be jailed and tried for what he did to me."

Garrett laughed. "The beating wasn't nearly as bad as the humiliation you've received. Most people in these parts felt you finally got your comeuppance, and those folks are voters. I intend to please them, not you and not the Ring, Dolan."

Dolan bolted up from his chair. "You can't intimidate me, Sheriff."

"Sit down, shut up, and listen, as I *will* intimidate you, Dolan. Talk back to me again and I'll have you arrested."

"For what?"

"For the murder indictments I hold. For helping Jesse Evans escape from the Fort Stanton stockade. I know what went on, and I've got witnesses that'll confirm you paid Evans seven hundred dollars to kill Wesley Bracken and Jace Cousins."

Dolan slowly settled back into his chair, his bruised face paling.

"I repeat, Dolan, it ends today or you will pay a price." Garrett turned to Bracken. "State your demands."

"They're very simple. My family is not to be threatened or harmed, that includes my wife, my children, myself, and my partner. Neither Dolan nor his hands are to set foot on my land, both at the Casey place and at my original Mirror B claim."

Garrett shook his finger at Dolan. "Do you understand that?"

Dolan nodded.

"In return," Garrett continued, "Bracken and Cousins will stay away from your property."

"I'm fine with that, Sheriff," Wes replied.

Garrett smiled, then lowered his pointed finger to his side and pulled out his revolver, placing it on his desk so the barrel aimed toward Dolan and the window. "I don't trust you, Dolan, because you're a vindictive son of a bitch."

Dolan slapped the sheriff's desk, sulling up like a bullfrog, then opening his mouth to respond, but halting when Garrett picked up the gun, cocked the hammer, and directed it at him.

"Here's the understanding I want you to leave this meeting with, Dolan. If a single hair on the head of Cousins, Bracken, his wife, or his kids is harmed, I will come looking for you, no matter how long it takes to find you, and I *will* kill you. Your political allies may stop me from arresting you on any indictment, but they can't keep me from killing you. As you saw with the Kid, I don't give up when I'm trying to bring a renegade to justice, and no jury in Lincoln County would convict me for shooting you, whether I'm wearing a badge or not."

Dolan's head shook like laundry in the breeze as he sputtered a response, his eyes wide as he stared at the gun barrel. "I can't control what my men may do."

"You better, Dolan. If I find out you or any of your men threatened, harmed, or plotted anything against the Brackens, I vow before God I will kill you."

"That's not right."

"Neither is what you've done to the people of this county for the past decade." Garrett lowered the revolver. "I've had my say as sheriff of Lincoln County, Dolan. You best abide by it. It ends today. It ends here. It ends this second. If you forget that, you'll end soon."

Dolan trembled with disbelief, so stunned he remained speechless.

Garrett turned to Bracken. "If you have any trouble at your place or anywhere you go in Lincoln County, you come to me. I'll take care of Dolan." The sheriff pushed himself up from his desk and slid his revolver back in his holster. "This conversation is over, Dolan. Get up and get out of here and, most of all, get over your vendetta against Bracken."

Grimacing, the former political and economic boss of Lincoln County stood. He glared a moment at Garrett, then Bracken. He took his hat from the corner of the desk, tugged it over his head, and marched into the hall and down the stairway, the heavy fall of his boots echoing up the stairwell.

The sheriff remained silent while Dolan tromped away. Wes realized he had misjudged Pat Garrett. Perhaps the sheriff would play as straight as he could within the restraints of county and territorial politics. Once Dolan was beyond hearing range, Garrett sat. "I don't know if that was legal, but it was right. Dolan's cheated folks for too long and gotten away with it until now."

"Thank you, Sheriff," Wes said. "Maybe we can look to the future instead of over our shoulders from now on."

"Perhaps, but Dolan is devious. I tried to put the fear of God in him, but I doubt it took. Between you and me, Bracken, I didn't feel good about killing Bonney. It was my job, and I did it, but I fear the Kid was blamed for many of the House's crimes. As for Dolan, it won't bother me a bit to kill him, if it comes to that."

"I'm obliged, Sheriff, for what you've done for my family." Wes arose and put on his hat.

"Just remember Dolan is as underhanded as ever. Whether his fear reins in his schemes remains to be seen." Garrett paused. "I half hope he tries something so I can kill him. He'll be a lot easier to kill than to arrest and try, politics being what they are in the territory."

As the leaves bared their fall colors along the Hondo Valley and the harvesting chores picked up, Wes gradually grew more confident that Garrett's threats had worked on Dolan. For the first time in years, he did not feel he had to wear his sidearm whenever he went out to milk the cow, work the fields, or chop wood for the coming winter. The crop would be another good one for 1881, and 1882 held promise to be the first worry-free year since Wes had arrived in 1873. Though Carlos came up for release in 1882, that day was months away, and Wes hoped that his time in Yuma Territorial

Prison had softened the bitterness that his brother-in-law carried. Perhaps that was a mere dream to hope that Carlos had changed, but Wes never thought someone could cow Dolan out of his vindictiveness as Pat Garrett had done.

Together Wes and Jace managed the major chores to prepare for winter, while Sarafina filled the larder for cold weather. Luis and Roberto, despite their youthful exuberance, could handle growing responsibilities like shucking corn. Blanca and the dog, though, remained oblivious to the work at hand.

As the days of September bled into October, Wes saw the fatigue in everyone's eyes. Knowing they would need a final run of supplies before a hard freeze sat in, Wes suggested they take a break and everyone ride to town to spend the day and relax a few hours before resuming the chores again. Jace liked the idea, but not everyone going at the same time. He proposed Wes take his family to town one morning, spend the night, and return the next afternoon while he stayed at the Casey place to watch over things and to work with anyone that brought a load of corn for grinding in the gristmill. Wes liked Jace's suggestion and mentioned the idea to Sarafina, whose tired face instantly sported a smile. His wife answered with a nod, and then a question. "Should I carry my revolver?" Wes rubbed his mustache, considering the matter and deciding the dangers small, thanks to Garrett. "Leave it under the mattress where you can find it. You shouldn't need it since the sheriff has made clear he intends to stop the mischief."

Sarafina hugged her husband. "I have longed for this day to arrive."

Two days later, Wes hitched up the wagon and loaded Sarafina in the seat and the kids and dog in the back. Wes wore his pistol and a gun belt full of cartridges. He also slipped his carbine and a box of ammunition in the driver's box, not to fight off attackers, but in case they spotted game that they could bring home. They rode without worry, though the brisk morning chill lingered until the sun topped the mountains and heated the landscape.

Arriving in Lincoln, Wes stopped at Juan Patrón's house, but no one was home. He then drove to the Wortley Hotel, registered to spend the night, and dined with everyone in the eatery. They visited the stores and purchased what supplies they could, the merchants delighted with their business because they paid cash. Wes and Sarafina placed blankets on their hotel room floor for the children and the dog, then shared a thick feather mattress together. Wes arose early, but left his wife, the boys, and Blanca to sleep late while he had a breakfast of bacon, biscuits, fried eggs, and coffee in the dining room. Between cooking and serving early patrons, Sam Wortley reported things were picking up in Lincoln, and Garrett had brought the security that people had craved.

As Wortley went to serve another customer and Wes finished his last cup of coffee, the front door opened and Juan Patrón poked his head in, smiling when he saw Wes in the corner. He strode across the eatery and nodded. "I heard you were in town. We need to talk."

"Have a seat, Juan."

"No," he replied. "Let's visit outside where no one can overhear us."

"Problems?"

"I can't say for sure, but certainly a rumor worth passing along."

Wes stood up, tossed his napkin by his plate, and grabbed his hat as he followed Patrón across the room. "I'll settle up when I check out of our room," Wes called to Wortley, who nodded his okay.

Once outside, Wes led Patrón around the hotel to his wagon parked in back. "You sound worried, Juan."

"It may be nothing, but there's a rumor

in the air about Dolan."

Wes felt his jaw clench.

"You remember your meeting with Garrett and Dolan a few weeks ago?"

He nodded.

"Word is after that Dolan convinced some of his county friends and territorial officials in Santa Fe to stop paying the prison bill for Carlos. Rumor has it he was released awhile back."

Pondering the gossip, Wes considered it a possibility, as it was a way Dolan might get back at Bracken without drawing Garrett's suspicions. "I suppose it's possible, but I'm hoping the prison time did Carlos some good. Whether or not he likes it, we're family."

"Maybe so, Wes, but Carlos is Carlos. I've heard a couple people say they've seen someone that looks like him skulking around near San Patricio. You should be careful."

Wes grabbed Patrón's hand and shook it warmly. "I will, Juan. You've always been one I could count on. I'll buy your breakfast."

"I ate early, Wes, because I'm leaving for Roswell on business. I was going to stop by your place on the way, but when I learned you were in town, I had to let you know."

"I'm obliged, Juan. Stop by on your return."

Patrón nodded. "If I have time." He turned and walked away.

Wes pondered whether to inform Sarafina of the gossip, finally deciding against it. Why spoil a pleasant trip to town? Come afternoon following a filling lunch, he loaded up, settled his bill with Sam Wortley, helped his family into the wagon, and started home, arriving an hour before dusk. Wes and Jace unloaded and tended the team, then ate a supper of tortillas. Jace stayed on the Casey place the next day, then headed for Lincoln the following morning.

Wes spent the day hauling and chopping wood, building a surplus from the upcoming winter. By suppertime, he was exhausted, leaving his hat, coat, and holster on pegs by the door. After eating a bowl of chili and moving into the front room, he lit two lamps and settled into his rocking chair to let the exhaustion melt from his muscles. After finishing the dishes, Sarafina joined him, the kids following her.

Luis and Roberto played with the dog, and Blanca headed for Wes, her hands outstretched, but she tripped and fell, screaming, then crying from the bump on her head. Jumping up from his chair, Wes picked her up and settled back into his seat, holding her in his lap until she merely whimpered. Once she calmed, she stood up in Wes's lap and wrapped her arms around his neck, resting her cheek against his shoulder and singing a song that only she understood the lyrics to.

As he enjoyed the girl's concert, Sarafina jumped up as Concho yelped at the front door. Sarafina looked at her husband. "There's someone at the door."

A voice called, "Sarafina, Sarafina."

Suddenly Sarafina smiled. "It's Carlos," she gasped.

Before he could shout a warning, Sarafina yanked the bar away. As soon as she did, the door flung back and Carlos pushed Sarafina aside, a revolver in his hand. As his eyes adjusted to the yellow light, Carlos swung his pistol around, pointing it at Wes.

And Blanca!

CHAPTER 27

Sarafina screamed. "No, Carlos, no!" She jumped in front of her brother, pushing his pistol hand downward.

Carlos shoved her to the floor, but she scrambled to her hands and knees, crawling to her sibling, grabbing him around his calves and pleading. "Please, Carlos, don't shoot *mi esposo.* I beg you, don't," she cried as her sons cowered in the corner and sobbed.

Slowly, Wes arose from his chair, holding Blanca aside. She wailed as he gently lowered her to the floor, then ran to her mother, bawling with each step.

Carlos wormed from his sister's grip, backing away from her toward the door and glaring at Wes. "I spent seven hundred and ninety-one days in that Yuma hellhole. All that kept me going was knowing one day I would kill you."

Wes judged if he could lunge for Carlos

and strip him of his weapon, but feared Sarafina or the kids might get hurt in the scuffle. Even if he hadn't left his revolver hanging by the kitchen door, he still couldn't have used it for the same reason. Besides, he had promised Sarafina he would never kill her brother.

"You put me in that hellhole, *bastardo,* and you and your kind soiled my sister."

"I kept you from the gallows, Carlos, or getting shot by the law like Billy Bonney."

Carlos just snarled. "Go for your gun."

"I'm not wearing a gun." Wes lifted his hands away from his side.

"Noooo," shrieked Sarafina, scrambling to her feet and jumping in front of her brother again. "Don't hurt my husband. Noooo!"

"Get out of my way, Sarafina." Carlos shoved her aside.

"I vowed to Sarafina I would never kill you, Carlos, and I intend to keep that promise."

"Don't hurt *mi esposo* or my family," Sarafina pleaded, then glanced at her husband.

"No, *mi esposo,* break that vow and save yourself and our children. He's a rabid dog."

Carlos glanced at Sarafina. "You choose him over me, your brother? I will not hurt you, *mi hermana,* or the little ones."

Sarafina spat at her brother. "If you shoot *mi esposo,* you will hurt us all, Carlos."

"He ruined my life," Carlos screamed. "He was never one of our people."

With Carlos momentarily distracted, Wes took a step toward him, but his brother-in-law waved the gun at Wes's chest and scowled. "I'll send you to hell tonight. You'll fry forever like I roasted all those days in a broiling cage. Do you know how hot it gets inside those walls and how little water they give you and how brutal the guards are?"

"You're alive, Carlos, not hanging from some gallows or buried in the cold ground."

Carlos cackled, his strange laugh frightening the children more. They wailed even louder.

"Don't shoot *mi esposo* in front of the little ones," Sarafina begged.

"Then get them out of here," Carlos shouted. "I'm tired of their howling."

"Okay, okay," Sarafina answered, "but they are children, afraid for their father." She glanced at Wes, "Your promise is not as important to me as you being here for our children. I love you, *mi esposo.*"

"Move," shouted Carlos.

She herded Blanca, Roberto, and Luis toward the door to the kitchen. "Just don't shoot my husband. I'll return."

"Ser rápido," he cried as he stared at Wes with venomous eyes.

"Killing me won't end your problems, only magnify them, Carlos. It's time to put the past to bed. I've tried to do that with Jimmy Dolan, for the safety of my family, though I still loathe the man. Think what this will do to Sarafina, to your nephews and your niece. They will hate you when they're all the family you've got now."

Carlos shook his head wildly. "Shut up!"

Slowly and defiantly, Wes lifted his arms and crossed them over his chest. "I'll not break my promise to Sarafina."

His eyes bubbling with rage, Carlos lowered his pistol to his hip.

Wagging his head from side to side, Wes caught a glimpse out of the corner of his eye of Sarafina returning from the kitchen. He pursed his lips and waited, knowing he could never make it across the room to wrestle the gun from his brother-in-law without first being shot.

"I'll count to three," Carlos said, "then I intend to shoot you."

"No, Carlos, no," screamed Sarafina, "don't make me do it."

Carlos ignored his sister, focusing on Wes. *"Uno —"*

Once Carlos lifted his revolver, Wes decided to dive for the wall, then scramble for him, hoping to reach him before he fired. Perhaps then he could wrest the gun from his grip and save himself.

"*Dos* —"

"Don't, Carlos, don't," pleaded Sarafina softly, resignation in her voice at what was about to transpire.

"*Tres* —"

"Please, no, Carlos," Sarafina called.

Slowly and deliberately, Carlos lifted his weapon, cocking the hammer and aiming at Wes's chest.

"No," cried Sarafina.

Wes dove for the wall.

The blast of a gunshot exploded through the room.

Falling hard against the floor, Wes grimaced at the shock of the fall, but certain he had avoided Carlos's first shot. Would he be so lucky with the second?

Carlos screamed in anger and frustration.

Wes scrambled on his hands and knees, lunging for Carlos.

The thunder of a second shot rumbled across the room as Wes grabbed an ankle. Once he did, his brother-in-law's pistol clattered on the floor in front of Wes's face. With his free hand, Wes shoved it across the room toward his wife. He drew a deep breath of the acrid stench of spent gunpowder, then seized Carlos's second ankle to yank his feet out from under him. Before Wes could pull him off balance, Carlos moaned and fell to his knees atop Wes's shoulders.

Wes pried himself from under his brother-in-law and rolled away, jumping to his feet to defend himself against the pending assault. Glancing at Carlos, Wes saw pain and bewilderment in his eyes. Two red blossoms on his shirt spewed blood from his chest. Then Carlos tumbled forward, making no effort to break his fall with his limp arms and landing square on his nose. Carlos twitched once, then never moved again.

Confused, Wes turned to Sarafina, who stood dazed before him. As he was about to ask what happened, he saw at Sarafina's side his revolver, smoke still seeping from its hot barrel.

By sunrise Wes Bracken worked at digging a grave for Carlos beside that of Luther on the Mirror B property by the Rio Ruidoso. Carlos's body, wrapped in a wool blanket, rested in the wagon bed, as he had carried it from the house so the children would not see their dead uncle. While he could remove the corpse before the little ones saw it, Wes could not hide the bloodstains on the floor, and Sarafina could not erase the memory of killing her own brother, even in defense of her husband. By midmorning, when the grave was sufficiently deep enough to keep varmints from digging it up, Wes maneuvered the wagon beside it and slid Carlos's sheathed body from the wagon bed, placing it in the grave as gently as he could. He took his shovel and filled the hole, mounding the dirt over after another hour of work. Once Jace returned in the afternoon from his trip to Lincoln, Wes planned to bring the family and him back to the site for a simple graveside service. Wes owed Sarafina that at least, if not Carlos.

When he was done mounding the grave, Wes climbed in the wagon and started toward the Casey place, stopping periodically to toss in the wagon stones he could use in the afternoon to build a cairn over the resting place. He knew the task would delay his arrival home and he dreaded facing Sarafina. He had kept his vow not to kill his brother-in-law, but at the cost of piling the burden of Carlos's death on his wife's shoulders and conscience.

Reaching the Casey place shortly after high sun, Wes secured the wagon in front of the house and marched inside. Luis and

Roberto both talked in hushed tones as they mother-henned Blanca. Though they didn't understand just what, the children sensed something was wrong. They looked up at him with sad eyes as he passed, but did not try to greet or run to him. Stepping into the kitchen, Wes saw Sarafina bent in her chair over the table, her head resting on her arms on the tabletop. She whimpered softly, not looking up when Wes walked in. He cleared his throat. Sarafina remained still. Wes stepped to her, placing his hand on her shoulder. Slowly, she lifted her face and looked at him with eyes reddened and moistened from grief.

Wes put his finger beneath her chin and lifted it, then leaned down to softly kiss her lips. He could taste the salty residue of her tears. Helping her up, he placed his arms around her and hugged her silently. He whispered in her ear. "It had to be done."

"I know," she answered, "but it still hurts."

"When Jace returns, I'll ask him to fetch his Bible. We'll all ride over to his grave to say a few words from the Good Book."

"There's stew on the stove," she said.

"I'll fix a bowl," Wes said. "Do you want to go sit with the children?"

"No, I don't want to enter that room, not after last night. The stains on the floor bring back too many horrible memories."

Wes nodded. "Let me pull your rocking chair into the kitchen and ask the children to come in. Have they eaten?"

Sarafina nodded.

Wes retreated to the front room and picked up her rocker, stopping as he passed the kids. "Your mother needs your hugs."

"Does she want a hug from Concho?" Roberto asked.

"Sure," Wes replied, "bring him along, too." He toted the rocking chair into the kitchen and placed it beside his wife. She moved to it, her face marred with sadness. Luis stepped to his mother, hugging her around the neck, while Roberto squeezed her legs. Blanca scampered to her mother, shrieking she was being left out. Roberto lifted her and placed his sister in her mother's lap. Then Luis darted into the front room returning with Concho, petting him with one hand and his mother's thigh with the other.

Wes turned to the counter and grabbed a bowl, then dipped two ladles of stew out of the pot. Taking a spoon, he went to the table and sat down. He took a bite and chewed it, flinching at the char. The concoction had sat too long on the stove unstirred and had a bitter, burnt taste. Even so, he finished the bowl, not wanting to show disappointment and add to his wife's grief.

When he finished, he turned to Sarafina. "Is there anything you need me to do for you?"

"No," she answered softly. "I just want to rock here with the little ones."

Wes nodded. "I've a few things to do until Jace returns, so I'll be outside." He started for the door and reached by habit at the peg where he kept his hat, but realized he had never taken his hat off while he ate. Wes went about his tasks, but he knew it was just make-do work until Jace returned, and they could visit Carlos's grave to say an amen over his short life. After two hours of menial jobs, Wes saw Jace turn off the road for the house, so he jogged around to the wagon where he awaited his partner.

As Jace neared, he stood up in the saddle and checked the wagon bed. "Is our crop so bad you're harvesting rocks now, Wes?" Jace grinned, but the expression melted away when Wes frowned in return.

"We've had a problem, Jace."

"Sarafina, the kids? They're okay?"

"Thankfully, but Carlos returned last night."

Jace whistled.

"Prison only embittered him."

"Did you kill him?"

"Sarafina did."

Jace sighed and dismounted.

Wes continued. "I wish I had shot him now because Sarafina's not handling it well."

Walking over, Jace hugged Wes. "I'm sorry, Wes, for you and her. What can I do?"

"Fetch your Bible, Jace, and ride with us to the Mirror B where you can say a few words over his grave. I buried him this morning next to Luther. The rocks are for his grave."

Releasing Wes, Jace returned to his horse. "I'll fetch my Bible from inside, but I've got presents for Sarafina and the kids in my saddlebags."

"Save them for tonight, Jace. Let's get this over with. I'll load the kids and Sarafina and we'll ride over." Wes entered the house and strode into the kitchen. "Jace is back. I'll take the children to the wagon. Why don't you take the pot off the stove and follow us?"

"I'm not going in that front room," she insisted. "I'll just meet you at the wagon."

"I understand." Wes turned to herd the children out the front door.

"Can Concho come?" Roberto asked.

"Yeah," added Luis.

"Me, too," Blanca mumbled.

"Sure to all of your questions," he replied, scooping up Blanca in his arms, drawing a cackle from her as they marched through the front room and outside. Wes put Blanca in the back of the wagon, then boosted Roberto into the wagon as Luis picked up Concho and slid him over the sideboard to Roberto. Luis grabbed the top of the rear wheel rim and stepped up the spokes and into the back.

Shortly, Sarafina came around the side of the house, a black shawl draped over her shoulders.

Cousins stood by his dun, his expression somber. He doffed his hat. "I'm so sorry, Sarafina, about Carlos."

Forcing a smile, she replied. "Thank you, Jace. It means so much that you will say a few words over his body."

"I wish I'd been here to help. Things might have been different."

She smiled again, but said nothing more.

As Jace mounted, Wes helped his wife into the wagon seat, then climbed in beside her, took the reins, released the brake, and turned the rig toward the Mirror B where he had first taken Sarafina after their marriage.

The ride to the grave was a solemn one,

save for the children in the back, playing with the dog and moving the rocks around. When they arrived at the grave and Wes brought the wagon to a halt, Jace helped the kids out of the back while Wes assisted his wife down, then grabbed the dog from the back and handed him to Luis. The adults stood at the head of the grave while the kids looked at one another, confused by the ritual.

Jace opened the Bible and read a scripture, but Wes lost himself in his thoughts about his first glimpse of Sarafina upriver almost nine years earlier and how they had married and hoped to breed horses on this land. He could never have seen how much trouble, violence, and death would follow. Wes prayed the killing was over, and he could raise his family without fear. He put his arm around his wife as she sobbed. The children, seeing their mother crying, edged toward her, holding her legs and comforting her.

When Jace finished his comments, he bowed his head and said a brief prayer, commending Carlos's soul to the Almighty. And then it was over. Wes pointed to the wagon. "Do you want to sit there while we cover his grave with the stones, Sarafina?"

His wife shrugged.

"No, Wes. Why don't you and Sarafina

walk around the place?" Jace said. "I'll back the wagon up to the grave and have the boys help me cover it with the stones." He turned to Roberto and Luis. "You boys would like that, wouldn't you?"

They both nodded, and Roberto released Concho, who jaunted away, chasing a ground squirrel.

"Keep an eye on Blanca for me," Jace instructed Wes, "so she doesn't get in the way."

Wes picked up the girl and held her on his left hip as he slid his right arm inside his wife's. They strolled silently away from the shade of the cottonwood tree where Sarafina's brother now rested beside her husband's sibling. Wes felt powerless to comfort his wife.

As they walked among the burned-out ruins of their first home, Sarafina finally spoke. "I miss this place. Can we rebuild and start again here?"

Wes hadn't considered that possibility as the Casey place was already built. "I suppose we could, though it would take time."

"I don't know that I can live in the Casey house anymore. The front room brings back the horror of last night."

"It might take a year to rebuild with all the other jobs facing us," he replied.

Sarafina looked up into his face and smiled. "I can wait, if you promise me we *will* return."

"And we can turn over the Casey place to Jace. He's been a fine partner who hasn't gotten as much out of our partnership as he deserved." Wes eased Blanca to the earth, and she bolted toward Concho, who barked at the ground squirrel.

Wes turned to Sarafina and flung both arms around her, squeezing her tightly as he kissed her lips.

The moment, though, was broken when Blanca tripped over a rock and tumbled headlong to the ground, wailing at the unexpected encounter with earth.

Breaking his grip from his wife, Wes said, "Let me tend our daughter."

As he stepped away, Sarafina grabbed his wrist. "What did you say?"

"I said I need to check on Blanca." He tried to pull away, but his wife's grip tightened.

"That's not what you said. Repeat it."

Confused, Wes shrugged. "I said I must tend our daughter."

Sarafina smiled and sobbed at the same time. "You said *our* daughter. Those are the words I've waited to hear you say." She flung her arms around him and kissed him with surprising passion. Then, arm and arm, they walked to comfort their daughter.

EPILOGUE

By the turn of the century, Lew Wallace's novel *Ben-Hur: A Tale of the Christ* had surpassed Harriet Beecher Stowe's *Uncle Tom's Cabin* to become the best-selling American novel of the 19th century. It remains one of the most influential Christian novels of all time. Even so, the New Mexico governor's betrayal of William H. Bonney became a stain on Wallace's legacy.

James J. Dolan was never tried for any of his crimes and ultimately took over the ranch land and store originally owned by the young Englishman John Henry Tunstall, whose murder precipitated the Lincoln County War. Dolan partnered in some of his ranching ventures with District Attorney William L. Rynerson of Doña Ana County, but struggled with alcohol in his later years and died an alcoholic in 1898 at forty-nine years of age.

Pat Garrett remained the Lincoln County

sheriff for another term. A year after shooting William H. Bonney, Garrett published a book defending his role in the death. Though the narrative was largely written by Garrett's acquaintance Marshall Ashmun "Ash" Upson, *The Authentic Life of Billy the Kid: The Noted Desperado of the Southwest* remained a primary source on Bonney for seven decades, though little of it was verifiable. Garrett was assassinated in 1908 by political enemies.

Like the decent men that tamed the West, usually in obscurity, Wes Bracken and Jace Cousins lived out their lives in peace on the land they settled. Cousins eventually married. Both men remained fast friends and raised families that became productive citizens first in the Territory of New Mexico and then in the State of New Mexico when it joined the Union in 1912. Though they both belonged to early settler/pioneer associations in their declining years, neither Bracken nor Cousins ever spoke of their experiences before, during, or after the Lincoln County War as emotions remained too raw and too painful for decades.

As for William H. Bonney, he died at Sheriff Pat Garrett's hand on July 14, 1881, in Fort Sumner, New Mexico Territory. Even so, Billy the Kid still lives today.

ABOUT THE AUTHOR

Preston Lewis is the Spur Award–winning author of forty-plus novels. He has received two Spur Awards from Western Writers of America (WWA) and a Will Rogers Gold Medallion for Western Humor for *Bluster's Last Stand,* a volume in his comic western series *The Memoirs of H.H. Lomax.* Two Lomax books were Spur finalists. He has earned three Elmer Kelton Awards from the West Texas Historical Association (WTHA) for best creative work on the region.

In 2021 Lewis was inducted into the Texas Institute of Letters for his literary accomplishments. A past president of WWA and WTHA, he resides in San Angelo, Texas, with his wife, Harriet. He holds degrees in journalism from Baylor and Ohio State, and a master's degree in history from Angelo State.

CPSIA information can be obtained
at www.ICGtesting.com
Printed in the USA
BVHW050722161222
654388BV00002B/2